Nigel Frith's epic adult fantasy brings together the deities and monsters of Northern myth into a fast-moving narrative, which blends mystery, horror, suspense and humour. It tells the story of Balder, the god of sunlight, and his love, the Vana Iduna, and how they are finally re-united and recounts the adventures of Odin, Thor and the wicked god, Loki, in their attempts some to preserve, some to end, the hero's life. Giants, dwarves and elves inhabit a landscape of forest and plains, through which the Aesirs of Asgard journey to avert prophesied evils.

D1578826

Asgard

NIGEL FRITH

London
UNWIN PAPERBACKS
Boston   Sydney

First published in Great Britain as *The Spear of Mistletoe* by Routledge &
Kegan Paul Ltd, 1977
First published by Unwin Paperbacks 1982
Reprinted 1983, 1984

UNWIN® PAPERBACKS
40 Museum Street, London WC1A 1LU, UK

Unwin Paperbacks,
Park Lane, Hemel Hempstead, Herts HP2 4TE, UK

George Allen & Unwin Australia Pty Ltd.,
8 Napier Street, North Sydney, NSW 2060, Australia

© Nigel Frith 1977, 1982

ISBN 0 04 823209 2

Set in Perpetua
and printed in Great Britain
by Hazell Watson & Viney Limited,
Member of the BPCC Group,
Aylesbury, Bucks

Contents

PART ONE

Asgard

OF THE BEGINNING of Ragnarok does this tale tell, Ragnarok, the day of doom, the twilight of the gods. It comes upon the Northern deities, the Aesirs of lofty Asgard, when their hope for the future, Balder, the sungod, is threatened by destruction. There is but one thing in the world which can prevent Ragnarok, just as there was found one thing in Nature which could bring Balder's death. Of the former, that is the tale of Pangaea, of which this book is the first. Of the latter, this is the tale of Asgard and the beginning of Ragnarok. But what was it first that brought these evils down upon the Aesirs?

It was the abduction of Iduna, the goddess of youth, on the eve of her wedding to Balder, the blond hero. For Loki, the scheming fire-god, allowed the giant Thiazi, demon of the Eastern winds, to fly away with her to his dark castle. Loki always bore malice against the gods, and loved to engage in plots to hurt them, and Balder especially was he jealous of. And so secret had the fire-god been in his dealings, that none of the gods knew that he had planned it, but they were all baffled when they discovered she had gone.

And to solve their perplexity, Odin, father of the gods, spoke to them and said, 'Let each of the Aesirs go forth seeking Iduna, and ask in the world below if any know where she has gone, for this next day was to be my dear son's wedding-day.'

And all the Aesirs went out to search for the beautiful goddess of youth, Nanna-Iduna. And even Loki himself, laughing inwardly, went out as if searching, but on another mission. And for nine days the gods searched, and on the tenth they returned to Asgard. Thor, the red-bearded god of thunder, returned from craggy Jotunheim, Vidar and Vali, the gods of matter and light, returned from Alfheim and Svartheim, the lands of the elves and the dwarves. But neither these nor Forseti, the god of justice, nor Bragi, the god of song, could find any trace of the auburn-haired Iduna. And the gloomy Aesirs made their way, battling against the pouring rain, to Gladsheim, to take counsel what they should do next.

It was a desolate feast they came home to, and the wedding wreaths and garlands mocked them, withering on the shield-hung walls, and Odin, wrapped in his blue cloak, sat by the high-seat pillars, gravely staring into the fire. And the gods entered the hall, and shook the rain from their dampened capes, and sat at their places, the twelve Aesirs together. And Balder paced up and down on the rushes of the floor, and Hermod, the messenger of the gods, sat next to Odin, silent.

And the father of the gods spoke and said, 'I see from your faces, Aesirs, that your search has been useless. In everything we do we are mocked by fate with failure. That we have built the strongest heaven, immune to all attacks, guarded by towering walls, counts little against fate. But oh my friends, a terrible knowledge has come. I repent the day that we began this enterprise. My heart is so heavy, I cannot speak.' And Odin covered his face, and was silent. And the gods looked from one to the other, for it was disheartening to see their leader at such a loss. But the goddesses went round filling the drinking-horns with mead: Freya, and Fricka, and Sif, the wife of Thor.

But as they sat dismayed, came in Loki, the scheming god of fire, and soon he had them in a different temper. For Loki laughed and cried out, 'Whose cat has died in the night? Oh great Aesirs, what a row of forlorn faces I see! Because Balder has lost his minion are you all stricken with woe? Perhaps you are remembering your own old flames? Freya, what of your lost lovers? There are some of the heroes in Valhalla could tell us a saucy tale. And Thor, what of your old amours? Hammers don't make weddings without some cause. Can Sif feel safe when you go deep into giantland? And Odin, dear brother too! You may well cover your face in your cloak. Who has not heard of the sweet maiden Gunlod? She thought she was safe in a cavern in the mountains, but you stole her potion and her maidenhead with it. It was a good deal you made, when you won Od-hroerir!'

And Odin looked up at this, and his one dark eye glared from over his cloak. But red-haired Thor spoke out and said, 'No more of these taunts, oh evil-speaking Loki! This is no time for flyting, for we are all sad here to a man. It is a shameful, bitter thing that Balder's bride has gone, with her sweet face and gracefulness, on the very eve of her wedding. Some black work is here. But do not you fear, Balder, we shall find that girl, once someone has worked out a plan.'

And Loki, who had been filling a drinking-horn, and pretending not to listen, turned round at this and said, 'We shall wait till doomsday, if we wait for your brains to turn over. Oh mighty Thor, if only you could think with your arms! But why are we all sitting here with knitted eyebrows? I take it none of the great twelve has sniffed any trace of the bride to be? But has anyone anxiously asked poor Loki? Balder, will you not ask me how I fared in my desperate quest for this innocent girl? But perhaps first you ought to tell us how you wooed this innocent. You have been strangely silent about your time in the Western Isle of Vanaheim. What did you two get up to there for so long? Is Iduna as innocent as Thor thinks?'

But now did the blond-haired Balder swell with fury at this taunt, and leaping the table he sprang at Loki and sturdily struck him in the face. And Loki fell to the rushes of the floor, and blood spouted from his nose, and Balder cried over him, 'Had we not been in Gladsheim, I would have struck you with my sword, you poison-talking son of a dwarf. I would have hurled you from the walls to break your cowardly neck. Ay, I would do it too, if Forseti, god of justice, were not here to look at me askance. For you are and always have been a pest among the Aesirs!'

And Loki got up, quivering with shame and rage, and he wiped the blood from his face with the back of his hand, and said, 'Madder you grow every day, Balder the beautiful. Once you were heaven's hope, so bright, so blond, so strong. And how greatly they all rejoiced when they discovered you had brains in your skull. Oh Loki, has met his match now, they simpered, when you made your first pun. But mad you are now, Balder, mad with lust. Ever since you had a whiff of madam Iduna's skirts you have raged like a bull getting close to his holiday. Ay, hit me if you please. No one will restrain you. No one cares for crafty old Loki. But I shall have revenge for this blow you gave me. If I'm there at your wedding, I swear I'll murder you.' And Loki spat out blood in Balder's face.

But Thor the Thunderer strode forward from his seat, and pinioned Loki in his arms, and forced him to the floor. And Thor said, 'And unswear your vow you will again, Loki. Such a shameful vow has never been spoken in this hall. And before this night is passed and this good feast, you will vow yourself to unvow what you have spoken. Either that or I will squash the breath from your body.'

[5]

But Balder shook his head, and gently released Thor's grasp from the fire-god, saying, 'Leave him, great thunderer. He and I were both rash in what we spoke. I spoke from anger and too much frustration, nor did he make firm his boast with a pledge from the cup. Let him go, and let us be friends again, for I have a certain question that I would put to Loki.' And Balder helped up Loki to his feet, and he picked the straws from him, and patted him on the back. And Balder said, 'There is a witch, Groa, lives in the deep dell of a black wood. She knows many things that happen in heaven and earth, and unlike many sibyls gives useful advice. To her I went in my fruitless search for Iduna, and laid my case before her, on which she took pity. Though she could not help me by telling me her whereabouts, she told me of an old saying, that now I tell to you: if there is anything missed in heaven ask Loki. Tell me then, Loki, whatever you may know. You said none had asked you of your findings. Now I ask you. Speak.'

Then did Loki smile, and bowing sarcastically to Balder, he then looked about at the rest of the gods, and said, 'Did I not say Balder had wits? If he and I were to rule Asgard how simple it all would be. You are right to ask me, blond one. I have longed to tell you all. For I know where Iduna is and now I'll tell the tale.'

Amazed were the gods, but speak they did not. They sat with their ears forward, hanging on Loki's lips. So Loki continued, warming to their regard. 'Iduna is in the castle of the great wind-giant Thiazi. He it is who sends the East winds in the white-spangled wintertime. Ashamed though I am to say it, I planned with him Iduna's abduction. I had Iduna abducted to save my own neck!' And Loki looked round now at the astonished gods.

But then he shook his head, and sighed, and continued. 'Thiazi, as you may know, gods, has two forms. At times he is as natural a giant as you could wish: Thorlike, tall, plodding, and rather stupid. At other times he assumes the form of Hraesvalgr – dreaded name – the vast eagle that blows evil thoughts over the whole continent of Midgard, and blights the buds that strive upwards in the spring. Well, this is how Hraesvalgr came to abduct Iduna.

'One day, Odin, Thor and myself – you will doubtless remember this well, my old comrades – were journeying in a wilder part of

[6]

Jotunheim. It was those far off days when we still spoke to each other. Finding no villages which could sell us anything to eat, we slaughtered a wild ox from a passing herd, and in a cauldron were cooking it over a fire. But strange to say, as long as we boiled it, the meat stayed raw, and would not cook. Every time wondrous Thor fished it out with a fork to look at it, it was just as raw and red as when we started. It was then that I noticed with a nasty shock – not having Thor's heart inside me – a monstrous eagle perched on the dead bough of a pine tree, glowering at us with saucer-shaped eyes. It was Hraesvalgr, and by his magic, since he might retard and hold up all progresses on earth, he was restraining the cooking of our side of beef. Greedy as we all are, and in spite of our being of opposite races, it was quickly arranged that if Hraesvalgr allowed the meat to cook, he could fly down with us, and have a share. Swooping from the tree and fairly blowing us all over – except Thor – he blazed the fire with his deathly cold wings, and soon it was roaring enough to cook the herd. The meat was quickly done, and we cut it into portions.

'Friends, you know I am an envious soul. I confess it myself. Whenever I see people enjoying themselves, sourness enters my heart, and I yearn to stop them. Thor gave the eagle a monstrous hunk of ox – far greater than my share – and I was naturally wracked with jealousy. Just as the eagle had sunk his ugly beak in it, I seized the other end, and tugged it away. Lord Odin, Comrade Thor, you know well what happened next. Our happy threesome were suddenly separated. I was whisked into the air, as the spiteful eagle flew off, and soon I was gazing down on the massive mountains of Jotunheim, which looked from that height like ribs of the crinkly sand. He hung me by my heels in his parlour back in Thrymheim, and there I dangled, a prisoner, as I saw it, for life.

'Well, my friends, I sigh to admit it now, but what could I do? Thor would have at once twanged himself off the rope, and crushed the giant's skull with a flick of his wondrous hammer. But I was not gifted that way. All I had to get me out of my predicament, was the poor tangled mass of grey brains in my head. Now Thiazi, it seemed, was a bachelor giant. Never once in my stay did I hear ringing through his halls the abrupt tones of a scolding wife. On

[7]

this I based my plan, and appealed to him, thus. "Thiazi," I said, "it is very little use to you to keep a poor little fire-god hung up in your window like seaweed. There are far more shapely and comely things to look at in the saintly walls of glorious Asgard. Have you never heard of a swap of prisoners? Let me go, Thiazi, and I will bring you something far better: a lovely goddess to adorn your spacious home." I was delighted to see that he warmed to my proposal, and oh so swiftly was a little plan arranged, and I was free again and bound for lovely home.

'Friends, forgive me. But what else could I do? I might have died if I had hung there any longer. And I was so worried as to how you would all get on without me. Goddesses are expendable – forgive me, ladies – but how would you all fare without Loki to get you out of scrapes? So I came home to arrange a crafty swap. The plan – it pangs me to admit it – was this: that I lure a goddess to a place near the walls of Asgard, and Thiazi flies over and grasps her in his talons. I was to select the one I thought best, and as I strolled about, happy in Asgard, I pondered which goddess would best suit Thiazi's lust. Now, every one at that time was praising Iduna. Daylong I heard nothing but the glutinous warblings of her name. She was so pure, so innocent, so happy, and Balder, the blond hero, was gloating in his conquest. Yes, I sighed sadly, it must be she. Everything worked charmwise. I got to work. The grove of Brunnaker with its mossy orchards was hard by the wall on the North-East – Thiazi's way. Iduna was so anxiously proud of her golden apples, which she kept in a magic casket, the fruit of eternal youth, that I had the perfect excuse to lure her thither. Rather naughtily I suggested I could show her better apples, and decoyed her stealthily into the perfumed grove. There among the ever-burgeoning trees, black Thiazi plummeted and bore her off screaming. Oh, I can still hear her shrill girlish screams!' And Loki clapped his hands together, and delight was enthroned on his face. But then, looking at the grave faces of the gods, he expanded his hands, and shrugged his shoulders with a weak smile.

But the gods were incensed at what they had heard, and murmured angrily at Loki's blatant joy. And Fricka, mother of Balder, stood up, her black eyes glaring, her breast heaving with fury, and said,

'Loki, it were well if you were banished Asgard for ever! Though you may be brother of my lord Odin, you are unworthy of this place. I would have you manacled in the blackest pit of Hela's realm, to undergo tortures until the ending of time. What meaner or more spiteful crime has there ever been?'

But Loki cried, 'Dear lady, did you think I could leave it there? I pray you, gods, hear me out, for my story is far from finished, and I have already been working to put all right. Do you think I am so callous to leave the case so? Hardly had Thiazi flown away but I was wracked with the pains of shame! I moped about heaven, struck with my unworthiness. And when all you gods found that Iduna had disappeared, I could do nothing but keep silent, and beat at my evil breast. However, when great Odin sent us forth to search for the goddess, I decided to scheme again to fetch her back to Asgard, and if you hear the rest of my tale, you will see I have worked a cunning way out.

'When the great Aesirs hared off, Loki went back to Jotunheim. First of all I found an extraordinary state of affairs. Happily for Balder, Thiazi had not been able to molest Iduna, for she had shut herself in a mysterious bird-cage. It was a cage quite big enough, and gave her complete protection, but there she was, shut in the thing and Thiazi not able to open it. You may well carp at this part of the tale. I cannot fathom the true mystery of it, but the cage once housed the king of the birds, or some such worthy, and had a spell put on it that once the door was shut, it might never be opened. It seems that Iduna fled thither to escape the giant, and escaped indeed. That Thiazi cannot reach her, this is certain, but it is also certain that she cannot get out.

'I spied in this a means to strike a bargain, and at once had at Thiazi to gain Iduna's freedom. I began by pointing out to the great oaf that even if he could get at Iduna, she was not really perfect for him. She was a good deal smaller, she had brown rather than blond hair, a roundish face, and something of a young figure. Would he not prefer a more well-formed, ample goddess, a lady of more obvious charms, well skilled in the rites of love? This was the idea I now put. Is it not strange the way one's mind throws up these amicable notions? My suggestion appealed to Thiazi, who was by now in a rather frustrated state, and it was fixed that in exchange for Iduna, I should bring him Freya, the goddess of love.'

But the Aesirs murmured in anger again at Loki's pranks, and again did Fricka burst forth in her fury, 'Can you do no more than heap wrong on wrong? How dare you go bargaining about the goddesses of heaven as though we were so many cattle? Are our charms to be discussed with giants, and the best and tastiest of us to be selected for their slobbering kisses? Forseti, god of justice, can we not have him whipped for this impudence?'

And among the tumult in the hall Forseti then spoke up. He was an old god, white-bearded, and knew a great stock of law, and coughing on his fist he rose to address the company. 'Aesirs, if my mind serves me correctly, there has been no public flogging of a god since Thor himself whipped Loki for stealing the hair of the former's wife. And this cannot be considered as an administration of justice, since no Thing sat in deliberation before the punishment was meted. An insult can always be countered by a nicely calculated insult in return, care being taken not to exceed the first insult, for fear of opening the progress to a blood-feud. But in this case, oh Aesirs, I am not sure that the goddesses can claim to be insulted, when they have had their charms so lucidly expounded.' And with a smile Forseti resumed his seat.

But now did the eager god Vidar speak out, for he loved to make his comment on whatever chanced, and he said, 'Well have you spoken, Forseti, and well have you spoken, Fricka, but has Loki spoken well: that I wish to ask. He tells us he was captured by a giant, who is also an eagle. He tells us that to gain his freedom he arranged for him to abduct Iduna. Can he be believed? Iduna is gone, certainly. But is she in Jotunheim? Could she not be any-where else, in Alfheim, or returned to Vanaheim? How do we know that Loki is not luring us into yet another trick? He tells us Iduna is locked in a magic bird-cage. Can we believe this? What is this cage? Why should Thiazi have it? These are the questions we must be asking, my friends.' And satisfied that he had said some-thing, he sat down.

And now did old Niord speak. Niord was a Vana, and once ruled over the seashores and the headlands. His flowing beard was tinged with green, and his cloak was sewn with cockle-shells. And Niord said, 'Strange are the ways of sorcerers. Thrymheim, I remember, where Thiazi lives, is a castle bordering on the very edge of Alfheim. Its stony walls overlook the land of the elves. In border countries breed the people of magic. This Thiazi seems like a sorcerer of some kind, and very like it is that he has enchanted cages. And I do predict there are more wonders in Thrymheim than we have yet heard of, yea, and perhaps ever shall.' And raising his finger to them all, he ceased speaking.

But now did Thor with frowning brow speak to the gods: 'Friends, I have been trying to follow your advice, but I cannot see what you mean us to do, for do you really mean that we are to take Freya and exchange her? How ever will she get out of Thrymheim if we do that? And perhaps the beautiful goddess is not willing to be taken to the foul giant's castle. None of us have heard what she has to say.'

And Freya, leaning against her bejewelled hand, smiled at Thor and said, 'You are ever the gentleman of the gods, mighty-muscled Thor. I have been listening long to those bargaining over my head, wondering if they will give the lady a chance to speak. Though I am flattered by Loki's kind report of me, charmed to be considered Asgard's prime bait, I am not a little frightened by the thought of being eaten up by a hulking Thiazi! Sif, my friend, do they really mean to sell me?' And Freya turned to Sif, the wife of Thor, with a smile.

And Sif replied, 'Surely they do not, my dear. But what they do mean to do I also cannot see. How, friends, are we to solve this riddle?'

But Balder at last, impatient of this talk, leapt to his feet, and spoke: 'Long enough I have sat here, Aesirs, listening to your talk, and quietly enough have I bided Loki's foul tale. But I will no longer stay for the plots and gossip. I am going to Jotunheim to win her back by force.' And Balder flung his great cloak on his shoulder, angrily he strode towards the door.

But before he might fully unloose even the latch, Odin himself spoke and addressed them in sombre tones: 'As bitter news as I have ever heard, even from the hard days, when we gods were young, must I now unfold to this company. Prepare yourselves, my friends, for words as sharp as death. Think to chew on ashes, such is the news I bring. You must go no more on journeys, Balder, but remain for ever in the bounds of Asgard. It has been prophesied that in Midgard you will die.'

The gods were silent, and the door blew open, and the harsh wind screamed into the smoky hall, and the rain was mingled with it, smelling of torn boughs and tempests. But the golden-haired Sif, her garments blown about her, shut the door, and restored the peace within. And Balder came back and sat again on his carved high-seat.

And Odin turned to Hermod and said, 'Tell them your tale, Hermod, and all that you have seen.'

So did the messenger god begin to speak, and say, 'Harsh things are assailing us, and tonight we must count them over. While the rest of the Aesirs went forth to seek Iduna, Lord Odin bade me go to the Finnish wizard Rossthioff, to inquire if he knew anything of the future for us. And though I went to the land of the Lapps seeking news of Iduna, I came back wiser only about her betrothed, for that was all his magic could show me: Balder of Odin's sons is doomed to die.' And as they heard these words, the company turned to gaze at Balder, but he merely stared at the ground before him, as if waiting for their talk to cease.

And Hermod continued, 'Hear then of my story, and I will tell you how I came to know so much. It was no easy journey, across the plains where the reindeers roam, and phantoms and monsters besieged me from Rossthioff's magic. But Odin's staff protected me, and at last I found the man. He was a squat magician, and I found him by his tent flattening a mouse-skin with stones and pebbles. When he saw me he did his best to keep me off with magic, and eventually he attacked me himself, but I was the stronger and I soon had him bound, and forced him to promise me a good insight into the hidden whereabouts of things. Then did I release him, and let him set about his enchantments. But alas. This was where I heard, not of Iduna, but of Balder's death.

'Muttering his outlandish spells, he padded with his hide-bound feet on the springy heather of the soil, and shaking his tasselled

[12]

wand, he soon enough dimmed the sun, and cast the marshy land in a terrible pall of darkness. He leered with his yellow teeth, and jogging up and down he started the earth trembling, and a cinder-choked wind sprang up, sounding like so many wolves on the chase of an elk in the marshes. Then he pointed to the horizon, and I beheld a great river of blood, and a woman and a boy, bathing in the foul reeking liquid, came up onto a kind of bank. The boy brandished a bow, and as I looked, he grew swiftly, until his towering head was hidden in the black clouds. At once these visions disappeared, and I was left with the grinning wizard.

'Then did Rossthioff explain the omens. The boy was a son of the Lord Odin's, who would grow as quickly as a day, and was born armed to revenge a terrible deed. The woman Rinda was a fair maiden that the lord of the gods would woo and win, coming from the land of the far Ruthenes, bearing him this son. The red river was the deed to be revenged: for one of Odin's sons would be murdered by another. This, Aesirs, is the bitter prophecy that I was given. This it is which Odin sees as a threat to the life of Balder. He bade me speak, and I have told my tale.'

But at once did Fricka speak out at this and said, 'But what is there in this that threatens Balder? He did not say his name: merely a son of Odin's. Why could it not as easily be any of Odin's sons? Why could it not be Vidar or Bragi or Vali? If we must believe with you the word of a dwarfish Laplander that calls up visions with mouse's skins, then why do we not take him at his word, for he never mentioned Balder at all? This is merely one of Odin's alarms, for always does he have to cry doom!'

But Odin answered his wife with wrath, 'Why must you be always disputing everything I say? Can you not understand me, woman? I say it is omened that Balder will die! Am I not the great seer of the gods? Is not this my spear carved with the sacred words of the Norns, and does it not make all plain that lies before us? Sometimes you presume too much that you are my wife. If I tell you it is Balder that Rossthioff means, when my word is the final law to all tribes of earth, is it not enough to satisfy your doubting feminine mind? What would you that I do? Stab him here myself?'

[13]

But Fricka turned aside from her husband's rebukes and addressed Balder, saying, 'My son, will you be cowed so by this old wizard? Why do you not speak with me? Have we not more sense than this leader, who idles his time with charms, and is no more worthy to be called the lord of the Aesirs? Why do you sit so meek and silent? Can you believe you are doomed to die?'

And Balder rose and pushed away his drinking-horn with a weary hand, and addressed them all, saying, 'Are we gods and we do nothing but bicker and sit at home? I care not if I am doomed to be struck dumb. My wife lies out there in the bleak peaks of Jotunheim. I can no longer sit here chewing air. Aesirs, I shall go now, this moment to Jotunheim. And with deeds shall I accomplish what we sit here nattering of.'

But as Balder went again to the door, Odin stood and cried to him, saying, 'No, my son, that you will not. You are to live no longer such a life of a hero. No more adventuring will you go, to bring back glittering plunder from the sea-girt isles. No more will your ship Ringhorn lurch on the wintry seas. The life of your heedless youth is over. I forbid you henceforth to leave Asgard's walls.'

But Balder spun round, his hand upon his sword, and glared with flashing, fiery eyes. And he debated with himself whether to defy the Lord Odin, and he stared into the grey eyes of his leader. And no god dared move for the sake of sparking some foolish action.

Then did Niord suddenly burst forth with speech, saying, 'Oh, this is a dire night and a horrid one! What things have we heard, enough to harrow the soul! And brothers, I sense there is a further evil flying hither. See, how the torches tremble and halt their flames. Such things are the bodings of a worse presence coming. Truly it must be that Balder and all of us are doomed!'

But Hermod spoke then, and said, 'Yet still we must be sober and weigh these things truly. Lord Odin has had me tell my tale of woe. But certainly it is his knowledge that tells us it is Balder among the sons who is threatened. Tell us then Lord Odin, how is this knowledge yours? For I know you have a tale to tell that speaks of such prophecy.'

And Odin sighed, and then he replied, 'I saw a vision of Hell, prepared for Balder's death. A certain witch gave it me. Hence is all my pain.' And he shook his head as he said this, and stayed a long while silent.

But then as the Aesirs looked on him, Odin continued: 'Troubled by the distress that attended Iduna's abduction, having already sent Hermod to glean what he might from Rossthioff, I still could not rest at home. I went forth to earth myself to read the signs. On Sleipnir did I ride, and wound about me the Wanderer's guise in which I tread the earth, my wide-brimmed cap and cape. North of the Throndheim fiord in Helgeland, Torgen, a lonely island, floats on the grey seas. Cresting its slaty slopes a hill, Torghatten, named by the dwellers of the coasts a market-hat, rears up a ghastly eye, for the winds over the centuries have bored into its head a sky-filled tunnel, which looks out blankly over the dotted islands, and slimy Leko, shaped like a giantess. The invisible witch Hyndla lives in that hole, and her voice is it which in the tunnelled winds shrieks prophecies to those who dare to come. To Torghatten I went, tied up my horse, and on the marshy, stony path ascended to question.

'I called out into the teeth of the wind, "Hyndla, howling prophetess, from glorious Asgard am I come to consult you. The bride of my son on the eve of her wedding-day has vanished from the land of Asgard, baffling us all. Howl to me now of her whereabouts, oh great seer, and you will have Odin your friend in the coming days." And crouching at the brim of the hole, I listened to the winds. Mingled with their frosty breath I caught these sounds: "A fool are you, Odin, to ask for my help. Do you not know that Hyndla never tells anything to the good? The whereabouts of Iduna I shall never speak, but there is a vision which it is doomed that Odin shall see. Peer down, oh great one, into the frothy, gnawing billows of this island. There beyond the tangled seaweed will you see a vision to haunt you in nights to come." I felt my sad heart grow colder within me, and turned a weary eye to the promised horrors.

'There among the pebbles of the shore, just as the wind told, I saw the sea grow misty and slide away from sight. Deep, deep did I peer into the very bowels of earth, and streaked with sulphurous light did I see the wild lands of Hell. And a hall loomed there, much like Bleidablik, my dear son's palace, though grey where that is gold, and hollow where that has riches, and in the midst of that mocking hallway was a banquet set out just as we feast in Asgard. Oh, how it panged my heart to behold that reflection of our joy. For the tables were hung with black and gloomy purple, and the feast was a feast of death, as for a funeral, and the whole vision rang in my heart the sombre bell of fear.

'Then did I turn back to the rock-strewn mouth of the tunnel, and cry, "Why do you show me this, witch Hyndla, and what can the funeral feast mean in Hell? How can they die there or celebrate a burial, when all are already dead and doomed to be lifeless wraiths?" And the shrieking gales that made up Hyndla's voice howled back, "What marks here as a feast of leavetaking, there in Hell is a feast of welcome. The banquet is set for one near to you, Odin. This vision shows you that in Hell there is preparation, for one of the great Aesirs is soon bound for that realm. Balder, your dearest son, is expected there soon, for on Midgard will he meet his death suddenly, unannounced."

'I groaned aloud as I heard the laughing wind shriek this weary news in my ear, and turning my gaze again into the sea, I saw the feast still, and sitting at the high-seat a spectre of Balder already there. His chest was gashed, and a great wound ran down, red blood bedabbling the purple cloths, and as he twisted as if still in pain in Hell from the wound, devils made mock of him, offering him the ashes of food on silver plates. And all manner of ugly creatures, too hideous to name, sported about him, until my stomach grew sick of this cruel mockery. I ran down the slippery slopes of Torghatten to the sea, and as I ran the vision slid away from me, vanishing under the waves. And when I reached the pale shingle of the beach the water that lapped at Sleipnir's hooves seemed stained with the blood of my son that I had seen. True it is that he is doomed to Hell. Certain that I will never suffer him to leave Asgard! If I have not spoken the truth, let Hell itself rebuke me with silence. But if I have told aright, let the great vault resound with thunder to my staff.' And Odin seized on his rune-bearing lance, the lance on which all the laws of men are graven, and he clashed it on the flags of the floor of the hall. And at once a momentous booming of the earth echoed that blow, and it seemed that the whole deep of Hell itself resounded with thunder. And all the Aesirs were wraught with the thrills of fear.

But Balder answered Odin at once and said, 'The threats to my life are mine to heed or heed not. And if I were imprisoned in Jotunheim would not you all look to save me? What law can force me to be a coward and sit at home? I must go to Jotunheim. Do not seek to stop me.'

But Odin grew furious and beat his breast and cried, 'Ah, now all things begin to turn against me, as I have always feared. Even the greatest bonds of all, of allegiance and of blood, are broken. Now do we feel the beginning of Ragnarok. Yet you will not go, my son. I am your lord still. Did not Hell itself confirm with its roaring the truth of the prophecy? Is not this, my staff, the law that we must all look towards?' And Odin held up his staff for all to see, and the light of the fire flickered on its runes, lighting the ash-wood cut from the great world-tree.

But Balder with a cry of wrath leapt forward, and seized on the staff. And Balder called out, 'How I am driven to madness with all this worshipping of witches! If all the mumbling sorcerers of the world must natter against me like so many old hags, let the great hag herself, Hela, the queen of Hell, rush up here amongst us and tell us the truth for good. Now, when I clash it, let her appear and speak!' And the blond-haired Balder struck with the staff again on the ringing flags, and the Aesirs looked with dismay at the bidding he had made.

But Balder's striking of the staff made merely a thin clatter, and it was followed by only a long silence. And the Aesirs began to breathe again. And Odin stretched out his hand to his son, and Balder returned to him the lance with its lines of runes. But then there was a noise of whimpering at the door, and then a sound of claws scratching the wood, and Loki said at once, 'Now Hela is coming. This is her dog, and she's taking it for a walk.' And the Aesirs then saw that the food on their plates was beginning to change, and slowly the meat and the bread and the broth grew pale and chalky. And as they watched, each piece turned black and crumbled in ashes. And there was a smell of sulphur and sour-tasting bronze.

Then did the ground begin to rumble and shake, and the lights of the torches that burned on the walls leaned all one way. And the whimpering noise of the dog began to be louder, and at last he barked and howled. Then did all the plates jingle together, and fly clashing into the centre of the room, whereat the door burst open and the dog Garmlet, the bunchy offspring of the great dog of Hell, hideously ugly and barking with deafening yelps, leaped boister-ously into the room, and howled a great howl before the high-seat pillars. Then was Hela there, the old crone of Hell, wrapped in the stinking rags of corpses, with yellow, aged face and knobbly hands, shrieking and laughing at her dog capering in the midst.

And Hela cried out, 'Have you fed well, little Garm? Will you lick the plates too? Seldom it is these great folk summon us to dine. But you will chew them all over soon enough, and bark them into pinfolds, and herd them about my marshy wastes, and cheer your little heart all day with fun and games.' And Garmlet leapt up at her warty face, and licked it with his tongue, as white as candle-wax, and the dog upset the tables, for he was as big as an earthly ox.

Then did Hela turn to the Aesirs and say, 'What is all this tap-tapping on my roof? If you cannot bide the noises of Hell, why do you live above us? Which kind one invited poor Hela to dinner? It was not him, that rascally lecher that fathered me off Angur-boda, Loki, the shrimp. He never gives a thought to the tatty, threadbare children he spawned. I'll soon have him howling when I get him downstairs. Which of you bade us here? What's your question?'

And Balder then spoke to her and said, 'Foul are you, Hela, and you defile our eyes to behold you. And fie, what a foul stench you bring with you from the marshes of Hell! Oh Hela, pity us so much as to leave quickly. But tell us this before you do. Am I to die and come to Hell? Was Odin's vision true? Be quick, I pray you, for see how your fleas and lice hop from you to us and sprawl over the floor.'

But Hela was a mad witch and would not answer, and her mind leapt from this to that. Crazed to be looking at so many of the gods, she paced up and down among them saying, 'Oh, you lofty

[18]

Aesirs, how you lord it up in the skies! But you will all come to me as swift as I spit on the floor. I'll have her with the golden hair for a pipe-cleaner for my old briar. Her, the plump one, I'll have a haunch of for supper. And that bulgy, tough one with the blood-red hair, he will scratch my callouses and reverently scrape the grease off my nose. It's medicine for lechers. Oh, I will make you all hop about, when you come to cousin Hela. But him, the shrimp there, Loki, the fire-spitter – oh I have such a lovely home awaiting him! In lava land, where hot rocks splurge and bubble, I have a pinnacle already manacled, and there the lover will languish on the flints, and a tidy little serpent, some miles long, will hover over his head, dripping venom in his eye. Come, clap your hands and dance, gods, to Hela's dance of death. Why bide the due time? Come now, come now. Oh Garmlet, will we not have fun with these snooty ones that are here?'

But Balder ran at her, incensed and seized her by the hair, and shouted, 'Here you raving crone, leave railing and answer the question, or I shall slit your throat and ensure your staying below. Tell us what I bade you: is Odin's vision true?'

And Hela grew quiet, and looked into his eyes and said, 'What blue eyes has this blond one! Will you serve Hela in Hell? But what is this thing you ask me? Was Odin's vision true? The vision he took of Hyndla, the witch of the hill-hole, which he saw in the sea? No, it was far from the truth. There are no banquets and rich cloths of purple in Hell. We are but poor folk down there, and can but bite and scratch. Only Odin the lordly, gloomy one, could have said such a lofty vision. But you will come to Hell in poverty soon enough. Ay, it is doomed that you will die. Not five days have you left to live on earth. And then you will be mine, to live with as my paramour.' And with her thin and greasy lips, Hela kissed him, and laughed. And Balder drew back in disgust, and wiped his hand across his mouth with a grimace, and wildly Hela shrieked with glee.

And then did she leap about, and lifting up her stinking skirts she hopped before the Aesirs in a filthy dance, and sang out, 'Ay, you are all to come to Hell, trooping to me hand in hand! First Balder the lovely-limbed. Strange will be his death. How you will all gasp with surprise! It will be a sudden thing, wiping off a thousand smiles.

And a few will be next who are not yet here. But then you, and you, and you, and you. Off you will dive, one by one to me, and Garmlet will catch you, snapping like he does for titbits. And even you great Thor, and great Tyr too, and even you, great Odin: crunched and burnt and poisoned and snapped, all will follow Balder on the lonely Hell-road. Whoohee! Whoohee! What I'll do to you big men too!'

But as Hela danced before the revolted Aesirs, Fricka, the dark-eyed, could bear the disgust no longer, and leaping forward she seized Odin's spear, even Gungnir, the great lance, written with many runes, and she whacked it down over Hela's back and said, 'Back to your kennel, you putrid bitch of Hell! Our menfolk you may make cringe with your flaunting filth and foulness, but I am a match for any woman the height or the depth of the world. Out, you runnion! Out, with your smelly dog-lover! Back to your dung-hill this instant or I shall have you howling for a thousand broken bones.' And Fricka belaboured the crone with the staff, as if she were beating all evil out of the world.

And Hela shrieked and laughed, and crying out to her dog, she quickly made a back for it, and Garmlet leapt onto her greasy shoulders with a grunt. Three times did Fricka chase her round the hall of Gladsheim, and each time she went Hela knocked with her knobbly stick the shields that hung glittering on the walls. Loud was the clanging and the bellowing they made, as witch shrieked, Fricka roared, dog barked, and shield on shield clashed down, revolving and revolving with brash circles on the flags. But on the third time round the hall, with a whoop and a crash of thunder, Hela vaulted through the door, and hopped madly away into the night outside.

But Balder raced after his mother, and stayed her, as she ran down the pavement outside Gladsheim. And he himself ran after Hela then. And Balder chased her as she leapt like a frog, and at each lurch Garm the hound yelped, and snapped back at him. And Balder chased her along the marble pavements, and all over the great plain of Idavold he chased her, where the fallen from Valhalla fight their fight. And past Noatun, the palace of Niord, he chased her, and down the rainy hills until at last they reached the walls.

And Hela climbed up the wall like a quick lizard, and she waited crouched on the top for Balder. And when she saw him below, she lifted up her skirt and showed him her bristly arse, and with a great fart she blew herself from the walls. And so she plummeted through the keen air. Down where the trunk of the great ash-tree grows, where the blue leaves that make the sky shimmered and rustled, she fell. Down she fell through Midgard to the smoke of Hell.

And Balder looked after her, and gazed into the dark night and said, 'Well are you gone, foul vision of the rot to come! Truly have you smeared us all with the stench of corruption. Bah, I taste it yet in my mouth! Well, come not again to our walls, Hell-hag. No more will I summon up your spirit to confuse us!' And Balder turned away from the walls and went back towards his own home.

But in Gladsheim all was busy and commotion, for so great a stink had the Hell-witch left behind her, that all the gods were a-work to cleanse the place. And when the tables were clean and the flags of the floor, they strewed new rushes, so that everything was fresh. And Hermod commanded that the two doors of the Hall were opened so that a wind might blow through to clear the air, and he had cast onto the fire sweet-smelling herbs and the smoke billowed this way and that, cleansing the corners of the hall.

And when all the gods were settled and returned to their places, did Fricka come towards them, and she gave back the staff into Odin's grasp. And the gods were weary now after their sweeping and scrubbing, and they sat silent also, for no one knew what to say.

And while they sat disconsolate, Fricka said to Odin, 'Well, my lord, it is late. But shall you tell us where we may meet tomorrow? Will you call us together that we may debate what to do? We cannot sit here all night plunged in moroseness.'

But Odin stood up and glared at her sternly and said, 'What good is it that I command anything? Are not my commands set at nothing by even my own son? I have shown you the future, and this foul woman has confirmed it foully. You must look to your own wits henceforth, for Odin's rule is done.' And in anger did Odin stalk out of the hall, and went to his own palace, the house in Glasir.

[21]

And Fricka stared after him, and said as he quitted the door, 'Oh, you foolish old man! Runes and wizardry have made a sop of you! No more worthy are you to rule the Aesirs!' And she sat down wearily, and there was silence in the hall.

But then did ancient Niord lift up his head and speak, saying, 'You would think that the ruler of Hell, that was a queen there, would be queenly, but you saw the crude stink and horror of the very monarch herself. Ay, in Hell is only misrule, and its captains are merely capricious, for what greater misfortune is there than to be ruled by brutes and fools? All that is wanton and bestial and mindless lives in that dark place, plaguing those who have passed.

'Oh Aesirs, repent then. So long you have spent in conquest, so mighty have you become by the power of your will alone. But not all things can be won by the strength of the fiery heart. Other races are there now which arise through the playfulness of mind. And you and I are like giants, and fall from unwieldy strength.'

And Hermod arose, and looking about the hall he said, 'It is late. We are all weary. Vain is it to sit here. Let us go to our beds, and think on these things alone. And tomorrow let us meet in the great hall of Valaskialf, and there let us hold a counsel of what we should do.' And the Aesirs nodded, and thought that this was wise, and they began to leave their places in the hall.

But as Fricka arose and drew her robes about her to go out into the cold night, Sif took her hand again and said, 'Will you come to our house this night, and sleep there? For Bilskimir is nearer than the lonely hall in Glasir, and though there are many thralls there who follow Thor, yet have we rooms and beds enough for an honoured guest. This is no night to be lonely and perturbed in mind.'

But Fricka shook her head and said, 'No, I shall go home. But first I shall visit Bleidablik, and talk with Balder a little. I should not sleep whether I were with you or at home.' And one by one the Aesirs left the hall, save only Loki, who sat still plunged in thought, stabbing the brands of the fire with a poker.

But when Niord and the three last Aesirs, which were Vidar, Vali and Forseti, walked all the same way home, Eastwards towards the walls, they came to Heimdall's house, Himminbiorg, which

[22]

looks out over the bridge leading to earth, and here they stopped to say farewell. And Niord shook their hands, and sighing he said, 'I fear the spirits of dreams will be winging in Asgard tonight, and none of us will be untroubled by the fylgies that bring us visions.'

And Forseti replied, 'As for visions and dreams they are but products of the mind. Whether I sleep ill or well, comrades, I hope I shall think soundly tomorrow, for it is then we must decide what steps shall follow our news.'

But Vali looked troubled and said, 'If Hela looks to see us all soon in Hell, can doom be far off, the dreaded Ragnarok?'

And the three gods and the Vana looked up at Heimdall's house, and far up on a high tower, they saw the god himself, leaning towards the earth, with his ear cupped in his hand. And Heimdall saw them, and turning down to them he said, 'Sad things I have heard you discussing in hall, oh Aesirs, and now you wonder if I hear the drumming of doom. Stay then. Harken. I shall tell you what I hear. It is a still night, and the rain has ceased. Over the roofs of a thousand hamlets the moon shines, and lights the mist. I hear the breathing of the tribes of men. I hear the slimy worms rising from the grass. I hear the year's wool growing on the pastured flocks. The torrents roar, the ice groans, the bleak sea chafes, and the wind in the gorges seethes. But afar off in the lands of our enemies, there is only silence. All's well, my friends, all's well.' And the great god turned back to the earth, and took up again his unwearying watch.

And the gods bade each other good night, and each went to his own house. Over the sloping hills of the floor of heaven they went, to the palaces that shone in fields of golden leaves.

And Fricka at that moment came to the door of Bleidablik, and pushing it ajar went into Balder's home. And very faintly by the far light of a torch that guttered on the wall, she found her son Balder sitting disconsolate in the darkness, and she went to him, and kneeling beside him took his hand in hers. And Fricka said, 'Odin is gone in high dudgeon home, and says his rule is done, and will command us no more. I came here to bid you have courage, my son, but now I am here I feel I have none of it myself. What way can there be to avert these omened evils?'

[23]

But Balder shook his head and said, 'Mother, busy yourself not with such things. They are old wives' tales. Tomorrow shall I go, let Odin say what he will. For how can I dally, when Iduna is in Jotunheim? She was not meant for such rough sports as we endure.'

And Fricka got up angrily and said, 'Tush, my son. She is a woman and she can bear as much as any of us. Do not we go through more pains in bringing children into the world than all you precious fighters that roar if you feel a sword in your side? Iduna is no fairy. She is from Vanaheim not Alfheim. And she has more guile about her too than you in your doating would ever see. Fie, my son, you allow your love for this woman to make a sop of you.'

And Balder seized his mother's hand then with a laugh and said, 'Now you do me more good than with all your sympathy! Do you think that she is well? Oh heaven let it be so! Leave me now, mother, for I shall go to bed. There is more spirit in you these days than there is in my father. If we have but spirit, we shall overcome.' And his mother left him without any more words, and quitting the great hall she banged the door behind her.

And Balder arose, and taking down the torch that flamed on the stony wall, he stared into its flames·and said 'Oh Iduna, keep well, stay safe but till I come. Now that I know your whereabouts, no force will keep me from you.' And Balder held the torch to him, and embracing the light he walked down the tapestry-hung hall and came to the alcove where he had his straw bed.

Now Balder's younger brother, the blind god Hodur, slept with him in Bleidablik, and when Balder came into the alcove, Hodur called out, 'Balder, is that you? Was that our mother here now, and why are you so late in coming home? I have lain here so long, yearning to question you, for I have heard strange noises tonight. There was a hideous barking and a shrieking of women. It seemed that there was a great tumult in Gladsheim. Have the gods quarrelled or what has come to pass? I have not been able to sleep here, so worried I have been.'

And Balder went to the blind Hodur, and sat on his bed, and stroked his hair and said, 'Worry no longer, blind Hodur, for Balder will keep you safe. The mad mood passed and all's well again. But the best news is, my brother, ·hat I know where Iduna is. Loki the wretch confessed that he had her stolen away. And tomorrow I go to fetch her. Oh Hodur, my honey, how I will squeeze her in my arms when I find her again!' And Balder hugged Hodur and gave him a smacking kiss. And Hodur cried out, annoyed, and pushed him away. Then did Balder leave him, and stripping off his clothes, he got into his cold bed. And he tossed and he turned and he sprawled, thinking of Iduna. And the night moved on, and the moon went round, and all the gods in Asgard were at last brought to silence.

But now high above the storms and the fret of Gladsheim, on the highest peak of Asgard, and the summit of the world, the Norns, goddesses of fate, sat spinning in the peaceful sky. For above them the very crown of the world ash-tree Yggdrasil, rustled and shook its blue and airy leaves. And by its roots did a sweet fountain, Urdar, spring forth, and its waters trickled into a flower-surrounded well. And the three sisters, spinners of the wyrd of the world, lazily spun the spindles which twist the twine of time.

And Urd, goddess of the past, smiled and said to her sisters, 'Time flutters on, and the temper of earth changes. See how these Aesirs already fall asunder. And were they not once the terrors of the earth? Hum on little spindle, and bring all things to pass.' And the goddess twirled the white thread that was coiled with the other three.

And Verdandi, goddess of the present, spoke as she spun and said, 'The Aesirs fight and fall, and we sit here and spin. Yet the bite of an apple will keep them from destruction. Did not Iduna bring some, that the lovely Balder wooed? Hum on, little spindle, and bring all things to pass.' And Verdandi drew out the red thread she was spinning, and playfully let it fall twined with the other three.

And Skuld spoke as she span, Skuld, that was goddess of the future, and said, 'Their frenzy and anguish are but a game to us. Are not all things a play to the one that watches within? But the giants were overcome, and their conquerors will be too. Loki the joker will bring them a swift end.' And Skuld chuckled, looking down at her twins, and she added to the three strands a thread as black as death.

[25]

But now came to the world ash-tree three fylgies, which were the familiars of three witches of the earth. And they flew up the dewy mound of the hill at the top of Asgard, and they hovered in the soft air before the Norns. And so that they might revisit their mistresses with the news of the coming days, they asked if they might drink of the well of Urdar. And Verdandi smiled and said, 'Never do the prophetesses get such toil, as when big things are born and great ones tramp the stage. You wish to drink, little fylgies, and taste our sweet well? It is a fountain of knowledge that can never run dry. Drink your fill. But as ye drink, tell us who you are and what it is you wish to know.' And the fylgies flew nearer and shyly looked at the fountain.

And the first fylgie swayed in the wind and cried out, 'I am the fylgie of Hyndla, the wind-witch, who granted Odin the vision of Balder in Hell. Let me drink of the future of a certain one of the gods.' And the three Norns nodded, and granted him a drink. And swooping down to the blank face of the water, the fylgie set it rippling with the wind of his wings, and as he drank, the bubbling fountain said, 'The gods shall be doomed by one that cannot weep.' And the fylgie rose up high into the air, and at once it flew downwards on the long journey to earth.

And the second fylgie bowed to the Norns and said 'I am the familiar of the wood-witch, Groa, who wishes to know what she may tell one of the gods, for already she has the knowledge that he will come to her this night.' And the three Norns nodded and granted him a drink. And the fylgie bent down to the fountain, and as its lips touched the crystal water, it heard the lapping waves say, 'The gods could be saved by a branch of mistletoe.' And the fylgie bowed again to the Norns and flew off, and it winged downwards through the whispering leaves of Yggdrasil.

And the third fylgie drank straight off, and without waiting to be bidden heard the water say, 'The gods shall be doomed without anyone doing anything.' And it gruffly turned to the Norns and said, 'Thurk sent me. You know what I wished.' And swiftly it flew away, and plummeted down to Midgard. And the three Norns looked at each other and shook their heads.

But before the Norns could resume their tasks, there appeared another fylgie, but it seemed less sure and confident than the others. For it strolled up and down, looking baffled at the sheer walls of the trunk of Yggdrasil, and the white foam of the fountain spouting into the sky. Then did the Norns call to it, and ask it what it was and what it wished. And the fylgie looked astonished when it saw the three wise women sitting together, with the yarn of fate heaped over their knees.

But then the fylgie cleared its throat and said, 'I am the fylgie of Balder's dreams. Confusedly have I made my way hither, for I am not used to this sort of journeying. The troubles of the night and the yearning in Balder's heart have forced me inwards to the land of eternal things. What is there to see? What is there to do? For Balder is perplexed and knows not what to think.'

And Skuld looked at it and laughed and said, 'Many this night have come in quest of Balder's fate. He it is where all the crossroads meet. Drink then of this fountain, little fylgie, which wrinkles with the reflection of all earthly things. But so small are you, you will have to drink and return and drink again. Several journeys must you make tonight, if you are to read of Balder's fate. Take your first draught then, and fly back to your master.'

And the fylgie drank, and saw a strange land reflected, and gulping flew back to Balder with his first dream.

And Urd looked after him, and said to her sisters, 'Now is the time of testing come to the North. For the old order is assailed by the new. And in these riddles is the shape of what will come. Sisters, spin on, spin on, for the tangle in our laps has all the answers here. Piece by piece let us find the meaning of these riddles, and then who knows? we shall learn of our own fate perhaps.' And the spindles twirled around again, humming like struck tops, and under the great ash-tree did the three women raise their arms.

But Loki, the cunning god, sat still by the fire in Gladsheim hall, and brooded as he looked into the flames. And grunting he said, 'That hag had great impudence to speak of me so slightingly. She must be crazed to think that I am bound for Hell. Is she not anyway supposed to be my daughter? That I should ask her mother, if I should ever find her again. But out on the old crone! Crags and poison for me? Perhaps she spoke of me like that before the others, so as not to excite their envy in that I was to be a favoured one. For I am not entirely Aesir. The blood of their enemies is in me surely. Well then, I will cease brooding on what she told me, for it is but air and means nothing at all.' And Loki got up from the fire, and kicked a brand so that the yellow sparks flew. And he watched them surge through the hole in the roof.

Then did Loki pull on his cloak, and walked out of the door into the squares and places of Asgard. And the night was still now, and the moon lit up the city and its land with a bleak and frosty glare. And Loki stood in a central spot and gazed about him at all the tall barns and great palaces that lay scattered on the turfy downs of heaven. For many roofs, shingled with shields of silver, glittered in the moonbeams, and many arching rafters were crossed over the night sky. And Loki said then, 'Will all these great ones in this mighty land be brought into Hell? Oh, what a mighty irony it is for these proud ones to be so destined! Did they rear up this great land, and fortify it with such rearing walls, and is it all to crumble and be overthrown? Long ago was it known that Ragnarok, the great twilight, would come. Oh, this feeds my soul for all the injuries they have given me!' And Loki laughed and strolled about the encampment.

And he came to Thor's home, Bilskimir, which was a complex of long-houses, and they were formed round a great square, lain with huge, slatey flags. And in the many halls were lying asleep all the thralls of the fallen heroes that went to Valhalla, for while Odin received the lords, Thor took the peasants to his care. And scattered about the square was hay from the stables, and in their roosting-places the hens and cockerels slept. And Loki said, 'Will even this red-headed, over-hearted oaf be brought low? His strength is great, and Thor's hammer Miolnir can crush anything he throws it at, and return again to his hand. But the brains in his head are no bigger than a nightingale's. Yes, he will fall. It is said that Jormun-gandr, the world-serpent, that coils about the earth, will kill him with its poison at the twilight of the gods.'

[28]

And Loki came then to Odin's house in Glasir, and Glasir was a grove of gold-leaved trees, that kept their leaves even in the wintry time of the year. And the moonlight played in their boughs, flashing and dancing from the twigs and foliage. And Odin's house was long and gloomy, its grey sides were of iron, and its roof inlaid with silver, and upon its rooftree a golden cockerel sat, glaring with ruby eyes towards the East. And Loki said, 'And will this great monster of gloom also meet his end? Odin, that was the father of us all, and won all we have in the olden days, for he it was that got the drink Od-hroerir, which brought us power, and he it was that gave his eye for a draught of Mimir's fountain, so that he may look into the coming days. Much good that has brought him! It makes him a spectre at every feast. Well, hurry on, doom, and swallow this lord up. The Aesirs have long murmured against his wintry rule.' And Loki turned back and walked another way, and he went up a long hill to a place which gazed afar.

And Loki saw then all the halls ranged about him. There was Glitnir, the house of Forseti, the god of justice: level was its rooftree, and each door balanced by another. And he saw Noatun, the wild palace of Niord, and it was daubed with pitch and sand like the houses by the sea, and seaweed hung up in its porch to tell the weather. And he saw Folkvang in the park of Sessrymnir, a delightful garden with many bowers and arbours to sit, and the house was neat and carved with intricate patterns of wood, and this was Freya's home, the goddess of love. And then did he see Valhalla itself, the mightiest of halls, where the fallen heroes live in eternal joy, the Einheriar, which the Valkyries fetch. And the great hall sparkled with walls of glittering spears, rank on rank in a ring of impenetrable steel. Over the great gates were a boar and an eagle, and their eyes shone out glaring to the ends of the earth. And the roofs of the palace were of shields of burnished gold, and they flashed back the moonbeams into the face of the moon.

And Loki smacked his hand against his thigh and cried, 'How mighty are these Aesirs! What palaces of power are these! And is all this vast strength to avail them nothing against their foes? Will the monsters and giants, whom they pushed back into the world's verges, be able to arise and break into these mighty walls? Oh, great day when that comes! And yet how can it happen? Even the moon this night seems anxious to placate them.'

But Loki's gaze then fell upon the far off house of Balder, the hall of Bleidablik, and its silver roof sloped down to a colonnade of golden pillars. And Loki smiled and said, 'There lies the key to the destruction of the gods. How all things meet in Balder, and depend on his overthrow. Long we have known that he has usurped all power. There is in him something unknown to the older ones, for his great strength is lit within by intellect. He alone now can destroy the enemies of the gods. But Balder is doomed. Witches cry it out. Then Ragnarok is coming. But how will I see it accomplished? I will straightway go to earth and take up the prophecies. Odin found out the most by consulting the wind-witch Hyndla. To her will I go at once to find out how Balder shall be doomed.' And Loki hurried off down the sloping hill towards the walls.

Now Loki had the power, alone among the Aesirs, of turning himself at will into any living object. Thus, once he had come but to the walls of Asgard, he changed himself instantly into a wheeling sea-gull, and diving with thin wings through the dark air, he plummeted downwards towards the fiords and shores. And busily did Loki skim the waves that led him towards Throndheim. And so Loki came to the strange island of Torgen, where Torghatten, the eye-tunnelled hill, looks bleakly out to sea. And Loki changed back into his own true shape and mounted upwards to consult the witch of the winds.

But when Loki came to the top, and stood against the mouth of the hole, he could make out no sounds of wind channelled in the prophetic tunnel. But then did he shout into the hole, and his lone voice echoed out of the other side, 'Hyndla, you witch of the winds, are you there? Answer me now as you answered the Lord Odin, for strange times are upon us, and these things must be known. Balder you prophesied would be soon dead and in Hell. Tell me now how he will meet his death!' And Loki set his ear into the great cavity and harkened.

And a small faint breeze that sounded like laughter came back to him, and it blew the thin hair of his head over his eyes. And the half-heard voice said, 'You must be mad, Loki, to think I would tell you such things. Do you not know that Hyndla never speaks of what you wish to hear? If I were to tell you how Balder will meet his death, how busily you would rush off and try to bring it about. But I tell you I will not. You will puzzle your mind, and wrack your poor brains a thousand times from this moment, trying to work out how Balder may be killed, but you will not stumble on it, though you split open your head with thought. Go then, you wretch, and leave Hyndla to sleep again. There will be rain-storms again this night, and Hyndla will be howling.' And the faint warbling breeze died down again, and left Loki no wiser.

And Loki sat there gloomy again, perched on the slimy boulders, and he rested his head on his fist, and stared ahead of him.

But as he looked out over the waters, he saw the fylgie returning from consulting the Norns. Then did the fylgie land on one of the great boulders and panting it recovered its breath and then said, 'Hyndla, Hyndla, I bring your consultation from the Norns. And the well of Urdar said to me, and this message I return: "The Aesirs shall be doomed by one that cannot weep." Such was your bidding, Hyndla, have I not done well?'

And Loki leapt up and shouted, 'Excellently well, little fylgie of the witch, for you have given me the prophecy that Hyndla would keep from me. Nay more, such a fresh one as she had not even heard. Now I know something to the bane of the Aesirs. I have gathered well from the dip into the occult!' And Loki laughed and capered about the slimy crags.

But the witch Hyndla now grew enraged and a sudden dark cloud grew on the other side of the tunnel, and a sudden wind sprang up and howled through the rocky channels. And with a great roar it blew Loki and the fylgie up into the air, tumbling together, somersaulting over the moonlit waves and islands. And the fylgie was distressed and shrieked like a sea-bird. But Loki decided to fly again home. So, turning himself into a great white hawk, he thrashed his snowy wings, and soared out of the black clouds to heaven.

And as Loki walked once more in the dark of Asgard, he looked again on the halls he had studied before: on Thor's compound, and Odin's secret grove; on Freya's sweet home and Niord's, and he felt exceeding joy in his heart and said, 'With each hour I walk the earth, my power grows and their doom comes upon them. How at first I doubted that such great ones could be overcome! But now do I see before me a great task for my mind, for brain is better than brawn: this is the lesson that my deeds will show. And step by step I have been led to this aim: that I shall kill Balder, and vanquish all the gods!' And Loki walked again to the mound, and he sat there to think how best he could begin his evils.

But the fylgie of Balder, that consulted the Norns, went ferrying to and fro its dreams to Balder. And the first dream that it showed him was of the land of smoking ashes, and Balder dreamed wearily of the mists and melancholy. And the second dream that it showed him was of a more mocking air. For Balder dreamed of a deep wood of oak-trees, and he was wandering in search of some fruit from their boughs. But search as he might among the grey-lichened boughs, the oak-trees had no fruit, for they were all completely bare. And he thought to himself how can there be fruit on bare trees? But far off he saw a green patch high up in the grey twigs and branches, lit by the moon with silvery sheen. And Balder ran and eagerly climbed the tree to fetch it. But just as he stretched his hand towards the green leaves, he saw that they were not leaves at all, but a green, grinning gnome. And the gnome hissed at him, so that Balder jumped with fright. And he found that he was but in his bed, and his coverings were on the floor, and the sharp sounds were his own fearful breath.

And Hodur said to him, 'Balder, why did you cry out? You have been restless and turning in your bed, and suddenly you shouted as if in fear. It is unlike you to have such frightful dreams.' And Balder replied, 'Oh Hodur, sweet brother, I have seen some ghastly things. What they mean I know not, but my heart is full of doubt and fear. Yet why should it be? I am not afraid of death. I will sleep again, brother. I am sorry to have waked you.' And the two brothers settled down again to rest, and soon they were asleep again in the wooden alcove.

But the third and last dream came to Balder that night. And the fylgie that brought it was heavy with the weight of it, and could go no more to the fountain. And Balder's dream was full of many weary things. For once more he found he was hunting in a forest. But now was the forest not of oaks but of pines and firs, and the forest was dark, and overcome with dead boughs. And Balder kept looking among the spiky trees, but for all his looking he could not think what he was looking for. And while he restlessly yearned to know what he should do, he caught a glimpse far off of his beloved Iduna, walking between the dark boughs, stopping and picking things from the ground. With a surge of joy then did Balder run towards her, calling her name among the echoing ranks of trees, and he ran as speedily as he could along the ferny tracks and paths. But suddenly when he felt that he was nearing her at last, he found blocking his way was an enormous giantess, clad in white robes, that swept up towards her face. And when he looked at her face, he grew sick and disgusted, for the face was fat and full of bumps, and the flesh was spread all over the face, so that the eyes could hardly be seen. And with horror did he see that grasped in the giantess's hand, shielded from him by the high walls of her white-clad thighs, was Iduna. But just as he tried to reach forward to pull her away, the giantess showed him her other hand, and opened her palm before him, which was huge and like a great table of flesh. And on the palm he saw three things: a hammer on a loaf of bread, a tunic hanging in a may-bush, and a woman's hand holding a weapon. And once he had seen these things, the giantess turned away, and with great strides began to disappear into the wood. And Balder ran after her as speedily as he could. But now were his legs so heavy and slow that he could not make after her. He strove and strove to make his legs go faster, and at last with a scream he leapt up out of bed.

But Hodur came up to him, And feeling his way, Hodur clasped his brother and said, 'Balder, you are tormented with some spirit. Let us quickly go to our mother Fricka. She will dispel this demon that keeps attacking you.'

And Balder stood panting at the door. Half the clothes of his bed were still draped over him, and the wolf-skin and bear-skin clung to his sweating breast. And Balder's eyes were like saucers staring out into the black hall before him. And he clasped his brother with his hand and said, 'Oh Hodur, never have I known fear like I have

[33]

felt tonight. And the fear is still with me, greater than ever. Let us go then, but let us go to Odin, for I have wronged him this night, and now do I feel it. He with his great wisdom can solve these terrors for me. For I have been blind to the horrors of the prophecy. For what if I should die before I can save Iduna?'

Then did the two brothers hurriedly dress, and Balder tied Hodur's shoes about his feet, and they left the hall and went over the fields towards Glasir. And coming to the house and the door that led to where Fricka and Odin slept, they knocked sheepishly at the door, and waited. And Fricka answered the door suspiciously, but threw it open on seeing who it was, and fearfully did she say, 'Balder, my son, and Hodur, what brings you here, for it is the middle of the night, when the moon is coldly shining? Yet if you are anything like your mother, you have not been able to sleep.' And she took them inside, and led them into a hallway, and going to a table she made them cups of the cheering honeymead. And bidding them drink she gave it them, caressing the two brothers as she put the cups into their hands.

Then did Balder speak and say, 'Hodur has come with me but for love and fellowship. Yet the trouble is only my own. Mother, let us go to Odin and wake him, for badly do I need his counsel. I shall beg his forgiveness for my deeds this last night, for I am sorely afraid that I have dreamed bad dreams, and I fear lest I shall not be able to rescue Iduna.'

And Fricka looked angrily and scowling at him said, 'Are you suddenly afraid now that you have brought her into it? And do you wish to go tamely to your father now, and cringe to be forgiven? What good could he tell you? He speaks nothing but woe from day till night. Yet if you wish, I will wake him, and you can see for yourself. It were better anyway not to have you two at loggerheads.' And Fricka took their cups from them and replaced them on the table, and beckoning them to follow her she led them to the door of her room. But then turning did she say before they entered, 'Balder, my son, let us see what Odin suggests. But for myself I have been thinking this night of a plan. If the old greybeard here cannot give us hope in anything, let us all three go to earth and consult this witch Groa. She told you something useful indeed when she told you ask Loki for what in heaven had disappeared. She is of more worth than all these other sorcerers.' And so saying she pushed open the door, and they entered the dark room where Odin slept.

And already at the creaking of the door was Odin awaked, for his bed lay piled with thick bear-skins and sleek furs, and his shield and spear lay glinting a little way from his bed. And Odin spoke out to them and said, 'Who comes this night to trouble my slumber? Can I not find peace even in sleep? Wife, why are you up at this ungodly hour? Are you come to pester me, and scold me some more?'

And Fricka said, 'Peace, great seer, and malign us not before we speak. We have come with no revolt. No, Balder and Hodur are here. And Balder indeed has suffered a great change of heart. He has been troubled, my lord, with all that he said tonight, and how he vowed to disobey you in the hall. Here is he come to beg your forgiveness, and plead with you to take him as your son again.'

And Odin hummed into his beard and said, 'Balder, is this so?'

And Balder knelt down by the bed and said, 'No son likes to cross his father, nor can he be at peace as long as there is a quarrel. Vile dreams and restlessness have plagued me tonight. I do not wish to tempt fate now by any intemperate acts or disloyalty. Therefore forgive me, father, and let us be friends again, for you are the founder of us and all we have.'

And Odin got up out of his bed at once, and laid his hand on his son and said, 'That will I do, my son, with all my heart. Do you think I would wish to hurt you in any way? Oh Balder, all might be well, if only we tread carefully. Let us quarrel no more, and do you remain in Asgard. Did I not build this land as a fortress against all fear?'

And Balder quickly got up again and said, 'Father, I thank you for your kind heart. But do not still lay that ban upon me that I must never leave Asgard. What I formerly pushed aside, that now do I dread and believe : that I may be doomed to die within some few days. But father, in my dreams I saw the captured Iduna, and my nightmare was that I was too weak to rescue her. And this is the substance of all my new fear. Oh father, tell us some way that this may be averted. You have great wisdom. In your wanderings over

[35]

earth, you have learnt the secrets of all things, and the inner myster-
ies they enfold. Give me but some hope, some way that I may save
her. Help me to put off death a while until I may do that.' And
Balder knelt down again at his father's feet.

And Fricka spoke also, joining him in pleading, and said, 'Ay,
Odin, now deserve the title of wisdom, which men bestow on you.
Easy enough it is to counsel fear, and to urge sitting idle, and waiting
for doom, but are not your great wits and knowledge above such
cowardly acts? You have traced all herbs of the earth, you know
each creature and stone. Is there not some spell you have culled from
the far Caucasian wizards or Arctic seers, that will but guard your
own son against serpents or poison or arrows or drowning? Come,
my husband, search your brains for some daring scheme. Let us
know the remedy to all these boded ills. There must be some clue
in the prophecies you have heard, which might divert their power,
and turn them to good.'

And Balder then spoke eagerly and said, 'Ay, my lord, this I am
sure there must be, because in the turmoil of my dreams did I see
strange things that had meaning. A vast smoky land did I see peopled
with mists, and an oak-tree wherein did a green gnome sit. Do these
symbols mean ought? Is there some mystery in them? And when I
dreamed of Iduna, she was in the hands of a dough-faced giantess.
And ay, I remember it now, most weird things she showed me in
her hand, for there was a loaf with a hammer in it, and a tunic
thrown onto a flowering hawthorn-bush, and there was a woman's
hand holding a blade. Surely these objects have some esoteric
meaning. Tell us, my father, how are they listed in the runes?' And
Balder tugged eagerly at his father's sleeve, and looked up at him
with pleading brow.

But Odin tugged his sleeve away, and lifted up his hands in
exasperation and he cried out, 'You are all come again just as
before! You win me with smooth words and then taunt me as you
did in the hall. See, this is nothing but a plot to make me rescind
my ban. Go, if you must, my son. Go to Midgard and your death.
Go, and bring doom upon us each and all. I am weary of waiting
for it to come. Oh my son, my wife, little do you know how you
torture me with your words. You put into the air the very voices

that have plagued me for all these weary years. Do you think I have
not searched my wisdom for ways out of this calamity? Nightlong,
daylong have I been pondering on it, before you or any of you knew
that it was foretold. Ah, how I curse the day that I went to Mimir's
well. I was young then, and foolish, and knew not that prophecy
was the vilest curse. Recently had I won the great draught of Od-
hroerir, and what power did it give me, and all the Aesirs! I thought
that the answer to all lay in drinking the right potions. So did I go
to the fountain of Mimir on earth, where the trunk of the great
world ash-tree Yggdrasil pierces Midgard, and ascends into the
heavens. They asked for a sacrifice to repay my taking of one sip.
I gave them my eye, and looked but one way ever since. Then I
drank, and instantly had knowledge of the future. Oh, that power
has plagued me from that day to this! It breaks my spirit. It saps my
will. No, I have long seen this curse coming upon Balder. And this
vision of Ragnarok, which some think is but a fable, I see yet
clearly before my eyes, and the day when we all shall die. My dear
ones, give up hope. There is nothing we can do. As surely that day
comes upon us, as the sun goes round. The signs you saw in the
giantess's hand, my son, they were your death-signs, and they are
approaching. Once you have seen those three things pass before
you, then you will know that your death is instantly come. Abandon
yourselves then to this wisdom of despair, and open your hearts to
the darkness that must be.' And Odin sat down on his bed with a
great sigh, and wearily he placed his head in his hands.

Then did Fricka take the hands of her children, and silently led
them out of the bed-chamber. And without speaking a word she
delayed a while outside, and from a large chest drew out robes and
piled them over her arm. And some pelts and rugs gave she also to
Balder to carry. And quietly she led them both out of the house,
Balder following her, and Hodur stumbling beside him, and they
went forth into the frosty fields of Asgard. And Fricka led them
across the sparkling paths towards Thrudvang, where Thor lived
in his hall Bilskimir. And the shadows of the three lay across the
cold grasses, which were silvered over with a sea of rime.

And when they came into the great compound where Thor had
his thralls, Fricka awoke the sentry who was sleeping at his post,

and she said, 'Take these clothes into Thor's hall, and in the morning give this message to Sif, your mistress: that Fricka came in the night to stay, and leaves these robes of hers to be put in a chamber. Say to her that we three: Fricka, Balder and Hodur, are going to earth to consult the seeress Groa. And we purpose to return on the morrow. Now let Thor in his absence, for he is always kind-hearted, lend us a horse for the travel through Midgard.' And Fricka gave the sentry the robes, and gave those also that Balder was carry-ing.

Then did the sentry lead them over to a great barn, and the place smelt warmly of horses and hay. Then did he go to the stalls and fetch forth, clopping on the cobbles, a great charger, whose sheen gleamed in the steaming air. And laying over it a blanket, and putting on the horse's reins, set forth towards Heimdall's gate that leads to earth.

Then did Fricka stay them a while and say, 'Oh my dear sons, my heart is light at last. We three are to go forth, and search out our own fate. It is strange times when a mother and woman has to take on the duties of her lord, but we are going to consult a woman for aid, and so it is fitting, and Balder can bide a while. Know then that I will crave from the sibyl a task to perform, I will beg from her a means to make Balder invulnerable. Whatever Groa shall advise, have no fear that I shall do it, for I sense that a great adventure is to be begun. Come then, my sons, be my children still a while, and let me lead you down to try the luck of the world.' And Fricka led Balder and Hodur to the great gateway, and they looked out from that vantage over Midgard.

And the path was pale and lit by the lonely moon, which had now drawn its chariot to the zenith of the sky, and the dappled lands looked peaceful sleeping below them. For before them lay the Northern nations, which met the sea with inlets and a thousand dotted isles. And the sea wind blew up fragrant with salt spray. To their left stretched out the massive forests of the Teutons. To their right were the snowy lands of the Lapland lakes and marshes. And touching their very feet, leading down in a great arc to the soil, was the bridge of the rainbow, Bifrost, whereon only the gods could pace. And Bifrost arose from the mists of the seashore, and a frosty colour invaded its hues, and each of its tints took on a silvery sheen: the scarlet and the fiery and the gold and the lime and the turquoise and the sea-green and the sea-blue and the mauve. And so did they descend and walk upon Midgard, and tread the winding ways that led to the sorceress.

Now Groa was a wood-witch and lived in a cave in the dark fir-forests of the land of Voss, where the trees of Rundall hedged in the river. And concealed by a tattered cloth she sat in the cave, a smoky fire before her, casting up its fumes, and she on a raised platform, to look down on men. And here after much wandering did the three gods come, bearing a torch to light their way through the gloomy woods, climbing the upward track with Hodur upon the horse, and when they entered the dwelling they sat all three on the floor, and here they looked up at the prophetess. And she had grey hair knotted and twisted into a thousand wriggles, and her face was wizened and wrinkled all over, yet behind these lines did the witch seem young.

And Fricka spoke to her and said, 'From high Asgard the impregnable fortress, in times of great trouble are we gods come a-begging. For evil times have come on us and the happy hall of Gladsheim is wracked with dissension and indecision. For it has been prophesied and surely you must have heard it, that Balder my son here is doomed to die. Oh Groa, you have helped us gods once when you told Balder to inquire of Loki, let me implore you to help us again, and lay on me the task of keeping Balder alive. Tell but the one task, be it never so harsh, which out of all these troubles will keep my son safe, and I will straight be about it, and the Aesirs may live still.' And Fricka finished her plea, and they sat still waiting.

Then did Groa speak: 'I will speak to you of these things. Let Balder and Hodur leave the cave, for I would tell it to your ear alone. And afterwards let Balder come in, and let me speak to him in private, for I have something to tell him that will also help the Aesirs.' And Balder and Hodur went outside the cave, and the two of them sat together on the mossy boulders. And Fricka stayed still looking up at the prophetess with hope.

And Groa sighed then and said, 'I speak to you alone and to yourself you must keep the words, for there are some amongst you who will seek to work against them. Go then, and bid everything in the world to swear to you an oath never to harm Balder, the god of sunlight, and when that oath is sworn your son shall be safe.' And once more the prophetess fell silent, and stared in front of her with impassive eyes.

But Fricka was puzzled by the strange advice and knew not what to make of it, and so she said, 'Alas, Groa, how might I or anyone do that? Who can even number or tell all the million creatures? Who can speak to them? Who might bid them swear? I beseech you tell me is this all the action you can urge me to? Oh prophetess, I beg you, is there not some other thing?'

And Groa chuckled and said to her then, 'Small thanks I get for the help I give you. But the task is not impossible. Listen and I will instruct you. The words of the gods can be heard by the world, but the world can only answer in the deeds of the world. To obtain an oath from all things on earth, three things must be done. Hear each one now and remember. For first the hearing of all things is to be summoned, and second all things are to be bid to take the oath, and thirdly must their answer be made plain. Prepare yourself then for journeys and tough work, work tougher than any man or woman has ever tried, for you are to ride forth swifter than ever horse went, and you are to sit on the highest mountain of the world. I read in your face, Fricka, that already you have begun to doubt. But settle your heart. It can and will be done. I will tell you your mission, and you may leave me then to think.

'The three things I told you are to be done in this way. When you return to the realm of heaven, take Sleipnir, Odin's steed, and prepare it for a long travel. Leaving Asgard then, fly on Sleipnir to all the regions of the world in Midgard: fly to Manheim, and Alfheim, and Niflheim, and Jotunheim, and Svartheim, and Vanaheim, and all the lands of the fires. In each place you go call aloud to every creature, and bid them attend to the words from the height of the world. Thus you may accomplish the first thing, which is the summoning of the hearing of everything on earth. When this has been done, fly then on Sleipnir's back to the great peak of the mountain Glittertind, for high above the wild ranges of the Northlands glitters this ice-summit, plunged in eternal snow. From this point on earth may everything be heard, and everything be hearing the terms of the oath: then you may speak out to all things the precise words of the secret vow. But hear me, Fricka, tell no one these words, for the terms of the oath must be known to no one but ourselves. And these are the words which you must speak: everything on the land, in the waters and in the air, swear never to harm Balder, the god of sunlight. The creatures will reply then, and you will hear them swear. Leave me now, and summon Balder to my cave, for I have something that must be heard by him alone. Remember to be secret about what I have told you. And for the rest, be of firm resolve.' And the prophetess, having recounted her long tale, fell silent once more, and sighed a deep sigh.

Then did Fricka go out of the cave, and motioned Balder to enter, and she sat perturbed by Hodur on the stones. And her heart was overawed by what the prophetess had told her. And she began to wish that she had not begun this enterprise. But she recalled each order of the seeress, and tried to imprint in her mind all the details of the plan. Meanwhile Balder sat down before the witch, and gazed up at her as she sat on the leafy platform.

Then did Groa speak again and say to Balder, 'What I have to tell you is not yet fully conceived. I have had news tonight, and know not fully what to make of it. My words to you, Balder, will be vague and halting. Yet something do I feel, and it is imperative I tell you. Listen therefore, and speak not till I have finished. For some days I have felt there was a loss suffered in Heaven. Thus was it I bade you ask Loki, when you told me of Iduna's abduction. But something other than she is missing from heaven still. And you are to retrieve it, as you are to rescue her. Yet this is my quandary, Balder, and bear with me. Something is missing, yet I know not what it is. And yet this do I know: that what is missing is now in Hell.

'This night did my fylgie fly to the Norns that spin the fate of things, and drinking at the fountain of Urdar did it bring me a prophecy that the gods could be saved by a branch of mistletoe. I searched my mind to fancy what this could mean, and I recalled there are old stories of men taking journeys to Hell, and the mistletoe is the plant which gives them secure access, and their deeds having been done allows them to retrace their way. It is a magic plant, and in some lands are those that cut it by moonlight for rites of their religion, and surely it has strange power to guard men going into Hell. Whereat, thinking what this prophecy could mean – and sorely have I been thinking these long days – I do now believe that there is something in Hell which has fallen from Asgard, and that this is a mighty enchanted thing, on which ye gods depend. Balder, my mission is for you, that you go out and find what thing this is, and that you then take the mistletoe and descend to Hell to fetch it. Go now, Balder, and leave me to silence. I have given you my rede. The rest is for you to further.' And Balder got up and left the prophetess thoughtfully, and the three gods began then their journey home. But as soon as they had gone, did a certain thought strike Groa, for she saw another meaning in the prophecy of Urdar.

And Groa gathered up the leaves which were piled at her side, and on them was written the runes of many prophecies and ancient truths, and she spread them before her and said, 'How long a life I have spent, carving with my nails omens on leaves, and prolonging vanity! How I have vexed my brains with seeking knowledge and making schemes! And a thousand times I have thought to catch the essence of things and make them into a charm. But charms are but words, and words but runes, and runes but leaves. How inevitable is the corruption they suffer, when the spirit of my dreams is put into such matter! I have sent forth my words now, and nothing can call them back, and the minute I have pronounced them, I see they are far from perfect. Go forth then, my commands. You are bound to chance like all things. Burn then, my leaves, for Groa has said enough. Burn, burn all my prophecies of help. What power have you flittering things against the coming storm?' And Groa threw down then all the sleek leaves, and as the smoke surged up from the hissing, crackling runes, did Groa close her weary eyes, and feed on the peace within.

And the three gods made their way back through the fir-woods. And Balder led on the horse that bore Hodur, picking his way through the dead bracken and the budding. And the tall spoked trunks of the fir-trees rose up all around them, filling the air with the black dust of their barks. And the torch that Balder carried spluttered and ducked with his pace, and the trunks multiplied the shadows so that the air seemed full of turning wheels.

But as they plodded on silently, Hodur breathed and said, 'I smell the coming dawn, and far off the birds I hear. Surely now the day comes, for the air is fresher and sweet. How fair it is on earth! How wealthy to live here! Surely this is better than our fortress for all its strength. In Asgard everything is hard and endures. But here I feel the tenderness of things that die.'

And they came to clearer ways now, and the dawn streaked the sky through the trees, and the river came in sight, which would lead them back to Bifrost. And they stopped a while by the banks for the horse to drink, and they ate a little and drank some honey-mead, and afar off they saw the fawns and deer coming down to the sandy banks to water. And the glittering stream led off into a bend of the dark fir-trees. But when the great day came it grew stormy, and the Eastern horizon was barred with bloody clouds and the travellers hurried on for fear of being caught in the rain. And so did they follow the pebbly stream now, and pace on through the rushes the way that they had come. Yet still did neither Balder nor his mother speak, for their hearts had not yet kindled to the tasks that lay before them.

But in Asgard meanwhile did Hermod summon all the gods to a counsel in the great hall of Valaskialf. And to the hall came Niord and Vidar and Vali, and took their places along the benches where the twelve Aesirs sit. And Thor the great red-bearded Thunderer came, and with him was the golden-haired Sif, who saw that all of them had the solace of wine and bread. And Loki came in from his long vigil on the hill, and his face seemed fiery and his eyes sparkled with eager thoughts. And the goddess of love, Freya, came in late, and her hair was swathed on her head in many a gleaming coil.

And when all the gods were assembled except Odin, then did Hermod rise and address them saying, 'It is strange and without precedent, oh Aesirs, to begin such a council without our leader, Lord Odin. But already this morning have I sent messengers to his house, and already his reply have they brought me twice: that nothing can save Balder or ourselves from death, and that he, our

[43]

leader, refuses to come. Yet I hold it wise, my friends, that we debate what is to be done, for in times of trouble it is best to think clearly. And to my mind there are two things that we must discuss. The first is: what preparations should be made for the rescue of Iduna from Jotunheim, and the second is what steps ought to be taken to protect Balder from the fate that has been promised him? Yet before we fall to talking about Balder, will no one say where he is? For it occurs to me that he is not in this hall, nor is his mother Fricka. Let us hope no ill has already claimed him.' And Hermod looked around the hall, but none of the gods answered, and left him only with silence.

But Thor, who had been sitting idly by, suddenly slapped his hands on his thigh, and he cried, 'Out on it! I have forgot the important message I was to give you all. For Fricka last night came to our house, and told our sentry that she was going to Midgard to consult the seeress Groa. And she has taken with her Balder and his brother Hodur, the blind, and they are to ask if there is anything to be done that may save Balder from the omens. It bodes well, does it not? That Fricka has a stout heart.' And the gods were glad at what they heard and murmured assent.

And Hermod replied, 'This is good news indeed. For Groa is a good witch, and has already assisted Balder. Let us hope that she will have similar good advice for Fricka. We all wait with eager hearts to hear the news of her mission. But gods, since with this news, the fate of Balder is presently being seen to, let us give thought to our other question. How might we therefore rescue Iduna?'

But then did Loki arise immediately, and looking pleased with himself say, 'It is a fortunate day for you, oh Aesirs, that I am in Asgard, and not about my travels among other races of the world, for the brain of Loki has been busy this night, and while Fricka can only consult and ask, Loki has speedily worked out a plan. For I know how to frustrate the giant Thiazi, and bring back Iduna to us, and if I cannot do it, call me a clod of earth and throw me over your shoulder. Listen what my plot is, oh Aesirs, and say if I have not done well. A body of us will go to Thiazi, and by a certain deception win our way into his castle, and when he least suspects, crack open his skull. And the deception will be such that not only

will he welcome us as friends, but that he will hand over voluntarily
the goddess Iduna to our safekeeping. For we will take him – as
he thinks – the goddess Freya – for you remember, do you not, that
I arranged with him to swap Iduna for a more ample goddess, since
Iduna had locked herself in a cage – and we will go so far as to have
a wedding ceremony between him and the goddess, who we will
say will not stay with him otherwise. And when Thiazi is intent and
overcome in his wits by lust, as he sits so close to the blithe
goddess of love, then we will attack him, and soon have him over-
powered. Yet do not worry, my friends, for I see already that you
are frowning at the thought of Freya being put to risk – for where
would your lives be without her to delight them? – the simple
deception is that Freya will not be herself. Since he is a strong god
and his hammer is necessary for the ratification of the wedding, let
Thor disguise himself, and make up the party. He in woman's
clothes will sit next to the giant, and his hammer will be placed on
his lap as part of the ritual, and when Iduna is safe in our hands and
the giant is unsuspecting, then Thor may well knock him senseless
with one blow of Miolnir. Is not this a good plan, my comrades, and
will not it do well?'

And immediately Thor burst out laughing and cried, 'Ho, Loki,
your brains have done it again. An excellent plan does it seem to me,
and full glad am I to be part of the adventure. Oh, I shall lay it onto
Thiazi with my hammer. I have been aghast that such a tender
maiden as Iduna should be swept away into the hands of a foul giant.
They are not graceful creatures, you know, as we are, for their
manners are most rough and they are crude in what they do and
say. But tell me, Loki, there is one thing that distresses me. Will I
really have to wear Freya's clothes, and mince about like a woman?'

And Loki replied quickly, 'Ay, that you will. And not only must
you be attired like the great lady herself when you come to Thrymheim, but you must wear these woman's clothes from the moment
you leave heaven, for you must enter Jotunheim, and pass the
frontier in such attire, lest the word goes round the giants that we
are impostors. And will it not also be a good thing if Balder comes
with us, and that he, I and Thor should make up the rescue party?
Though it has been prophesied that he will die if he goes to Midgard,

[45]

yet I do not think it would be on such a journey, for Thor could look after him, and I only wish him well.' And Loki pouted his mouth, as if he spoke of a minor matter, and shrugged his shoulders deprecatingly.

But then Hermod spoke again, and the gods murmured in agreement: 'That I do not think should be. For Balder is in danger, and in his danger is our danger, and for him to go on an enterprise to Jotunheim at such a time would be most unwise. Moreover his father, Odin, has forbidden him to leave Asgard, and Odin is our leader and his words should not be gainsaid.' And the gods agreed with this and applauded the speech.

But the goddess Freya then arose, and settling her garments neatly about her divine shoulders, she smiled at the gods and spoke: 'Most flattered am I to have played such a key role in your affairs, my brothers, and delighted above all that it needs no action of mine to bring any of this about. I must only be myself, which, as you know, is my chief entertainment. Yet who could be idle in such stirring days as this? Gods, let me play my part also in this glorious enterprise. Let me assist in Thor's disguise, and dress him in my best clothes and trick him in cosmetics. Yet one small flaw do I see in Loki's plan, which to my trained eye is obvious. If Thor is to impersonate me to the satisfaction of even a brutish giant, how is he to seem convincing when he sports an enormous red beard? Yet have no worry, friends, this even this, I shall overcome – nor shall the vicious snip of scissors despoil him of manhood, that mighty man. For the fashion is abroad on earth now that women getting married wear veils to cover the lower half of their faces. I have such a one, offered me by a descendant of Charlemagne's living in the Frankish court. This do I donate to help along our schemes. And now please continue with the urgent matters in hand.' And with a gracious wave, Freya seated herself, and arranged about her sumptuous hips the flowing folds of her gown.

But now did they hear far off the trumpet sound from the gates of Asgard, where a servant of Heimdall's signalled the approach of Fricka, and Sif, the golden-haired, spoke out and said, 'Surely this is Fricka and her sons returning. Let us go forth to meet them, and hear the news they bring.'

[46]

And the gods agreed, and went out of the hall of Valaskialf, and over the pavements towards Himminbiorg. And talking amongst themselves and with spirits full of hope, they saw Fricka and her sons afar off, where Balder was leading his horse through the gateway and into heaven. And the gods greeted them, and took their hands, and Thor lifted Hodur down and stood him amongst them all. Then were they joyful to be together again.

And Sif cried out, 'Welcome, Fricka, back home, for you have been a-work, while all we have been idle. But come now, tell us, for we are all bursting to hear: what advice did Groa give? Is there new hope now?'

And Fricka smiled at her friend and replied, 'Ay, there is so. I think that now we can do something. For Groa was helpful and has laid on me a charge, and though it seems arduous I believe I can accomplish it, for she has found a way to make Balder invulnerable, and once this is done, then are we all home and dry.'

And the Aesirs were delighted with this news, and chattered amongst themselves now, with hope renewed. And Hermod spoke then, and said, 'This is great news, for now do things take cheer, for also have we great news for you too, for Loki has devised a way whereby Iduna may be rescued, and if once you can assure that Balder is safe from harm, then he may join in the plot, and the bride be fetched back to heaven. Then shall we all be as happy as we were. But see, it is threatening rain, and a foul storm looks as though it will fall on us. Let us return all to Valaskialf, and let food and drink be brought for Fricka and her sons, and let us hear what is this great quest, and all put our mind to helping the goddess Fricka.'

And with that did the gods go back the way they had come. But or ever they could enter the hall by the swinging door, did a dark wind spring up, and water-spots come down, and the smooth paving-stones were dappled with the rain.

And when they came into the hall, so eager had all become, that straightway they embarked upon another breakfast, for hardly had the meat and drink been laid for Fricka and her sons, than the other gods began to help themselves, and soon were they all feasting in the early part of the morning.

[47]

But when they had eaten and drunk did Hermod arise and say, 'Indeed we have a plan now to take Balder and Thor and Loki to Jotunheim, and to meet with the giant and rescue Iduna, and this may they set forward the sooner the better, for Thor is to disguise himself and to be passed off as Freya. But come now, Fricka, tell us what is your plan, for we are all eager to help, and wish to see it accomplished.'

Then did Fricka arise and say, 'Aesirs, forgive me, but I cannot tell you all, for parts of my plan are to remain to me a secret, since the plan involves an oath whose wording must I keep to myself. Yet this much can I tell you, and I will confess it daunts my courage, for I am to ride on Sleipnir about the whole world, and get everything to swear never to harm Balder. Indeed you may look astonished, and I assure you so was I, when Groa first told me that this was what I had to do. But truly there's no way out, and she has revealed to me how to do it, for first I am to travel about the land of Midgard, and summon all creatures with a horn to hear my request, and then I am to fly to the highest spot on earth, and speak to the creatures the secret words of the oath, and last am I to listen to the reply the earth will make. Such are the steps which I must take this day. But say then Aesirs, will you consent that I should go, and will you help me now prepare for this mighty journey?'

And Hermod answered at once and said, 'That we will, Fricka, and gladly will we speed you upon such a mission. But fie, this is a tough test for any man to accomplish, and must you, a goddess, be about such perilous things? Has any of us before flown around the whole of Midgard? And did the witch tell you to do it, as if it were nothing? I am dismayed that she had not some easier way to do it. Yet Balder must be protected, and Lady Fricka, if you feel you can do it, then who are we to gainsay what you have undertaken? We will give you all the help we can. And truly, now you think of it, it seems a fair plan, for if all things in Midgard swear never to harm Balder, then how may he come to any harm, when he goes walking there? I begin to see the logic of the wild witch's plan. Come then, let's about it, and discuss what has to be done.' And here did the gods murmur in assent, and they stirred eagerly to get the plan into action.

[48]

But Balder then arose and spoke to them saying, 'Aesirs, before we all fall to planning my mother's journey, let me merely ask you gods a question, for the seeress Groa laid on me a charge also. And this shall I ask you: is anything lost? It was a theory of the witch's that our present woes stem from the loss of some important thing in heaven wherefrom our energy and strength is born. She laid on me the charge to recover this thing, but yet could not tell me what this thing might be. So answer me gods, and we may dismiss it from our minds a while: is there anything lost that any of you do own, or do you know of anything which presently is missing?' But the gods were all silent, and they looked at him strangely, and when the silence had lasted long enough, then did Balder say, 'Well, then, to our tasks. Mother, let us begin your venture, for you are to be a hero now, and do deeds worthy of fame.'

But here did Niord rise up, and with a gesture call for quiet. And his face was perturbed and lit with a strange mystic light, and he said, 'Friends, there is one precious thing in heaven, wherefrom indeed do the Aesirs take their strength. This it was in the old days which made them irresistible conquerors. Who knows not of Od-hroerir, the drink of will? We grow daily more set on feasts and debates, and less and less is our strength tested with achievements and deeds, and slowly are we forgetting the deep things from which we took our life. Tell me then, anyone, has Od-hroerir been seen of late? Has anyone looked to the potion or cared for the cup? Ay, you greet me with silence. That is eloquent enough. But if Od-hroerir has been stolen, then it is woe indeed, for the last few drops of it might have been power enough to resist the coming doom. You may often scorn me for remembering those things, but that brew of Od-hroerir was the source of you all, for Odin won it far off in olden days, and you warriors would drink of it, and go forth to kill and overcome. It came from the dwarves, though Odin got it not thence. From the blood of Kvasi they made it first, and it suffered many journeys ere it came into Odin's hand. For Odin, our lord, found it in the care of a maiden, Gunlod. And Odin seduced the maiden to gain the drink, and he bore it away, leaving her wretched behind him. This drink gave you will, and made you fight us Vanas, and were it not for that stolen brew, there would

[49]

be no walls of Asgard. Let us see, therefore, if we are truly doomed.'
And while the Aesirs looked on, unsettled by Niord's words, the
old Vana himself went to a small cabinet behind the throne of
Hlidskialf, and opened it with a key and put his hand inside. And
the cup of Od-hroerir he drew forth for all to see.

And then did Balder laugh and cry out, 'Then we are all made
merry men! Come then, Aesirs, let us be about our tasks, for my
mother is to bid for the furthest journey, and make her son safe
from the combats to come. Oh, every vein in my blood rages to be
questing, and mother, though yours is a hero's task, I wish it were
little and over quickly, that I may at last be gone.' So did they begin
preparations for Fricka's journey round the world.

For Fricka and Hermod fell to conference together, for Hermod,
being the messenger of the gods, had maps of the various lands of
Midgard over which Fricka was to fly, and he spread them on the
table to see best how to reach the whole world. For Fricka explained
how every point of Midgard was to be reached, and together they
pondered how she should fly thither. For wide was the world she
saw on the maps, and huge were the spaces of the air above them,
and ever to the West of all the known land there stretched the blue
colours which denoted the boundless seas. But then did Hermod
decide best where to voyage, and turning aside he sent to fetch
Sleipnir from the stables, and the goddesses were sent to fetch
Fricka some travelling clothes.

And turning back Hermod pointed with his finger at the maps,
and explained to Fricka how she could fare. And he said, 'It will
be best, dear lady, if you voyage in a circle, to leave Asgard from
Himminbiorg and return that way again. Now the earth's seven
kingdoms are placed in this way, that six of them lie on the land
mainly to the East, and the final region Vanaheim lies in the Westward ocean. Let Vanaheim be last then, and the spaces of the air,
and the rest you may tackle from an arc from the North. When you
leave Asgard therefore, fly directly North, and the immediate
region you will encounter will be Manheim. Threading through
these regions fly swiftly into the snows, and among the mists of
Niflheim ride and blow your horn. Then when you have summoned
them, swerve Eastward and Southwards again, and leaving the

Arctic wastes will you come to the Jotunheim ranges. Here you may safely journey over the mountains and plains.' And Hermod here pointed to the wide steppes of the East, over whose spaces the winds beat the giants.

And Fricka puffed her cheeks out and said, 'It is long so far, and I have not done half. I tell you, messenger, I begin to grow tired already. Yet go on with the journey. These lands I shall find, and over them all will I blow my horn to summon them, and so will all creatures be bidden to hear the oath.'

And Hermod continued, 'The way from henceforth is pleasanter for a while, for you see what land lies on the boundaries of the giants: Alfheim it is, where the happy elves live, and Frey, our comrade, rules the woody realm. Pass then over Alfheim, and summon its elves to hear you, and you come to Svartheim, which fringes the inland sea. Here also may you dally and breathe a while, for the country is pleasant, and warmer than here. So far have you visited the chief tribes of the earth, for Jotunheim houses giants, and Alfheim the merry elves, and Svartheim the dwarves, who are cunning in artefacts. But South of these countries is an inhospitable land, for there burns the furnace of Muspelsheim, the land of fire. Steel yourself, Fricka, for a hard journey here, and keep a tight rein on Sleipnir, who else may fear. But if you have courage, you will ride through the flames safely and piercing the fires will you reach the cool of the ocean. There lies Vanaheim, and the islands of paradise. This then is the voyage which lies before you. And surely we all know that Fricka will fly fast.'

Now the gods in Gladsheim were peering over Hermod's shoulder, and they followed with their eyes the journey as he pointed it, rolling the vellum maps with scooping and grating sounds. And they marvelled at the distances which lay before their queen. But when Hermod finished, they applauded his words.

Yet Fricka still looked serious, and searched the maps with a frown. And she said, 'Yet when I have finished this journey, Hermod, and summoned with my horn all the lands to attend to me, then must I fly to the highest mountain of the Northlands, and speak from the heights of Glittertind my secret oath to the creatures. So only will I hear when they reply to me. But where is this

Glittertind? I do not see it marked.' And Hermod then pointed to a place to the East of Asgard, and such was the snowy mountain, that vaunted above all the rest.

And now did the goddesses bring Fricka her fresh clothes. They combed her hair, and dressed her, and busily bustled about her. And Sif lent her a waterproof cape of oiled skins, to protect from the storm that was now coming on. And they fetched Fricka a helmet from the hall in Glasir, and such was it she wore as the leader of the Valkyries, the girls that fly the world and bring the warriors that die in battle. And the helmet was shaped like a Viking's, and sprouted horn on either side. And a bangle of copper was she given to protect from lightning, and a lance with which to deflect the rushing clouds. And Fricka felt like a mighty warrior to be so tended, and armed herself as if going out to battle.

And Vidar and Vali meanwhile went to the stables, to fetch Odin's Sleipnir, the great horse with plumy wings, he that could fly faster than anything in the world. But the two gods worried that missing its master, the steed would refuse to come with them, and kick with its iron heels. So they took with them some honeycake in a bag, and the horse took it gratefully and was led out onto the cobbles. Then did they harness it and saddle it, and fit it out with its glittering trappings, for the trappings were precious and inlaid with silver, and decorated about with many a swirling dragon and snake. And they hung down from it the jingling bells and iron rings which were to ward off the evil spirits. And Sleipnir, sniffing the stormy air and scenting adventure, flapped out his great multi-coloured wings, and beat them, so that the feathers flew amain, and then he settled them again at his sides, biding flight. And Vidar and Vali led him back towards the doorway of the hall.

And when they arrived back, Fricka came forth and all the Aesirs, and everything was ready for the great journey. But the wind blew harder now, and the thunder rumbled afar off, and the rain came in big drops, and rang on the armour Fricka wore. So hurriedly did they all move towards Himminbiorg and Sleipnir was led whinnying in amongst the gods. And when they arrived Heimdall turned down to them from his tower. And since Heimdall had heard all their talk in the hall, he sent down a servant to Fricka who bore her a horn of silver, and this was for her to blow as she flew over the lands, and would summon all creatures there to attend to her words from Glittertind. And he said that when it was time for them to answer, would he then blow his own Giallar-horn. And then were the great gates flung open for her again, and before her lay the storm through which she must fly to Midgard.

But just ere Fricka could mount Sleipnir and fly forth, Niord called to them from afar off, and came toiling towards them on his old legs from Valaskialf, and he held up the cup with Od-hroerir offering to them. Then did Balder race back swiftly to Niord to help him. And Fricka meanwhile kissed the goddesses farewell. And Sif, embracing her, said, 'Take care, great queen, and do not try more than your strength. Remember you are a woman, for all your soldier's heart, and though you work for the safety of us all, do not risk your own welfare or dare too much.'

And Balder then came running up with Od-hroerir in his hands, and he lifted up the cup to his mother on the horse and said, 'You would fly round the world sooner than Niord will get here. He says there is yet enough for you to drink and one more. So drink hearty, mother, and let it give you power to your task.' And Fricka took the cup and she drank one draught of the potion. And there was one mouthful left, to be reserved for darker days.

And so did Fricka take in the reins of Sleipnir, and turning the great steed to face the gate, she called to the gods and said, 'Aesirs, do you fly, or you will all be soaked in the rain. This is not a time for long partings, so I leave you. Have no fear, my friends, that I shall achieve this task. But if poor Fricka you never see again, what shall I say? Flee from the storm. Remember me.' And bidding them adieu with her upraised hand, she spurred Sleipnir towards the gate, and launched forth into the darkening air.

Then did the thunder crash about their ears, and the rain come bucketing down by the gate, and the Aesirs drew their mantles about them, and fled in a body back to the warmth of Valaskialf. And even old Niord, who had just at that moment arrived at the gate, turned back and hobbled his way with them. Vidar and Vali supported him on either side, and sometimes the old man's legs did hardly touch the ground.

[53]

But Sleipnir at once plummeted into a sooty cloud. And the great horse beat at the turbulent air with his muscular wings, and the substance of the clouds was hurled this way and that. But the great storm rallied and struck at him with its power, and the lightning fell about them singeing the plumes of the horse, and the flashes flamed on Fricka's horned helmet. But throwing forward the spear over the head of the horse, Fricka immediately cleaved a way in the cloud. But now did the vengeful rain pound over Fricka's head, and soak into the feathers of Sleipnir's wings, standing out in bubbles and running over them in little rivulets, so that the wings grew heavy with the water they had drunk, but Sleipnir beat them hard, and thwacked the freezing air, and it seemed as if Fricka rode on a waterfall. And so through the storm they plied with a will, and soon did they float away from the blackened clouds.

And when they were winging happily through clear air, then did Fricka pat Sleipnir's side and say, 'Well done, oh mighty horse, for that great thunderclap could not detain your wings. I know we shall conquer these leagues that stretch before us. But come now, steed, let us get into our stride, and strive not so sturdily to eat up the miles, for long is the way before us, and we must not tire. Float with the winds and let us relax and watch, for many and multi-coloured are the great lands we shall see.'

And so did Fricka guide her horse towards the world, and they winged their way downwards through the ether to dappled Midgard.

And they came then to Manheim, and flew over the fiords and channels. And below them, moored in safe heavens were the dragon-ships of the Vikings, and the shields on the sides glittered in the morning air. And the silver birches were budding now, and the reeds grew green, for the Spring was coming on, and afar off in the hills the cataracts smoked down, and the ibex roamed on the crags above the treeline. So over the land of Manheim Fricka then blew her horn, and summoned all creatures to attend to her words from Glittertind.

And flying speedily up the teeming coasts of the Northlands, Fricka struck out for Niflheim, where no men can live. And she drew her cape about her as the air got steadily colder, and even

Sleipnir shuddered as he felt the pinching frosts. And they flew over Spitzbergen, where the glaciers meet the sea, and mists and fog enveloped them, when they came to Niflheim. And they flew close to the ground so that they might know when they were above land, and the dry snow flew up in their faces at the beat of the horse's wings. And all they could see was drear wastes of snow: snowy mountains, snowy icebergs, snowy hills, snowy plains, and the air was dark and black, and scowled over all. And Fricka blew in summons her horn over that land, and at the sound below them there looked up the polar bears. And they stood on their hind legs and roared at the flying horse.

And Fricka patted Sleipnir's flank and said, 'Fly Eastwards and Southwards now, oh mighty steed, and let us leave this inhospitable land. Woe to those who go exploring in this waste, for surely they will feel they have come to Hell itself. Fly on, my Sleipnir, let us come to better lands.' And Sleipnir wheeled round, and sniffed with his nostrils at the air blowing from the South, and scooping the frozen air eagerly with his plumes he sped that way eager for the scent of grass.

And so they flew over the gloomy peaks of Jotunheim, and Jotunheim was divided into two, for part of it lay mountainous, and bordered onto Niflheim, and part of it lay rolling in endless steppes, where the breezes sweep all day over the shimmering sedges and weeds. And the blue mountains reared up, scraping the clouds with their sharp chins, and their black sides plummeted down with many a jutting crag, and the eagles wheeled about them, screaming into the echoes. And Fricka blew her horn there for all the creatures in the land, and she blew it again over the steppes, for the creatures that roamed there. The tundra was locked in winter. The marshes were frozen over, but the great river Volga flowed on in the South, and reflecting the grey clouds sought the Caspian Sea.

And they came next to Alfheim, which was a sunnier land. For here do the elves live, with Frey who is their lord. And Frey was the son of Niord, and a Vana, but he did not stay like his father with the Aesirs, but loving the sunlight and the golden woods of earth, he took up his home in the fertile land of Alfheim. And sometimes did he ride through its beechy woods and flowery meadows on his golden-bristled boar Gullinbursti, and sometimes did he float down the tree-lined Danube in his boat Skidbladnir, which could sail on the waters or in the air, and when not needed be kept in a pocket. And over the great forests where the spotted toadstools grow, and the squirrels hide their nuts, and golden orioles fly, did Fricka sound her silver horn.

And as it should chance, as Sleipnir flew on, they passed over Frey as he walked in the fields, for Frey was busy sowing fertility on the seeds, for the year was advancing, and soon they would sprout up. And Frey cast out of a rank-smelling sack mill-refuse and manure to enrichen the sleepy soil, and he saw Fricka overhead and waved to her laughing. And he called up as she passed, for his elves had brought him tidings, 'Fare on, brave Fricka, and good luck go with you. It will not be long before Balder is safe, and his sweet little wife is draped about his neck. I will see you at the wedding, and come to wish them well, oh Queen. But do not let me detain you. Fly on, and Spring will follow!' And at this did Fricka feel full of a sweet joy, for the earth seemed kindly and shining again.

And so did she come to Svartheim, which is the land of the dwarves, and the dwarves were cunning workers and great artists, and had made many a prized thing which the Aesirs had squabbled over. And the dwarves lived by the shores of a purple sea, and rocky were their lands and burnt with a gilding light. And the lands were teeming with the riches of the dwarves, and ships ferrying rare cargoes plied this way and that, and fishermen dragged forth red mullet and speckled squid. And Fricka blew her horn over the chalk-blue slopes of the shores, and round the marbly hills did she see the goats go grazing, and the yellow gorse blooming, perfuming the sultry spring air.

And flying Fricka said, 'This is the sweet land where Balder went questing, for down the great river Dnieper did he sail in his shining ship Ringhorn, and through the Black Sea down to the Golden Horn, to bring back fine dishes and crosses of gold from the dwarves. Blessed are the temples that wear such finery. But farewell, happy lands, for we are of other mould, and must strive against the darkness for our destiny. Come then, faithful Sleipnir, for the direst part of our journey is to come. To Muspelsheim must we fly, land of flame and heat, and its furnace must we penetrate to come to the ocean's domain.' And so Fricka left rich Svartheim's sea-fringed soil.

And afar off did she see the sky lit up with a hot glare, and rolling dunes of sand were wobbling in the heat-haze, and Sleipnir spluttered to sniff the singed air. But they flew on to Muspelsheim, and wafted over its deserts. And as misty and cold as were the first of the far lands she visited, so stifling and hot was this land below her. And Fricka felt hot in her waterproof cape, and taking it off she wrapped it in a bundle. And so they rode towards a great block of flame. Beneath them was the land bleached and barren with the sun, and nothing grew there but a few spiky cactuses, nor nothing lived but insects and salamanders. And over this dreary sand did Fricka blow her horn.

And so she came upon the wall of fire. Harsh were the flames, belching sparks into the sky. Brilliant was the light that flashed from the limitless fire. And the sands below were all melted into glass, and flapped and glinted like a boiling sea. Sleipnir whinnied with fear at the flames, and three times did Fricka wheel him round before it. And on the third circuit she dug in her spurs and urged him forward. For a while there was scorching heat, and darkness and light all at once, and choking, and pain, and a sharp smell of singeing, and they were hurled upward and downwards by the mighty currents in the fires, and Fricka feared least she should be pitched off into the glass. But then piercing the fire's blue eye, they floated smoothly forth over the cool waves of the sea.

And Fricka patted the neck of the flying horse and said, 'Well done again, Sleipnir, for now is the direst moment passed. For there remains now but the creatures of the water and the creatures of the air. And the waters will be favourable I do not doubt, for the Vana live there, under Aegir, their king, and the air has but birds and the lights of the heavens. Come then, noble horse, and eat up the miles towards the peak of Glittertind.'

But as Fricka flew on, there appeared in the West, in the great stream of ocean, the circling water that surrounds our world, the floating islands of happy Vanaheim. And it was from these islands that Balder wooed Iduna, when he first caught sight of her walking in the orchard.

[57]

And Fricka pulled in the reins and then spoke to Sleipnir, saying, 'See below us a peaceful isle, set about with apple trees that try out their spring leaves. Let us sink down to the young lawns of this land, and rest a while, and breathe its sweet air.' And as she spoke Sleipnir turned back his ears to hear her. And thirsting for the cool waters of a stream, did he plummet down to the island, and fly toward its shores. And there was a calm bay, where the sea surged quietly on the sands of a little beach, and leading from the beach through a wall that ringed the isle was an arch with an iron gate, and the black gate was ajar.

And so did they alight on the dewy turf, and leading Sleipnir to a stream nearby, Fricka left the horse to drink, and wandered among the trees. Still was the place and full of pearly mist, and it seemed there was no sound but the unfolding of the buds, and a few pipings of birds came through the haze with a lazy noise. And clustering at her skirts as Fricka sat down were pale-faced primroses with their floppy leaves, and shy blue crocuses opened their petals.

And suddenly before her, she saw an armlet lying in the flowers, and picking it up she turned it over with wonder and said, 'This is my son Balder's armlet! I know it by these runes. What marvellous chance that I should find it here, in one small place on the solitary island. For this place must be the very island that he came to in his ship, wooing Iduna. Often I have wondered what it must be like, and how he found her. What a reckless thing he is to take his armlet off and lose it! No doubt his wits had been suspended by the charms of that girl. And yet I can laugh at it, for all is peaceful here. How strange it is when you find in a far away place the objects that take your mind immediately home! In truth there are no journeys. All is always home. I will tie this ring onto my belt and return it. And with this I will get Balder to speak of his wooing, for he keeps deadly silent, when it is time to speak of that.' And so did Fricka get up, and thread on the golden bangle to her side.

And now did Fricka begin to look about the island, for she was curious to see what a place Iduna had come from. And she saw that it was a round, dome-shaped island, and the clammy sea-mists billowed in among its hills. And in most places were the chalky cliffs falling sheer into the sea, and the bay over which she had flown was the one safe approach. And gaily around its shores romped the little orchard wall, piled up from rough stones, and covered in growing grass, and the red-haired mosses that are soft and moist. The trees that it guarded were ancient apple-trees; their grey-patched trunks were frail with age, and opening to the heavens they twisted into strange shapes. But at the highest point was a great tree growing, and though it was early spring it was hung with golden apples. And afar off through the mists its mysterious branches stretched, and the apples glinted in the sun of the afternoon, and flashed light on the idle sea.

And Fricka, sighing, said to herself, 'Indeed this is the place they call the gardens of the West, where the fairy Vanas live, and the life is sweet and idle. But why is it walled about, and whence this ever-fruiting tree? And what purpose attaches to that little gate, where brown apple cores litter the rocks towards the sea? It is an intriguing, happy place, and I feel I could walk here long, sitting among its warm stones, and picking its spring flowers: for see where the coltsfoot and violet strew the grass. If care would fly our hearts, earth would be paradise. I will indeed ask Balder to tell us of this isle. But alas, the sun goes low in the sky, and I must continue my journey. Farewell, farewell, oh little happy isle, for you have reminded me that life is full of sweetness.' And Fricka took up the reins of Sleipnir and led him away, and mounting the great steed's back once more, she launched forth into the realms of the keen air.

Now the realm of the Vanas was the great ocean, and over this now did Fricka make her way forward. And at first did the silver fishes look up with scaly snouts. And there were black-spined herrings and dappled mackerel, and shoals of sprats glinting in the tumbling foam. And greater fishes came, the tunny and the sword-fish, and the ballan wrasse with fiery hues. And narwhals broke the surface with their curly horns, and dolphins mimicked Sleipnir as Fricka hurried by.

But human faces were there also seen, for Aegir, lord of ocean, stirred the sunny billows with his trident, and so ruled that the high seas would be choppy. And Ran was with him, his wife, the sea-queen, and men call Ran the Robber, since she lures sailors to their death, and in the shapes of sea-gulls do their souls ever haunt her realm. But now were the two monarchs idling their time, for the afternoon sun was sultry and pleasant, and cast the Vanas' shadows a long way on the waves. But afar off sporting among the hills of the sea were the nine wave-daughters of Aegir at their play, and as Fricka flew past they pointed up at her amazed, and drew their dank yellow hair and shaded their eyes from the sun. But when Fricka blew her horn to summon the things of the water, the daughters flapped on the surface of their sea with their palms, and wobbling up came the denizens of the deep: the green-haired undines, and nixies with scaly cheeks, and stormcarls frowned upwards with puzzled black brows. And thus all the creatures of the water heard the summons.

And Aegir god of ocean pointed to the flying horse and said, 'Look, wife, there goes the queen of heaven on Odin's horse. What can she mean to summon us so, and to call us to harken to an oath she will speak? The Aesirs seem to be learning new ways, for long it is that they have shut themselves in Asgard, and now are they venturing very much abroad. Let us send them calm days, and bring the spring on faster, for Iduna from our realms is to wed Balder soon.' And so did Aegir hold his trident horizontally over the sea, and the weather grew calm and hushed was the afternoon.

And so Fricka rose through the keen realms of air, and flew past the shining car of the sun, which drew its axle downwards now, and flashed from the Western horizon. And Sol, the bright sun-maid, could she see guiding the reins, and Arvakr and Alsvin were the names of her sleek steeds. And their gleaming hooves touched the rim of a great cloud, and the cloud glowed rustily and shot forth red rays. And Fricka saw palely in the sky at the same time the chariot of Mani, whose grey mare stepped out proudly. Alsvider was the name of this horse, and it drew the tides behind it, and frostily did its white mane show over the pearly seas. And summoning both creatures to listen to the oath, Fricka sank again towards the dappled earth.

And so in the last silence of the deep evening, at that time when all hearts relax to tenderness or regret, Fricka came to the peak of Glittertind. On the shore she dismounted, and looking forth, she said, 'How silent and vast is this land of the height of earth! And how I feel unworthy to command it anything! Surely we do but trouble the spirit that broods under this all. Well, my journey is done, and weary am I. The great warrior Fricka is much in need of rest. Oh all you little creatures of the earth, forsake me not now. Let not my one quest be in vain. Nor do not remember that I am but a woman, for I have done as much as any man could do. Yet answer me, little creatures, and do not think on any malice. What has my son Balder done to harm you, when the sunlight is our joy? But give your sweet blessing on Balder and on his bride. Keep them safe. And the rest let the winter make sleep. All things on land, in the water and in the air, swear never to harm Balder, the god of sunlight.'

And now did Fricka hear sinking down from the dark sky the low sweet tone of the Giallar-horn, which summoned all creatures to answer the oath. And the sound went echoing in the snow-drifted vales. And the mountains were full of silence and stillness was in all.

But the gods meanwhile, hearing that Fricka's journey was near done, went to a high hill, to attend the outcome of her quest. And when they heard Heimdall blow his horn, they strained their ears to listen to the reply, and they doubted not but that they would hear the murmur of all the things of the earth. But after they had listened a while, they heard nothing, and began to look at each other with dismay.

And at last Vali, the talkative god of light, spoke and said, 'We hear nothing, do we not? We all stretch out our ears, but none of us have heard a sound. Brothers, should we not ask ourselves what this means? Does this mean that the creatures have refused to swear the oath? Can it be that not one single thing on earth has responded to Fricka's summons?' But the gods did not answer him, but looked at him frowningly, for they were all not speaking since they wished to listen still.

But at last did Hermod address them, saying, 'What use is it us listening here? Our ears are not placed to hear the whispers of earth, nor are they sharp enough if they were. There is but one of us in Asgard who might hear whether Fricka's cause is safe. He sits eternally harkening to the world, listening for the warning sound of the approach of doom. Let us then go to Heimdall, and call upon him that he may satisfy the anxiety in our hearts.' And so the gods descended the shadowy hill, and came to the tower of Himminbiorg, and on it with his hand cupped to his ear they saw Heimdall, his helmet flashing with the rays of the dying sun.

And then did Hermod call up to him and say, 'Heimdall, our guardian, and the watchman of heaven, tell us what sounds waft up to you from the dappled earth? For Fricka has gone from us a full day's journey, and we have heard ring out the noble Giallar-horn. Say if you hear anything that answers Fricka's oath, for we long to hear some comfort to quiet our fearful hearts.'

But Heimdall sat still, and lifting up his hand he signalled the Aesirs all to keep silence, and he leant even further forward, straining towards Midgard. But his brow was furrowed and dark was his face, and the gods felt their hearts grow cold, as they saw that he did not hope. And Niord sighed wearily and shook his grey head. And the gods questioned Heimdall no more, but as if fleeing from bitter news, they turned and streamed away, and went to Gladsheim again. And mighty Thor swung open the great door, and Hermod led them silently into the chamber.

And Loki did they find toasting his shins at a fire, chewing on a bone. And when he saw them enter, he wiped his moustaches and called out to them, 'Oh here come the merry crew of corpses! Is Fricka then not back? Has she fallen off Sleipnir, and ended up in the sea? You gods are all too childish. You but feel a thing, and it is written all over your face. But come, what has happened? Will no one tell little Loki?'

And Thor at once answered and said, 'Nothing has happened. That is the disgrace of it. Poor Fricka of the mighty heart has journeyed so long, and Heimdall has heard nothing. Fie, what scornful days! Surely I tell you I am tired of tameness and suffering.' And Thor sat down on a bench along the weapon-hung wall, and the swords clashed together with the buffet of his shoulders. And slowly all the gods sat also, some by the crackling fire, and Balder sat afar off and stuck his two hands in his dishevelled blond hair.

But at last did Hermod speak to them saying, 'This is no night for feasting, and idle is the time we spend in this hall. Let us go back each to his separate dwelling. And let each god think of the dangers which are before us, for if Fricka has been unsuccessful, and doom is advancing, then manifold are the preparations which we must undergo. Odin is to be placated, for he commands the fallen heroes of Valhalla, the Einheriar, who are to fight with us against the monsters. Our allies in Midgard are also to be wooed, and wise must be our proceedings with the tribes. Let us then give deep thought to these things, and on the morrow meet yet again to discuss what we must do.' And Hermod got up then, and turned towards the door, and the other gods rose wearily, ready to leave the hall.

But just as they had begun to file out, they heard a bugle from Himminbiorg, announcing an arrival in heaven. And the gods fell silent, and gazed that way. And then did they catch sight in the moonlight of Fricka on Sleipnir galloping from the gateway, and her clothes flew fluttering on either side. And the gods raced towards her, and met her on the way, and they caught Sleipnir's bridle and held him as Fricka leapt down, and they saw that her face was radiant with joy.

And Sif the golden-haired spoke to her saying, 'Fricka, dear friend, do not keep us in suspense, but tell us at once what answer made the creatures.' Fricka answered, 'Then rejoice this night with me. For the great journey is done. My mission is accomplished. All things on earth have sworn never to harm Balder.' And the gods when they heard this burst into rejoicing, and loud were the sounds of joy in the courtyard.

And red-bearded Thor smacked his hand on his thigh and said, 'What! Fricka, you are a woman and a half! And you have accomplished something greater than a man. What a mighty warrior you are, and how you look it in that armour! The warlike Valkyries could have no better queen. But tell us of your journeys. How did you accomplish so much? And how was it you heard just now the answer of all creatures to the oath, for neither we nor Heimdall heard a peep!' And the gods nodded eagerly, and clustered about Fricka.

But before Fricka might reply, came forth Balder from the hall, last of the gods, but drawn by the joyful sounds, Balder, the god of sunlight, now invulnerable, and Fricka rushed and embraced her son. And Balder stroked her hair and said, 'Mother, welcome home!

[63]

I have been sitting here fretting all day, that you are adventuring, while I am idle. Yet how brave you have been! What perilous paths you have threaded! What greater daring than a mother shows for her child? Come then tell us how you fared on your journey, for you are the great adventurer now.' And Balder laughed and took his mother's hand.

But Fricka looked up at him for a while, and she caressed his cheek with her hand, and tilting up her face she kissed him on the lips. But turning then to the rest of the gods she said, 'Some have sat idle while the true ones have worked. Sleipnir and I have earned all your bread today. But we wish for refreshment, before we give you any further entertainment. And if you wish to keep in my favour then whisk me into the hall, and give me a soft seat to sit on, and let my only labour be to lift food to my mouth. For I hunger and thirst greatly, and the horse does too.' And smiling Fricka turned to her son, and thumping him between the shoulders she pushed him to the door. And the gods applauded her, and were at once in festive mood. And when Sleipnir had been led away to be groomed, and watered and fed with fragrant hay, then did all the gods return to the hall of Gladsheim, and soon the chamber rang with laughter and jest.

For there were brought forth busily bristly boars which were roasted whole, and the tables were set with flagons of golden mead. And servants bustled about attending to the gods, bringing them napkins and baskets of the round, flat bread, and loud were the shouts of the marshals of the attendants. And the gods eagerly sat at the tables as the trestles were put up, and their countenances beamed with the light of pitch-torches. Then did a fragrant scent of cooking puff up into the air, and the great hall grew warm and hazy with smoke and steam.

But when they had begun feasting, did Thor strike on the table with his fist and say, 'A health and a toast to Fricka the mighty mother! Why, if she could have been a man, how powerful we would be then! Look at her flashing black eyes and her determined brow, and how splendidly they glower at you from under a horned helmet. But tell us though, Fricka, for we are all eager to hear: how was your travelling, and what sights did you see? Yet first for our curiosity, satisfy us of one thing, for that is how you knew things had taken the oath. For truly, queen, you must have ears like a bat or a wolf or whatever has mighty ears, for we were straining to hear till the blood sang in our heads, but nothing we could note when Heimdall blew his horn. Nor nothing could he either, for we went to him and asked. Tell us how it was ye caught the voices of earth.'

And Fricka smiled and replied to the revellers: 'That will I do, if you can hear me now. But Heimdall you misunderstood, for he heard well enough. He told me to excuse him to you, when he bade you be silent and would not answer, for at that time he was intent on the sounds, and listened to them carefully to check that all things replied. But of the sounds themselves I shall now speak, though the rest of my journey I'll leave to another night. Yet, oh fellow gods, what long ways did Sleipnir fly. How I wished at times that I might have taken you all with me. So many lands, so many fair realms; they kindle to one sun, but are rich in difference. But yet to my answer, and the answer that earth made me.

'As anxious as were you, biding in Asgard, so was I on Glittertind, waiting to hear if the earth would take the oath. For first there came, when I had spoken the terms of the charm, only a ghostly silence that filled the ranges of the hills, and I began to think that my travel had been in vain. How lonely I felt then with Sleipnir beside me. How I and he felt cut off from all friends and home. Little love did I feel for the life of a lone adventurer. And I looked at the harsh cold peaks, and they seemed hostile to me.

'But before I had truly noticed it, as I knelt in the snows of the peak, I found myself listening to a trembling sound. It was a hum that came neither from without nor within, and it seemed that both I and the mountains were filled with this vibration. And as I sat up, peering forth to search its cause, I heard a crack shiver in the air, and it seemed to be that the whole earth had split. And just as the buds split in spring and the ice breaks apart and the juice in things starts flowing, so did I hear then a thousand splitting and sundering sounds, and the liquid hum filled the space between. Then below me the glaciers rang aloud, and with a noise like thunder and a shape like tumbling smoke, I saw miles down the slopes an avalanche of snow. And the avalanche sailed downwards into the breathless valleys, and the boom of it rose up again, scaling the black crags. And after a jingling of metal and a clanging of stone, the air grew purer and all was calm again.

'But then from further and deeper in the vales, came a noise of dripping waters, filling the air with sharp splashes like rain, just as a bright day in April when the willows are sleeked with green. And mingled therewith was a sound of rushing rivers, bounding among rocks and hissing through reeds. And the tumult grew louder of cataracts and fountains, until all was merged into a roar of waterfalls, and this too was hushed into the beating of the eternal sea. And once more all was silent, and I was left alone.

'And then did it strike me with joyful surprise, that I had heard replying all the creatures to the oath. For this was the sound of dumb things, and already much of the world had taken the oath. And I stood then and looked forth joyfully, and even Sleipnir lifted his head, and stared before him with pricked ears. And so we heard a rustling in the wind, and my skirts fluttered and cold hair streamed. And there was a noise of beating wings, whirring and sailing and thrashing. And the voices of creatures was mingled with this, of roars and bellows and miaows and barks, echoing in the vales as though they were filled with war. And there was a great wrenching and squeaking and sighing of leaves, and a clicking and grinding and squealing and shuffling. And then a piping of birds made the whole sky ripple and sing, so that it shrilled in my ears like the rinsing of water. And as these sounds kept forth, others that had finished arose again and joined them, so that all sounds were mingled into a universal concert. For every note in the compass was struck in that concord, from the deepest, enveloping boom to the sharpest, sweetest trill, and it felt as if my poor body was pierced through with the noise, and sounded also in harmony with the notes. And then did I feel again that all sounds were one, and that hum came from my own inner spirit, and I found I was that thing.

'Oh what a sweet surety did then invade my heart! I felt then such content as I had not felt for many years, for all evil things seemed to be rolled away, and there was only gladness, all else was vanity. Oh then did I know that my dear son was safe, for what harm could there be wished him among such a universe of concord?

It was as vain to fear then, as to doubt that the world was good, for how could so many things exist together, without harmony being? So was it that all things with such sweetness gave me my answer. So was it that they swore never to harm my son Balder.

'Oh my friends, it would be idle to say that I did not fear on my journey for surely I did. And I began to be glad I was a woman, and that such exploits were not expected of me always. So also did I see how much I loved our halls and company, for though some far places were pleasant enough, and some fearful, yet in both did I often wish that I was back home. Yet, my friends, though I have been through ice and fire, and have ridden through whirlwinds, and pierced the thundercloud, now I am with you again, and all is familiar fellowship. And Balder sits there, thinking I am talking too much, but the cloud that I saw over his head is all blown away. I drink to you, my friends. I have tasted the wide world, but yet I still drink to the great hearts of Asgard!' And Fricka lifted up her curly drinking-horn, and brandishing its mellow curves she drunk deep of its cheer, and the Aesirs applauded her, and banged the oaken tables.

And then did Thor leap up from his seat and roar out, 'By God, Fricka, you give it to us strong! My heart burns within me with such lust to do great deeds again, that I could leap over the wall of heaven this minute and take on Jormungandr again or throttle the monster Fenris in the sky. Truly it is inspiring to hear of great things well told! But tomorrow, Aesirs, when we go to Thrymheim, I well fetch that crude bastard of a giant Thiazi such a whack over his head, yes, I will crown him over the temples that he will shoot out of the roof of Hell. Oh pass me that great cauldron of brimming honeymead, for now do I have a raging thirst to be drowned drunk!' And Thor reached over to a mighty bowl which stood by waiting for the flagons to be dipped in it, and lifted it in the air, and poured it between his teeth, and did not finish gulping until the cauldron was bone dry. And the Aesirs cheered in a body this great feat.

But then in a quieter moment did Niord arise from his seat, and stroke out his beard and say, 'Aesirs, we have heard a remarkable story. The world is wide and the heart of things is mystery. Surely the mother of the gods is in tune with the deep, and rather than treat her like the hero of a battle, we should honour her as a seer and a wizard. But is it not strange how inexplicable is fate? And how soon are upturned the hopes of fears of men? For but this last night we met here in this hall, and Gladsheim was then as full of fear and foreboding as it is now replete with gladness and mirth. Let no man say he is blessed or he is damned, for fortune is two-faced, and sees both ways at once.' And Niord threw up his hands, his palms facing right and left.

But then did Fricka take the golden bangle of Balder's from her belt and draw it forth, saying, 'Inexplicable is fate indeed. For who would have thought that of all the islands in the world and all places on that island, I should alight where an Aesir had been before? Now Balder, you have some explaining to do. Did you not before I left heaven ask us all if anything were lost, for the seeress Groa had told you you must recover such a thing? Well, it seems that the one who asked was the loser himself, and had he wracked his own brains he might have saved everybody else the trouble. Do you not recognise this armlet? I found it in Vanaheim where you were wooing Iduna. Now how did it come to be there among the grasses, and why did you take it off from your arm? There's a little story here, I should think, which might entertain next.' And Fricka held out the gleaming circle of gold, and the gods gazed on it, raising their eyebrows.

And Balder smilingly took the bangle, and slipped it onto his arm where it was held tight by his flesh, and he looked at it and said, 'Indeed this is the armlet which I lost on Iduna's island. I never thought to see it again, and it bodes well that it is returned. But how it came to be there, do not ask me to tell you. Yet do not laugh at me, for there is nothing to tell. I know I have kept silent about the course of my courtship, but you were all too eager to jest and poke fun, and Iduna is a modest girl, and I wanted to spare her blushes. But now alas the sight of this bracelet does not stir me to tell you tales. It fires my heart all over again with such feelings that I long to be off on my journey to rescue her. Oh mother, it is ungrateful when you have travelled so far for my sake that I should be silent, and wish only to be gone. But I have no heart for joking, and I do wish I was gone. Yet alas this golden bangle is not the thing which is lost, nor is heaven safe now that it is found, for the prophetess told me that the thing which is lost is biding in a bitter

[68]

place than happy Vanaheim. But let us think of that again, when Iduna is safe. On with the feasting, gods, I'll be merry another day.' And Balder withdrew again, and sat in his dark corner.

And so did the Aesirs feast into the night, and with talk of the next day's venture they now cheered the time. And now did Thor and Loki fall to boasting, and Thor bragged that he would bring Balder safe to Thrymheim, and Loki boasted that he would outwit the giant, and they pledged both that they would destroy Thiazi and his reign. But when it was Balder's turn to speak of his next day's task, they found he had already gone, and slipped silently from the hall. And so did Bragi, the bard of Asgard, come forward with his harp, and he sat before them, and sang of good things. Of the great deeds of the past did Bragi sing, and the time of war between the Vanas and the Aesirs, in the far-off days when even the gods were young. Yet he told how the threatened battle had been averted, and hostages were exchanged, and peace was made assured. And so there grew up a great age in Midgard, when life was vigorous and great things were done. And the night moved on, and the stars went round, and at last did the Aesirs quit the merry hall, and they dispersed in their companies to the palaces of Asgard.

But Fricka returned with Thor and Sif to Bilskimir, for she had foresworn the company of Odin and gone to live with her friends. And so weary and faint did she feel, leaving the heat of the hall, that Sif had to support her in her arms, and lead her over the fields to Thrudvang. And so did Sif place her in an easy bed of down, and she wrapped her in glossy furs of bears and wolves and foxes. And while Thor went about the camp, talking with the sentries, Sif sat with Fricka, and talked with her a while. But then did the red-bearded god and his wife retire. And Fricka lay for a long while unable to sleep, for the fury of the day kept her mind always running on many things. And it seemed also that Sleipnir was beneath her still, ceaselessly journeying over the vasty fields of air. And Fricka began to worry then whether she had indeed summoned all things, and she went over in her mind everything that she had done, and her heart was still troubled in spite of her triumph.

Now Loki had also followed her unseen, and when the time was ripe, he speedily changed his shape. And drawing down his shoulders and hunching his back, he shrunk himself, and became an old, wizened woman, and in that guise he shuffled into the hall. And he came to Fricka's bed and spoke to her thus: 'Do not fear, Fricka, nor do not cry out, for I am only an old woman, and am come friendlily to your bedside. But perhaps you recognise my ancient careworn features, for I am a person of some note in Asgard? I am one of the Norns, the old hags who spin the web of fate. And that is my purpose in coming to you this night. For my sisters and I note and remember everything in the world, as it comes from the confused wool of the future, and is spun into the thin present thread. Yet of your great adventure we are slightly in ignorance, and one particular thing remains to be wound into the coiled distaff. What was the wording of your vow you spoke to the world? Yet do not look fearful, my dear. Though you were bidden to be secret, you can surely tell me, for I am the recorder of events, and how may the vow be kept if it is not recorded? Indeed such is my mission in coming to you this night. Let me hear the vow, and fate will record it, and by this you may ensure that your vow will be kept. The Norns themselves will ratify your oath, and nothing on earth will dare henceforth to break it.' And Loki knelt down and took Fricka's hand, and encouraged her to be frank with him, as one woman to another.

And Fricka grasped Loki's gnarled hand and sitting up in bed she peered at him with earnest eyes, saying, 'How well you read my thoughts! For I have been lying here tortured with the doubts about the vow, wondering if I have accomplished all, and whether Balder is safe. Yet should I really tell you? I was bidden to keep all to myself. Yet so weary am I now, and so spent with all this journeying, that it is sweet to have such an ally as yourself. Will it not ensure my son's long life and safety? Oh then grant him a happy fate, and do not withhold your blessing. For the vow was this that I spoke from the mountain: all things on land, in the waters and in the air swear never to harm Balder, the god of sunlight. Now do I feel a great weight gone from my heart.' And Loki smiled a smile and nodded his head to Fricka, and hardly had he done that before Fricka fell asleep. But Loki at once changed himself again, and now he became an albatross and immediately he flew away, and as he flew, he laughed, and thus cried out: 'What a fool is this Fricka to fall for this guise so easily! You struggle about all earth, and are duped at your own front door. All things on the land, in the water and the air, swear never to harm Balder, the god of sunlight. Such were the exact words, and now will I test them.'

And Loki flew Southwards and saw the hot regions of the fires. And there in the land of flame, among the deserts of burning sand, did he see the violent Sturt, the maddest monster of earth. And Sturt was like a giant, and his skin was the colour of fire, and over its orange pores there burst out sweat in great sheets of flame. And his hair was vivid red, and twisted upwards in licking tongues, and his eyes were violet blue and bulging, and they stared at the albatross nearing. And Loki called out to Sturt and asked him a question: would he be the one to kill Balder the god of sunlight?

But Sturt thrashed out with a sword of glaring glass, and swiping at Loki he cursed him and said, 'Away, away, you Northern imp. Come not to me in these borrowed skins and plumes. And to Hell with your fine questions, for what business is it of yours? I will never harm Balder, for I have taken the oath.' And thrashing again at Loki he drove the albatross away, and Loki flew on then and came to other regions.

And Loki rose in the air, and soared up to heights near the sun. And behind the gleaming sun he saw Fenris, the wolf, approaching. Cloudlike was its body, entirely made of shadow, and its fur was frosty and shone with the crust of rime. Hungrily did it lope perpetually after the bright one, but for all its persistence it gained no mile on her course. And as Loki came near it, it bayed with its dripping jaws. And Loki called out to Fenris his fine question.

But Fenris the wolf panted and bayed out, 'Never shall I harm Balder, for why should I hurt your enemies? You spawned me in the wild days from Angur-boda the giantess. Out of a rank womb I came, and into a foul spot am I now cast. For here through the clear air I have continually to race, while devouring famine gnaws my sunken belly. Out with you, you albatross, or I will forget you are my father and eat you as a bird.'

And so did Loki fly off again, and leaving the lands where the day was in full, he swooped out over the seas to search his last creature.

[71]

And busily did he skim over the surface of the waves, and gazed with his beak downwards into the depths beneath. And at last he saw Jormungandr, winding his monstrous way. For far below in the green darkness of the waters, Loki could see sliding an army of glittering scales, for the sides of the serpent wind on and on, and they clasp the whole bounds of earth in the slithery touch of their coils. And deep in the silent shadows he saw the monster's head. Fanged it was, with tusks like a snake, and its eyes burned evilly so many miles below, and its nostrils sniffed at the black ooze of the seabed, and puffed it up into clouds when it spewed the waters forth. And Loki called down to it his one fine question, and he hung over the regions like a bird looking for fish.

But the voice of Jormungandr came in bubbles from the deep, and as every great bubble burst did a certain sentence break out into the air, and thus in parcels Loki heard his reply: 'I am Jormungandr, serpent of the earth. Nothing is there larger than my monstrousness. Deep in the gloom do I perpetually circle the world. Some men call me Time for I have no beginning or end. But even Time is earthbound and a prey to the laws of the world. So have I sworn not to harm Balder the god of sunlight.' And at that no more bubbles came up, and Loki took wing towards Asgard.

But as Loki flew upward, he passed a certain region of the earth, where there was a fissure that looked deep into Hell. And through this gap did he see the shape of Hela. And when she saw him looking, Hela screamed out with laughter and called, 'Hi there, my lovely dad! What great plots are you about! But for all your flying high, Hela can see your arse. Hoo, what a hope you have of finding a chink in the oath! Scheme on, little fart-face. Screw your eyes up tight. For all your pretty quarrels, you'll howl together in Hell.' And Hela stuck out her tongue, and shrieking with laughter, she showed him the other side to her body, and held up her filthy skirts. And Loki with disgust flew on from her swiftly. And he came again to Asgard, to settle for the night.

PART TWO
Jotunheim

WHEN A NEW dawn had swept her roses from the streets, and melted the frosts on the roofs of Asgard, then did the gods prepare themselves for the great journey. For Thor and Loki and Balder were to go into the land of the giants, and rescue Iduna from her mysterious cage.

For Thor went straightway to Freya's abode, Sessrymnir, to have himself disguised as a lovely woman. Now Freya was already up, and was directing her blond-haired maids, and the maids brought soft linens and robes of wool, and they tried out the various clothes on a dummy that stood stiffly in the middle of the hall. But when Thor entered the perfume-smelling apartments, with a laugh they all set about dressing him as a ravishing bride. And since brides wear red, they swirled about his sturdy hips great skirts of crimson, shot with rose, and they drew over his manly shoulder a blouse of fine linen. And to fill out the folds which lay over his breast, in it they shoved two pillows, full of goose's feathers, and they puffed them up giggling, so that they took a fine shape. And lastly Freya tied on the wedding-veil that was to hide his bushy, russet beard.

But Loki also became busy in his way, and rising from his itchy bed, he set out into the streets. And he went to the empty kitchens of Gladsheim, where the slops of rubbish from the feasts stood about in bins, waiting to be boiled up for the pigs, and he broke into the scullery, and with rash hand sorted through the knives and forks and spoons. And Loki selected himself a fistful of strange kitchen implements, of needle-like daggers of iron, used for gutting fish, and of steel prongs which held together roasting meat, and copper pins and forks, all of different metals. And he went out again, looking guiltily about him. For the different piercing things of many metals he wished to try out on Balder to see if they might harm him. And stuffing them in his pockets he stole into the great square.

But Balder meanwhile arose sighing from a long watch over the lands of Midgard, and he went to Thrudvang, where Thor lives, and he found the homestead surging with life, for servants dashed hither and thither, fetching food, and blankets and clothes, and in the middle of them all was the great cart of Thor, and tethered to the cart his two goats, Toothcracker and Toothgnasher. And Sif greeted

Balder happily, as she stood ordering the preparations, and at last did they drive the cart forth to the gates of Himminbiorg.

And there now did all the gods congregate in the fresh morning, and they greeted each other with merry shouts in the cold, misty air, and there was a sound of dogs yelping and of horses clopping their hooves. And the older gods looked on at the cart, exchanging comments, and remembering old times, and the younger ones drew nearer and sought to help, for there was always something dropped or something that would not wedge in, and the more people that helped the more there was to do. And so out of all the sleeping fields of Asgard, the square by the tower of Himminbiorg was seething with colours and noisy with life. And at last Loki drew near to the cart, and testing its springs jumped into it. But when Thor approached, attended by the maids of Freya, then was there loud laughter at his flowing robes and embroidered hems. And his own dogs sniffed round him, unable to be sure of their master.

But when Thor was climbed into the cart, and all was ready, then did Sif approach him and say, 'Now husband, you look truly the biggest fool that has ever been. But so expertly has Freya made up your disguise I have no fear you will fool the giant Thiazi into thinking you are beautiful. Yet here, take this pouch of sweetmeats which I have had prepared, for they were boiled up specially for you last night, to keep you amused on the long journey before you. I have wrapped them in leaves of mint, so that they should not stick together. Farewell then a while, sweet husband, and though you are dressed as a woman, forget not your great strength, for your own safety and Balder's and Loki's depends on the might of your arm. Now let me just see Miolnir once more to make sure you have your hammer with you. All's well then, and adieu. Oh, do but take care, my dear sweetheart. We have so long been married you and I, yet whenever you leave me, I feel like a young girl again. Take care. Take care. And now lift up that pretty veil a moment, that I may kiss your old bristles once more.' And Sif lifted up her lips to Thor's face, and he lifting his veil did kiss her sweetly.

And then strode Fricka forward, and she took Balder's hand and said, 'Now Balder, it is your turn to journey, and I am full glad to be able to sit at home. But do not let this adventure go to your rash head. You are with powerful strength, but this is no excuse to go raiding. Take on no more than is necessary for your aim, and come you straight back with Iduna to Asgard, for we shall have the wedding-feast ready as soon as you return. But now take this little present I have brought you. It is a keen dagger made of steel, and this sheath must you fasten around your ankle with these buckles. Wear this and always have a weapon ready about you. So then, farewell, my warrior, and fight well. May the fates watch over you, as I think they shall, and hold everything to the oath, which forever guards your safety. When you return you will have a wife, and for me will a mother's power be lost. And so this is a great farewell, Balder, between you and I, and with it I release you from my care and power.' And Fricka sighed and drew back into the crowd.

But as no one especially seemed to be bidding Loki adieu, and the three of them in the cart were ready to leave, Niord threw up his hand, and spoke to the whole crowd of gods, saying, 'It is a long way these travellers go, and the lands of Jotunheim are wild and wide. Far otherwise than in Asgard is it that giant-haunted land. So I would say this to the voyagers, and hope they will note my words. Thrymheim is a strange place, nor is it far from mysterious Alfheim. Indeed the castle of the giant Thiazi keeps the very borders of that other land. Beware then, my friends, of all manner of weird enchantments. Beware them on the journey and when you reach that place. For I have heard wild tales of the power of Thiazi's magic. Look deeply into things, for they may well not be what they seem. And it is said that he has strange creatures, which serve him in strange ways.' And with a gesture of mystification Niord fell silent, without explaining any further.

And now did the cart roll forward, creaking upon its axle, and the hairy goats strode to the archway of the great gate. There did the voices and footsteps echo under the gloomy stones, and above them, as Heimdall saw them pass, the great watchman gave the order for the wide gates to be thrown open, and loud was the grating of their hinges as the way from Asgard was revealed. And before them stretched the rainbow bridge of Bifrost, and the sun flooded the gateway with ruddy beams of light. But just before the cart could move off onto the bridge came Freya from her house and greeted the gods in the cart, and she handed to Balder a great bundle of falcon-wings wrapped in cloth, and leather thongs coiled out of the wrapping, with gleaming buckles bound.

And Freya took his hand and spoke to him saying, 'In the cause of love, sweet Balder, what would not Freya do? Take then with you these magic robes of mine. Long I have looked after them, and preened their sleek soft feathers, and they will be enough to bear you and Iduna flying in the clouds, for there is magic sewn in every falcon plume. Take then these enchanted falcon-wings, and should you need a swift escape, or flight over any obstacle, tie them to your shoulders with these thongs, and command them to start flapping. Merrily then will you be wafted along, and you will be able to tread with your toes on the damp-misted clouds. Farewell then, Balder, I wish you well in your quest, for what better object to go adventuring could there be than winning back lost love from weary climes? Ah, you are enough to steal any lady's heart.' And patting his cheeks with her soft, perfumed hand, Freya drew back at the relentless rolling of the cart-wheels, and lifted up her skirts from the mud of the great gateway.

And so did the cart creak forward onto the rainbow bridge, and begin to descend towards the distant lands below. And Thor guided the goats down the shimmering multicoloured stairways, and they moved past the scudding clouds that swirled up from the seas. But as he and Balder turned back to wave at the gods, Loki sat screwed up in the front of the cart, and quietly selecting a long needle of iron he turned round secretly, while Balder was waving, and sharply stuck forth the pin into the region of Balder's kidneys. It bent and sagged at the impact as if it were a slither of copper wire. And angrily did Loki cast it out of the cart, where it plummeted through the sunlit clouds to earth.

But the gods at the gate waved long at the travellers, for Fricka and Freya and Sif stood together, one swathed in her dark robes, one tricked in a rose-sewn blouse, and one whose blond hair blew lustily in the wind from the earth. And when at last they had waved long enough, the goddesses turned aside, and moved back into the shelter of the gate. And Forseti and Hermod went before them into the square, and to the goddesses they looked but sombre men. And so they went back to their homes, and settled down to their familiar tasks: sewing the long robes, and weaving at the harplike loom. And the days unfolded as they had always been.

But when Thor and Balder had descended from the bridge, they set out at once over the turfy hills towards Balestrand, for it was here that they were to embark on Balder's ship Ringhorn and sail on the fiords deep into the land. And the birds were singing in the merry middle-earth, as the creaking cart crested the rolling hills before them. And for a while they silently checked all that they had brought with them. And Balder outspread the falcon-wings on the benches in the great cart, and examined the soft beauty of their fawn plumes and white down. And the long shadows of the goats nodded their way over the hills, and the hares on the dewy grass ran madly in the morning air.

But thus journeying through Manheim, they passed a mysterious oak-wood of tall and ancient trees. And as they splattered along a muddy road they saw far off a strange figure of a man. For he was old with a white beard, and clad in flowing white robes, and twisted in his hair were the dark green ivy leaves, and he wielded in his hand a sickle of shining gold. And when the travellers came to him along the meandering path, they saw that he held in his hand a green plant, which was stiff and branched roundly and full of leathery, oval leaves. And with a start Balder saw that this was the mistletoe: that very plant which the witch Groa told him to pluck, and bear as his safe-conduct into the deeps of Hell. And so Balder spoke to this ancient man and said, 'All hail to you, venerable man of venerable woods. We are three gods who travel towards Balestrand. But speak to us fair for a moment, and tell us: what is that plant which you bear in your hand?'

And the old man answered, and he spoke in a singsong voice: 'All hail to you travellers, that follow the two-hooved goats. You go a-questing, and ask of the prince of all questers. For this plant is the plant of mistletoe, gathered from the branches of the mighty oak. See where its brothers grow high in the creaking branches, for it spreads a spring magic over the wintry woods. Know then, oh gods, that this is the plant of detachment. It keeps the soul of the oak alive through the frozen days, for being detached from the body

[79]

that dies, it lives for ever green, neither in heaven nor earth. And so has it the power to lead you through the lands of death. Receive it from me, oh youth with the golden hair. Keep it for ever with you, and you will not come to harm.' And the old man stretched out his hand towards Balder, and Balder took the plant, and they all three looked at it wonderingly. But when they looked again to the old man – lo, there was nothing but the grass and the trees.

And leaving the oak-wood they passed through scattered shrubs where the black-spotted elder was twirling its spring leaves, and came to the shores of the great fiord of Sognefiord. And afar off, moored safely in the deep waters, could they see the striped sails and the glittering tackle of the long-ship Ringhorn. And soon was the cart clumping over the pebbles of the shore. And the travellers let down the gangplanks and led forth the goats and carts into the wide belly of the ship, and they unfurled the sails and made all things ready to be off. And the morning mists were fading from the cold-clear water as the great ship puffed out her cheeks with the breezes and forged with its dragon prow towards the grey hills Eastward.

And when they were all settled happily in the boat, and the goats had been watered and hay was thrown down for them on the deck, then did Loki call the two together and address them thus: 'Comrades, let us now discuss the intricacies of my brilliant plan, by which Thiazi is to be outwitted and dear Balder relieved of his bachelorhood. As I see it the drill ought to be thus. I myself, who perhaps have the quickest wits, and am most experienced in all forms of negotiation and trickery, will take charge of all dealings in person with Thiazi. Thor, who is hampered from his usual fist-flying by the delicate finery he sports, will have to play a subdued role, and concentrate solely on looking alluring, until such time as he may bring his hammer down on Thiazi's head. Balder, I suggest, is responsible for securing the release of Iduna, and getting her and her cage – since at present we cannot get her out of it – into the cart and away home. Alternatively, if he can put his stunning mind to helping her out of the cage, he might very well fly away with her on Freya's falcon-wings, which are a welcome addition to our resources in this adventure. I think you must agree this is a fair distribution of labour. Unless you have any objections, let us take so much as settled.' The gods had no quarrel with this, and as the ship was running freely before the wind, they sat on the well-scrubbed boards of the deck, and ate a small breakfast of loaves and mead.

And they sailed away from the rich land of Balestrand, and rode past the gloomy headland of Vangness where the tribes of men had erected a great shrine to Balder the god of sunlight, and they went Eastward into the deepest reaches of the waters. And as they rode the woods and greenery of the banks grew more and more sparse, and they slid by frail birch-woods with white-striped trunks, and the sides of the fiord became sheer and threatening. And Balder sat at the prow gazing with wonder at the craggy slopes, and peering ahead for the end of the channel.

And so at last did the travellers come to the boundaries of the gloomy land of Jotunheim. For they moored the ship under the shadow of a cindery range, and they drove up a rocky track towards the grey crags. For the crags were the frontier between Manheim and the giant land, and the pass through them was guarded by the watchmen of the giants. And as they went on the mountains became overcast with cloud, and foul vapours surged about the jutting heights above them.

Now the frontier was watched by two lazy giants, who sat side by side on the slaty slabs, slumped in idleness and dribbling from their mouths. And when they saw the cart approaching they swore and struggled to their feet. But when it came alongside them their evil eyes lit up, and they told Thor to get down from the cart to be searched.

Then did the giants poke through the lady's pockets, and look in her little purse, and examine her belongings. And then did they feel about her bodice, and see if she concealed any goods. And having searched her hips, did they begin to feel her phoney breasts, whereat the steel grip of Thor descended on their wrists, and the giants were surprised at the strength of the woman's hand.

But just as Thor brought up his leg to remount the cart, one of the lumbering giants pinched him a mighty squeeze on his buttock. At first the giant was pleased and grinned like a madman, but his grin started to fade when Thor gripped him again with his

[81]

hand, and he let out a great 'Oof' when Thor dug his elbow in his ribs. For a long time the giant's eyes rolled round and round in his head, amazing his fellow who stared at them dumbfounded, but when eventually he recovered his wind, the cart and the travellers were no more to be seen. For Loki had cracked the whip, and they had hared away into Jotunheim.

And so did the gods pass the looming peaks and passes. They picked their way through forests, and fir-woods on slaty hills. And so did they clatter by the boiling mountain streams, and the eagles flew above them and bears sniffed at them from their caves. But when they had journeyed for a long while through Jotunheim, and had left the craggy country for the rolling lands of the plains, in the forbidding light of evening they came to an empty land, for this was Thrymheim, where Thiazi had his home.

And now did the winds leap upon them with great force. For their clothes and their capes were flung back from their shoulders, and the hair of the goats shrieked and whistled as they laboured on. And when they came to the summit of a hill, they found swooping at them great balls of twigs and sticks and seeds. And these tumbling plants raced towards them like horses charging, and bouncing high into the air did they fly past with shrieking noise. And the dust too billowed in the air, and flung darkness at the gods.

Then did they see the dark stones of Thiazi's fortress, for it lay black against the sky, looming and fearful. And it seemed like a vast prison that kept its secrets still. But before the travellers might gaze at it further, thankful to be heading out of the wind, the gods drove the cart down to a hollow where they might pitch camp. For in the dunes they found shelter, where the grass was springy and lush, and here they unloaded the cart, and drove home the poles and supports for the tents of hide. And very soon were the goats set free from their ungrateful task, and browsing happily on the violet-studded turf.

And then did Loki speak and say, 'Now are we here. You have seen the castle of Thrymheim. There does the ugly giant live, who we must deceive and send off to his ancestors. And this night must I go to the castle and present myself to Thiazi, and I shall arrange with him about the marriage tomorrow. And I will fix it that we

[82]

three shall go to him in the morning, and partake of a wedding-feast, and there exchange our girls. But before I go to the tall one, and to revive our flagging spirits, let us now set all the camp in order, and cook up a meal to feed us this night. And then when I have eaten, I will see about my plots.'

And so did they agree to this, and speedily they built a fire, and they set a pot over the flames, with broth and good meat to boil. And they laid out their straw beds, and set everything comfortable inside the tents. And they stretched out the canvas and hide, and pegged it down stoutly into the sandy earth. Then when they had emptied the cart, and arranged the wedding-gifts and provisions in the tent, they sat about the fire and waited for supper to cook. And soon were they feasting and cheering their tired hearts. But Balder felt all the time, as he stared into the flames of the fire, the presence of the silent castle where he knew his love must be.

But after dinner, by way of a crafty game, did Loki urge Thor to try striking at Balder with his hammer, for he told the thunder-god that he could not do harm, for Balder was protected by the terms of Fricka's oath. But Loki then drew out the various daggers and knives he had collected, and to encourage Thor, and satisfy himself, he showed how a needle jabbed into Balder's arm would make no puncture, and the point be turned away. And while they were still astonished, Loki tried out his other weapons eagerly, and he stuck Balder with an iron fork and a piece of copper prong, and a steel knife, and he took a long, sharp piece of flint, and plunged it with all his might into Balder's chest. But all the weapons melted and turned aside. But then Thor picked up his hammer and tapped him on the elbow. But the hammer bounced off as soon as it touched the skin. Then did Thor's eyes pop open with amazement, and he fell back on a bundle, and laughed at his wondrous comrade.

But now did Loki draw round himself a cloak, and put on a helmet of bronze, and grasping his spear, he went out over the plain towards the giant's castle. But after he had gone a little distance from the camp, he turned about, and a mean look came into his face. And drawing the weapons which he had tried on Balder from his cloak, he petulantly threw them down onto the grass. And sneering at them, he kicked them about with his foot. And he cried, 'Away with you asses, you bits of metal straw! Can you not dig into the beautiful pure skin of that fatuous hero? Must he be like adamant, and not subjected to earthly laws, all because he has a doating mother, that watches his every toddling step? Well, I shall defeat him. I shall find a way. For I alone know the charm that Fricka made, and I alone shall have the wit to pierce it. Gloat on then, lover-boy, for your end will soon come. There are but three days of Hela's five left.' And with these malevolent thoughts Loki went on his way, and walked with a gloomy heart towards the castle of Thrymheim.

But Thor meanwhile was romping about, all eagerness to enjoy the new game he had been given. For continually would he strike at Balder with his hammer, and incessantly would he be astonished when it hurt him not. And so with sudden dashed from the side, and playful ankle-blows, and enormous smashes on the head, did he dance about Balder, amazed that he could not be hurt. But when Thor had grown weary, and Balder was becoming impatient, they packed away the meal-things and lay back to finish the mead. And the wind had all died down now, and the day was dying in the West with saffron hues.

And then did Thor pat his friend on the back and say, 'This Miolnir of mine has brained a thousand giants, but you, my friend, it cannot even dent. This cannot but mean you are destined to be a great one. I knew it when you were little, for how you howled and shrieked to have your way. There is nothing to stop you now, for nothing on earth can harm you.' And Thor let out a 'haha!' and smashed Balder once more about the bonce, and then did he lie back, winking at him, and chortling to himself.

But Balder replied, 'Alas, though, I feel nothing like conquest or battle. For I can only think one thing, as I have done for these months on end. Oh God, Thor, my friend, you must know what it is like to be in love, for your Sif is almost as sweet a one as my Iduna, though she is growing old now, and has girls of her own. But I marvel that you recovered from this. Yet I will fight well enough to fetch Iduna from this monster. Come, Thor, let us not sit here gassing. Let us be up, and reconnoitre this castle here, for there may be some escapade I can be up to tonight. If I could but find out where Iduna is, I might be able to see her.' And Balder leapt up impatient again and restless, and Thor, always eager for adventure, agreed to his plan to spy.

And so did the two gods go out into the dark dunes, and catching the last light of the sun they studied the shape of the castle. For there was a keep, wide-spaced and built of spacious stones, and a large gateway led into it, hung over with ivy and crumbling, and the moat in front was dry and a haunt for rabbits. But the castle had a mighty tower, pierced with three windows, one above the other, and the tower was huge and mysterious in its purpose. And the third window up was the greatest of them all. And long did they look at this, pondering where Iduna might be, and the two gods were disquieted to view the extent of the stones, for the castle was mighty and seemed impregnable. And the wind began to howl again about its flinty walls.

But then did they leave the castle and study the land to the East of the keep, for running along the very border of Jotunheim and Alfheim was a high wall that bound in a large estate. And it seemed that there must be a gentle garden hemmed in with the stones, for the tops of trees could be seen above it, rustling sadly in the evening air. And further down beyond this wall was a hollow, where lay a budding wood, and between the trunks of the copse a lake glimmered. And the two gods spoke of the strangeness of the things they saw, for objects seemed haunted by spirits, as though many things were there enchained, and trees and walls seemed to stare back at them as if they were people.

But Loki meanwhile came to the gate of the castle, and paused awhile at its looming door, for he seemed but a small thing on the mighty drawbridge, and he could not reach to the knocker to summon attention. And so did he kick against the hard impassive oak. And at last the great gates swung apart. Harsh were the clanking of locks and chains, and loud was the echoing crash when it clanged in its jambs. And the black lodge seemed like a dragon's mouth, and Loki went forward to be swallowed.

So did Loki move through the gloomy castle once more, and leading him with wind-tugged torches were the strange servants of Thiazi's slavery. For there hobbled before him things which were neither men nor bird, but a creature between the two, with a man's bones but birds' feathers, a man's face but bird's crest. And these were the menfowl whom Thiazi had long ago enchanted. And the menfowl beckoned him to follow along huge corridors where the dust lay thick and there were strange things left decaying. And they past door upon door which seemed as though they had never been open for years, for everything was rusty and full of worm-holes, and even the stones inside were flaking off, and littering the uneven floors with their splinters and slabs. And the menfowl took Loki towards the great chamber where Thiazi ate his meals. And at last they came upon the door that led to him.

But the menfowl were afraid to go in, or to announce him, and when they had brought him to the door they scuttled away, and disappeared into the shadows. And so Loki himself climbed up and undid the latch, and leaping down to the flags again, swung open the door with his foot. And there did he see Thiazi at his supper, for the monstrous giant hung over a house-sized table, and devoured a massive feast with slobbering, greedy jaws. For before him on six-foot plates were whole rows of pigs, skewered on great spears, and a brace of lumbering oxen, dressed neatly on a side-plate, and the giant scooped up forkfuls of five or six swans at a time, and crunched them bones and all in his chops.

But the giant himself towered over the table, and darkened with his shadow all the fare before him. For he was massive and bulky, with arms like oak-trees and a head like a boulder on a mountain, and as he chewed the sound of his grinding jaws echoed all about the chamber. And Thiazi wore a thick-spun smock, gathered about his neck, and baggy trousers which were shoved into boots the size of barrels. And his face was wide and pitted with many lines, and his nose was covered in blackheads, and his eyebrows swirled up in brushlike bristles. And there were black bristles from his nose and black bristles from his ears, and sprouting all over his upper lip, about the size of a large bed, was a big black moustache, that turned down at its ends in handlebars. And thus did Thiazi glower before him, a perpetual look of suspicion in his eyes. But Loki was undeterred, and climbing up onto the table before the giant he leaned on a loaf of bread, and addressed him.

[86]

And Loki said: 'Hail, Thiazi, your bawd is here. I have returned at last with everything as I suggested. Freya the mighty goddess is ready in my camp, and tomorrow I shall bring her to be wedded to your glorious self. What extravaganzas of carnality I may then leave you to. I am here merely to sharpen your appetite for tomorrow's feast. Thor's hammer itself we have brought with us to legalise the ceremony. Do you have ready for us in the morning a marriage-feast to make Freya feel at home. But be mindful of our bargain, and in order that all may go well, do you also have ready Iduna in her cage. What do you say then? Are you willing to do so much? The goddess Freya, I may tell you, is very anxious to meet you. For she feels at last she might satisfy her lusts.' And Loki wiggled his eyebrows at Thiazi and waited for his answer.

But the giant gazed back at Loki with an impassive face, and stared at him menacingly a long while to frighten him, and he wiped his moustache with his hand, and the sleeve fell back to reveal a brawny arm. And then did Thiazi slowly reply: 'I could have a wedding-feast with you as the principal dish. And I could seize you and the goddess, and keep you here prisoners along with the caged one. And there are things I could do to you which would while away these stormy days, and give me some amusement in this gloomy castle of mine. Do you not know I only lured you here to practise my tortures on you, and bring you to scream and weep? And you thought too you were such a clever little fellow, and were getting the better of the wind-demon Thiazi. Well, well, you may be right, you may be wrong. Bring this woman to me tomorrow and we shall see. I want to get a good look at her before I agree to anything. No one deceives Thiazi. No one. Never. For my castle is a refuge for all the tortures of earth.' And Thiazi sneered and nodded his head slowly, and then he nicked his finger and thumb together, as if he were snipping off Loki's head. And he chuckled to himself at the thought of giving pain and fright.

But Loki was used to the giant's lumpish malevolence, and he merely looked at Thiazi awhile, as though considering something in his mind. And at last he said, 'You would not have in your castle, Thiazi, a method of killing one who could not be cut or sliced by anything on earth? For we have in our city a certain god, that is proof against harm from all things on the earth. Think hard though, for it must be no stabbing or throttling or drowning or squashing. None of your ordinary murders, but something special.' And Loki gazed at the giant again, and smiled at him with an encouraging face.

But the giant stared stupidly at Loki for a long time, until Loki grew weary of waiting for his reply. But then did Thiazi lumber up, and he walked over to the fire, and suddenly did he seize on a lame manfowl that was sitting sadly in the hearth, and he picked him up, and showed him to Loki. Then did Thiazi skewer the manfowl onto a toasting fork, and the manfowl screamed and twisted in agony. And Thiazi then held him out over the fire, and the feathers on the manfowl's back immediately caught the flame, and with shrieks and groans was the little creature burnt up, until there was nothing on the fork but a blackened lump. And all the time Thiazi grinned slyly, as though he were doing a very cunning thing.

And Thiazi laughed, and he pulled off the manfowl and held it up by a leg. And smiling he said, 'The best death I ever heard was when Suttung was burnt under the walls of Asgard. He was an oaf, that Suttung. He had no brains or cunning. Like a greedy fool he flew after Odin, when Odin had stolen the draught of Od-hroerir, and when he came to the walls he was burnt. For the sluggish fool was disguised as a great hawk, and his feathers caught fire when they threw burning straw on him from the walls. He didn't think of that, did he? It never struck him that feathers catch fire. Well, you see how they do, don't you, with this little shrieker. Oh, I have had much fun with these slaves of mine.' And Thiazi looked at the shrivelled form of the lame slave, and then slowly with a smile he pulled its legs off, and then skewered the body down onto the table. And long did he gloat on the blackened corpse.

But Loki did not speak, but looked aghast, for suddenly as if in a vision he saw a picture of Balder blazing and on fire, falling down from a great wall and screaming as he fell. And then with wonder did he suddenly think, that of all things on earth was fire the one that could harm Balder, for fire was not of the waters, nor did it grow on the land, and neither did it fly in the air like a bird. And he was thrilled with this thought, and stood rapt by its power. But then did he recover his seriousness, and set himself to think.

And after a while did his face change wondrously, and a hesitant smile began to light his features, and when he walked he walked as if on tiptoe. For quietly now did he draw near to the giant, and quietly did he gaze into Thiazi's eyes. Thiazi looked at him as though he were suddenly ill.

And smiling then Loki addressed the giant and said, 'There is in my camp, oh great one, a god who hates you, and he has come here with Freya and myself on purpose to kill you. His name is Balder, and the reason for his hatred is this: he is Freya's lover, and does not wish you to have her. Now I have worked on your behalf in this, and though pretending to sympathise with him, I have quietly thought out a plan for his destruction. Now first tell me if you are with me in this, Thiazi, and wish to hear my plan, for if you are not, I will bid you good night, and leave this Balder to kill you in his own time.' And Loki looked up at the giant, who scowled at him, and it took a long, long time for the words to register in the giant's head, but eventually he seemed to understand, and he sat up and said, 'Ay.' And then did he glare at Loki with great concentration, and thus staring waited to hear further.

And when Loki was satisfied that all was well, he continued with these words: 'Then hear me well, oh giant, and listen with all of your brain. For this Balder is a very strange hero, for he is the very man that I have told you about, and he is it that cannot be killed by anything on earth. Think then what a ferocious enemy he is to have. It will indeed be well for you to kill him this night. And yet think how helpless you are without me, for I am alone the man who knows how to do it. For I am alone the man who knows the one thing on earth – and there is only one thing – that can possibly harm him. And if you are with me in the plan then, oh giant, you will I tell what that one thing is. What do you say then? Are you still with me?' And Loki looked again at Thiazi, and for a long time he paused, and then the giant's black moustache twitched, and he nodded and said, 'Ay.' And so did he stare again at the little fire-god.

[89]

And Loki then laughed and said, 'That one thing is fire. You spoke of it now yourself. It is also my own element, for I am its god, and am like it. And with fire you will bring this terrible enemy down. What do you say then, Thiazi? Will you hear how to do it?' And thus Loki stopped again, and the giant said, 'Ay', after quite a short space of time.

And Loki then sighed, and drew in his breath, and he went to Thiazi, and placed his arm on his shoulder, and leaning on it he whispered in his ear: 'Go then this moment, Thiazi, and fetch about you your slaves, and tell them to take up into the top of the tower a cauldron, some kindling wood, some straw and some oil, and get them also to bring a tinderbox to light the fires at once. Now when you have all these things on the top of the tower in the moonlight, set the cauldron over a fire, and boil up the oil till it seethes, and keep the whole thing ready by the walls, on a tripod with a good swing. And when you have these things, then may you sit and wait, for the next part of the plot, you must leave to me. Have you followed me thus far, oh Thiazi, and are you sure now what you have to do?' And Thiazi began to nod before even Loki had finished, and he said, 'Ay', in an interested voice and coughed.

And so Loki felt more assured, and thus he recommenced his plotting and said, 'Now I will go forth now, and persuade the monster Balder that you, Thiazi, sleep in the top chamber of the tower. And I will tell him that if he wishes to kill you, he is to scale the walls of the tower, and climb up to the third window. He will be certain to do this, for I shall play on his lust for slaughter, and fear you not, Thiazi, but he will come that way. Up the craggy walls will he climb like a cat, and you and your slaves will be sitting, waiting above him. And now shall I tell you, Thiazi, what you have to do?' And Thiazi roared, 'Ay', before Loki had finished, for even he saw now what sort of thing was to happen.

And Loki continued and spoke to him thus, 'Once he is on the wall, you have him at a disadvantage. He cannot fight, or move, or he will fall off. He is thus a great target for anything to be thrown on him. So what you will do, oh giant, is to throw at him the lot. You will push the cauldron to the turrets of the wall, and pour the great load of boiling oil all over his body. That will give you a great cause of cheer, when you see the steaming mixture slosh all over his head. Think of the pain and the burning he will feel. Think how he will howl and grimace to you with his face. Will you not do this indeed, my great friend?' And, 'Ay', bellowed Thiazi, becoming animated at last.

And Loki chuckled to himself, and thus spoke again: 'The last part of the plan may then be put into action. The coup de grâce you will deliver, my hulking fellow, and see something to delight you for the rest of your life. For the straw you will set fire to then, and get it to burn brightly, and then will you cast it over the turrets, and let it fall on the oil-covered hero, and once the new fire has struck against the oil, the whole man will flame up and burn like a mighty torch, and down will he plummet like a bonfire to the ground. What do you say then, Thiazi? Will you not do as I suggest?' But the giant sat there, grinning to himself, and he smiled smugly, as if overcome with sleepiness, and with one eye did he gaze at Loki cunningly, and then did he wink, and nod his huge head.

And Loki sighed then, and felt comforted, and he patted Thiazi on the shoulder once more, and using the giant's knee as a step, he climbed down onto the floor, and began to think of leaving. But as he turned back to the giant, prepared to bid him farewell, Loki said again, 'Forget not my instructions, Thiazi, and be sure to see about it straight. For I shall go to Balder now, and deceive him to climb up the tower. And you must be up there ready with your men, and the oil to throw over him, and the lit straw to set it on fire. But I know I can trust you, for you are a great thinker. They say you giants are fools, and as often as not it is true, but you, Thiazi, must have other blood in your veins, for you have a cunning and a craftiness that quite surpasses the whole of your race. And so handsome you are too. I cannot think why you have never married before.'

And Loki was just about to wave goodbye when he saw the giant's face had clouded, and he paused and looked back, wondering what was the matter. And Thiazi curled his lip and said, 'I have been married. Do you think I am a fool? My wife was Thurk, the giant-witch. But she did not please Thiazi, for she was too hard-hearted. I banished her to a cave in Galdhopig in the plateau of Ymesfield. And she is known the world over for the nastiness of her heart. We call her in Jotunheim the one that cannot weep.'

And Loki froze when he heard these words, but then did he walk out of the hall without saying anything further. And he was astonished, and overwhelmed, and knew not what to think, for this had been the prophecy he had heard at Hyndla's: that the gods would be destroyed by one that could not weep. And so did he decide that that night he would go to see her, and he would fly to her on the falcon-wings of Freya and see if he could pierce the secret that she knew. And so did he make off across the dunes again.

And he found Balder and Thor sitting by the campfire talking, and at once he went to the cart and took forth the falcon-wings and smoothed their brown feathers and tucked them under his arm. Then did he turn and address the two gods: 'Friends, all is fixed for the wedding tomorrow, and Thiazi is amenable to our whole plan. But I now must leave you, and go flying on these wings, for I have promised to fulfil an errand for the giant. Expect me therefore to return just before dawn. But Balder, now harken, for I have great news for you, for I have spoken with Iduna, and know where she is this night, and I can tell you how you might climb up and see her. For she is imprisoned in the top chamber of that tower. Do you see where the third window looks out onto the moonlight? That is her own room, and there she is pining for you. If you have daring and spirit enough for the task, you could climb that craggy wall, and visit her this minute. I told her you would try your best, and I privately betted you'd do it. But enough, I must be off. And now I'll bid you adieu till dawn.'

And Loki took forth the wings and then concealing his bounding heart, he began to fit them onto his shoulders. And he fixed the sockets about him, and tied the leather thongs in front of his scrawny chest, and he hopped about the turf a little, getting accustomed to their ways. But then the wings flapped of their own accord, and swiftly bore him up into the air, and so with a hurried wave to Thor and Balder below, Loki climbed up into the darkness of the sky. And Balder remained staring, quite ravished by this news.

But then did he leap up at once and cry, 'Oh God, can this be true? Can she be really in that strange third window? Oh Loki, I have hated you a thousand times, but I could forgive you everything tonight. Oh Thor, is this not wonderful? I shall go this minute. I shall fly.'

And Balder swiftly got ready for his task. But his hands shook with fever so much at the thought of seeing his beloved Iduna, that he could not easily don his clothes. For he tied onto himself shakily a thick leather tunic, and he wound gauntlets about his wrists, over the linen of his sleeves, and onto his feet he strapped the supple ankle-boots. And the dagger that Fricka gave him he tucked inside. And when he was ready he seized his ashen spear, and so went forth to the gloomy walls of the castle. The chariot of the moon stole into the innocent sky, and the tower was lit silverly by Mani and his steed.

And Balder looked up at the tower and said, 'Oh looming tower of Thrymheim, what great secrets do you hide? Three windows do you sport, and in the third is heaven. Will your walls stay beneath my fingers as I climb, or will you rebel against me, and spurn me from my love? Well, I shall take each stone as it comes, and each window of your wall I shall explore and probe for the truth. Let me but study the juts and fissures of your stones, that I may work out the best route to those chambers.' And Balder gazed up at the sheer walls of the tower.

But Loki meanwhile had not immediately flown off, for though his soul lusted to hear what Thurk would tell him, he first wished to see Balder reach his fiery end. And when he saw Balder fall to studying the tower, then he flew like a great bat to the turrets of the keep, and there he settled to watch the sports of the night.

But Iduna meanwhile sat disconsolate in her cage, not in the high tower to which Balder was striving, but in the deep copses of the garden walled by the castle. Her auburn-coloured hair glinted in the moonlight, and fell in crisp ringlets over her pale green bodice, which was dotted with daisies like a meadow in spring.

And Iduna sighed, and thus did she speak: 'The nights roll on, the moon goes about, and still am I a prisoner to a giant and a cage.

Alas, I could laugh at my fate, if I did not rather weep, for what a fool must I look, shut up like a human bird. And thus has my life been a tragedy and a farce, since I left Apple-Isle, my sweet and golden home. Oh Balder, where are you this bright and frosty night? Do you sit by the fire in Bleidablik, fretting where I am gone? Do you range about the world, searching in dusty corners? Oh my love, I am here, in a bird-cage, in Thrymheim. But how ever can I expect you, even you, to know that?' And as Iduna spoke the trickling tears ran down, and they dripped on the leaves which littered the cage's floor.

But as she lay lamenting, there grew up a sparkling light. And there appeared before her a great blaze of bright mist. And the mist swirled and condensed into a form, and hovering in the air came the vision of an immortal. For a goddess there was, swathed in rich robes, that glowed with a subtle fire, and her face lit with pure love, and she looked gently on the form of Iduna. And then did the vision speak to her and say: 'Long have you grieved, my daughter, in your prison, and long have I suffered with you, sharing your misfortune. But yet you are blameless, and so all will come well. Cheer then your spirits, and begin to smile again, for I have come this frosty night to tell you that help is on its way, and that the temper of things is changing, and soon you will be free. But there is a thing I would remind you ere this comes, and which you must look to no matter what may happen. The apples you bore with you have fallen from your hand. On them depends the life of the gods. Seek them again therefore, and return them to Asgard. Adieu, my child. Be easy in your heart. And the vexations that are to come about this night, do not too much consider. For now is a mad time coming upon Thrymheim, and before this night is out there will be much to make heaven laugh.' And the shimmering vision then faded before the trees.

But Thiazi meanwhile decided to visit his captive, for he wished to take another look at Iduna, to ensure he was not getting a bad bargain. And he kept forgetting, in the tumble of his thoughts, the plan that Loki had given him. And so he lumbered down the booming corridors, and came to the yard. And the menfowl all scattered when they saw the great enchanter. And so Thiazi passed through a gate in the boundary wall, and came into the grove of rich trees, which he had once stolen and walled in from the land of Alfheim. And in this grove were many birds singing and fluttering, but as soon as Thiazi entered, they all fell silent. And he went straightway to the tree, wherefrom there hung the great bird-cage, and he stared straightway onto the form of Iduna.

And when Thiazi had stared at her for some time, he addressed her saying, 'Indeed you are not the one for me, for you are but a puny, whining wench, who always sits disconsolate, gazing at the floor. Nor do I like your face or your figure, for there is not enough fat on you to get my hands round. Glad will I be to be rid of you, for the embassies from Asgard have come, and they have brought me the goddess Freya herself, who is to be from this time forth my paramour.'

And Thiazi peered at Iduna through the bars, and she was just so tall as from his chest to the top of his head. And Iduna was thrilled by what she heard, for the embassy from Asgard was a delightful thing to hear of. But she was made fearful when she heard Thiazi further. For the giant continued at last, and said, 'Yet I have not time to waste talking to you, for there is a mission I have to execute this night. I am to put in practice a little plot I have thought up. For I hear from my friend Loki that a certain Balder from the gods is to scale my castle walls, and I am to pour oil over him, and burn him up like a tinderbox. Well, that will be amusement to see how he flames and screams. I cannot bear these people who sit and suffer in silence.' And Thiazi spat at Iduna, and went back into the courtyard of the castle.

And coming out into the moonlit air again, he seized on a passing manfowl that was called Birdbrain, and grabbing him by his ear, Thiazi spoke to him saying, 'Birdbrain, I have a mission for you, which see you execute directly. Over on the plain there is a camp of Aesirs, who have brought with them the great goddess Freya to be swapped for Iduna and her cage. Sneak out now to the camp, and without being seen, spy on this goddess and see what she is like. If she is sleeping, slip off her clothes and examine her body well. Make sure she has fat round hips and good breasts with outstanding nipples, and look at her teeth also and make sure they are not decayed. And when you have examined her come back to me and tell me every word. I do not trust these Aesirs, and I would not be surprised if they tried to shop me with a bad bargain. Off then with you, bandy-legged feather-flesh, and come to me in the hall, and wake me if I'm asleep.' And the startled manfowl Birdbrain, who had large popping eyes and breathed in and out quickly as though he was having a fit, backed away from Thiazi and ran forth from the great gate towards the camp. And forgetting about Loki's plot Thiazi went back to the hall. And collecting another manfowl on his way, he nailed his foot to the table, and continued his meal. And all during his feeding he watched the manfowl's attempts to release himself, and he chuckled at his failure, and laughed aloud when he screamed.

But Iduna was left fearful in her cage, and she stood up and grasped the bars and said, 'Could I have heard of anything more fearful than I have heard this night? Balder is here. That is such sweet news. He is plotting to release me. Oh, that I knew he would! But this hideous giant is to set a trap of fire for him, and he is to be burnt as he tries to rescue me. And what can I do that am stuck fast in this imprisoning cage? Oh, that I had never entered the grove that day, or entered this ridiculous cage, which keeps me safe, but now holds me from Balder. How wretched has my life been since I left Vanaheim!' And collapsing on the floor, then did Iduna weep, and the birds were all silent in the grove listening to her sobbing.

But at last she stopped, and looked up at last and said, 'A woman's tears get nothing done. Some way I must think of avoiding these dangers. If only I might warn Balder that he is threatened. If only I might draw him to me, and gaze on his sweet face. But see how the little birds cluster about me, and sit in a line on the branch trying to console me. They remind me so well of my little birds in Vanaheim, that would hop about with me in the orchard, and help me tend to the gardens. But why does this strange one press so closely to the cage? Is it a hoopoe with its flourishing crest, and barred wings? I think that is what he is called. It seems he wishes to help me. I'm sure they have understanding, for I have often noticed how they work together in the garden, and warn each other when Thiazi comes hither. Then could he not help me? He could take a message to Balder. I could tear a strip off my skirt, and send him with it in his beak to find Balder, and when he had attracted him he could lure him to this garden. And see how the little creature hops up and down and cocks his head from side to side. I'm sure he understands me. I will do just that. Come then, sweet one, and take this cloth from me. Bear it to my love Balder, and lead him back to my care.' And with that Iduna knelt down on the floor of the cage, and tore off a strip of her sea-green skirt, and held it out to the bird through the bars of the cage. And the hoopoe immediately took hold of it in his beak, and flew off from the orchard out into the wide world.

But Thiazi meanwhile, who had just begun to nod in his chair, suddenly woke up with a start, and slapped his fist on the table crying, 'A pox on these menfowl! They have distracted me from my work. For I was supposed to boil in oil this evil thief Balder that hopes to break into my castle. Let me haste about it, and get these idlers working.' And Thiazi leapt up from his seat, and throwing all the dishes to the floor in a rage, he stormed out of the hall to where the menfowl lived. And straightway he shouted his orders in threatening tone, and told one group to take a cauldron, and one to take a tinderbox, and others to gather straw, and others to fetch a great many pots of oil and animal fat, and he bellowed at them all that they were to take their burdens to the very top of the great tower of the castle, and meet him there. And lashing with a whip that he snatched off one of the walls, Thiazi started to belabour the menfowl, whom he considered dull-witted and slow.

And now was the castle in a turmoil of activity, for menfowl ran everywhere, bumping into each other. And some ran down the huge cellar steps to fetch oil from the great jars that leaned together in the darkness, and some went flapping madly to the stables to dig out great forkfuls of straw, and tie it into bales. And one ransacked the kitchen for a tinderbox, and a whole tribe of others wrestled with the enormous cauldron, which was used to boil up whole oxen, dozens at a time, and the cauldron nearly flattened them as they tried to heave it. And the whole castle was full of shrieks and hubbub, as though it had been raided and was being put to the sword. But finally they assembled all things necessary, and congregated in the courtyard at the entrance to the tower, to wait for Thiazi to bring them the key of the door. And the whole yard was filled with peculiar things.

And while the menfowl stood up at the tower from inside the castle, Balder walked about looking up at it from the outside. And he peered at the three windows overlooking the plain, one above the other, marking three floors within, and the highest, so he had been told, was the one that imprisoned Iduna. And so he tried out the jutting ledges made by the ill-fitting stones, and lifted himself on his fingers to feel what he must attempt.

But just at that moment did the hoopoe sent by Iduna spy him, and fly around his head making its whooping sounds. And at first it tried to fly in front of his eyes, and then did the little creature strut about before him on the grass, and at last did it try to perch on some of the jutting stones. But Balder did not seem to take any notice of it, so fiercely was he planning out in his mind the way that he would ascend. So the hoopoe now perched on Balder's shoulder, and daring all it waved the little slip of green garment in his face. And Balder started back with astonishment, and stared for a long time at the bird. But then did he angrily shoo it away, and without more ado began to scale the wall. But so desperate had the little bird become, that it flew ahead of him right up the wall, and coming to the top of the tower ascended even further, until in sheer frustration it was shooting up into the sky.

Now it so happened that at that time of night, winging back from a distant journey to the far ocean of the East where some Viking sailors had been slaughtered in a sea-fight, was the Valkyrie Waltraute on her flying horse, vexed to be journeying empty-handed home. For Waltraute was one of the keenest of the Valkyrie maidens, and would travel the world over to find Odin more recruits for the Einheriar, and sometimes she went even to the furthest Eastern reaches of Midgard to get her hands on the lovely fallen heroes. But as it chanced, the hoopoe, in his perpendicular flight, came across Waltraute. And Waltraute noticed the strange bird, and the shred of tattered green cloth, and immediately became intrigued. And as the hoopoe flew off and began to glide downward, Waltraute, yearning for some sort of adventure, followed the coloured creature and descended towards the earth.

Meanwhile Thiazi had opened the door to the tower stairway, and cursing his servants, he drove the unhappy menfowl up the twisting steps. Those with the jars of oil were fortunate; those with the bales of straw were blest, but those struggling creatures who bore upon their shoulders the enormous and unwieldy bulk of the great and mighty cauldron were damned to numerous and conflicting tortures. For first there was the great weight of the cast iron which nearly drove them through the stones of the stairway, and then there was the lashes of the whip, which being the hindermost they felt from Thiazi's hand, and lastly there was the geometry of the staircase. For though the cauldron was large and round, it had a rim to it, and three bold legs which jutted out in emphatic directions, and the stairway, though circling peacefully upward, was perforce staggered by sharp-edged steps. Nor did the two objects come together in concord. But at last the exhausted menfowl arrived on the cool of the tower top, and fell about in heaps under the glittering moon.

Then did Thiazi address them all and say, 'Now, you idlers, listen to what you must do, and do not omit anything or make mistakes, or I shall gut you, or string you on a line by your ears, or shut you up in a sack with a cockerel and a mad dog. Build a fire now, and let it burn hotly, and put the cauldron over it, and the oil in the cauldron, and so heat it up until it is singeingly boiling. There is to come here tonight a certain evil person, who wishes me harm, and threatens me with the evil eye, and he hopes to climb this very tower and despoil me of my gold. But I shall be ready for him. The enemies of Thiazi do not have an easy time. When he climbs this wall of the tower, throw over him the burning oil, and then kindling this straw here till it flames, pitch the straw over the walls onto him covered in the oil, and he will light up like the finest pitch-torch. To it then, you fowls! Why have you not begun? Let me lash you a few times, and get your muscles working.' And Thiazi, having given his instructions, hastened about beating his servants and quenching his nasty heart.

But then did two things happen which caused great turmoil among Thiazi and his minions, for first did a manfowl called Quill-face report that Balder was already climbing the tower, and second did another manfowl called Beak-natter observe that they had no wood or shavings to start a fire, and that a cauldron could not be set boiling from bales of straw alone. And so was there great consternation on the tower, nor was it made any easier by the need for silence, for the brainier of the menfowl persuaded even Thiazi to cease bellowing, since it was necessary to keep their tactics a secret from the climber below. A tribe of menfowl ran hastily down the stairway, while Thiazi took to thumping the others with his quiet fist, and after a while they returned with logs and sticks for the fire, and only the latter part of the force was wedged in the stairway by a tree-trunk.

But now did Balder reach the first window, and to allow himself a respite did he climb in. But he found dark things there, and the room was vile and unwholesome. For he saw a number of racks and torturing pieces, and great iron clamps and spiked boots hung rusting from the walls. And on some of the racks, half-decayed, part skeleton, part flesh, part bird, were the corpses of the men-fowl whom Thiazi had tortured to death. And vile lumps of brains or pieces of flesh lay dusty upon the boards, festering and bitten by rats, filling the room with a vile smell. And Balder grew enraged at such a monster as this giant and speedily he swung himself out of the window and began climbing again.

And before any of the excited crew above might do anything to wet him or set him alight, Balder came to the second window, and since his fingers were aching, climbed in to take another rest. And this was a strange room, full of many magic things. For here also was a corpse, but the corpse was that of an old man, whose white beard still clung to parts of his skull, and the skeleton lay back in a carved wooden chair. And the robes of the skeleton showed that he had been a wizard, for they were embroidered all over with signs of the zodiac, and a tarnished ram pursued some silver fishes around the fading hem. And about the room were old books and talismans and stones engraved with runes. And there were bat's wings, and the glands of new-born deer, and there were wands and jewels and unicorn's dried hearts. And Balder wondered at this, and resolved to solve the mystery, and find who was this victim of Thiazi's cruelty. And spoiling for a fight then did Balder take to the wall again, determined now to get to the last window.

But the menfowl meanwhile had been working well, and they had a fire flaming under the cauldron, and were breaking up with sticks the slabs of fat that had not yet dissolved, and it sent a smell of cooking for miles around. And a manfowl named Leonard devised a tripod of logs, on which the cauldron might be swung over to the turrets and emptied of its contents without burning their hands. And as they waited for the oil to boil they heard Thiazi's snores, for he had stupidly dozed off. But when they awoke him to tell him that Balder was reaching the third window, he leapt up and straightway ordered them to pour out the oil. And they heaved it over, and upturned the cauldron with a tree-trunk, and the half-melted oil fell with a splodge over the wall, and engulfed Balder with its stinking mess.

Then did Balder see that the tower was thronged with people, and that he had fallen into an ambush of a noisome kind, for the oil that had half melted was rank and foul, and the oil that had fully melted was hot and scalded him, and it billowed upwards in clouds of smoke and steam. And yet for all the pain and discomfort, the substance was yet bound by the oath, and it did no harm at all to Balder's smooth skin. But the sleek, skiddy liquid made his fingers slip on the stones, and twice did he lose his grip with one hand. Whereat with utmost effort, clinging to the wall and gritting his teeth, Balder made on up the last few inches, towards the stone ledge of the third window.

And the sight of this set the menfowl in a turmoil, and they ran about gathering up the straw, and brought it to Thiazi, who was supposed to light it. But Thiazi with the tinderbox fumbled so much with his fingers that he could not get the steel and flint to spark, and sensing the ridicule of his servants, he lashed out at them, and claimed that the steel was faulty, and immediately he sent down a bevy of menfowl to the kitchen to bring up another. But there came cries from the menfowl he had sent off that they could not get down the tower, since the way was blocked by those

[101]

who failed to bring up a tree-trunk. And at this Thiazi ran mad and chased all those on the roof round and round trying to smash their faces.

And while this diversion occupied those on top of the tower, Balder on its side heaved himself up the final inches to the window. And his heart bounded with joy as he clutched onto its craggy ledge, and pulled himself by degrees onto the sill. And at last did he swing himself forward and tumble into the room. And far from falling, though stickily, into the arms of Iduna, he found himself pitched onto a pile of prickly twigs. For this highest room was the strangest of them all, for the whole chamber was filled with an enormous nest. Twigs and branches were plaited about it, revolving in a circle and deepening towards the centre. And as Balder fell into this centre, he found that it was foul with bird-droppings and downy feathers. And Balder saw then that he had found Hraesvalgr's nest, which was the eagle-form of the wind-giant Thiazi, and here was the centre of all his tyranny.

And then did Balder fly into a towering rage, for he saw that Loki had tricked him, and that Iduna was never in that place, and that he had been duped merely to lead him into the ambush he had just felt. And knowing that he was invulnerable, and spoiling for a fight, he decided to climb outwards and upwards, and to see who was plotting against him. And so did he leap out onto the ledge, and wiping his hands and feet all over with eagle's down, he clung once more onto the wall, and furiously climbed upward.

But the tower by now was a scene of confusion, for the brands of the fire had been kicked about by Thiazi, and now set burning the floor on which he stood. The menfowl were panicking, since the way down was blocked, and Thiazi was cudgelling them with a flaming torch. It was as this bedlam reached its height that Balder appeared climbing up over the turrets. Then was there a ghastly silence on the tower, for menfowl stood frozen, Thiazi seemed stunned, and an expression of disbelief stole over Balder's face as he gazed at the flaming floor, teeming with half-birds and filled with a giant, all clasped into immobility by the sight of a glistening hero. And long the surprised parties stared at one another.

But Balder unluckily was close to a flaming rafter. The oil over him caught fire with a sudden whoosh, and flames poured off him and flashed on the scene like lightning. The menfowl shrieked. Thiazi stumbled backward. Skidding from the ledge Balder fell into darkness. Then was there pandemonium as the menfowl caught fire themselves, and Thiazi hurled them this way and that as he trudged to the edge of the turrets. Afar off did Loki watch also with eagerness. And so fell Balder down from the tower. The fiery tongues swept from him, leaving a trail of smoke. Like a falling star he flew, and like the mane of a charger at the gallop. But when he hit the ground, harmed neither by the flame or the fall, he got up at once, and walked disgustedly over the dunes.

But now was the whole fabric of the tower burning brightly, and the menfowl that were on fire were shrieking in a chorus, and Thiazi enraged fell to beating them all over again. But as at all times, when his passion reaches a peak, Thiazi can turn himself into the dark enchanter, so now did he begin to desert his giant self, and the fury surged upward, and blocked off the currents of human thought. For the box of his nose hooked downwards, and his eyes became fixed and black. His body crouched forwards, and his shoulders were hunched on his chest. His fingers grew stiff and sprouted with quills. His legs became scaly and shrunk into thin spikes. And his pore-dotted skin, which oozed foul grease, was suddenly dappled all over with brown feathers. Then from his toe-nails, splitting the leather of his shoes, did harsh talons burst out, and cling to the flaming boards. And so he became Hraesvalgr, demon of the Eastern winds. And he settled with his wings and smothered the fires of the tower. Loki opened his own wings at this and flew dismayed to the snows of Ymesfield.

But when the fire was put out, and everything in the castle had grown calm again, then did Hraesvalgr's rage cool, and he stood up upon the tower, and hopped off it down into the courtyard below. And when he had landed he folded his wings about him, and strutted in birdlike fashion towards the hall. And there did he look through the door at all the left-over meats that littered the table, and as he looked his feathers melted into his skin once more, and he became Thiazi and entered. And Thiazi sat greedily at the table, and at once began to eat, but no sooner had he put into his mouth a forkful of a brace of boar than he fell asleep, and his great face slid forwards into a dish of greasy bones. Then did his snores resound about the hall and its corridors.

But the menfowl that were left alive, after Thiazi's beatings and burnings up on the tower, signalled to those still below in the castle as to their plight, and soon were these from above and those from below working to free the middle ones who were trapped about the tree-trunk. And they brought saws, and sawed the trunk in half so that it could be carried again downstairs, and the ones in the middle were set free. But then did the menfowl gather up the dead bodies of their fellows, and they took them one by one to a secret place near the gardens, to bury them. And when this mournful duty was done, they went back to the great barn where they slept, and rested themselves in preparation for another day of slavery to Thiazi. And soon they and their feathers were asleep in the straw.

But Balder meanwhile had fled in flames from the bottom of the tower. And though the flames were not burning him, yet it was uncomfortable to be covered all over with ignited oil, and remembering that he had seen with Thor a small lake among some trees to the left of the castle, he ran that way across the spaces of the dunes. And as he ran he was like a beacon burning in an invisible hand. And he ran along the grassy slopes, and downhill past the rabbit-warrens, and he threaded through the trees towards the glimmering of the water. But by the time he reached the shore his flames were dying down, for most of the fat and oil had by now burnt itself away. But at last he flung himself headlong into the cool, wide water, and buried his whole body under the moonlit waves.

Balder's skin rejoiced in its fresh, clean bath, and he swam for a while among the dappled billows. And as he looked about, he rejoiced in a land of fair and muted hues. For the duckweed had on it a bubbling silver sheen, and the marsh marigolds were white against the muddy banks. And the gathered trees that stood around the pond were mottled by the moonbeams with trunks of pillared grey.

But when he grew tired of cruising about the water, and had swum to the bank, and climbed out onto the oozy shore, in the cold glitter of the moon, he saw that he was naked, for the flames of the oil had burnt all his clothes away. Nor did anything remain but the sheath strapped to his ankle, and the little dagger in it, glinting in the wet. Whereat Balder sighed to be so caught out in the cold. But at last he grew weary of the strange turns of fortune, and not having the will to go any further, he lay down on the banks, and looked out over the silver tops of the trees.

And Balder spoke to himself saying, 'What a fool I have been made by love! Surely I have lost my wits since I lost my heart to Iduna. For where is the cunning that in the old days would have saved me from any such stupid ambush? I walked into it goonishly, for I was crazed with the thought of seeing her, and so I stood there like a solitary target, while those idiot monsters poured oil all over my head. It would have served me right if I had not been protected. I would have fried then, like a chop, and that would have been just. Am I a baby again, that I have to be guarded by my mother? Oh Balder, how you have changed from your old self!

'And surely that is it. For I am changed indeed. Ever since I saw my sweet, and went to that misty island, I have been haunted by this strange feeling in my heart. What is this love then that seems to take precedence over all? It is pain and it is comfort. It is heart's fire and ease. And truly I am worn out by all its trouble and fret!' And sighing a great sigh did Balder close his eyes, and after all his exertions he was soon asleep.

But the Valkyrie, Waltraute, in pursuit of the bird, found herself taken into a copse of beeches. And she had not followed the crested bird far, before she saw it fly up and perch on Iduna's cage. So leaving her horse tethered to a bush she came forward, and looking up at it, saw that it was Iduna, Balder's newly-found betrothed, who was sitting disconsolately propped against the bars. And with surprise she called out her name, and awoke her from her troubled slumber.

And when she had gained her attention Waltraute said, 'Iduna, it is you here, the betrothed of the sun-god Balder! Do you recognise me? I am Waltraute, a Valkyrie and servant of Fricka. We were

together once at one of the feasts in Gladsheim. But can it really
be you, shut up in this strange gilded cage? This then must be the
castle of Thiazi the giant, for the rumour has gone round Asgard
that you were captured and taken here. And perhaps you yet do not
know that Balder and Thor and Loki are a-work to set you free.
Did you know of this, Iduna, or is this news to you? But tell me
is there anything I can do to help? For this strange little bird led
me hither, with what I see is a piece of your hem. How clever
you were to think of catching me with this little trick! I swear
it was only by chance that I happened to be flying by.'

But Iduna replied at once and said, 'Oh, it is happy news indeed
that they are planning to rescue me. And fortunate that you,
Waltraute, should come here. Yet do I greatly fear that Balder is in
dire danger, and the little bird that kindly took forth my hem was
really intended to reach him and lure him to me. For I believe that
Loki is plotting against him, and that this very night an ambush of
fire is prepared for him. Wherefore I plead with you, fair Waltraute,
go at once, and see if you can find Balder, and quickly tell him to
look for me no further, but to come at once to this grove, where I
am imprisoned, so that I myself may warn him what dangers he is in.
Oh say you will do this, my dear friend, and do not let us waste
any more time, but do it straight.'

And Waltraute smiled at the anxious look on Iduna's face, and
replied, 'Would it not be extra danger to ask him to come in these
walls, and might I not warn him as well as yourself against danger?
But have no fear, Iduna, I will do as you say. I am always eager to
help young men, for I care for them when they fall, and come to me
in Valhalla. I will seek out Balder indeed, and will woo him to you.
Yet do not fear either that he will be in much danger, for while
you have been away has his mother Fricka gone forth and bound all
creatures to an oath, and there is nothing in the world now which
can cause him harm. Lucky are you indeed to have won such an
invulnerable warrior.' And smiling at Iduna did Waltraute again go a
little way up the hill. And she flew off on her horse to scour the
ground for Balder.

But the manfowl Birdbrain, who had been despatched to spy
on Freya, had for a while got lost in the dark dunes, and he wandered

about fearfully, falling down rabbit-holes and chiselling the sand with his chin. But at last he stumbled upon the very ropes and stakes of the tent of the travellers, round which he peered about with popping eyes to look out for signs of the lovely goddess.

Now Thor, as it happened, had been helping the night gently on its way with many a brimful goblet of honeymead, and though he still wore dutifully all his female trappings, yet when he went to piss, he did it as a man. And it chanced that the manfowl, as he slid around a rope, hearing a trickling sound, came upon him at it. And he was astonished to see the lovely goddess standing up with her back to him, and a little later jiggling something in front just as a man might. And Birdbrain's eyes grew round as he thought, 'Assuredly these Aesirs are a peculiar race. How may their goddesses stand up to do such things, when every other female on earth squats upon the ground?'

But then did Thor stroll back towards the tent, and ducking under the canvas flap, he brought out a sword and a sharpening stone, and then did he roll up the woollen sleeve of his under-bodice and he bared an enormous, muscular arm, with biceps as big as a young girl's waist. And once again the manfowl's mouth fell open with surprise, and Birdbrain thought to himself, 'Assuredly these Aesirs must be very strong, for if that is what an arm of their goddess of love looks like, who could imagine what the great Thor's would be!'

And to see more plainly, and to try to get a close look, the manfowl nipped behind Thor, and crouched down beneath his legs. And Thor stopped sharpening, and threw away the whetstone. And then did he let rip a deafening fart, and the impact of it nearly blew the manfowl off his feet.

And once again did Birdbrain mutter in surprise, 'These Aesirs are almost as gross as Thiazi! This is not much of a lady for sure, to do a thing like that. Why, it sounded as though a thunderclap had exploded over my head, and the wind would have driven a good ship towards Vinland.' And as Birdbrain went forward, to gather even more to report to his master, Thor rolled up the veil in front of his face, and having done this he turned round to look back at the tent. But when Birdbrain saw that the goddess had a mighty beard, bushy as a hawthorn and as red as mulberries, he could not restrain himself further, and gasped with surprise.

But now did the great Thor hear this little birdlike gasp, and spying at once the strange creature lurking among the guy-ropes, he darted forward and seized Birdbrain with his sturdy fist, and Birdbrain struggled and croaked with horror. And Thor picked up a rope, and wound it about Birdbrain's body as if he were a bird ready for the spit, and when this was done he dangled him by a string from his wrist. And Thor debated whether to chop his head off, or to squash him with a boulder, or to peg him to the ground with a spear. But at last he approached the cauldron on which their broth had been kept warm, and he held Birdbrain out over the still bubbling water, thinking that he might parboil him, and see what he tasted like. But Birdbrain shrieked so, with his little eyes popping out of his head, that he threw him still trussed up into a corner, deciding to await Loki's advice when he returned. But his appetite was whetted, and Thor compromised at last by pitching a leg of mutton into the cauldron, and he lay down on the grass to await its cooking. And the steam puffed up fragrantly into the sky.

But now did Waltraute fly on her horse over the land about the castle, and spy down for any signs of Balder. And at last she thought she saw an intriguing sight by the side of a lake, for there was the body of a man stretched out like a dead warrior. And at once did Waltraute settle her horse on the springing turf, and she tethered the steed to a bush, and went forward to the man. Then did she see by the moonlight that it was Balder lying there, and she was much surprised to find him completely naked, and she cast loving eyes over his smooth body. But then did she think of a scheme wherewith she might wake him, and perhaps tempt him to her own love.

For Waltraute had with her, as many of the Valkyries do, a pair of swan's wings, which sometimes they may use in place of their flying steeds. And so it is that they are thought of as swan-maidens, and many legends have been told of these arts. And there is also an old tale that if a man would hear a prophecy, he should steal to a lake where a swan-maiden is bathing, and capturing her swan's wings, hold her to ransom, and so force her to speak to him of the tune of the coming days. And Waltraute decided to adapt this ploy. And she drew forth the creamy swan's wings from their sheath in her leather saddle, and she settled them carefully along Balder's warm flank.

But then did Waltraute step back, and say to herself, 'Now Waltraute must you be resolute, for not often do you find such a man as this, alive and alone with you in the woods. You must strip off your clothes, and swim in the lake, and then you may wake him up, and claim that he holds you to ransom. Yet alas, for one thing, that water looks freezing!' And she tested it with her toe, and gasped with horror. But then with a spring she stripped off her clothes, hid them in her saddle-bag on her faithful steed, and returning to the bank immediately plunged in. And before she might allow herself to scream at the impact, she at once started splashing the cold lake-water onto Balder. And Balder awoke at this, and gazed at her in the lake.

And Waltraute called to him in angry tones: 'I only pray that heaven may see you, you wicked lustful man! Oh, it is an old plot to try to capture us innocent Valkyries by stealing our swan's wings, and holding us to ransom. Yet I know only too well what you want. And I am forced to come out of the lovely water, in order to obey your overmastering strength.' And Waltraute ran out of the lake with a shiver, and immediately stretched herself by Balder's side.

Whereat Balder looked sidelong at her and said, 'Waltraute, I pray you have more sense. It is strange that you and I should meet in the middle of the night by a lake in Jotunheim. It is very strange that both of us should find ourselves naked at the same time. But that I should steal your wings, and keep them to ransom, and so fall asleep, and awake remembering nothing of my own plot – this is a sight too far-fetched, and I rather doubt it is true. Yet it is always pleasant to meet friends in foreign parts. And I am also most flattered by the friendliness you have shown me. Please tell me a prophecy. I believe that is the custom.'

But Waltraute turned aside and glowered angrily, and she said, 'It is easy to mock. A Valkyrie's life is not so pleasant as a god's.

Can I help it if I like to relax a little and talk? I only wanted to be kind to you, and stay with you for an hour or two in this pretty place, but I see you are so full of dotage for Iduna that you cannot spare any time for any women but her. Well, go to her then, for it was she who sent me. She is over the wall there in a grove by the castle, strung up in a great bird-cage in the boughs of a beech-tree. She told me to tell you to go to her at once, and she will warn you of certain dangers. As if I couldn't have done as much, talking to you now!' And Waltraute got up, and went to her horse, and shamefacedly climbed back into her clothes. Then she returned to Balder, and snatched her wings from under him.

But Balder was still astonished at what he had heard, and taking her hand he stopped her and said, 'Is Iduna in that place? And does she know that I am here? And did she send you to fetch me to her? Oh, why did you not say this before? Tell me how I shall find her?'

But Waltraute mounted her horse, and settling herself in the saddle she shrugged and said, 'What a changed man are you suddenly by the mention of her name! I would not want you to talk to me now, for you are grown soft with this doting on Iduna. Wait but for the dawn, and then if you will find her. Go that way where the little birds are singing. Farewell, then, Balder. I shall return to Asgard. But a prophecy indeed I shall speak before I go. Loki wishes you dead. He is searching for a way to kill you. If you wish to stay alive, then never give Loki a weapon.' And with those words, Waltraute spurred her flying horse, and she swept up from the lakeside, and sailed into the air. But so dark had it grown now that the moon had set, that she soon disappeared into the blackness of night.

And Balder then sat down again, his mind racing with thoughts, and he said, 'Indeed I know that Loki wishes me dead. For did he not swear at the feast in Gladsheim to kill me on my wedding-day? And this ambush tonight must have been of his invention. Ay, Loki, I will beware your words from henceforth. Though I'm in love, I'll be no longer a fool. But oh, haste on, fair dawn. Clear this idle darkness. And let the birds sing loud now to lure me to my love. This time I shall find her: that I know for sure.' But though Balder

[110]

looked about in all directions, there came yet no light to his impatient gaze.

And Thor now also could only see by the light of the fire, for he gazed at the crackling cauldron and hungrily wished with equal impatience that his leg of lamb would soon be boiled. And he got bread ready, and some capers to spread on the meat, and he walked up and down in the darkness like a hungry lion. But when at last he had fished out the meat and begun to gnaw on it and smack his lips with relish, then did the manfowl speak at last, and he startled Thor completely, coming out with a man's voice. For he said, 'Assuredly, you are no more the goddess Freya than I am, for no goddess eats like that, nor has such an arm, nor sharpens swords, nor makes loud noises from her behind, nor passes water in a standing position. You are an impostor as sure as I am a manfowl, and as sure as I have been sent to spy on you, so I have discovered your trickery. How my master will rave and shout when he hears of this! I would not be in your great boots, brawny though you are. For he will go mad, and you will be the one to suffer.' But the manfowl could get no further in his indignant speech, for Thor leant over towards him, and smartly cracked his hammer down on his head. Wherewith the manfowl was laid out cold on the floor.

But here began a great wonder, which astonished Thor even more, for no sooner had he laid him out in a swoon than the little creature began to undergo a change. For at first was his face contorted with the blow, but then did his feathers drop out and fluttered to the ground. And the grey down which covered in patchy tufts his whole body began also to fall away, leaving a man's skin underneath. And the claws of his feet dropped off, and the plumes attached to his arms, and gradually did he take on the complete appearance of a man. And the man now bowed low before Thor and addressed him.

And the man said, 'I salute your hammer, Miolnir, and its magic powers, for this hammer is greater than all Thiazi's magic. By striking me upon the head with its beneficent flat, you have reconverted me, great god, into the form wherewith I wandered the earth. For many years have I lingered a slave of this wind-giant Thiazi, for he has subdued thousands in his cruel reign, and his influence holds back the whole Western regions of the earth. I am Ladislav, the Pole, and ere this foul shape overtook me I was a subject of the great King Mieszko. I lived in Biala Podl, on the banks of the fast-flowing Bug, and though many men turned Christians when Mieszko turned so, I did not desert the service of the pagan gods. My faithfulness has been rewarded by the great Thor himself. Henceforth I shall serve him who has saved me from vile serfdom.' And again did Ladislav bow down before Thor.

And Thor laughed to hear this, and patted the man on the shoulder and said, 'Greetings then, faithful Ladislav. Never has my hammer affected its victim so favourably, and I rejoice that I have done some magic without my knowing it. But come, you need not treat me with so much respect. We Aesirs may be gods to some, but we are very much like people to each other. Therefore fall to this meat which I have just boiled. But while you eat, dear little sir, tell me how it is you came to be enslaved to the giant? And are there any more like yourself in slavery this minute?' And Thor pulled off a good strip of meat from the leg of lamb, and laying it on a large hunk of bread, he handed it to Ladislav with some mead to wash it down.

And Ladislav, when he had eaten and drunk, replied, 'Indeed, great Thor, there are many more in the castle like me. For Thiazi is a cruel tyrant, and loves to keep enslaved far many more than he can ever feed or look after. Wherewith I hope devoutly that you will ransack his castle, and free as many of my fellows as you can, for the blow of your hammer will be their happiest stroke of luck. Oh how long have so many of us suffered, bound in the keeping of that sly, slab-faced villain! How many of us he has tortured, and imprisoned and left to die! For always is he imagining that we are stirring up a revolt, and daily he strikes at those whom he thinks plot against him. Yet what can we do, our manhood taken from us, and chained in this ridiculous state of half-man, half-bird? But I will tell you how Thiazi came to over-rule us.

'It was in days far off, when there were many tribes and factions in our country, and men lived by the strength of their arm in pillage and plunder. Thiazi captured a tribe of us as we went on a raid into the East. And there was already in his prison a certain magician or wizard, and this was the secret of Thiazi's great power. For not only was he strong, being a giant, and as powerful as any of that race, but in appropriating the magic of this wizard he extended his power even over the whole world. For with such power did he change himself in Hraesvalgr, the giant eagle, and so did he blow his freezing winds over all the West, holding back the development of plants and men. And with such magic did he turn us into menfowl, and being as impotent thereafter as birds, we became his slaves and could not ever escape. That magician is long dead now, and Thiazi no longer has such power. But the damage is done, as far as we are concerned, and as Hraesvalgr does the madman still rule earth. Oh mighty Thor, you have the chance to save us now, and to benefit all mankind by driving the monster away.' And Ladislav bowed low yet again, and tenderly touched Thor's foot.

And Thor looked down on the man, and was moved by his beseeching, and he laid his hand gently on his shoulder and said, 'That will I do, Ladislav, for my heart has been touched by your sad tale. All tyrants do I hate, and love to dethrone these hulking giants from their evil rule, for they are no better but worse than you or I, and they inflict their evil minds on all the tribes of earth. But as to how all this shall be accomplished, you had better wait now for the return of better minds than mine. When Balder comes back, and Loki the guileful, they will be able to speak of a way of freeing your comrades. Till then, friend, let us feast and make merry, for so much of the night has gone by that there is little point in trying to sleep the fraction left. And as we eat let us talk of old things, for it delights my heart to hear of the deeds of the past, and great men of earth, and the ages they brought in.' And so did Thor and Ladislav sit together by the bubbling cauldron, and pouring out great horns of mead they warmed their stomachs and their appetites for stories. And the fire they sat at flickered and was cheerful, and so burned this merry spark, a sign to the deep skies, alone in all the darkness of the rolling steppes.

But when the dawn that is so pure that only the saints and labourers behold her had stolen into the East and cast light on the cloud-hung sky, then did Balder at last begin to see his way. For he followed the bird-calls to the groves in the castle walls, and the walls he soon scaled, and looked into the mystery within.

And he saw a tangled copse of larches and black-budding ash, and briars went rolling in thorny coils, and all over the slopes were the brown skeletons of ferns. And Balder jumped down and went that way where the birds were singing, and he capered nimbly through the scratching prickles, and his bare feet grew frozen in the glittering frost.

But then did he come to a copse of evergreens, that was hushed and still with a soft floor of pine-needles. And in the middle of this place was a small bubbling spring, and he found then about him a sudden carpet of flowers, for the clearing by the well was filled with wood anemones, and a strange rank fragrance lingered in the still air.

But then, suddenly looking up, did he see a hoopoe perched on a bough. Rarely before had he seen such a gay crest, which swooped up from its head with pink and black stripes, or such a long, thin beak or such barred wings. And the bird seemed to burn before the dark foliage, as if its cinnamon-pink plumage were full of enchantment. But then did Balder see that there was a thrush perched also nearby, whose brown-mottled feathers blended with the dead leaves. And then did he see starlings and nuthatches and yellow wagtails, all dotted about in the bushes of the grove. And a bullfinch showed peach-red above a branch of green, and in the mists sat two woodpeckers peering down, and one was checkered black and white with a crimson tail, and one was plum-green on a smoky branch, and it laughed at Balder and shook its scarlet crest.

But as he sat there gazing on the many wonders, did the hoopoe flutter down to him, and seem to call for his attention, and at last, when Balder was watching it fixedly, the hoopoe hopped onto a stone by the side of the well, and dipping down its long beak it took water, and tipping up its head it drank. And when it had done this thrice, it nodded with its head at Balder. And it seemed that the hoopoe wished Balder to drink of the spring. And so Balder leaned forward from where he was sitting, and scooping up a palmful of the clear water he held it to his lips and drank.

But now did the birds all begin singing, and the grove was filled with a mingled sound of many cries. For the owls that were there hooted and shrieked, and the stonechat sang his short, cheerful song. A blue tit cheeped on, and a sparrow nattered quarrelsomely, and the chiffchaff chaffed, and the warbler warbled. And as the grove filled with the thronging notes, at last the tiny nightingale, pale and quiet-hued, filled the haunted woods with its nostalgic voice, and sung low tones of sadness and trills of sweetest glee.

But then did Balder feel he was entering a dream. For each bird seemed to change, and to become no longer a bird. For he seemed to see into the soul of every one of the songsters, and so was he aware that they were not birds at all, for what he saw were light-elves hovering in their places. Where there had been an eager little swift, there hovered blossom-elf. Where there had been a chaffinch there was now a sylph of the wood. And the tiny wren became hopping nut-elf, and the robin a door-elf that haunts the kitchen doors, and drinks the elf-blots which men put out at night. And the titmouse was a mischievous elf that ties knots in horses' manes, the raven was a death-elf that haunts returning murderers, and the cuckoo became a will-o'-the-wisp that leads men over marshes. And so was the grove full again with strange creatures, and Balder grew even more perplexed with the magic sights.

But now the hoopoe had landed in a little tumbling circle of red-spotted toadstools, a fairy-ring in which the elves often dance at night. And as soon as the hoopoe landed among the floppy-hatted fungi, he too seemed to change his shape. And Balder saw a weird man entirely grown over with hair, and the light glinted madly in his big green eyes, and the eyes stood out boldly over his slaty-blue cheeks, for the blood of the forest-elf was blue, and gave a blue tinge to every part of his skin. And great spiky tufts of green hair stuck forth in all directions, and his hair was bushy, his eyebrows were bushy, and his beard exploded outwards in a great green tangle. And this elf was dressed with a red sash round his middle, and he wore his left shoe on his right foot and his right shoe on his left. And he laughed shrilly like a hysterical woman.

But then did the elf address Balder saying, 'Now Balder you had the sense to drink the well, and you can see us birds for what we truly are. But alas, what a great indignity it is to have to strut about manacled in that absurd bird's form! How ever I came to be a hoopoe baffles me continually! Do I look to you now anything like a hoopoe? Yet answer me not, for I have a great thing to tell you. Nor have I appeared merely to chat, but to talk business. But first let me ask you if you have drunk enough of that magic well? Can you see me clearly, in my true stately figure? For it is pointless talking to you, unless I can be assured.'

But Balder could not help laughing at the peculiar green worthy before him, and he said, 'Indeed I see you well, strange sir, and hear you well, and am completely impressed with your true shape. And I do now see indeed that the birds of Thrymheim are not what they seem. And indeed thus much was I told this night, for a Valkyrie bade me in searching for my love, if I wished to know her whereabouts I was to follow the birds. Wherefore I earnestly beseech you, my new-met friend, if your business is to tell me where is my love Iduna, then speedily let me know it, and let me go to her.'

But the green man answered with a scornful laugh, 'Indeed we birds are not what we seem, indeed! And thank the heavens for that. For I seem to be that idiot thing that can only whoop and whistle, that nods about on the grass like a demented puppet. But do I look to you anything like a hoopoe? Yet answer me not, for I have asked that question already. Know then, Balder, that I am Leshy, the forest-elf. In Alfheim I lived, where Frey has his kindly rule. Yet I and my fellow-elves fell prey to the wind-giant, Thiazi, and with the help of a magician he imprisoned us in this wood, stole the very ground from Alfheim, and turned us into birds. Dvovoroi here, the yard-spirit, he turned to a black and white woodpecker. Ovinnik beside him, with wrinkled belly and tufty beard, he became a woodpecker too of green and red. And I Leshy, the wood-emperor, he made me into a – yet I shall not mouth the word again, for the very pursing of my lips brings on me the sickness of distaste for my worldly form. Alas, Balder, in our souls we are all angels, yet how many of us boast an outward form so fair?

'Yet hear me now, Balder, and listen to me well, for we know why you came here, and are set to help you. For you wish to rescue

your love, and I will tell you the way to find her. But let this be
the bargain between us this day. In return for helping you, you
must overthrow Thiazi, for once the giant's will is broken and his
power has been reversed, we shall no longer be bound by his
ghastly spell, and can fly free and leave these gardens. And once the
giant is killed, and his breath is spent, we can return to our old
and handsome selves. What do you say then? Will you agree
to it? I warn you, we elves can be very irritating if you don't.'
And Leshy raised up a craggy blue finger and shook it in Balder's
face.

And Balder laughed again and said, 'There is no need to threaten
me, Leshy, I shall be happy to help you, for I am sick to death
already with this ogre, Thiazi, and long for nothing more than to
smash him into a pulp. So content me now this minute, Leshy,
and do not let me delay any longer, but straightway show me which
way Iduna is.'

And so Leshy lifted up his hand, and pointed with a scaly finger
further up into the wood, and with a strange popping sound the elf
vanished and became a bird again. And Balder turned away and
walked towards the taller copses.

And he went up the hill, through the stately grey trees that
swept up their smooth trunks and interlaced their arms. And a
gentle mist lay among the deep woods, and the sunbeams pierced
it high up in the beech-tree branches. With what grace did the
slender boughs bow down to the coming of the sun, and green
shoots dapple all the cascades of the trees! And the dawn air
smelled of the scent of the rotting leaves, and the little flies and
moths went careering with the spring.

And Balder felt reassured, and smiling to himself he said, 'Now
do I know that Iduna is in this place, for there was just this air of
blessedness when I came to Apple-Isle. It is as if all has been washed
clean and is rich, and everything about me part of some great
festival. But where can she be? Does she hide in those foggy dells?
Is she behind a tree-trunk, drawing patterns on the green lichen?
Or will she be covered up in leaves, as if hidden in winter sleep?
Oh, I am mad with the thought of her, and here stroll talking
nonsense to myself. Come then, Iduna, show yourself to me.'

And now did he hear a faint little sleepy sigh. And looking up did he find to his surprise that a great flat disc hovered immediately above his head. And as he moved to one side of it, he saw that it sported a burnished golden flank, and rising from this some gilded bars, and when he strode out from under it he beheld that it was a bird-cage, and in it was Iduna, asleep and hugging her knees.

And Balder at once leapt up to a branch of the tree, and crawling along it gazed at his love. Her little sculptured face was just as in his dreams: just so did her peachlike cheek swerve round to the dells of her temples; just so did her lovely eyes sprout out in front in a thick mass of lashes; just so did her tiny nose twist round into rosy nostrils; just so did her bitable chin sneak forth from the swoop of her cheek. And with just such a smoothness did her full, sweet mouth brood over the air before it, as though on life that slipped away. And once again did Balder feel his senses suspended, and felt he could hang there for ever, without even a bough. But then did he reach forward and gently kiss her cheek.

And Iduna sighed a delicate little sigh, and smiling she looked at him, and quietly said, 'Well, you have come at last. And high time it is. All night I have hardly slept a wink, expecting you to come. And here it is the dawn, and at last you find me.'

But Balder laughed and cried out, and said, 'Oh Iduna, Iduna, I shall now run mad! Nothing in my life has meant so much as rescuing you. I have dreamed of nothing for nights but you, thought of nothing but how to get to you, wished for nothing but having you with me again. At times I thought I was going mad with thinking about you. Everywhere I looked I thought it was you. Every step I took was but one more nearer or further from you. I have gone climbing up sheer walls for you. I have been made invulnerable to all weapons because of you. I have crossed Jotunheim, consulted witches, challenged Odin, scorned Asgard, and seen a flock of elves because of you. Oh my God, Iduna, you are more to me than my whole life, but how can I get to you, for even now after crossing the major part of Midgard, I am dangling by one hand from a creaky branch, and can't get down sufficiently to hold you in my arms!' And in desperation then he leapt up onto the cage, and clinging onto the bars with his hands and feet he pressed his face between the gilded metal, and Iduna took his face in her hands and kissed him on the lips.

Long was their kiss, and after Balder's struggles passionate. And all the force of their love went into that meeting of lips. And then did they murmur many things each to the other, and call each other by many sweet names. And Balder, though he might move nothing but his head, kissed her madly, until his lips were aflame.

But the cage by now was set swinging and jolting so much that it came off its hook and plummeted down, and crashed squarely onto a heap of branches, twigs and beech-leaves. Whereat there was a sudden shower as in the winds of autumn, with many bronze and russet leaves swirling in the air, and the sunlight turning them into showers of gold. And when Balder and Iduna found that they were both unharmed they laughed happily and fell about on the floor.

And Balder slapped his hands on his thigh and said, 'Wow, what a kiss was that! Such a kiss opened up the ground under my feet. But yet what a hefty thing this bird-cage is! I thought I might have lifted it and carried you off, but alas, I will not manage your escape as easily as that.' And he pushed the cage, trying to lean it over from its base, but for all the strength of his bare, muscular arm he could not shift it, and he gave up and sat back on the ground.

But Iduna did not answer, for she was looking at Balder with a quizzical expression, and at last she spoke out and said, 'Balder, why are you naked?' And Balder laughed and replied to her at once, 'I was climbing the tower this last night on Loki's suggestion, and the giant poured boiling oil on my head, and lit it with burning hay. As Waltraute may have told you I am protected by a certain oath. What the words of that oath are nor I nor anyone knows, but all creatures have taken it, and vowed never to harm me. And so I was safe from the licking of the flames. But alas, you see the result. No oath was taken for my clothes. Everything was burnt off my back, except this little dagger on my ankle. Had I had time or my wardrobe in Jotunheim, I would have taken care to put on my best for you.'

[119]

But Iduna turned aside, and a powdery blush stole over her cheeks, and looking at the ground with shameful lashes, she said, 'You need not dress for me, for if we are to be man and wife, then there is no need to be modest before each other. And besides Balder, you are so lovely to look at. Oh Balder, I do love you so. I wish you were locked in this bird-cage with me.' And Iduna sighed a great sigh, and looked at Balder so plaintively, he clasped her fully at last. And so wild was his passion that he almost squeezed her to death against the cage.

But Iduna cried out, and pushing him away she sat back further into the cage, and pantingly she said, 'Oh Balder, you nearly pressed the breath from my body! And how my head swims now, and how feverish I feel. I fear that you will hurt me, for look how you breathe so fast, and your eyes flash so that they frighten me. For now is that rashness come over us, just as we felt in Vanaheim, when the dragon arose and tried to chase us away. Oh Balder, what is this fire which overtakes us? I am afraid of it, and do not like to give way. But why are you turned aside my love? And why do you hide from me?' And stretching out her hand, she touched Balder on the shoulder.

But Balder was facing the other way, for his manhood was rampant and he did not want Iduna to see it, and after his lust had cooled a little he said, 'Do not be afraid, my sweet, for you know I can do you no harm. We are overtaken with Freya's sweet fever, and when the time is ripe we may give way to its rage. But as to why I turned aside, ask me again on our wedding night, and I will show you soon enough. But come now, let us speak of more serious things. For the dawn is now complete, and the day is advancing, and soon I must return to the camp, and meet with Loki and Thor.' And Balder looked about him, and the frosts were now melting in tawny woods.

And Iduna said, 'Alas then, for I have also a serious matter of which we must speak. The goddess, my mother, told me of it tonight. Those apples, Balder, which I brought from Apple-Isle, those which fell from me when I was abducted, they contain all the hope of life for the gods. You must regain them, for none other can do it. For unless we find them, surely the gods are doomed.'

And Balder was silent, and then he said, 'Then alas indeed, for that will be a bitter journey. For I see that those apples are the thing that heaven has lost, and I see that those your apples have fallen into Hell. A witch told me of them, and that I must go to fetch them, and that for my safe-conduct I must take the mistletoe. I do not relish going on such an errand. Yet will I have to do it, when the time is come.'

But then did he shift his seat and continue: 'But now, my dear one, let us immediately consider the urgent things before us. As Loki and Thor and I have planned it, this day's device to fool Thiazi is thus. The giant expects that the goddess Freya has been brought him, and he has agreed to exchange you for her. The goddess, you may laugh at this, is none other than Thor himself in an elaborate disguise. But Thor has a stronger arm than any one else, and it is his hammer that is needed to do the trick. When he is close to Thiazi in the mid-part of the marriage ceremony, and the hammer is placed before them, Thor will take advantage of the giant's befuddlement and strike him down with the very hammer that is to consecrate his wedding. This done and Thiazi over-thrown, we may run off with you, and release the castle from his tyranny – for there are many elves, I discover, who are all prisoners like you to this giant. Now the urgent question is this. You are locked in this cage, and Thiazi cannot open it, but is there any way you can think of in which we can get you out? Just tell me how it was you came to be in it.'

And Iduna sighed and said, 'It is a foolish and soon-told tale. Once the giant had brought me here, he treated me fairly gently, for he was intrigued to have one of the Aesirs in his castle. But he kept me none the less locked up in a room inside the keep. I was both wise and fearful enough to know that Thiazi would soon want to force himself on me, but I could see there was no escaping from the castle or the grounds. It is easy enough for me to tell the tale now, but at that time how I feared, how I repented I had ever left Vanaheim! I think I have grown ten years since that day you arrived on my island. At any rate I found I had some cunning, and was shrewd enough to avoid a certain fate.

'I heard from one of my guards, who was a weird creature, half-man, half-bird, that there was an enchanted bird-cage in the grounds, whose door once shut might never be opened: a legacy from an enchanter who used to be Thiazi's slave. This, I bitterly thought, might be my last refuge. When it became obvious that Thiazi was lusting for me – I do not know how I knew it, but he certainly seemed so frightening – I plucked up my courage, and pretending to be sweet to him, I got him to take me into the gardens and show me the magic bird-cage. How grateful I was when I saw it! How I prayed that the magic would work! When I reached it, I leapt in and clashed the door. And then I waited to see what my fate would be. It was horrible what Thiazi did to try and get me out. I shut my eyes and rolled myself into a ball and pretended that nothing outside in the world could touch me. And by the blessing of the magic, he could do nothing to harm me. After days of threats and schemes and bludgeoning he gave up and left me. I would have died had not these sweet birds in the gardens fed me. But at any rate I escaped Thiazi's evil. And thus it was I became a willing prisoner from love. And here am I, Balder, suffering the same fate, although your love and your arms it is keeping me from. What a foolish tale I've told. But there seems to be reason in it. And yet alas, my sweet love, I know no way of getting out.' And Iduna looked at Balder, and she did not know whether to laugh or cry, for her eyes were full of tears and yet her lungs were full of laughter, and her smile hovered between both, knowing not whether to go up or down. But Balder gently pressed her lips with his.

But then did he stand up and say, 'It is high time that I left and consulted with Thor and Loki. But wait but a little here, and I will show you a wonder. And you will see why the little birds have been so helpful. I may also learn a good way of getting you out of the cage.' And Balder at once hared off, and ran down the slopes towards the copse of the elves. And soon was he hurrying back through the grey and misty woods, with the hoopoe flying after him, fluttering its pink wings.

And throwing himself on the ground before Iduna he said, 'Now my love, drink of this well-water from my hands, and then look carefully at this little hoopoe here, for you will see him as he truly is. I will question him of the cage then, and ask him if he knows the secret of its charm.' And tipping up the quivering water in his palms towards Iduna's lips, Balder gave her to drink, and she sipped it all up.

Then was Iduna astonished to behold the strange form of Leshy, for before her also he showed himself with his blue skin and green beard, and he laughed to see her eyes grow round with wonder. But then Leshy spoke, and his weird voice rang out: 'So Iduna, you see me in my true self. Do you not realise now how you have been deceived, for what you took to be a loonishly coloured bird is really such a man as myself, noble, stately and green. Yet do not be overawed, for the world is full of wonders. Now Balder to your question. I shall answer it quickly, and then must you fly to your comrades. You may leave me here with Iduna, for I have much to speak to her of the days we have spent together. Of the history of the cage you must hear in other days, but of the charm that binds it: these are the words of the oath: that the latch may not be lifted, nor the cage opened, by anything on the land, in the waters or in the air.' And Balder nodded, and took care to remember the words.

And then did he snatch one last kiss from Iduna's lips, and ran away quickly as the dawning grew warm around him, for the Spring seemed to be coming now in a torrent to the trees. And he climbed swiftly up the great garden wall, and leaped down onto the grass on the other side, and made off then towards the hollow and the camp. And as he raced he felt entirely a different person, for where before all his going had been full of effort, now did he find that his limbs bounded along. Every thrust of his thighs seemed like an enjoyable leap, and every breath of his lungs seemed filled with a sweet fire. And so did he arrive at the camp again.

But far from finding Loki and Thor busy at the cart, and preparing for the wedding, the camp seemed empty and there was no sign of life. For Loki he could not see anywhere about the tents, and Thor at last he found sprawled sound asleep. And Thor snored loudly with his head propped on an old jar of mead, and beside him, snoring almost as loudly, Balder was surprised to see a sleeping man. And so Balder picked himself a light breakfast of bread soaked in ale, and took his plate and went and sat against a tent-pole. And as he started on his meal, he gazed out before him towards the gloomy castle. And then did he begin to think again, and he pondered how he might solve the charm that was on the cage. And so he turned over in his mind the words of it, that the latch might not be opened by anything on land, in the waters or in the air. And long did he rack his brains for what might escape that oath.

But as he put down his plate, his hand touched against the branch of mistletoe. And Balder picked it up and gazed at its stubborn leaves. And it had a thick, tough stem, for the whole plant grew about the length of his arm, and its branches thrust out all about it, completing a circle of green. And he felt the leaves were stiff and waxy, and there were little flower-buds on it, since the Spring had now come in. And Balder shook it, and the leaves rustled with a strange noise. And he thought then of what the old man had told him: that the mistletoe was the plant of detachment. And he felt it strange that such a thing should be held of such great mystery, and that it alone might conduct him into and out of Hell. And then did he see that it would penetrate the charm on the cage.

And Balder's lips parted in a smile of amazement, and his breath grew faint and almost stopped, and he looked at the plant with wonder and said, 'How strange that this gift should be such a gift for me! Does it not haunt me, this plant, and hover within my reach? For I was bidden to take it, and without asking I was given it, and without thinking does it now give me the means to release Iduna. Oh magic growth of the soul, you will set free my love for surely you are not of the land, nor the waters, nor the air, but your element is life itself, and you grow from the living tree. And thus you are detachment, not of the world but of the soul. When men henceforth shall think of Balder, let the mistletoe be my emblem, and be linked with my name.'

But then did he begin to wonder how he might use the plant to free his love. For he saw that as it stood, it could not be of much assistance. And he saw that the mistletoe needed to be slender enough to slide into the lock, and that also it needed to be long enough to stretch a great way, so he decided to trim off all the

[124]

branches from the trunk of the mistletoe, and sharpen the trunk into a bladelike point, and when this was done to tie the whole trunk onto the end of a pole, and by this means would he have the right device. And so did Balder set himself to make it. And he shaved off the bark, and thinned it into a blade, and fixed it on a pole, so that he made a kind of spear.

A faint breeze stirred the grasses where he sat, and scattered the leaves which the mistletoe had shed.

But though by now the dawn had well advanced and struck with its beams the castle of Thrymheim, far away in the West the sun had not yet risen, and the mountains of Ymesfield were still plunged in darkness. For it was here that Loki had flown to consult with the witch that cannot weep, and at last in the silence of the blue-black snows he found towering up the high peak of Galdhopig, and he landed here, and searched about in the cold for Thurk's cave. The footsteps of Loki were the first for many years to disturb the smoothness of those wide, white slopes.

But Loki found the cave, hidden under a great overhanging crag from which the spiky icicles hung down in their masses and were like a ragged beard over the great gaping hole. And a smell of smoke did Loki scent as he came on a narrow, ice-greasy path, and from the cave there glimmered forth a flickering light as if from a cauldron's fire. And Loki stopped a while, and thought to himself ere he went into the cave: 'It would be as well to test this witch in some way, to see whether it is really true that this monster cannot weep. For unless she is the one to whom tears are unknown, it will be no good to ask her how the Aesirs may be destroyed. Then I have a good excuse to do some cruel deeds this night.'

But at once did he hear a sound that filled him with dismay, for out of the cave came the sound of howling and tears, and immediately he cursed and swore that he had come a long journey for nothing. But then did he hear another deeper voice, railing from within, and a stone bounced out of the cave and into the dark drop before it. And Loki saw then a snivelling giant baby girl shuffle out of the cave and stand whining in the snows. And he marvelled at what he saw. And Loki thought to himself, 'All is perhaps safe after all, for this is not the witch, but an offspring of the foul creature, and as ugly, I should think, as she. How might such a witch as this, so old, so vile, conceive babies up here in the reaches of the mountains of Jotunheim? These giants are vile things. But now might I have an excellent chance of testing the strength of Thurk's stone-heartedness, for if I were to murder this, her little girl, then that would surely of all things cause her to weep. For this idiot child must be the only creature she has in the world. I'll lure the girl over, and slit her throat.'

But now did the child spy Loki for herself. And immediately she stopped weeping, and advanced to him curiously, and leering at him, she stood with her finger in her mouth. And the baby giant was slightly taller than the fire-god. And Loki smiled at her, and showed her his sword. And he tapped her on the head with it, playfully, and the child laughed. And since she was friendly to him, and did not seem to be a nuisance, Loki decided not to slit her throat, which would be bloody, so he fell to tickling her ribs for her, which the girl enjoyed. And counting them off, he selected the place where the sword might penetrate her heart, and spitting in her face, he quickly jabbed it in. And the sword pierced her heart at once, and all life fled from her limbs. And the huge child choked and swooned, and her knees gave way, and she crumbled onto the snows, and her black blood seeped into them, expanding in a dark pool. And Loki recoiled from her, and wiped his hands on the snow. And for a while he seemed crazy, and fell to kicking her corpse. But when at last he grew tired, he sat for a while panting, and then did he compose himself, and prepare to confront Thurk.

And searching his clothes for spots of blood, he went to the cave-mouth, and entered, smiling kindly. And he saw Thurk, filling up the greater part of the cave deep inside, and she sat by a cauldron that was bubbling and throwing up steam onto the roof. And the roof dripped continually with the water from the steam. And Loki saw that Thurk was huge and monstrously fat, and she seemed like a great quivering plug that had been shoved to block up the cave, and the smell in the cave was thick, rank and greasy. And Thurk's clothes were all damp with steam, sweat and oil, and they clung to her blubbery arms and her whale-sized thighs. And her head was enormous, and like a great sphere of flesh, and so greatly did the fat bulge on her cheeks that her mouth was nothing but a crease in the folds, and from her nose ran down great streams of green rheum, which bubbled as she breathed, and squeaked in the wind. And Loki was disgusted by the ghastly sight.

But yet he steeled himself to find out what he wanted, and he spoke to her, saying, 'Hail, oh ugliest of women on earth. I congratulate you on the power of your looks. After seeing you I feel I will not eat for several weeks. But tell me, oh monster, are you Thurk, the giant-witch? And are you that woman that used to be married to Thiazi, the wind-giant? For I have a grave question that I wish you in your wisdom to answer. But first tell me if it is true what I have heard: that no matter what misfortunes befall you, you cannot weep? For one that cannot weep I am especially seeking, to help me in my plots against the proud Aesirs.'

And Thurk did not seem at all surprised to hear a sudden voice or to see a god in her cave, and she answered him at once in a voice without any expression: 'Hail, Loki, god of fire and deceit. You did not announce or yourself or tell me who you were, but yet I know you well enough. And you know me well enough too, although you are too bewildered to see it. I am indeed this Thurk, whom you seek. I have sat here in this cave for year upon year, marking nothing, noting no seasons, listening to the winds. And without my willing it do all things present themselves to me, so that I have good knowledge of the past and the future. I am neither bored nor interested. It neither excites me nor depresses me. And so with you. I do not care if you go or stay. You are right in supposing that I cannot weep. No tears have passed the lids of my eyes for all the long years that cover my origins.' And the witch grunted and sighed, and suddenly did she stop speaking.

And Loki was at first disturbed by her strangeness, and could not think for a while what he should do next, and he began to feel guilty that he had killed her child. For since the giantess did not seem to threaten him or fear him, he had lost the impetus of his natural hatred. But then did Loki feign to laugh, and he cried, 'Ha, I do not believe your words, you blubbery old hag. And it is no good trying to impress me with knowing my name. The whole world knows of Loki, for his brain is brainier than anyone's, and written down in the runes of time are the many deeds I have done with my power to plot and deceive. And since I am such a man, and since I scorn to be weak and pitiful, for these are the ways women hold back the march of time, I have compounded a test for you, Thurk, to see if your proud boast is true. See what I bring you now. Look on it well. And then we shall note whether the tears you have foresworn do not course down your cheeks. Behold what a present Loki has brought you.' And with that Loki hurried out of the cave.

And he grabbed hold of the carcass of the girl-giant by her ankle, and dragged her bloody body over the icy path, and he brought it to the cave mouth, and took a deep breath. And with a jeering cry then, and a sudden shove from his hands and feet, he rolled the girl's body into the cave, and hurriedly pushed it so that it rested below Thurk's gaze. And he stood on it with one foot, and triumphed, and he gazed up into the slitted eyes of Thurk. And Thurk looked down on the body of her daughter, and its arm was flung up over its head, and its mouth gaped, and was full of congealing blood, and its hair of snow from the drifts outside. And Loki peered up fearfully, to see if Thurk would weep.

And Thurk stretched out an arm, and taking the girl's leg, pulled her towards her, with many a grunt from the effort of her task. And she reached up, groaning again to a shelf in the rock of the cave, and took down a long knife, and held it before her. And Loki flinched back, fearing that she would attack him. But Thurk wrenched off the leg from her daughter, and taking the knife she began to slice pieces from the thigh into the boiling water of the pot. And in this way she cut up into pieces a whole leg from her daughter, and stirring the stew with the end of her knife, she said, 'Since you have come so far, you might as well stay for supper.'

And Loki was appalled, and thought that he would be sick, and he staggered back towards the cave-mouth, staring at the witch in horror. But then he stood for a long while gazing at her impassive face. And Thurk never looked at him again, but merely kept stirring the pot, and she fished the meat out now and then, and bit it, to see if it was cooking, and then spat it back into the steaming stew. And it did not seem that she cared one jot for her daughter, nor even that it had made any impression on her. And the more Loki thought of the strangeness of her case, the more he grew fired by her easy-going evil. For it seemed to him that with her all barriers were taken away, and there was not any feeling that could restrain any action that could be contemplated by the mind. And it was as though he had suddenly been offered infinite riches. And he rejoiced suddenly, and went back into the cave, and sat with Thurk, peering into the cookingpot.

And Loki then said, 'Assuredly you are a great one. You are a mighty sage. For now you are divorced from the odious loves of human fools! For when I brought you your daughter that I had killed, not one trace of emotion showed on your face. And when you tore off her leg and stripped off the great bleeding chunks, oh then you made me ashamed to have so much weakness in myself, for at first I was horrified. Yes, I even felt sick. Oh teach me now, great teacher, the secrets of your wisdom. For I have come here fired by a prophecy that I wrenched from the ears of Hyndla, the wind-witch. It was meant for her alone, but Loki in his cunning got it. And the prophecy told me that one who never weeps would be the cause of the destruction of the Aesirs. Tell me then, Thurk, tell me the great secret. How is it that through you I may destroy the tribe of the Aesirs?'

And Thurk sighed and spoke again, saying, 'If a thing is prophesied then why bother your head with how it is to be accomplished? For if it is prophesied and the prophecy is true, then it will happen without your tiny mind working away. You admire me for having no tears, but you yourself are as much a part of the tear-breeding races as any of the Aesirs. For if you fret yourself so greatly with how to do this and that, then you are yearning for something, and when your hopes are dashed, you will feel like weeping, whether you do nor no. Oh, you have much to learn, that think you are so drenched in evil. For evil is the same as good, and its perfection lies in the same detachment. And yet for all this, you will play your part. Your actions will bring Balder's death, on his wedding-day, just as you swore.'

But Loki's eyes flashed with joy when he heard her final words, and he seized on her huge hand and pressed it to his lips. And Loki cried out, 'Oh such words I have longed to hear! How they put a crown upon all the troubles of my life! For I was always a great one till Balder came along. Reprove me how they might, the gods were dependent on me, and many a sticky corner did I get them out with my plots. But this Balder is not only a great bully, but he thinks and acts as though he had a brain as good as mine. Oh Thurk, oh mighty empress, tell me how I may kill him. Oh but speak the words to me, for he is defended now by such a host of charms. For now does he boast and brave in my sight, for he knows that I can do nothing to harm him. I am an older god than he. I was here in the beginning of time with the other gods. I myself in those days spawned the ugliest monsters on earth. I and the foul giantess Angur-boda: a howling witch, a demon of passion and hatred. I set up the brood that are all-powerful in destruction. And yet this beautiful one, this smooth-face, this grace-walker, this crooning lover, this oily, unctuous, childish, feeble boy: he has usurped my power. And he it is I must kill. Oh, I beseech you, great and wondrous goddess, but speak to me the words how I may bring about his death. For all things have sworn never to harm him, all that exists on land, in the waters or in the air, and though I have tried a thousand things to kill him, nothing can I find which will go against the oath. I kiss your foot. I prostrate myself before you. I will do anything you ask, if you will tell me what will kill him.' And Loki cringed and ducked like a dog begging for titbits, and he wrung his hands before the giantess and squeezed his face into pleading shapes.

But all the time Thurk looked at him with the same dead face, nor did she speak for a long time, but watched his whining antics. But then at last did she reply to him and say, 'To achieve Balder's death, you have merely to do nothing. A weapon will be given you. You need not even look for it. Nor when you have it, need you make any effort to kill him. For in truth we do not act, but are the instruments of fate. And you have been chosen to bring all this about. So long you have thought upon it, that the deed must fall on you. And your final triumph will be achieved not through strength, but from a moment of what you call weakness.' And Thurk drew out from the cauldron a piece of the flesh of her daughter, which was now cooked and tender enough to eat, and she held it towards Loki, and thrust it into his mouth.

And Loki chewed on it, and the flesh tasted sweet and delicious, and he looked up at Thurk, overawed by her words. And such joy burned in his heart that he felt like worshipping her. And the taste of the meat and the thought of what it was maddened him into a strange lust. And the more he gazed on Thurk, the more did she seem to be everything he had desired, and he began breathing hard as his passion for her mounted. And at last with the juice of the meat dribbling from the sides of his mouth, he arose up, and unbuttoning his belt, he showed himself to her, to see what she would do. But the giantess was eating now, and feasting on her child's meat, and she merely chewed and neither looked ay or no. And so Loki lifted up her greasy skirt and stripped it back from her thighs, and exposing her stinking, hairy womb, he threw himself on her and fucked her. And as he did so he squealed and shrieked with glee, and the giantess lay back, immobile and unconcerned. And so they passed away the night in food and love.

But when at last the dawn stole to Ymesfield, and lightened the iron sky above the snows of the ranges, Loki ceased from his sports, and grew weary. And a feeling of disgust began to invade his heart, and he grew repulsed then by the foul sight of Thurk, sprawled back in the cave, and he drew away his eyes from the sights she showed him. So he looked to his falcon-wings, and smoothed them ready for flight. And Thurk looked at him coolly from her sprawl at the back of the cave.

And Loki then said, 'I shall go now, foul one, and speed back to my friends in Thrymheim. You have told me all I need to know, and have sated my lusts too, and fed my belly. It is not easy to resist my charms, when I have a mind to woo and be wanton. But if anyone asks you who visited you this night, tell them not it was Loki, or you will be made a laughing-stock, and your name will be added to the shameful lists of my conquests. Farewell then, Thurk, you are ugly enough, and many men would have shrunk from your foulness, but I am not an ordinary soul, and I can match any-one, whether evil or good. You can dream about me now: the quick witted fire-god. But I can only pity you, wedged in this cave.' And Loki turned about, and went towards the entrance.

And Thurk replied to him and said, 'You change your tune, Loki, now that you have enjoyed me, and I fill you once more with nothing but disgust. And yet you will remember my words, for in many ways tonight in the things that I told you did I fulfil your heart's wishes. Yet you are disappointed now, and want nothing more than to get away from me, and repudiate what you have done, for you are overcome with the strangeness of a revelation: that it is a great disappointment to get your heart's desire. But why do you spin me this foolish tale that I must keep secret about your love? This is not the first time you have loved me, Loki. Why, we are old lovers, and have humped it together many, many times. Do you not recognise your old wife, Angur-boda? Ay, I am that very demoness. From your lusts did I bear in the old days the great monsters: Fenris the wolf, Hela the goddess of Hell, Jormungandr the serpent that encircles the globe: the monsters that will bring about the destruction of your world. Rash was I in those days, and you were lured by my wildness. Just as tonight you came to Thurk, so then were you attracted by an evil greater than your own. But from bearing all those monsters I grew fat and gross and full, and gradually I turned into this giantess you see now. You have but made a sentimental journey, Loki, and resumed where you left off, and paid off old scores. And even the girl you slaughtered was not unknown to you: she was your daughter too, and I bore her when I had my last child, Jormungandr. She was made up from a lump that was left over. And so, Loki, you have eaten your own child. The worlds revolve with intricate balance, and all your deeds have their conclusions.' And Thurk sighed once more, and pulled down her greasy skirts to cover her white thighs.

But Loki turned away and ran from the cave, and so great was his haste and so disturbed his mind that his foot slipped on the icy path outside, and he fell over the ledge down into the drifts of snow. And as he went rolling the drifts began to slide, until an avalanche of snow was shooting down the valleys, roaring with a sullen note, and throwing up mists in the sun. But the falcon-wings were undamaged by this descent and, since they were magic, kept all the bloom of their beauty, and as Loki was thrown up in the air, the wings started beating and bore him up to safety. And so he sailed up into the blood-red morning sky, while below him still roared on the avalanche he had caused.

But in Thrymheim at the castle were the menfowl bustling about preparing for the wedding, for they knew that if everything were not prepared for Thiazi, there would be wild scenes of wrath and much pummelling for their number. And so they clattered in the kitchens, getting ready the quantities of plates and dishes for the wedding-feast. And the cooks were a-work, stirring the great stewpots which all night long had been bubbling on the fires. And they laid out the roast boars and the swans and the peacocks, and skewering them all on spits set them to roast over the flames. And great heaps of bread was pulled out from the ovens and set aside to cool, and massive flagons of mead were drawn off from the barrels in the cellar, and pepperpots and salt-cellars set out neatly on the sideboards.

But while in the kitchen there was great commotion, the menfowl whose job it was to decorate the hall for the feast had to go about on tiptoe and move furniture without the slightest noise. For Thiazi was still asleep with his face in the dish of bones, and still did his snores resound about the hall. And so without waking him did the menfowl put up new hangings of coloured tapestries, and garland with wreaths and flowers the gloomy walls. And they set the benches by the tables so that the visitors could feast, and they cleared away a part of the smooth floor of the hall so that the jugglers and entertainers might gambol. And when all had been arranged for the banquet, they set two chairs close together and a small table in front of them, and these were the seats where Thor and Thiazi would sit together when they were to be married, and the table was there to rest the hammer upon.

But the major part of the menfowl were engaged in another task. For the order had been given for the great bird-cage, in which Iduna was imprisoned, to be brought into the hall in preparation for swapping the two goddesses. Now this was a forbidding labour, for the cage was exceedingly heavy, and the manfowl Leonard had devised for the manoeuvre a large trolley on wheels, with a special flap up which the cage could be pulled, and articulated front wheels to steer the whole contraption round the castle corridors. Great was the effort with which the menfowl heaved it onto the cart. Enormous was the labour with which they guided it around the jutting walls and awkward doors. But when they got to the hall and had to position it without making any sound, their strength and ingenuity was stretched. And Iduna watched it all with nothing but admiration. And when at last it was set on its trolley at the head of the hall, she joined them all in the sigh which nearly awoke the giant.

But in the camp, meanwhile, there was also a bustle of preparation. For they got ready the gifts that they were to present to Thiazi, and set by in the cart a shield decorated with many a twisting snake and monster, a helmet crested with a glowering boar's head of gold, and two goblets which gleamed like the sun itself – all of which were far too small for the giant. And Balder at last got dressed, and put on his other clothes. And so he robed himself in a tunic of green which was sewn with white flowers, and he combed his blond hair so that it gleamed like the back of a horse. And he and Thor joked about whose wedding-day it was.

But as they stood together in the morning sun, with fluttering wings and a hasty face came Loki onto the scene, and smartly addressed them: 'Hail, gods, I am back, so let us get to work. There is not time for you to ask me how I fared in the distant land of Ymesfield, but let me just tell you I learnt what I wanted, and it is most necessary that I went. But now we must busily prepare for this wedding to the giant, and ensure that everything goes as I planned it. Let me just remove my wings, which are rather ill-fitting, and a slight pain to me – but necessary I do not doubt – and then I can be with you, and arrange everything.' And Loki immediately fell into a sort of fight with the falcon-wings, trying to get them off. But when Ladislav came forward to help him out of them, Loki started with amazement at seeing a man, and looked round in a panic to see what the others thought.

But Balder reassured him, and laughing said, 'Have no fear, Loki, for this is not an apparition, but this is a man, Ladislav, a dweller of the Western plains. Nor do not fret that we have everything prepared. All is ready for the wedding, and we were waiting only for yourself. But now listen to what we have arranged. Ladislav here is one of the many captives of Thiazi, and Thor's hammer has the power of releasing them both from their slavery and the slavish birdlike shape which is forced upon them by old magic. He will secretly go into the castle, and tell his fellows about our plan to save them. For if Thor can overpower Thiazi and strike him dead, then are the slaves released from their captivity.

'Now what I wish you to propose, Loki, oh cunning fire-god, is that the giant releases Iduna into my charge before the wedding begins. In that way I may have the chance to get her out of the castle, and set about opening the cage at my leisure. For to ward off the spell which has made its lock unlatchable, I have made a device which I am sure will open the door. However, if the giant will not grant this request, then everything will depend on speed and quick-wittedness, and so I will crave the falcon-wings from you now, oh Loki, on which I and Iduna might make a quick flight.' And with that Balder stretched forth his hand, and Loki who could not just then think of any reply, handed over the falcon-wings, and stood back scratching his chin. And Balder smoothed the wings, and folded them neatly, and then tucked them under his lithe arm.

But before they got into the cart and rode off towards the castle, did Balder and Ladislav check Thor's appearance and ensure that he gave the impression of a lovely lady. And they puffed out his soft sleeves, and pulled straight the gathered skirt about his mighty waist, and Ladislav kneeling down made sure that the hem was level all around him. Then did they adjust his slipping boobs, and squeezing them into appealing shapes, tug out a little more of his bodice to take them in. And finally they saw to his headdress, and the red ribbons that covered it, and they bound on tight the wedding-veil which had the luck of screening off Thor's red beard and burning face. And so did they mount the cart, and cracking the whip over the billygoats, set off over hills towards the gloomy castle.

But Thiazi meanwhile had been inadvertently awoken, for there came into the hall the manfowl Gwillim, who was a minstrel, and

Gwillim had prepared a great song to sing in praise of his master Thiazi, which exalted him as the blower of all cold winds, the shriveller of the springtime, and the death of flowers, and proud of his composition he entered coughing and clearing his throat, and immediately rang out a silver note to ensure that his voice sounded well that day. But Thiazi was not enchanted, and stumbling up from his sleep he roared about the hall, blaspheming against Gwillim, chasing him about and hurling at him goblets and knives for waking him up. But when he grew aware of the decorations in the hall, and came up against the bird-cage with Iduna sighing in it, he remembered that it was his wedding-day, and roaring out at Gwillim again, he chased him around the hall the other way, hurling chairs at him and plates for not having woken him up sooner. And Gwillim having befuddled the giant by suddenly hiding behind a tapestry, Thiazi went swearing off out of the hall, to change into some new clothes in preparation for the feast. And once he had gone menfowl crept out of the hiding places and appeared from all over the hall.

But then did Iduna speak to them and say, 'Alas, poor menfowl, you are as much an unhappy slave of this giant as I, for being a giant his strength is far greater than any of your poor selves. But there is to be a wedding today, as you know, and I can only bid you to be more cheerful and hope for better things, for the bride who is being brought to this castle may well be a great help to you in withstanding this brute. But now, minstrel, since I feel sure you are to sing at this marriage, may I make a request? Would you sing for us, if you know it, the story of this bird-cage, for I have recently heard it, and think it a sad and happy tale, and I would like our guests to hear it too. And don't forget to mention, for it is such a charming point, that the latch alone is where the spell can be broken.' And the manfowl Gwillim, who felt no more like singing the praises of Thiazi, graciously bowed and granted her request.

Meanwhile the cart with Thor, Loki and Balder in it arrived at the castle, and rumbling over the old drawbridge, stopped before the great iron-studded door. And Balder leapt out and banged with his fist on the wood, so that a great booming echoed in the gatehouse.

Then did a gatekeeper draw back the gate on its runners and grating hinges, and clattering on the cobbles of the lodge, the goats pulled the cart into the castle itself. And menfowl ran about them, guiding the goats, and greeting the guests with bows and pecks of the head. And busily they led them into the festive hall.

Then was Balder overjoyed to see Iduna. But as he went to run towards her, Loki stopped him with a sudden hand, for he did not want any of the menfowl to grow suspicious. And so Balder merely gazed from a long way off, and signalling with his eyes to her, did he show her the pole with the mistletoe's magic at the end, and the falcon-wings on which they might make a sudden escape. But then were the travellers bidden to sit down, and they seated themselves at the table, which was overlaid with good fare, and steaming pies, roast fowl, joints of meat and boars' heads spread about before them, tempting the pallet into innumerable delights. But for all that they could not begin to eat, since Thiazi had not yet appeared to welcome them as host. And Thor sat sighing with hunger and slobbering over the food, and it was only with great self-discipline that he stopped himself from falling on a goose. And since nobody knew quite what to do, there was an anxious silence, as sometimes happens at great feasts.

But Thiazi meanwhile had not gone to change his clothes, but instead went to a secret chamber, and stealthily closed the door. And this secret chamber had in it a spy-hole through which one might watch and hear whatever happened in the hall. And Thiazi came close to it, and looked down with suspicion on his guests. And thus did he cup his ear to hear what they would say. But at this point the menfowl thought it best to entertain the travellers, and after some jugglers with shrill cries and much clapping of plumes had thrown plates about the hall, and a small band played on harp and tambourines, the hall was given over to an impressive pageant. For Leonard had devised an interlude, and the menfowl in costumes and with mime set forth a play of Thiazi's triumph over the Western world. For a group of menfowl representing humans at their wanton pastimes were assailed by menfowl devoted to Thiazi's slavery, and at the high point, when the humans were actually attacking those who remonstrated with them, an engine

[137]

of Leonard's invention entered to universal wonder. For made of canvas and wicker and paint came in a great eagle, representing Hraesvalgr, and the eagle was so cunningly made that it opened and shut its wings, and crowed with a roaring sound. And in the play the eagle confounded all the humans, and the pageant ended with a military parade of menfowl, who, happy to enslave themselves once more to a stern order, marched out with strutting claws, and were gone from the astonished hall. But Thiazi was not impressed by the interlude, which prevented him hearing anything his guests were saying, and he left his spy-hole and went down towards the hall. And it was plain to the audience in the hall that the actors representing the humans had performed with real relish, and that the triumph at the end was more sombre than glorious.

But then came Thiazi into the hall, and the rest of the menfowl cowered. For he still wore the soiled garments he had on before, and the hair on his head was long like thatch, and bristles grew out of his ears, and his great moustache hung down to cover the sneer of his mouth. But when he entered did Loki stand up and greet him, saying, 'Hail, great wind-giant, mighty Thiazi of wondrous Thrymheim, we three Aesirs greet you, and welcome you as our friend. Behold these gifts which we bring you as a sign of good will. This mighty shield, this helmets and these cups. But behold of far greater beauty than all gifts of the earth, this wondrous goddess, Freya, the goddess of love, whom for your eternal delight and fond care we bring you in exchange for poor Iduna. I am only sorry, oh great one, that my plots did not satisfy you at first, but I promise you on my honour that you will surely be proud of this new goddess. Yet before we feast or ratify this contract, let me ask you but a small and insignificant reqest. My comrade Balder here wishes that you may allow Iduna in her cage to be taken from the hall before the banquet commences, for it will be a difficult task to remove her, and one we think best to do while we are still sober. Apart from this we have no further demands on you, great sir, than that you make our dear beloved Freya a good and loving husband.' And with this gracious speech did Loki smilingly sit down.

But Thiazi glared at him for a long time with small and evil eyes, searching his face and those of his guests for signs of deception.

And at last he replied, 'Do you take me for a fool? I do not trust you Aesirs. If I were to let this girl go, you would be instantly plotting how you could run away with this goddess as well. And I need protection against that unburnable fellow too. Do you think you are the only ones with wits on the earth? That moping one in the cage will stay, nor have I said yet whether I will consent to the swap, for first I have to satisfy myself that this goddess is all she seems. How do I know this is Freya you bring me? How do I know she is not someone else? And these gifts you bring me, what use are they to me? I am not a midget. Do you not know how strong I am? Even if these trinkets fitted me, I would need no protection, for not all the Aesirs clubbing together could hurt me. Not Thor himself – look how puny you all are beside me – not Thor the greatest of you with his hammer in his hand could make even a bruise on my head. Do you not know who I am. I am Thiazi, master of the Eastern winds. I have ruled the Western world for centuries on end. With the power of my eagle-wings I have en-slaved everything on earth. With my own power as Thiazi I can match any creature in the world. And as for these goddesses you bring me – do you think they really match my lust? But come, why do you sit there like fearful rats? Stuff yourself with my food, since you think to benefit from me. And let me sit by my goddess here, and see if I will have her. For if she does not please me, I swear I will keep you all prisoners.' And smiling to himself for having made his guests so silent, Thiazi sat by Thor's side, and immediately began to eat. And he tore at great oxen and bullocks roasted whole, and stuffed them into his face, and showed each of his guests how greedily he could chew.

But then did Thor at his side also begin to eat. And not to be outdone did he seize on bullocks and oxen too, and though they were almost as great in size as himself, Thor lifted up his veil and turning his face aside, so that Thiazi should not see his beard, he sank his teeth into them, and devoured them limb by limb. For so long had he sat there gazing at the food that he had not listened to a word Thiazi had said, and was only too happy to munch on the tasty things. And Thiazi was amazed at how much his betrothed ate, and ceased chewing himself to gaze at her with astonishment. But

Thor now drank, and downed a huge barrel of mead. And then did he eat again, whole swans at a time. But when he tore apart a great cow that lay roasted whole, Thiazi grunted in disbelief and dropped his knife on the floor.

But now came Gwillim forward to charm them with a song, and he sprinkled a prelude into the heated air. Gently did his harp sound, and cast a dreamy spell, for there is a time in all banquets to sit back and attend old tales. And Gwillim began to sing then of the tale of Iduna's cage. An idle story it was, of a prince and a restless heart, and a wily magician that built a golden cage. But Gwillim remembered Iduna's request, and in a prelude he told how he would speak of the cage of Thrymheim, whose magic was centred in the latch of the lock. And as he sang of this, Iduna stared long at Balder, and she pointed with her eyes to the lock, and Balder nodded his head. And so did they listen to the tale of the prince of Alfheim.

But alas for Desiderio – for that was the prince's name – he got nothing but grief from the making of the cage, for the object which he hoped to capture he never saw again, and lamented all his days, and died unsatisfied. And the thing which he had lost was the phoenix of Arabia, which goes to Heliopolis every five centuries, and burns itself on a pyre so that a new phoenix may arise. For Desiderio had found such a bird, a maiden phoenix, while hunting a long way from his wealthy home, and at night he caught it and brought it to his palace. And it stayed with him each night and sang him magic tales, but at every dawn, no matter how he would try to keep it, the phoenix flew away and left him all alone.

For strange it was that the prince should love the bird so much, for all his life he had been difficult to please. In his young days he would go questing great beauties, and he wooed many a maiden, and came to win her heart, but each time his ministers began to talk of marriage he tired of his love, and found many faults in her, and grew to yearn again for the beauties he had not met. And such was the case for many years upon years, until Desiderio seemed as if he would die unmarried. But when he found the phoenix it seemed that he was content. For the fiery creature, with its russet and golden plumes, would perch on the bed of Desiderio each night and beat its flaming wings, and sing to him of past ages. But at every dawn would it fly away, and leave him all alone.

And so the prince commanded a magician to make him a cage which would hold the phoenix and keep it with him for ever, for all the devices which they had tried on the bird had failed at a touch of its wings, and allowed it to escape. But magic alone they had not tried. And so the magician built him his golden cage, and brought it from his house, which lay in the grove of Thrymheim, and he presented it to the prince, swearing that it would work and that once the phoenix was in it and the door was latched nothing on earth could open the door again. And so they waited for the night and the visit of the phoenix. And this is the end of the story, for alas, it never came.

Now when Desiderio died, his old nurse came to his funeral, and hearing of his story she exclaimed in surprise, for his minister in describing the appearance of the phoenix reminded her of a strange event which happened long ago. For one day while she was watching Desiderio in his cradle, a gold and russet bird had perched on the foot and sung a sad song of ages far away. And the magician was dismissed, and brought back his cage to Thrymheim.

But Thiazi had not attended to this tale, for he was too far sunk in mead, and too far taken with Thor at his side, and he fell to grasping him about his waist and seeking to kiss him. But every time he sought to lift up Thor's veil, Thor tugged down his hand with an appalling grip of steel. And Thiazi grew angry, and could not understand how a mere woman could keep him off so long. So Thiazi arose and cried out in a loud voice, 'What is this coyness, woman? Are you not my wife, and cannot I kiss you if I will? Why do you keep knocking my hand away from your veil as if I was going to pull off your nose? Well, I will pull off your nose, if you do not keep your hands to yourself. Loki, what is this thing you have brought me? If she does not like my games, you can take her back, and I'll have that caged one again, for I have not given you this banquet to be made a fool of. Why, I will teach her who her husband is to be, and now I will box her ears to make her more amenable.' And Thiazi clanged his great fist around Thor's left ear, and the god's eyes went round in pain and fury.

[141]

But then did Loki jump up fearfully and dart between the two of them, and he cried out in a falsely cheerful voice, 'What, are we having a lover's tiff so soon? Shame on you both! But it is out of anxiety before the ceremony. Wherefore I say let us conduct the ceremony at once, this minute, without further ado, and then Thiazi, we will haste away, and leave you to do whatever you like to your new and lovely wife. Beat her, love her, humiliate her, tread on her, exalt her, wipe her over the walls. She is all yours, once the ceremony is done. Come then, let us have the two lovers sitting side by side, and I shall speak a few words, and place Thor's hammer before them.' And Loki bustled about the two, and he drew back their chairs for them, and kept darting between them to try and break the look of venom that held their eyes, and eventually he fell to shoving them from behind in the direction of the two chairs.

When at last Thor's rage cooled, and he restrained his desire to thump Thiazi through the floor, he went and sat in one of the wedding chairs. And Thiazi himself grew calmer also, and allowed himself to be led towards his bride. And so the loving pair were seated in the two chairs. And Loki stood before them with a saintly smile on his face. And as if he did not pay it any heed, he drew forth Thor's hammer from his shirt and placed it on the table.

But Balder, meanwhile, unfolded the falcon-wings. And slipping his shoulders into the thongs and straps, he bound them upon him, and tied the laces sturdily round the front. And having donned the wings, he took up his mistletoe spear and quietly held it ready in his hand. And he turned his eyes to the cage again, spying best how he might slip the mistletoe blade into the latch.

Then did Loki begin speaking of the marriage, and gently tapping the hammer a little way towards Thor, he said, 'Blessed are we, dear children, that we witness here today a wondrous joining of races that promises well for the whole of Midgard. Too long, too long, oh far, far too long have we Aesirs and you hulking giants been at war with one another. For why, why, why indeed, there is no reason why the intelligent and the less intelligent races of earth should not live in harmony and sweetness together. And so let it be on this joyous day. For now do you, oaf Thiazi, alias

Hraesvalgr, the bludgeon of civilisation, solemnly swear to the best of your intelligence, to take this Freya, goddess of love, sweet, lovely creature of glorious Asgard, to be your wedded wife? And do you, by the same token, oh wondrous Freya, take this wind-giant here to be your husband? Answer me now together at once, and let the lady lay her gentle hand upon the hammer and lift it up as a token of her promise to give her husband all that he deserves.'

But Thiazi was not to be hurried, since his wits being sluggish and his nature suspicious, he never liked to set his name to anything without first throwing doubt upon the enterprise. For Thiazi had been thinking also, and a number of things about Thor had struck him as odd. And so he spoke in a slow voice and said, 'I do not trust you Aesirs, and before I consent to marry this woman, I must satisfy myself that she is Freya, the goddess of love. For I do not think she is. I suspect that you have been trying to deceive me, and that this woman is none other than another goddess, and not according to the bargain we had made. For if this is Freya, the lovely goddess of love, then tell me why her arms are so hard when I pinched them, for they felt more like lumps of iron ore than the soft flesh of a goddess?' And Thiazi looked at Loki with menacing black brows, and his moustache twitched, and turned up at the ends.

And Loki smiled and looked up at the ceiling and replied, 'I am astonished at your ignorance, oh wind-giant, for do you not know that tight arms are looked on as the greatest mark of loveliness among the Aesirs? All the goddesses in Asgard have brawny, hard arms, but Freya is queen of them all, and has won many a beauty contest. And do you not want to be held tight, when you come to the sports of the wedding-night? Come then, let go of the hammer, and let Freya take it in her hand.' And Loki tapped the giant's hand lightly to make him let go.

But Thiazi would not release it, and he spoke again, saying, 'Then if hard arms are such a sign of beauty, which strikes me as a stupid thing – but then you Aesirs are stupid – why has this Freya got such a thick waist? When I put my arm round her to squeeze her, she feels like the trunk of an oak-tree. You cannot tell me that it is very beautiful. I think I have a bad bargain here, and should keep that one in the cage to make up for it.' And Thiazi pointed over his shoulder with his thumb, to where Iduna was looking on with anxious face.

But Loki laughed and cried out, 'Of course it is not beautiful! There's nothing fair in a fat waist. But Thiazi, are you not growing old now, and should you not wish to have the patter of enormous feet booming about your corridors, as you spawn an unsightly brood of little wind-giants to keep up the honour of Thrymheim? We have delicately thought of these things. And this is especially why we have chosen Freya for you, for being the goddess of love, who knows not that she has two wombs, and might easily bear you two sets of twins at once! And for such wonders as this, you must expect her waist to be a little wider than most. Come now, let us proceed with the ceremony.' And Loki grabbed hold of Thiazi's hand, and tried with all his might to prise it from the hammer.

But Thiazi was growing more doubtful at every moment, and he at once spoke out again saying, 'Then if she has two wombs, does she have two stomachs also, for I have never seen a woman eat as much as she? For when she sat at the table beside me, she ate three oxen, two goats, five swans and thirteen boars' heads. What sort of a woman can do that? She is a kind of monster. I would not marry anything so gross. And now that I am growing more and more suspicious of you and your devilish schemes, I would not be surprised if you did not plot to kill me here today, and have an army camped outside. So I shall command now that all the doors of this hall be locked, and that you are kept my prisoners until I am satisfied. Ho, there, you menfowl, lock all the doors quickly, for I do not trust these folk, and will not have them run away.' And as Thiazi cried at his minions they instantly sprang up and did as he bade, and before the Aesirs might act in any way, they heard the great doors clang together and the bolts were drawn. And from outside they heard the scrape of shields and the drawing of swords and the tramping of many feet.

And Loki feigned to be angry, just as he was frightened, and he said, 'What a disgrace and a shame this is to our honour! I have a good mind to call off this wedding at once, and to go back to Asgard with Freya, and leave you to die childless and miserable.

[144]

Have I done all this for your delight, and I get nothing for it but slights and suspicion? Did I not arrange for you to abduct that girl there, and when you were not satisfied with her, and she had rather cleverly shut herself in a cage out of your reach, did I not sympathise, and immediately offer to help you? And have I not at very great trouble to myself journeyed all the way to Jotunheim in an uncomfortable cart, and brought you the very peak of loveliness in all heaven? And do you still doubt me? Such is the gratitude of giants! Why do you think this poor goddess has eaten such a lot? Because of the terrible journey we made, she has not eaten to my personal knowledge for four days. And now she has found her dear one, will you deny her even a decent meal?' And Loki feigned to be so upset, that he drew his hands across his eyes, as though he had burst into tears.

But Thiazi was still not satisfied, and he said in a sneering voice, 'You do not impress me with your rage. What do I care a jot for what you have done? You would not have done anything if there had not been something in it for you. This goddess may be hard-armed, two-wombed and not have eaten for four days, but why does she have such a red face, tell me that? And why do her eyes flash at me, as though they could kill me? Is that a very womanly face to look at? Tell me these things, wise one. I am tired of being deceived.'

And Loki pretended to walk away in disgust, and he threw up his hands and cried out to the whole hall: 'When will this idiot see the truth of it all? When will the fool realise how fortunate he is? Oh Thiazi, you brute, you dolt, do you not realise how you have set all heaven on its head, how you have shamed the Aesirs, how you have done something which no man or god has ever done before? Why do you think I suggested that I should bring you Freya? How might I have dared – little me, the most insignificant of the Aesirs – to promise you, a doltish ogre, the hand of the greatest lady in the world? She loves you, you fool! She has loved you silently for years. Endlessly she has filled Asgard with her sighs for the great wind-bag of Jotunheim. It was only because of her love and her constant pressing that I came to you and suggested that she should be swapped for Iduna. It is love in her face, you see!

[145]

Her eyes burn with desire. She has not slept for weeks thinking about mating with you. Her face flames lust. Can you look on it and not see? Oh fortunate giant that have become the greatest lover in the world!' And Loki threw out his arms and clasping Thiazi's face he kissed it, and then turned away quickly to spit on the floor.

But still Thiazi looked with suspicion, and still his black brows beetled, and snarlingly he said, 'This had better be true, Loki. The doors are locked now. You can't get away. I might well have some fun with you anyway, since you are so cocky. And that smooth young one there, and that girl, if I could get at her. I could have you all stretched out on my instruments. But whatever you say, I still wish to be satisfied of one more thing before I agree to marry this woman. Let me see her face. Let me take off that veil, for she has been holding it down as if she were holding onto her skirts. And I want to see what her mouth is like before I agree to anything.' And with that Thiazi seized hold of the veil and tried to pull it up.

But Thor had not relaxed his grip on it for a moment, and he held one side and Thiazi held the other, and one pulled down and the other pulled up. And so did they wrestle red-faced for some time. But the veil was only thin stuff and could not endure for ever, and after it had been tugged for a good while, with a rip it split in two and fluttered from Thor's face, and Thiazi was left staring at Thor's great red beard. And Thiazi was so astonished that his other hand slackened its grip on the hammer, and Loki darted his fingers over it and slipped it out of the way. But immediately Loki cried, 'There are not many bearded women in the world, and it is one of life's ironies that the goddess of love should be so. Yet it is true, oh Thiazi. She is the goddess. Examine her more fully. Feel her. See for yourself. For you must be satisfied that she is a bearded lady.'

But Thiazi by now was so befuddled with the staring vision of Thor's furious face, which was now as red as his beard with the effort of keeping himself in check, that he was for a while influenced by Loki's words. And so he moved his hand, and felt Thor's left breast. And he moved his hand again, and felt Thor's right breast. And then he bent down to look under Thor's skirt.

But as he bent down, Loki handed to Thor the hammer. And as he peered between Thor's legs, Thiazi made a perplexed and querying grunt. And suddenly he shot up his head in horror at what he had seen. Then was he smartly clanged over the head by the great hammer Miolnir. And Thiazi fell to the ground, his eyes crossed, unconscious. And his tyranny was over and the mission was done.

But now did the menfowl peer at their master, for they could not understand how anyone had been able to fell him to the floor. And so struck were they with surprise and wonder that none of them knew what to do. And Loki looked fearfully and suspiciously at Thiazi's form, for the great giant lay sprawled back, and he had kicked the chair with his leg, and his head had crashed over some benches which were shattered. But for all his looking, he could see no sign of life in him, for a deathly stillness had slunk into the giant's body, as if a strange chemistry was working in his form.

But then did Balder spring forward with his spear, and easily did the thin blade slide into the slit in the lock. And the latch lifted up without any effort at all. And Balder called out to Loki to catch, and he threw him the spear, and bade him bring it back with him to Asgard. And the great golden door slipped open on its hinges.

But the menfowl seeing this began to whimper and protest. And so they ran about the hall and picked up cudgels and lances, and in doubtful rage they began to harass the travellers and threaten them. But so did Thor immediately spring in front of the cage, and standing on guard did he wield his hammer about his head. But Loki, who had not spirit for a fight, picked up the spear that Balder had thrown him, and pretending that he saw someone lurking among the curtains, he darted in amongst them and sought to hide himself.

But Balder was now reunited with Iduna, and once in the cage he took her in his arms. And carrying her close, he walked back towards the door. But the menfowl were all now menacing Thor, and at any moment it seemed they might spring towards the cage. So Balder checked the straps of the wings about his shoulders, and he leapt from the cage over the rushes of the floor, and bounded up onto the craggy sill of the window.

[147]

But the sight of the lovers being about to escape made the men-fowl forget their fears and swarm into the attack, and though Thor tried to fight them off, they thronged to snatch back the flyers. And then did Thor instantly shout out, 'Leap Balder, quickly, for the falcon-wings are enchanted and will easily bear you both. Fly back now to Asgard, and fly quickly too. These strange things will fall in time to my hammer.' And saying this, Thor began thrashing at the creatures. And Balder took a deep breath, and his love closed her eyes, and thrusting with his thighs he leapt out into the buffeting air. He fell like a plummet straight downwards towards the trees. But hardly had he clenched Iduna enough to squeeze her to death, than the sudden wind in the wings set them flapping together happily. And so from the gloomy castle and the dells of Thrymheim they flew through the sky of the late afternoon, bound to the Westward, and Asgard's cloudy walls.

But Thor was covered with squawking menfowl, and they cheeped and chirruped and screeched and howled, and they hopped from the empty window-sill and flung themselves upon him. Thor laid about him continually with his hammer. And those that were struck sank back motionless on to the flags, and lay about in heaps littering the banqueting floor. But as often as he knocked one over the head did another one crawl out from under a bench, and Thor doubted whether it would take him all day to slaughter them. And so he lunged and thwacked and shoved and crunched, and in the centre of the chamber was a great heap of warring strength. A whirlwind of dust and splinters and feathers, converged in a hub of champing teeth and tearing claws, and amongst them, glinting as it swirled in arcs and thudded, was Miolnir the great hammer, dealing the menfowl death. And at last the onslaught slackened in its fury and Thor stood alone, surrounded by stretched-out creatures. And Thor went to a table and poured himself a mighty flagon of mead, and he drank it off in a throw and poured half of it all over his sweating head. And then he shook his flaming beard and hair, and spattered the dust with droplets.

But by the time he had got his breath back, he saw that it was strangely silent in the hall and outside. For it was obvious that those guarding the door were listening doubtfully to the commotion

[148]

within, and those inside the hall lay as still as the grave. And when Loki came out from behind the curtains, groaning as if he had been engaged in many a fight, Thor stopped him from speaking to listen to a strange sound. For the hall was filled with a pattering noise, as the feathers and plumes of the menfowl dropped off them. And when the two gods looked at the bodies that surrounded them, they found that just as Ladislav had changed, so did the menfowls' bodies turn back into men. And when they had completely turned into warriors and peasants and people of the Eastern plains, so did the new men arise, and look about them with wonder.

And Loki was amazed, for he had not seen this before. But Thor let out a great laugh, and cried out to the host, 'Ho now, you are free, my fine fellows, and it is Thor and his hammer that have brought about this wizardry. Not Thiazi. His tyranny is done. But you are all restored to the men you really are. But come, stop not to wonder, nor rejoice. Your fellows remain yonder locked in the shapes you were. Help me then to strike them as I struck you, and soon we will make the whole castle free!' And Thor strode at once to the hall doors, and he took hold of the round iron handle with his bulging fist. And the new men, full of resolve, drew up behind him in a warlike rank. And Loki tiptoed away once more, and hid behind the curtains. But then did Thor heave at the heavy, barred door, and with a mighty clang did he snap all its bolts and locks, and the splintered wood was thrown open by his tug. And the hosts of men confronted the fowl they used to be.

And then did an even greater battle burst out again, for while before it was but Thor and the rest, now were there two camps of creatures opposed, breast to breast, face to beak, and they fell on each other with cries and squawks of fury. The corridors and chambers were filled with many noises: the shouts of the combatants, the cries of the stricken, the steps of those that fled, the oaths of those that pursued. And in every corner was some weapon or fist being wielded, and loud were the grunts and wild were the scuffles.

But as these legions were engaged in the major part of the castle, Ladislav had secretly been round to the sleeping-quarters of the menfowl, to stir up his former comrades to revolt. And demonstrating that he had once been Birdbrain, he wooed them over to the cause of being struck by Miolnir. And when he had persuaded a sufficient number, he sent them about to assemble all the menfowl from every occupation in the castle, and so there came to him not guards but cooks, and bootboys and waiters and all the staff of the castle. And everyone came except the bodyguard of Thiazi, for that was out on a patrol of the castle walls. But the rest now met in a large body in the courtyard, and Ladislav harangued them in a martial speech. And so did he fill them with a determination to be beaten.

But hardly had they surged towards the entrance, when the menfowl bodyguard of Thiazi, warned by certain spies, came running into the garden gate, their swords at the ready. And they shouted bloodthirsty cries at the rebels. Then did one of the bodyguard, when he saw the numbers of the revolt, smartly mount the steps towards a watchtower, and cresting its turrets he blew out a horn-call, which was a signal to all the giants that the castle had been attacked. And when the rebels heard this call they hurled themselves at the bodyguard. Then were sharp swords and mighty axes pitched against carving-knives and broomsticks and ladles. And the yard was filled with clashing forms, and puffed with a thousand feathers.

Now did a rebel lunge at a guard with his sharpened pole, and send the guard's helmet spinning from his head. Now did a guard slice down on a manfowl's head, and split the skull open and reveal his bird's brains. Now did a rebel leap from a wall onto a fowl-pack, and falling to the ground he kicked with his scaly legs. Now did a group of bodyguards, their lances stretched out before them, run the length of the yard into the rebels' ranks, and with a squelch of bodies were they spitted up their pikes. So did the great battle rage on in the castle yard, and the bellows and howls of the armies was lifted up into the skies. A cloud of dust covered over the sun's face, so that the castle was hidden in fires and murk.

But Thor meanwhile was battling in the corridors, and the might of the troops oppressed him not so much as their numbers, for he could hardly move for the press of menfowl mingled with men. But at last he and the new men thrust the menfowl out of the castle. And so like a stream of life they began to drive from the hall. Thor strode forward sturdily, swinging his muscled arm, and they fell down before him like wheat to the scythe. And as the troops burst into the yard and ran screaming from the terror of the hammer, the yard was flooded from the castle side with double the numbers it already held.

Then was there fury and battle indeed. For the rebels were fighting, and the guards were slicing. And now came on another troop of menfowl fleeing Thor. And those who fell onto the guards were thought by the guards to be attacking them. And the rebelling menfowl, seeing the guards attack the other, considered the fleeing menfowl to be on their side. Nor could these menfowl know whether they were being attacked or assisted. Nor was it possible for the new men to distinguish those who were for them from those who were against.

And so was the courtyard filled with innumerable warring factions, and man struck bird, and god struck bird, and bird struck bird, and bird struck man. Screams and roars, grimacing mouths and flying fists, slashing swords and lunging pikes, kicks and blows and buts were everywhere seen. And in the midst of the fighting was a tight pack of locked combatants whose arms and claws and thighs were painfully entwined. And this twisting, writhing mass struggled and twitched, and drew into itself more and more of the maddened attackers. And so did the fight take up the supreme power of all.

But at last was Thor making way against the menfowl, and around the walls of the castle now were row upon row of the creatures that he had knocked out. And those that had turned men were eager to help him, for having got back their old minds and courage, they were raging to join sides in attacking the power of the castle. And so there were less and less menfowl for Thor to crown on the head. And finally there only remained the mass of locked bodies in the centre of the yard. And Thor strode towards it and regarded the pile.

And it was like a great rubbish-heap of discarded limbs, which convulsed as some that were in its centre collapsed. Round and round did the legs and wings twine, like serpents knotted, or worms on the grass at midnight. And beaks and fingers jutted from the pile. And thighs and claws were twisted about each other. And he saw that the rebels and guards were all so far interlocked, that the might of his hammer might serve for all, if he could but strike the pile at its centre. And he saw a glowing, sweating, feathery head peeping up from the middle, with veins standing out on its skull. And the dome was the very centre of all the writhing pile. And Thor leaned over towards it, and lifted his hammer in the air. And then with an almighty wallop, he banged Miolnir down. The whole pack went rigid. There echoed a sort of twang. And the mass then fell apart, and opened, and was released. And spreading out like a squashed fruit were all the bodies of the menfowl within. Then did great rejoicing burst out in the castle, for the slavery of Thiazi was thus undone for ever.

And Thor, when he saw that his fight was done, walked among the growing men and spoke to them, saying, 'Welcome, you stirrers, is it not good to have two legs again? Is it not brave to bear arms, and to have the smoothness of muscle and flesh? I shall rename my hammer Miolnir the man-maker, for he has made men out of you scrawny fowl and sparrow-hearts. Up then, my men. Dance and make merry! For now you are human, you can feast at last!'

The new men cheered their hearts out. They ran and leapt and hopped. And weeping with joy did they clasp hands with friends they had known.

But then from outside came a ringing horn-call, and at once the company fell fearfully silent. And Thor ran to the walls, and looking out over the dunes he saw far off the shapes of giants advancing, for the news had spread of the rebellion in Thrymheim, and the fellows of Thiazi were coming to put it down. And Loki saw them too, and at once did he cry out, 'Now then, you new men, it is time to be gone. Whole armies of giants are approaching to attack this castle, and there is no help but immediate flight. Come then, Thor, let us be off double-quick. Back to the camp, and crack the whip over your goats.' And Loki at once darted out of the yard.

Then was the place seized once more with confusion, and the men ran to the walls to see for themselves. And gloomy the giants

looked, advancing over the hills. And since they all wished anyway
to get back to Alfheim, and a fight with giants would be a foolish
enterprise, they too decided on flight, and so streamed from the
hall. And they raced along the corridors of the castle, and got
ladders and ropes from one of the holds, and placing them against
the Southern walls, they poured over into the safe regions of
Alfheim, for there the giants from old treaties could not come.
But one man there was who did not run Southwards. For Ladislav
yet wanted to try fortune with Thor. And so he ran forth out of
the castle and hared after the two gods to catch them before they
went.

Now Thor was harnessing the two goats, who had been feeding.
And without a word of what he wished or why he had come,
Ladislav assisted them, and helped to take down the tent. But hardly
had they got the cauldron into the cart, when the distant voices of
the giants gave them cause to hurry even more. For they were hard
upon the castle now, and coming on with great strides. And Loki
leapt into the cart, and hid himself under the cauldron, and he
shouted to Thor to be quick and drive away. But Thor still went
about collecting the camp equipment, and he took on board the
straw beds, and the remainders of their food. And he shoved the
tent-poles into the cart, and went back to kick out the ashes of
the fire. But as he did so a great boulder dropped out of the sky.
He climbed into the cart, and cracked the whip over the goats.

But the ferocious giants were nearing fast, and the ground began
to tremble with the tread of their great feet. Over the dunes they
came, like sudden woods or rearing mountains. And the noise of
whistling leaves could be heard approaching as they tore up great
trees and bunged them after the cart. But Thor drove on steadily,
and guided the goats down the slope. And he began to whip them
towards the end of the castle wall, for just past this boundary was
the frontier of Alfheim. And Loki peered from his hideaway under
the cauldron, holding out in his hand the sharp prong of Balder's
spear.

But the giants did not chase the cart and the travellers, but
coming to the castle went in to cope with its rebellion. And they
saw all about them the traces of a great fight, and here and there

a scurrying man, haring towards the South walls and climbing over into Alfheim. But for all that the rest of the place was silent.

And when they saw that there was little they could do, they gazed about idly to look for Thiazi himself. And they came to the walls and looked over in Alfheim. But there they saw the fugitives filling the fields and woods, for they saw Thor and his cart wheeling about the tribes of men, and there was great rejoicing among them in the leafy dells. And teeming about the men and the cart were innumerable birds, trilling and chirping with glee. And it seemed as if down in the meadows there was a great festival, for there was a long procession driving towards the West.

And so the giants left the walls and came back to the courtyard, and shrugging their shoulders they decided they would go home. And so they drifted out of the castle, and away the way they had come.

But alone in the hall was Thiazi still lying. And a strange chemistry was working in his body, for the giant could only die in one of his forms, and now was he hovering between the shapes of eagle and man. His skin alternately grew goose-pimpled and feathered, and then fell back into smooth and hairy again. And his face, which was black in death, changed also into the eagle. And sometimes was his mouth hung over by its dark moustache, and sometimes did it jut out and harden into a beak. And as he lay there raging, his eyes swivelled round in his head, and they were like saucers and flecked with burning gold.

And Thiazi raved and his beak chattered with these words: 'Beat, beat my wings. Beat that hammer. Beat your plumes! I shall prey on them all. Oh change, change, flesh. Let me be bird again. Oh harden mouth into that cutting, slashing bone. Ha, I have him, I have him! I give him the eagle-look. Now is he paralysed. All is good, good. Oh wings, arms, wings! My heart is bursting. It's sharp. It's hard. Oh everything in the world, let it freeze and die with fear, for I am the rager and gnasher of mankind!'

But as he raged and thrashed around on the floor, he banged his changing head against the tables and benches. And the blow made Thiazi so froth with rage, and the tumult of his heart grew now so strong, that it brought the eagle's form upon him and made it stick. And so for the last time the beak split open his skull. The arms were wreathed in feathers, and the feet put forth their claws.

Then the monstrous eagle leapt, and the timbered roof was shattered, and beams and tiles and stones went showering out to the hills. And when Hraesvalgr was high above the castle, he flew on a last journey towards the bloody-coloured sun.

And Balder and Iduna were also already winging thither. And Iduna still clung about Balder's neck, as they sped through the clouds and swept over the mountains. And Iduna called out to Balder above the whistling of the wind and said, 'Oh Balder, let us fly like this for ever over the winding lands of earth. For ever let me make a soft noose about your neck, and wind my legs over your thighs as we pace above the grainy clouds. I feel we are like two spirits who are made of air and will never die. Oh what sweet release it is to be out of that troublesome cage, and to be fleeing from the harsh realms of the giant, and all his tyranny. I never knew there were such people in the world. But Balder, I am with you again, and even though we are dangling above those frosty rivers, yet I feel I could never be harmed now, though one slip of my hand would mean death.' And she looked down over his back onto the canyons and blue glaciers below.

And Balder smiled to feel her clambering over him, and laughing he said, 'Is this not a fine way to travel? Better these wings than Thor's cart. We shall be back in heaven a good day before he comes. But are you comfy peering over my back? I can't wait till we are home, and we spend our days together. Oh Iduna, let us be married tomorrow, as soon as the sun rises. Let us be wedded before any further harm can come to us, and then we will have our fill of love, for which we have waited so long. Oh my sweet, I sometimes feel I shall burst if I soon do not hold you in my arms, and all this trouble we have suffered came from delay.'

But Iduna was perplexed by Balder's words and did not know what to say, and for a while she was silent, so that he wondered what was the matter. But at last did the auburn-haired Iduna answer and say, 'Yet Balder, we cannot get married so soon and you know it. You have rescued me, my sweet, and so half your task is done. But have you forgotten the golden apples of immortality?

[155]

They are still in Hell, and they have more worth than me. Them must you rescue next, my dear heart, for the whole future of the gods depends on them.'

Yet Balder cried out, 'But what is this? What are you saying? Will you not even have us married before I am to go on this quest? Must I dash off as soon as my feet touch heaven, and leave you about to be snatched up again by some virgin-hunting giant? Have I not covered the leagues of Jotunheim, have I not climbed towers and been boiled in oil, and am I not even to get what I came for? What an extraordinary perversion is it to dote on such apples! Will they not bake well in Hell for a while?'

And Iduna cried out, 'Alas, I knew it would be so! I felt in my bones those apples would be a source of discord! For who would believe me among the gods if I told them the truth? And who would not hate me for telling them the truth? And thus I kept it all to myself, and it has been like a great burden laid on my little shoulders. Oh, you brute, you care only for carrying me away! The fact that I have left my home, suffered terrible dangers, given up everything for you, and am now asking you to do what is most painful for me, merely for the sake of the gods to whom you belong – all this means nothing to you. You only want my body! Well, I swear you will not have it, for if you do not make that journey tomorrow, I promise that I will have nothing to do with you from this time forth!' And Iduna fidgeted as she flew through the air, and many times she was near to falling off into the snowy wastes.

And Balder was silent, and he looked at her with stern face. But at last he looked glum, and sighed and said, 'Very well then, I will go on that wretched journey. Fortunately for you I have been already bidden so, and the witch of the earth has confirmed your words. I will go, since you insist, tomorrow in the afternoon. And whether I come back or not will depend on a branch of mistletoe. But hear me this, for this I will swear: if you have your wish, I'll have mine, and if I must go tomorrow, you must marry me tonight. So say what you like, and promise what you will, I'll not go away again and leave you around a maid.' And Balder wound his arms tightly about Iduna, and he raced with all his might

[156]

towards the land of Asgard. And Iduna laughed then, though tears were in her eyes.

But Thor meanwhile was making slower progress, lashing his goats on over the budding dells of Alfheim, and all around him still flocked the crowds of released birds. But Thor was puzzled by them, and said, 'Sweet birds, why do you plague me like this, and what is it you wish? For have I not killed Thiazi, the giant, and so given you release? And yet it is strange and accords not with what Balder said, for were you not all supposed to be elves? And I wish I knew what it was that you were bent on telling me.' But for all that Thor could not think. And Loki, who might have applied his mind to it, had gone to sleep in the cart, the mistletoe spear clutched in his arm, and every now and then he grunted and swore as the cart went over a bump.

But suddenly did all the birds shriek and pipe in terror, and with one accord they hid themselves silent in the hawthorns and hazels by the roadside. And Thor saw far off a black shape winging in the sky, and as it neared he saw that it was slowly beating mighty wings. And so did the form of Hraesvalgr fly towards them. But the great eagle approached and he passed over them Westwards, and the air of his wings flattened the bushes to the ground.

Then did Thor cry out with rage and dismay and said, 'Alas, that is Hraesvalgr, the form of the wind-giant Thiazi! Either my hammer did not kill him outright, or he turned in death back to his other shape. Yet curses and devils take the foul, vengeful beast! He is flying towards Asgard to intercept Iduna and Balder!' And Thor leapt out of his cart and stamped up and down on the road, and so mighty was his anger that even his goats flinched away from his gesticulating arms.

But suddenly all the birds left the hedges and fluttered about. Colours and shimmering patterns flashed from the darkened air. Sheeny blues and shot pinks hovered over the grass. And one moment there was a riot of crests, tails and pink, scaly legs, and the next moment there was nothing but the silence they left behind. And Thor saw the cloud of fowls swoop away to the West. And he watched the flocks teeming towards the light of the setting sun.

[157]

But Asgard meanwhile was heavenly calm and quiet, for it idled its time in the late afternoon, and the sun encouraged the grasses to relax their limbs and grow. And the gods, hearing from Waltraute that all went well in Thrymheim, had made cautious preparations for a sudden wedding, and they brought forth from their stores the finest food and the richest dishes. Servants were setting the great tables of solid oak, and sorting through the best plate and matching it with the goblets. And the yards were full with people carrying wedding-garlands, and bearing great salvers on their heads, and rolling kegs of mead.

But the gods of Asgard were lazy and at ease. Some of them marked how the daisies were coming on. Some of them sat in window-bowers in the sun. But a group of the gods sat on the very walls of heaven, yawning into their hands and playing a game of dice. There was Hermod there, and Niord, and Vidar and Vali, and a little further off Freya and Sif among the turrets. And while the men threw sixes and ones, the goddesses spoke of Balder and Iduna, and long they spent analysing the character of each, and deciding that they were ideally suited. But as the lazy day wore on, and Vidar silently drew to him the gold coins which the other gods had lost, Heimdall called idly that he could see a great flock of birds.

And the birds neared Asgard, and they swept up towards it in a mighty flock, for they had sped there by magic on the fastest route of all. And when they had soared up through the mirky clouds, and scaled the granite and bronze walls, in a feast of feathered numbers they perched on the sloping turrets, and ruffling their tired feathers they sang like a sound of the sea.

But all the gods were astonished at this sudden invasion, and they wondered if all the birds in the world had gone mad and staged a revolt. And so they looked with astonishment on the nodding pigeons and the ring-eyed mallards, and they pointed with amazement at the black-headed gulls and the red-bosomed robin.

But the hoopoe came forward and tried to tell the gods the news. For first did Leshy point to himself, and shake his head. And then did he point to the others and then did he shake his head, as if it might fly off. And next he pointed to the gods, and swinging his head, he threw out a great wing gesturing to the East, and then

[158]

he nodded along the wall like two goats going to Jotunheim. But then with lumbering step, and his wings stretched out on either side he strode in great strides like a giant of the East, and then he flew up in the air like an eagle of the East. But the gods only stared at him, and Sif sent a servant to the house to fetch some birdseed.

Then did Leshy throw himself into a fury of activity. For first he flew by the turrets like two lovers, and then he flew by the steps like a single eagle. Then did he loom as a giant again on the walls, and throw himself onto a poor sparrow as a captor. Then did he imitate a cage, and Iduna in it. Then did he mimic the menfowl in Thrymheim. Then did he climb the wall, and reach the top, and fall back as if on fire. Then did he bite all his fellows. Then did he leap into the air. And finally he gave a blow for blow account of Thor's wedding, his female dress, Thiazi's suspicion, the examination, the blow, the fall, and at last he ended his performance with a rendition of the giant's swoon, which left him prone on his back with claws grimacing. After which he lay stunned in a weary heap before Hermod. And Hermod sighed and gazed at his fellow gods.

But Leshy's efforts were not in vain, for when Hermod looked back at him, he examined his leg with care. And there tied on it, was the green strip of cloth from Iduna's hem. Then were the gods convinced that the birds had a message to deliver. But to solve all their dilemmas, Niord returned from his house bearing a magic draught, and thus he smiled and spoke to the gods: 'Friends, wonder no longer at these little birds, for I perceived at once that they were under an enchantment. I have here a magic draught, which will enable one of us to see their true forms, for it is my belief that these creatures are elves or dwarves or men, who have been turned into birds by a sorcerer. Hermod, you are the wisest of us. Do you take the drink, and see what they are. Then perhaps they may tell you why they have come.' And Niord handed Hermod the cup with the potion, and Hermod drank it off, and returned his gaze to the birds.

And so at last did the hoopoe appear to be appeased, for it let out a great sigh, and while the gods looked on, it began to whoop and sing at Hermod. And it seemed to tell him a story, in a language the gods could not understand. And when the hoopoe had finished, Hermod left the wall at once, and shouting for servants to follow him from the gateway, he ran off towards the halls on a swift and important mission. And the hoopoe preened its cinnamon-striped feathers.

But then did a great horn-call ring out from the tower of Himminbiorg, summoning the garrison to man the walls. And Heimdall came over and shouted down to the gods, 'Prepare yourselves, gods, for danger is upon us. Balder and Iduna are flying back to Asgard. But behind them, gathering speed, is another and greater shape. From what I can see of it, it seems to be a monstrous eagle; not a natural one surely, but a creature of outlandish size. Wherefore I think that this must be Hraesvalgr.'

Now was there great consternation on the walls, for the gods were horrified at what they heard, and strained their eyes to try to see how the pursuit was going. And guards and soldiers of the watch came running, and there was a clash of shields and a scraping of spears. Then did the gods also arm themselves, and they fetched forth their long ashen lances and their swashing swords, and they put on their heads helmets, and fixed cuirasses about their breasts. And Niord strode up and down the walls, wringing his hands and crying out.

And at last did they see the shapes approaching. And they made out the form of two dangling bodies, and pursuing them like a vast cloud the eagle of Jotunheim. And they saw the eagle overtake the lovers, and hang over them with its great talons outstretched. But then did Hraesvalgr hover and look towards Asgard, and when he had sniffed, and spied the gods upon the walls, he flew towards them suddenly with great loping strokes. And the monstrous bird reared up before them, and gazed down upon them with his evil eyes.

And his great beak opened, and Hraesvalgr said, 'Asgard, I have ye. Hraesvalgr comes to the carnage. Tremble ye petty gods whose doom is now arrived. For I shall cast away these walls that hold you in, and with my talons drop ye into the singing abyss. But first shall I catch these lovers as they come home.' And with these words Hraesvalgr swooped down, and faced with his jagged beak the flight of the homing lovers.

[160]

But the gods exclaimed in anger and horror, and with one accord they hurled forth their weapons at the eagle. Vidar cast his hatchet, Vali his long spear. Fricka in her fury hurled forth lance after lance. And many a watchman flung pikes and shot forth arrows. But like the trickling water they but bounced and flowed away. And when the lovers were nearing the walls, and their two forms could be clearly seen, the eagle wheeled downwards and hid under the land of heaven.

But now came Hermod from the hall with a body of men, and they bore great cartloads of hay and straw, and huge barrels and cauldrons of bubbling pitch and tar, and in a great hurry they lugged them up the steps. And from the carts they dragged forth pitchforks and they stood ready by the haystacks, as if to toss them in the air.

And Hermod addressed the gods and said, 'When Odin stole the draught of Od-hroerir, Suttung pursued him to these walls in the shape of a great hawk, and we to save ourselves set his feathers alight. Here is the weapon then with which we may kill Hraesvalgr.'

But Niord cried, 'Alas, that such a good plan should be spoiled by mischance! For the eagle is flown under the very land of heaven, and your straw will never reach him, burn as ever it might. And see now how the two lovers haste towards us! They hurtle on as though they had never seen the monstrous fate that awaits them.' And throwing up his hands Niord went down the steps, unable to watch more.

But from underneath the walls now blew up a mighty tempest and a freezing gale. For the air was thickened and brought to be dark as smoke, and a tumbling mixture of sleet and hail began to pour forth and assail the gods on the walls. Then did hurricanes fall and puff blizzards in their faces. And many of the guards ran cowering to the turrets. And there rose up the great shape of Hraesvalgr once more, and he hovered before the walls, gloating over his prey.

Yet the straw-bales caught alight, and the kindling cracked, and soon were vast flames pouring up from the battlements. And Hermod shouted to the guards to stoke the fires up high, and to pour over them the oil and pitch from the cauldrons, and the very pavements of heaven were made too hot to stand upon. And when Hraesvalgr was hovering just below their sights, Hermod with a yell bade the guards hurl forth their fires, and with shovels and with pitchforks they threw on him the flaming wood.

But Hraesvalgr lurched forward now, and before he might reach Balder and Iduna, he began to feel the heat that seared his down, and twisting his head he saw fires among the feathers. So with a roar he realised that the Aesirs had tried to trick him. With sudden rage then the eagle flew back towards Asgard, and thrusting out his talons he attacked the walls and the gods.

But now at close quarters could the Aesirs soak him in flame. With spears and forks they threw conflagration about him. Strike as the eagle might with the overhanging beak, the shavings and the straw-bales were biting among his plumes. The longer he stood fighting the fiercer the flames raged, and at last his whole plumage was singed and smoking blackly. Hraesvalgr leapt forth and roared among the clouds.

And now the burning eagle rattled across the sky. Flames poured forth from him, fed with the streaking air. To the West he swooped, and then to the East as fast. A plume of black smoke followed him, writing over the air. But as the flames burnt away his plumes he could no longer fly. Roaring he zig-zagged over the fields of heaven. He lurched and tumbled. He twitched and swivelled. With flame for his feathers he hung a while, and then fell earthwards. Down the eagle dropped over the silver surface of the sea, and beating the sleek mirror with a slap that echoed over earth, he plunged into the brine, and was lost in the boiling waters.

The gods drew in their breath, relieved from dread. For in the wild rebound of water, whose spray almost touched heaven, they saw that their sudden foe was finally overcome. But before they might cry out and rejoice that the lovers were safe, Hraesvalgr surged up again. The waters gave him back. With a darkening of the surface and a sudden whoosh of sea, he lunged up in a thunder-cloud of foam. Then did he fall back again, and was sunk in bubbles and breakers. The sea was sewn with broken plumes and talons, and took on the colour of the eagle's muddy blood.

[162]

But now did a strange sound fall on the ears of the gods, for there was a noise of tiny cheering and a thump of elfish feet. And looking about where the flock of birds had perched they saw that they had changed back into their former selves. For a thousand odd and grotesque little shapes were ranked about the places where birds had been.

And so did Hermod shout out his orders to some servants: 'Hasten, some of you, and tell those in the hall of Gladsheim to prepare a banquet at once, for there is to be a great celebration this day. For Hraesvalgr is dead that kept the world in chains. And see, just as Niord thought, were all these birds under an enchantment. Welcome then, oh folk of Alfheim. Welcome, especially, Leshy, you to whom I spoke. For without your timely warning we would not have been prepared.' And Hermod shook the hand of the green-skinned Leshy, and Leshy reciprocated with a graceful inclination.

But hardly had Leshy drawn in the breath which was to launch him into a lengthy polemic against birds, when a flutter of wings made the gods all spin round, and Balder and Iduna alighted on the walls.

And at once Nirod rushed forward and took both their hands in his, and in a voice full of emotion he cried to the skies, 'Praise be that these lovers are come safe home! It seemed as though doom itself was upon them, but by the grace of their chastity are they returned to the fold. Oh welcome, Balder, welcome, Iduna, our youngest hope, and our dearest joy. You have been through strange lands and harsh adventures, but now are you back in the safety of heaven's walls. Now let us rejoice and make merry at last, for we have a feast prepared, and tonight will be all joy!'

But Balder at once spoke out loudly and said, 'It is a custom among the tribes of the North lands, that if two witnesses see a man and a woman plight their troth, and watch them enter the bridal chamber together, then that is counted as a legal marriage. Now I have a long journey to make tomorrow, and might not be back for many a long day, and do not ask me what it is I go to do, but it is a matter of great importance, and the fate of us all depends on my going. Wherefore I call upon you all to witness that Iduna and I are getting married this instant. And since the bridal chamber is in my house,

[163]

Bleidablik, you can watch us from the walls walk over to that place. And since I have seen so little of my love, then we'll hie there this minute, and bid you hail and farewell.' And with these words Balder stripped off the falcon-wings from his back, folded them, brushed them, and handed them to Niord. Then did he take Iduna's hand in his, and lead her shamefaced down the steps from the walls. And the gods watched them go in complete and utter silence, till Balder carried Iduna over the threshold of his house.

But at last Fricka broke the silence and cried, 'Is that then the wedding? Are they now married? Do they sweep in one minute, and walk off man and wife? Is that botched ceremony all that we shall have? Is our standing here enough to make it legal? Is this the beginning and end of the marriage we have been squabbling over for so long? And is this all the satisfaction we'll have for all those months of grief and sweat and perplexity? This is her work, upon my word it is! She has never liked us Aesirs. She thinks we are brutes compared to her Vanaheim fairies. And all the time Balder has been away she has been planning this, and wooing him, I don't doubt, to throw the wedding in our faces! Oh, this is a disgrace and shame to us all! And after all I did for him too, to be treated in this way!' And Fricka turned aside, biting her lip, for her proud spirit spurned that the gods should see her cry.

But golden-haired Sif went to her and said, 'Come, Fricka, do not be upset. We are all of us surprised out of our wits by such a sudden resolve. But Balder may be rash, but I am sure he is not unreasonable. And I am sure there is some urgent reason for this act. But yet can it really be lawful to do what they have done? And is our witness all that is needed to clinch it?' And Sif turned about and sought out the eyes of Forseti.

And Forseti the god of justice nodded his head and replied, 'The ceremony will suffice, for we made no objection. Had there been any lawful impediment it was our duty to announce it. The law is an old one and was fashionable with the Vikings in more urgent days. It served well on campaigns and has not been abolished.' And smiling at the company, he leant his head the other way.

But old Niord shook his white locks, and sighing he spoke his thoughts saying, 'Time-honoured and hallowed are the ceremonies of man, and not lightly to be put aside unless there is great need. I hope that Balder's words are not empty and that this was not merely a feint to have his way. For we all know that Balder is a hasty young man, and it is not good for rashness to overrule the sage.'

But then did Freya speak, the resplendent goddess of love, for she had joined the party on the walls when it was clear that the invading monster was gone. And she laid her silky hand on the wrinkled hand of Niord, and smiling she drew in her breath and said, 'Love, old Niord, love. Customs may change but love last out them all. Poor Balder has been kept for so long from the arms of his dear sweetheart, and what arduous tasks has he accomplished to win her back! How can we blame him for being a trifle impatient? I feel we should salute such an overpowering show of life. What does it matter if the act is legal or illegal? What does it matter if this journey is not as he says? Why, there is tomorrow to see about that, and no doubt we'll hear all. Let it be, gods, for it has worked out so. We should be grateful that they waited till they got home, or love would have happened surely in mid-air.'

And at last did Hermod cough a while and say, 'The day fades fast, and the chill of night comes on. It is time that all of us were home at our hearths. Let us make the best of a baffling job. If the marriage is legal, as Forseti has told us, what right have we to carp or seek to alter it? And Freya is right, we cannot disturb them now. Let us leave things as they are, and meet again tomorrow. Yet if Balder as he said is to go on an urgent journey – and I have good trust that his words were no wit in vain – then I think that it behoves us to succour the lovers and help them. For who would willingly leave his wife the day after their wedding? But now another thought strikes me, which may be a happy compromise and resolve those disappointments of ours and the haste of Balder's scheme. For since Balder is to leave, as he said, in the afternoon, let us have a wedding-feast all tomorrow morn, and then rejoice together and celebrate in full. What do you say, gods? Is not this a fine idea? For having first the wedding-night and then the wedding-feast, what is it but to have a wedding backwards, and we can make good sport of that.' And the gods laughed at this, and agreed to the plan. And so with many a jest and a gossip, they descended at last the steps from the walls of heaven and began to wind their way across the fields to their homes. And Heimdall returned to his watch, smiling at all that had passed.

But the elves were disappointed to hear that the feast that night was ignored, and at once they flew after Hermod to talk with him of this. And so did Hermod listen to their pleas. And taking them in a great body over the square towards Gladsheim, he opened the door of the hall and showed them the supper spread out. And then did Hermod speak to the hungry-looking elves and say, 'Gracious creatures, you are all most welcome to the wedding-feast tomorrow. But since you have this night flown a long way, and need some hall to sleep in until the dawn, then partake, I beg you, of this supper we were to have eaten with the homecomers. For it will only go to waste if you do not attend to it. Feast, and feel free. And I bid you good night all.' And Hermod waved them into the chamber of Gladsheim, and smiling he bade them farewell and went home.

But the elves had lived now for year after year upon birdseed and hips and haws, and they craved for the juicy food which their beaks forbade them to eat. So with wild cries of glee they flew to the groaning tables. And when Leshy had done scrabbling his fingers in the air with eagerness, he bade them all be seated and the feast to begin. Loud was the squeaky chattering that echoed to the raftered roof, as a hundred skinny arms thrust out and sliced off hen-leg and rabbit-foot. Ecstatic was the chewing, and neatly went the teeth. And so did the light elves feel themselves again.

But Balder and Iduna were not so happily satisfied, for they seemed doomed to quarrel that day and be at loggerheads. For hardly had Balder dropped Iduna in the bridal chamber and thrown his back against the stout oak door, than Iduna began to weep, and thus complained: 'Oh Balder, I am sure that we have hurt all those poor gods with our rash acts. For how much they must have waited for our wedding, and now we do nothing to please them, but say one word and rush off. And alas for me too, for this is all the wedding-day I'll have. One minute snatched out of the prison of the giant, and the next shoved into the bridal chamber with no more ceremony. It is very hard for a girl to be so deprived of the thing she has dreamed of so much. If it were not you that I was marrying, I would never consent to it. And I know that it is only done for my sake to let you go on that journey, but alas again, for there is nothing I want less in the world than you to go off into Hell itself of all things, and leave me lonely again and put yourself in frightful danger. Oh, it is so unjust that all these woes fall on us! And where is my wedding-dress and where my feast with you? Shall I have nothing to remember of the day I was married but flying through the air and rushing into this room?' And Iduna sat down on the bed and gave way to tears.

But Balder was impatient and sighed and cried out, 'Oh, I know it is hard, and don't I feel it myself? Do you think I wish to haste away the very moment that I clasp you to my breast? It is like a refined torture such as Thiazi has invented for us and plagues us with after his death, that I should be so continually frustrated every time I seek to take you in my arms. Well, I only go on this journey for you. So you will have to forego something for me. And that something is a proper wedding with all its flowers and red dresses and hammers and nuts and nonsense. But now for God's sake, let us no longer quarrel or mope about it, but take off your clothes and get into bed, and let me make love to you before I go off my head.' And Balder knelt down beside her on the bed, and put his hands about her hips and reached forward to kiss her.

But Iduna pushed herself back from him and turned away. And after a silence, she spoke in a fearful voice: 'Oh Balder, must you really do that to me? I have heard what men do, and it seems such a horrible thing. You know how I love you, my sweet, but I am afraid that you will kill me with all your passion. Could we not just kiss a while, and lie in each other's arms? I am afraid of you when that light flashes in your eyes. Look what happened when we got that way in Apple-Isle. We were chased from the orchard, and that was the beginning of our grief. And it seems to me so horrible that love should end as they say, and that the most ugly parts of us should be the part love aims for. Could we not leave all this till another day?'

But Balder got up, and he did not speak another word. And he looked for a while out of the window at the darkening sky, and he began to take off his clothes and get ready for bed. And he took off his tunic and his hose, and his shoes and the little dagger tied on to his ankle, and he removed everything so that he was naked, and then with sullen face he got into bed. And he pulled up the sheets over him, and turning his back on Iduna he prepared to sleep.

And so did the long day die in the West, and the halls of Asgard buried their heads in darkness. And Iduna sat in a little tapestry-covered chair and watched Balder as he lay under the coverlet sulking. And since the room had grown dark, and the moon had not risen to cast its milky beams, Iduna got up, and striking a flint, she threw a tiny spark on to a small glimmering lamp, and a warm, soft light hovered and lit the walls. And as her shadow loomed about the chamber, she took the lamp to the bedside and placed it near Balder's head. Then she bent down and tried to kiss his cheek. But Balder stiffened and turned over in the bed.

And Iduna smiled then, and putting her hands behind her head, she undid the little buttons that held her green bodice, and opened the buckle that held her leaf-hued skirt, and she slipped out of the garments and hung them on the chair. And then throwing out the tresses of her chestnut-coloured hair, so that it flashed in the room like a sudden amber cloud, she unhitched the shoulder of her slip and pulled it down. And so did she reveal to the soft light of the lamp her full, swinging breasts and her hips so lithe and buxom. And then did she creep into bed, and settle between the sheets that warmed towards Balder.

But since Balder had again turned his back on her, she tugged at his shoulder, and whispered into his ear, 'Balder, come, don't sulk, my love. Don't be annoyed, for you know I love you so. Indeed I do. I really do. For you are the sweetest and most noble man that could ever be thought of since the beginning of the world. And you are the kindest and most loving of sweethearts, and the quickest and cleverest of planners, and the strongest and most powerful of warriors, and the fieriest and most passionate of re-solvers, and the loveliest and most handsome of gods. And besides all that, you are Balder, who I love till I die. Oh come then, my sweet, take me in your arms. Strain me to that mighty breast, and kiss me once more. For I feel I shall die now if you do not hold me soon, so much I have been suffering, and so sweet it is in your arms. Oh Balder, come, love me. Do not be so cruel as to lie still. For my love for you now is so strong that I feel my head spinning, and I shall faint if you do not kiss me. Oh you wretch, why will you not turn to me? How is it you can be so strong?' And Iduna began pulling and tugging at Balder's shoulder, but still she could not force him to turn round. And she fell over him and tried to roll him, and she grabbed his neck and tried to pull it, and she pushed and slapped and heaved and hugged, but nothing could make him turn towards her in the bed.

But after a while, when she was panting with all the effort, her hand was straying down his body to grab something to pull him over by, and without knowing what it was, she took hold of his cock, and so did she prepare to give it a mighty pull. But when it struck her she had gripped a peculiar thing, she snatched her hand away, and sat baffled for a while. And then did Balder laugh and turn towards her at last. And seizing her hand he squeezed it and said, 'That has given you pause for thought. You have pulled everything else on me, so what makes you stop at that? Oh Iduna, now your face does look such a picture! I don't think you ever felt anything like that on the isle in Vanaheim. But fret not, my sweet, I will love you tenderly. It is not such a monster, nor so ugly as you might think. And after a time you may even grow to like it. But come then, lie back and let me hold you tight. For now do you know what I hid from you that day, when I turned away from you in the grove of Thrymheim.' And Balder then leaned over to his love, and he took her chin in his fingers and kissed her on the lips.

And the lovers twined each other about, and hugged and sucked and strained. And they toyed and squeezed each other's bodies, as though to wring out all love's sweetness. And Balder fell to kissing her sweet face, and he covered her soft cheeks, and her fluffy eyes, and her bony brow in kisses. And he kissed the roots of her hair and her curly little ears, and he browsed down her neck, and about her plumy shoulders. And then did he settle on the ripe buds of her breasts, and long he sucked there, until she grew full-lipped and broody. And then did Balder sink down to the feathery flesh of her belly. And he disappeared under the sheets to nibble on those creamy pastures.

But when Iduna felt him still descending, she grew amazed and pulled up the sheets. And she saw his tangled, blond head below, and she felt him open her legs, to kiss between her thighs. But when she felt his lips there, her strength soon melted away, and she fell back on the sheets and surrendered with a sigh. And she wondered what would happen, for she felt she would explode.

And then did Balder lay her soft legs over his sturdy thighs, and brought his manhood to touch the lips of her womb. And he broke her maidenhead, and crammed inside her. But Iduna felt little pain, and she suffered it well enough, for pain was but a little thing to the strange other things she felt. And soon she began to warm to his work, and she started to cry out again, and moan and tremble and writhe. And so did Balder thrust into her more boldly. And so did they move together showering pleasure on each other. And at last she came, and collapsed on the pillows. And Balder too spent his seed and sighed as he did so. And rolling away from her, he lay down at her side, and chuckling then did he draw out his fat tool. But Iduna's little face was set in a mask of amazement. And Balder teasingly popped his finger into her mouth, for her mouth was dropped open and round with surprise.

And at last did Iduna sigh and say, 'Oh Balder, what happened? For I thought I was fading away. I was swept by this fire, and I thought it would stifle me. What can it have been? Did you give me something to drink? Oh, we must be careful, my sweet, that it doesn't happen again. Yet Balder, my sweet, do not leave me now. You must not go tomorrow. Do not bother about that journey. For I cannot bear to think that you should be away from me.'

But Balder looked down, and sighed, and spoke to her saying, 'Alas, no, my love, that can never be. For the sake of all the gods I must go forth to Hell. For the sake of all the gods must I risk my happiness and yours. Such is the hard task which fate puts on us. But fear you not, my love, for I know all shall be well. This task I was bidden to do before you told me of the apples. And I know that it is well I do it, no matter what the dangers are. But do you think with you here in Asgard I could ever be detained in the region of

Hell? Not in a thousand years would I be hindered by those fiends.
For you, Iduna, are now Balder's wife. With you he shares his bed.
From you will his children spring. That is a bond of union which
will outlive Hell itself. Oh therefore, my sweet, my fire, my death-
less heart, let us to it again now and of love gorge our fill. For I
have not shown you anything of the madness of love's ways.' And
Balder threw up his hips, so that his cock stuck vaunting into the
air, and then did he roll Iduna onto her back. and stretching up her
legs, he lay them over his shoulders, and he bore down towards her
with his manhood throbbing at her gate. And gently at first did he
slide it into her cunt, and so they fell sighing, and sucking the air
through their teeth. But then did he begin to pound it and to
thrust it deep into its sheath, and Iduna came to gasp and cry out as
she felt the fever once more. And Balder roamed it round, and
swung his hips from left to right, and he bucked and swirled and
circled and dived, and each movement wrung from her sweet
whimpers and sighs, and each thrust he greeted himself with growls
and lusty groans. And so did he ride her until she grew quite
frantic, and at last when she came she collapsed back on the bed,
and after a moment she burst into tears. And Balder stopped a
while, and kissed her tenderly.

But Iduna sighed and groaned, and at last she said, 'Oh Balder,
stay, stay, or you will kill me, I swear it. I cannot take any more of
your wild thrusts and shoves. Oh have pity on me, my darling,
though I know you love me so. But if you love me any more like
that, I swear I shall swoon away.'

But Balder laughed softly, and he drew back from her, and he
eased out his rampant manhood, and lay down on the sheets beside
her. And so he took her in his arms and comforted her, and said,
'Have no fear, my little one, for I shall never harm you. I love you
too much, and my lust is too strong. Come then, dry your tears,
and let us laugh at our loving. And let us just lie and talk and kiss.
For there is as much sweetness and we are as much together. For
you, my love, are like a thousand white horses, flying and shying
over fertile plains. And you are like a mad house of otters, thwack-
ing and tumbling in the green-weeded streams. And you are like
the rich moonlight of Midgard, that floats on the mists among the

birches of the vales. And you are like a seam of gold in the black earth, that hides its great wealth in the passes of the eagles. And whatever nights we two shall pass from now, for ever shall I be your servant, and make your bliss my own. And through all the coming days whatever they may bring shall I be your keeper, and guard you from all harm. And for ever and for ever, my sweet and honey love, I shall be your own true soul, and love you till I die.'

And so did they talk in the silence of the room, for the night had now advanced, and the stars were all a-roaming. And the room was so still that it seemed to contain all. And yet there was a tiny fly, that with the growing warmth of the days buzzed now and then busily about the window. And sometimes would it settle on the embroidered curtains, and dart along the woven scenes of battle and coiling serpents. And sometimes would it caper along the bedpost, and go climbing on the coverlet in the hills and valleys of the lovers' limbs. And so went the wedding-night of Balder and Iduna.

PART THREE
Balestrand

IT WAS NIGHT, and all in Asgard slept. Under the light of the moon was the whole land still, and the earth shimmered with a greyish green as it rolled towards the glittering breakers of the sea. And further inland, by the banks of Sognefiord, was the glade of Balestrand stirring with new life, for even in the depths of the night did the gleeful sap go creeping, and the flowers of the meadows take heart from the loosening earth.

Yet Odin, father of the gods, could not sleep. And he tossed and turned on his bed in his inner room, and he could not rid himself of the thoughts of the coming doom. Each time that he lay back his heart hardened within him, and each time he got up he felt merely sick and faint. And at last, unable to bear the torture further, he arose from his bed and donned his travelling cape, and pulled down his wide-brimmed hat to hide his vacant eyes. And he decided to go at once to the witch Hyndla by Torghatten. He strode over the squares to the stable where Sleipnir is kept, and led him forth for a night-time journey. And so did he walk towards the tower of Himminbiorg, whose mighty granite gate gazes implacably towards the East.

And Odin saw Heimdall at his watch, and called up to the god and said, 'Heimdall, hear ye anything? When will it come to us, the doom of all the gods? When will we hear the rumbling far off as our enemies mass for our overthrow? Alas for that black day which we must all face! Alas for the terror and the horror and the fear! How many years I have waited, dreading to hear that sound! How often I have started from my sleep, appalled that I heard it mingled with the winds! I leap up, strain my ears, my heart thuds in my breast. But I cannot tell if I hear it or not, and I sink back lost in the mists of despair. Yet Heimdall, Heimdall, hear ye anything?' But Heimdall grimly smiled, and slowly shook his head.

Then did Odin mount his steed and hurl himself towards the earth. And it was not long before they were coasting the bays and inlets of the land of Manheim, and the iron-coloured waters gnawed at the stubborn shore. And soon was the mount of Torghatten seen, and in the depths of its eye could he see the stars on the other side. And Odin dismounted, and climbing the slippery hill did he come to the hollow inhabited by the witch.

And at once Odin slumped down by the tunnel, and he grasped the cold slabs of the slatey entrance, and groaning he cried, 'Lo, where the mightiest of Aesirs is not humbled before you! Since that day you showed me the vision of my son in Hell, is all my power bereft me, and all my dominance gone. I beseech you now, Hyndla, have pity on a broken man. For long have I lived with the notion of doom, but always in my thoughts did I keep one place of hope, that Balder, my son, would survive the day of doom. How often have my tormented thoughts played with such a vision, for I seemed to see him, towering over a sea of golden light, ruling from the clouds in a time where wars were done. Oh Hyndla, cruel prophetess, you took that vision from me. Now I have nothing, but crawl like a beggar on earth. Yet tell me, I beg you, was there not yet some truth in my tender hope? Is Balder really to die for ever? Is there not some way that he yet may be saved?' And for a long time was there silence, with nothing but the boom of the sea.

But a faint breeze played about the hair around his ears, and a voice he heard inside the little buffets, and the small voice said, 'Fading and fading is the life of the Aesirs. You feel now the symptoms of laying down your power. Nothing is there can prevent Balder's going into Hell. This day is he doomed. Nothing can save him. Nor if there were would hard-won Hyndla tell you, for do you not know I never tell anyone good? Yet Odin, you are a seer, and long ago did join our company, and your eye you gave; that was a sacrifice. Something I owe you for the sake of our mystery. This then is a prophecy I gathered from the Norns: that the gods would be destroyed by one that cannot weep. And one thing further will I tell you, which is yet hazy in my mind: that all your evils come from Balder's stay in Vanaheim. Ask him what occurred there, and you may have a clue. Yet this day will the doom of the gods begin.' And the wind died out completely, and Torghatten was silent.

And Odin gazed forth over the waters before him. And lo, in the East, over the craggy horizon, the black sky was glimmering with a sea-grey light. It sharpened the cutting hills that blocked the landward way. And Odin turned and stared down at the flinty rocks on which he sat, and they were jagged and twisted into painful shapes.

And he closed his eyes, and ground his knuckles against his skull, and like a ghastly wind he groaned a grating sigh, and the despairing cry vanished into the limits of the sea.

But at last did Sleipnir climb up the slippery crags, and with big eyes looked down at his grieving master. And Odin laid his hand on Sleipnir's great head. Then wearily did he climb up, and heave himself into the saddle. And the horse climbed the skies as the dawn rejoiced about them, and returning to Asgard, he landed and went home. And so did the day of the death of Balder begin.

But while Odin greeted the new day mournfully, the rest of the gods were all in good heart, for they looked forward cheerily to a morning of feasts and sentiment. And Hermod, when he saw the first glimmers of day, arose from his bed and dressed himself in his tunic and hose, and taking his staff, Gambantein, he went out into the cold air. And the moon was setting, casting a farewell light upon Gladsheim. And to this hall did Hermod go, to set the servants a-work. But when he got inside the porch, he found that the men-servants of Asgard were already there, yet they had not gone inside the hall, but sat about leaning against the walls of the building. And there did they talk in murmurs, as if waiting for time to pass. But when Hermod approached, they shuffled to their feet and led him towards the door, and one of them swung open the door to let Hermod look inside.

And inside the hall, dotted about the benches, seen in the glimmering light, was a sight of sloth and confusion. For all the elves had feasted themselves into a stupor, and without exception they lay unconscious about the hall, their bellies bulging, their eyes stuck fast, their greedy mouths open, their throats racked with snores. And a great noise of grunting and groaning filled all the chamber. And Hermod gazed at a mushroom-elf, who had stuffed himself with roast boar, and had slid under the table until he was supported only by his chin. And he saw a berry-elf who had glutted himself with bread until his stomach was as round as the moon, and bulged up in front of him on his chair. And Hermod saw a pine-needle elf who had fallen into a pie, and a milk-stealing elf who floated in a great flagon of mead, and there was even an elf who had fallen asleep while swallowing a goose, for the head was inside him, but the body lay on the plate still, waiting to be devoured.

But Hermod struck his staff on the table and awoke them all, saying, 'Elves arise, and wake to eat again! For you have not done half the feasting, and what you have so far devoured is a mere supper to the banquet that will now follow. Arise, therefore, and set yourselves to rights. Wipe the grease from your mouths and the sleep from your eyes, refresh yourselves with cold water, and walk about for a while, for this morning are we to celebrate the wedding of Balder, the god of sunlight, and you are to join the gods in a feast indeed. But to allow us to make haste and prepare the hall for this festivity, let me entreat you, dear guests, to stir yourselves quickly and leave the groaning boards, for there are many servants awaiting outside who wish to begin to deck the hall and set ready the tables, but as long as you lie here they are able to do nothing.' And Hermod began to go round them then, stirring them to life with a tug of the shoulder or a touch of his wand.

But the elves, having been so long the captives of Thiazi, were not used to being woken in a friendly way, and immediately they leapt up in terror of their lives, thinking that some torment was ready for their bodies. And they knew not where they were, but imagined they were still birds in Thrymheim, and some of them shrieked and ran about, and some of them flew up into the air, as if to escape to the safety of the trees, and for a while there was confusion in the hall. But when at last they remembered where they were, they sighed with relief, and their eyes lit up with joy. And then when they had taken in Hermod's words, did they dance with glee at the thought of more feasts, and pleased at their new freedom, they offered to help all they could. And so they joined in with Hermod and the servants, and set about to tidy and deck the hall.

Then was the hall filled with as much bustle and business as it had been filled before with slumber and lethargy, for the servants came in and swiftly shifted the plates, and they scraped off the left-over food, and piled up the dishes on planks to take away. Then did they scrub down the tables, and set neat the benches, and clear away the ashes of the fire, and take down the old torches from the walls. And Hermod supervised the cleaning of the chamber. And when this was done the servants began to get ready for the next feast, and the kitchens were full of bustle and steam as stews were set turning again. But the elves meanwhile, following their natures, fell to decorating the hall in all the colours of the Spring, for they made garlands of the leaves that had freshly been gathered, and they stuck into them the flowers that had come forth in the meadows, and so did they fill the chamber with a fragrance of greenness and pollen. The walls did they cover with wreaths and nosegays, and upon the tables they set out the speckled flowers in rows, and around the wedding-seat did they build a great arch of blooms, and white were all the flowers that waited for the bride and groom.

And while Hermod watched the elves with amazement, old Niord arose and came to the chamber. And he gazed at the preparations and nodded his head approvingly. But then did he sigh and say, 'Hermod, the hall looks well, and the feast promises much merriment, but alas, is it not sad that Balder should be so hasty? It would have been better to have postponed this day, and waited for Thor's return, so that the marriage could be ratified with his hammer. Yet now are things done backwards: the bride and groom wedded before the feast, and the groom to leave suddenly, before the ceremonies are half done. I do not like the traditions to be overlooked.'

But Hermod smiled and put his hand on the old man's shoulder, and he said, 'Alas, my old friend, yet it is not an ideal world. But yet things are not black, Niord, look at this flowery feast. And think: for Thor and Loki may well be back in time for this wedding, and the great hammer Miolnir may give its blessing on this pair. We must wait a while, and hope for the travellers' return, for someway over there in the lands of the East must Thor's cart be jogging along, taking the road to home.'

And indeed, while Asgard was full of life, in the far-away realms near the borders of Jotunheim Loki and Thor were on the last stages of their journey. For in the gloom by the fiord they went forward, lighting their way with a torch, and the reflection of the blaze followed them in the water, and they wound a fiery way towards Ringhorn, moored at the shore.

But just as they caught sight of the tackle of the craft, a lonely figure came towards them in the gloom and ran to the cart with fluttering skirts. And the woman called out to them, and said, 'Greetings, sirs. Is that great ship yours that is moored by this lonely shore? And do you sail Westwards, for that is where I am going? For I am Sigyn, a country maid of Manheim. In Telemark I worked on the farms, and was good at making hay and milking the brown-blotched cows. But now am I journeying Westwards to Asgard, for there am I to go to find my husband again. Many years ago did the handsome Loki, the beautiful fire-god, woo me in Telemark, and there make me his wife. And before the year was out he promised to return and fetch me, and take me with him to Asgard, and make me a rare goddess in my own right. But I think that he must have forgotten the way back to me, or has fallen ill, or with business has been detained, for though I have waited him for ten years now, still has he not come back to the haystacks of Telemark. Will you not be kind to me, oh travellers, and take me towards my goal?' And Thor raised his eyebrows, amazed at what she had said.

And before he might reply, Loki began to speak, and he covered his head with a blanket to hide his face, and he altered his voice to that of an old man, and he replied to Sigyn, saying, 'Alas, we cannot help you, girl. The ship is our ship indeed, but we are not going anywhere near Asgard, for once we have left here, we are sailing up a creek towards the East, and will only take you further out of your way. But my advice to you, my girl, and I am a wise old man, is to go back home at once to Telemark, and forget about the marriage, and find someone of your own sort: a healthy young farmer, who will use you on the farm. For have you not heard the terrible news? It has set all Asgard weeping and wailing, and the gods now fear for their very lives. Loki is dead. He had been sent to Hell. And there he shall live for ever, and you will never see him again.' And under the blanket Loki kept his fingers crossed.

But then did Sigyn stagger back from the cart, and she cried out, weeping, 'Alas, is my love dead? Have I come all this way, and that dear little fellow is gone? Oh, I would have covered the whole earth for his sake, for his little gleaming eyes and his tufty hair,

and his sharp, beaky face were so sweet to me! He cheered up my
sad heart with his funny talk and his winning ways. Why, all the
other lads were like dunces to him. He could outwit them all,
and make me laugh fit to bust! And is the poor little fellow gone
to Hell, my own dear husband? Oh alas, then Sigyn will have to
make a longer journey. For if he is in Hell itself, I shall have to
go there now. Oh what a weary way I have before me!' And Sigyn
wept, and sat down on the ground. And Loki seized on the reins of
the goats, and urged the animals forward.

But Thor stayed him with an angry hand, and leaping from the
cart he went to Sigyn and comforted her, and he urged her to get
up and dry her eyes. And he said, 'Weep no more, honest Sigyn, for
you have a true heart, and deserve better. Such devotion is worthy
of a god himself, and you will be rewarded for all the troubles you
have suffered. Know then that Loki is not dead, nor is he in Hell,
for he is here in this cart, and was the very person who spoke to
you. He said those words to test you, and to see if you were faithful,
and surely you have shown yourself a most true wife and a brave.
Climb then with us into this cart, and once more greet your
scheming, fine-witted husband. For I swear to you now, and my
hammer shall make it true, that Loki will keep you henceforth and
never desert you again.' And so did Thor help Sigyn up into the cart.

And when Sigyn had climbed up, and was seated on the bench
next to Loki, she looked at his hidden form, for he was still
cowering in the blanket, and she could not fully believe what she
had heard. But gradually she saw that the shape was Loki's shape.
And at first she opened but a little of the blanket, and then did she
hold up a large flap and peep inside. And when she saw that it
really was Loki, she flung away the cloth, and roughly did she hug
him, and cover his face with kisses. And so did they travel the final
path to Ringhorn. And when they came to the vessel they dismounted from the cart and heaved it up the gangplank onto the
deck. And then they embarked on the ship, and drew up the
anchor. And letting down the sails did they catch the dawn wind,
and at once were driven Westwards away from the lonely shore.

In Asgard, meanwhile, the gods arose happily, for they were
eager to start the celebrations and to see the bride and groom.

[181]

Forseti, the god of justice, arose in his palace of Glitnir, awakened by a reliable cockerel on the first light of dawn, and combing his hair from a level parting in the middle, he went out past his law-giving throne. And he called on Vidar and Vali and aroused them from their slumbers, and together they went along the brightening paths towards Gladsheim. And as the three gods walked, they came to the house of Bragi, and already they could hear issuing from the wide-flung windows the sprinkling sound of his harp as he sent out a prelude to the day. And the gods called in to him, and bade him accompany them, and Bragi came forth, and the road showed four long shadows.

And now did Freya make ready in Sessrymnir, and her maids bustled about her as she chose her robes for the day. And in the rosy light of dawn which slanted through the casement window, they drew forth from a great oak chest the glittering dresses. There were dresses of glossy pink and dresses of rusty hues, and there were long skirts of purple and vivid crimson, deeply-dyed. And Freya sat musing as the maids combed her golden hair, and she sighed for the day when she was young and a bride. And at last did she choose a robe the colour of saffron and crocuses, and she slid her soft sides into its yellow embrace.

Now when these gods had arrived at Gladsheim they found Hermod standing outside the hall, and when they approached him and greeted him, he said, 'Assuredly gods, we have been outdone this day. And we know nothing about festivals compared with some races of earth. Do but go in, and look about the hall, for you will see a change in it, thanks to its new tenants. But I shall haste now and fetch Sleipnir from his stable, for on his back will we lead the lovers to the feast. And when you have satisfied your eyes, come out again to me, and we will all go then to Bleidablik, and arouse the newly-weds.' And with those words Hermod bade them farewell, and he went off over the paved paths to the stables.

But when the five gods had gone eagerly into the hall, then did they see before them a magic spectacle. It was as if they had stumbled into a magician's cave, or had come into fairyland, where all delicate things are teeming. For fluttering about every inch of the chamber was a red-spotted elf, or a fairy with rainbow wings,

[182]

busily arranging a festoon of flowers or food. For there were some with paint-pots that blotched the petals of hellebores, and there were some that made branches of sticky-buds sprout with tender shoots. And some were lining the crocuses with gold, and some were streaking the snowdrops in pale green, and others were twining into the very rushes of the floor the wilting purple of the shy bluebells. And everywhere was filled with streaks of colour and glee. And long did the gods gaze enraptured at what they saw.

But Hermod meanwhile went to the stable of Sleipnir, and he strode down the tiles of the stable and came to the great steed's stall. And Sleipnir looked at him, munching the fragrant hay, and he resettled his wings when he saw Hermod come to take his bridle. And the patient horse let the messenger-god lead him forth, and so went clopping on to the cobbles of the yard outside. And there did the grooms spread over him a cover of tapestry which they tied about his neck and bound around his girth, and the cloth shone with all sorts of different coloured silks, and depicted the old times when the gods were young. And they fixed over this a saddle of leather worked with runes. And so did Hermod lead the steed towards Gladsheim.

In Thrudvang, meanwhile, and the palace of Bilskimir, Fricka had arisen and sadly donned her clothes, and she combed her dark hair, and wound about her a cloak of dusty scarlet, and then did she go forth into the chamber of Sif. And Sif was already up, and the servants had led blind Hodur to her chamber, and Sif had sat him down, to tie up the laces of his shoes.

But Fricka sighed, and greeting her friend and her son she said, 'Alas, it seems only yesterday that I was tying Balder's little shoes, and setting him to rights after a fall in the mud, but now is he to be married – now is he already married – and little joy have I got but a dish of disappointment. Oh how soon, how soon do the years roll away, and snatch hence our youth, and cloud over our happy days! And now is Balder to be taken from me for ever, and I should not be surprised if he leaves us all in Asgard and goes to live on some dreamy island, to be alone with that tempting Vana. And on this indeed have I been thinking this last night, for I have remembered certain other things that I saw on that island in Vanaheim, for not only did I see trees with strange fruit, and apple-cores, and bangles, enough to make anyone suspicious, but now I remember a host of other things: half-noticed at the time, half-forgotten until now. Oh my friend Sif, do you think this woman is an enchantress? Has she lured away my son to be a prey of some Vana magic?'

But Sif got up smiling, and patted Hodur on the hand, and turning to Fricka she smiled and said to her, 'You are too suspicious, my dear, and have been brewing up strange thoughts. All women are enchantresses, and so is it they get husbands. But of this little Iduna have no further fears. She is young, she is sweet, she knows little of our rough world, and all her magic is the magic of innocence. And think, my dear, how she must be overawed by all us Aesirs. She has not been brought up in a city of fighting men and shields and helmets and forays against the giants. She has lived all her life in a secluded island, with nothing but apples and birds to take her thoughts. You must learn to forgive her for the sin all women commit. And so accept with grace the post of mother-in-law.' And laughing then did Sif turn aside, and gazing into a mirror did she arrange her gold-hued hair. And then did the three of them set out for Gladsheim.

And when they arrived at the hall they found all the other gods in a company by the door. And when they all met was there great bustle and chatter, and the excitement grew as the feast came near. For the goddesses gossiped, and whispered in each others' ears, and the gods strode up and down, discussing weighty matters, and their dogs sniffed about and looked up with pricked ears, as a servant or two hurried off over the fields on some mission.

But then did Niord cough into his fist, and he addressed them all thus: 'Aesirs, we are all gathered, and now is it time to go to Bleidablik, and on the duly-decked-out Sleipnir fetch these lovers to the feast. Short time is before us, for Balder must go after the noon. So let us feast well, and sanctify this marriage as we can. It is to be lamented that the due rites have been forestalled. Yet what pains me more today is that our company is lacking a great favourite, for the mighty Thor is not with us, nor may his sacred hammer Miolnir bless this pair as is proper. Yet let us not be downhearted, and let us make the best of this bad job. And let us remember that marriage is a sacred thing, for this that we make today is to last the lifetime of us all.' And so saying, Niord upraised a warning finger, and then did he turn his back and strode out as fast as his old legs could go towards the far-off hall of Bleidablik.

And so did all the gods make out over the fields, and where they walked did the new daisies spring from the ground. Niord led the procession, and behind him came Hermod, and keeping up with this group was Vidar, leading the great horse. And Sleipnir as he strode with his sturdy thighs sniffed at the dewy grass, which was sprouting deliciously. And next in the line came the goddesses together, for Freya and Fricka and Sif made up a talkative trio, and eagerly did they discuss each others' dresses. And next with the dogs came Vali chattering to Forseti, and last in the group was Bragi the god of song, and as he went he cocked his ear to his harp, and he tuned the strings in preparation for an ode. And so at last did they arrive at Bleidablik, and they fell silent before the door, and smiled behind their hands.

And then did Bragi come forward and stand by the very window of the bridal chamber, and he sprinkled into the air a nostalgic prelude, and then did he begin to sing an ode to the Spring. And Bragi sang of how the Winter's ice was cracked in a thousand pieces by the melting heart of the year, and how the rivers and torrents were released from their rimy fetters, and how the brooks began to sing again as they raced down the pebbles. And then did Bragi tell how the birds were set singing, for the dark tyrant of December had slackened his frosty rule, and at last he had been overthrown by the forces of the gold sun. And so coaxed out by birdsong did the daffodils burst their blooms, and shedding their withered cases did they flounce their saffron skirts. And so did the primroses and bluebells fill the woods, and the violets went rioting over the autumn's leaves. And when the gods had heard this song, they sighed and were silent. And for a while they forgot the purpose of their journey.

But the silence had not lasted long before the door of Bleidablik was thrown open, and Balder himself strode out. And bowing to the gods, he addressed them hurriedly and said, 'Good morning to the gods. Welcome to my house. Please enter and take a morsel of bread and wine, and let my servants look to you, and make you feel at home. For I must be gone at once, and cannot stay to talk with you. And very glad I am that you have brought Sleipnir with you, for him I must borrow for an urgent mission, and Iduna and I on his back must ride down to earth. There is a certain plant which I know grows in Balestrand, and thither must I go now to get it in good time.'

And with these words, Balder turned to go again. But Fricka, his mother, cried out in great rage, 'What is this you tell us? You are running away again! Are we perpetually to see nothing but your back, as you go haring off rash-headed from one wild scheme to another? Oh, let me give you the speech and rebuke that I should have given you yesterday, when you ran from us at the walls. Did we not save you from death, and did you not spurn us all to run off for a hasty wedding? Balder, this rashness of yours will have a deadly end. Have you no respect for the gods, for custom, for your mother? Where would you be if I had not flown about earth to save you, and make you invulnerable from all things in the world? Is this how you repay me for a mother's devotion?' And Fricka banged her foot on the ground, and shook her fist in Balder's face.

But while Balder gazed with a long-suffering face at his mother – for one thing was certain: things were not as he desired – there came forth from the house, clad in her robes as a bride, Iduna. For she wore scarlet and mauve, speckled over with flowers of green. And as she took Balder's hands, could the gods see she had been weeping. And such a sad picture she looked, and so fair in her bride's dress, that the gods let forth a great sigh, as if they were looking at puppies.

And at last Balder said, 'Aesirs, I am sorry to be continually frustrating your plans, and it must seem very rude the way I dash off and ignore your greetings. But alas, the times are so, and to do otherwise would be neglectful, and stern things take precedent over the pleasures of life. This plant must I fetch, and the journey must I go on, nor either of the two things do I desire to do. Wherefore do not let us quarrel any longer about what I do, but let what must be be, and the rest of the day be ours. For though

I must fare forth as soon as the day passes noon, yet that leaves us all the morning to rejoice and be merry together.'

And so did Hermod come forward and say, 'Necessity must be obeyed and he's a fool that quarrels. Go then, Balder and Iduna to the earth. Stroll about on Balestrand, and enjoy the scenery well. Leave Sleipnir tethered by the meadows rolling to the shore, and go a-wandering on foot about the glades. Now do not feel you have to hasten back, for there is still plenty to do, to set all the feast in order.' And Hermod smiled and encouraged them to leave.

So at once did Balder lift up Iduna, and putting his foot in the stirrup, he swung himself up into the saddle. And so did he wave adieu, and set Sleipnir in motion. And the gods watched the pair fly off over the walls. And when they had disappeared, the gods looked again at Hermod, for he stood there with a secret smile on his face.

And Hermod said to them, 'Aesirs, you look at me strangely. But have I done anything that should not be done? Balder had a mission, and had to go to earth a while, and what have I done but accept it with a good grace – for is a wedding-day a day to quarrel about small things? Let us return to Gladsheim and see once more to the feast, for who knows, there may be yet a thing or two to be done.' And Hermod strolled off the way he had come, and the gods watched as he nonchalantly went.

But then did they follow him and make their way back to Gladsheim. And some of them puffed out their cheeks, and some of them frowned, and some of them flicked their fingers angrily against their thumb. Yet also were they all slightly baffled by Hermod. And when they had advanced half way to Gladsheim, they found that Hermod had stopped and was waiting for them to catch up with him.

And when they had drawn around him did Hermod say, 'A fine day, is it not, gods? The air is balmy, the Spring is come in. Balestrand must be beautiful on such a day as this. How long it is since we went strolling about the earth! And the woods and meadows would look sweet today, decked out with flowers, as if for a wedding. Would it not be pleasant, if we could enjoy it too! For might we not also go strolling among its groves? And who knows that if we did so we might bump into the lovers. Wouldn't that be pleasant! All together on earth! But if we decided to go for such a walk, then it would be a good idea, in case any of us felt hungry, to take down a good store of food and mead, and tables to eat it off, and a few flowers and garlands, and some flagons and loaves and boars and mead – just in case, as I say, anyone should feel peckish. And while we were at it, we could carry down the whole banquet, for it seems silly to neglect it, now it is all prepared. I was thinking that since Balder has given us so many surprises, it might be a fitting revenge if we were to surprise him now, for if the lovers came upon us all, and turning a corner should find the wedding-feast set out amidst the trees, this could well be a fitting way to begin the party. I don't know what you think, gods, but it seems an amusing idea.'

And Hermod looked at the gods to see their reaction. And he saw a few smiles began to dawn on their lips, and soon were they all grinning from ear to ear. One moment they stood smiling, and the next moment were gone.

And so did they race to the hall of Gladsheim, and call their servants about them, and at once were they all set working even harder, and garlands and nosegays were lifted down from the walls, and food was restacked and fires were put out. Furious was the work, for time was pressing, and never before had Gladsheim been in such a turmoil. And Hermod stood in the middle, attending to a thousand questions, directing the dismantling, and thinking where everything should go.

And Vali stood by him, continually talking: 'Oh will not this be a great surprise for the bride and bridegroom! Will not it be wonderful to bear all the feast to earth, and set it up under the trees and hedges? And will they not be amazed when they see it? Surely they won't believe it. It will all be such a jape. They will be strolling in the fields, and suddenly will they see us all! Oh, shall we not all laugh then? Won't it be a wonderful reunion?' And chattering in this way he badgered Hermod unmercifully.

But Sleipnir meanwhile bore his travellers to Balestrand. And Balder and Iduna, though bound on an urgent task, felt their hearts relax as they gazed down at the springtime earth. For the tops of the trees were dappled with lemony leaves, and the slopes of the grassy dunes were dotted with tribes of daisies. The earth seemed to yawn and to stretch herself lazily, and the rabbits came tumbling from their winter burrows. And the horse swooped down, and floated over the hedges.

And Balder tethered Sleipnir to a bush, and letting him graze on the year's best grasses, he turned to Iduna and kissing her he said, 'Come then, let us find this branch of mistletoe, for the sooner I get it, and the sooner I depart, the sooner will I be back again, and can forget about those apples. And then we can spend all day doing nothing, wandering about in pretty woods like these.' And so did they go to search in the forest.

The air was full of fragrance, mixed with the smell of bark, and there was a rustling of branches as squirrels leapt among the trees. They followed a nimble stream that splashed the mossy stones, and came to groves of ash-trees, that spread their fans in the breeze. And by gnarled oaks they passed, foisting the yellow shoots of spring, and beech-trees, whose smooth trunks were like the limbs of some grey giant. But when at last they pushed through the brambles and set whirring away the pheasant with his scarlet eye, they came among some crab-apples trees whose branches were just beginning to flower. And among the speckled white, nestling in an elbow of the tree, they saw a branch of the green mistletoe.

And Iduna, taking Balder's arm, said, 'Oh how I fear that plant! Is it not a kind of evil plant, that will take you away from earth? And yet it is by such a plant that you and I are together again. Oh Balder, how shall I bear it, when you are gone away from me? I think I shall go mad if you go away today. I cannot even bear to think of you climbing up this tree!' And laughing, Iduna clung onto Balder's arm, and would not let him catch hold of the branch. And so they had a kind of merry fight, until they both fell in a heap on the turf. And then did they kiss beneath the mistletoe.

And as they lay entwined, as though kissing were something new, a robin hopped onto a branch above their heads, and cocking its head it looked down upon them. And the crab-apple tree was stirred by a gentle breeze, and sprinkled the lovers with natural confetti.

But when the lovers had had enough of cuddles Balder arose, and dusting off the clinging grasses, he swung up in the mossy tree and climbed towards the mistletoe. And when he reached the plant, he took out the dagger from the sheath on his ankle, and then he cut at the very root of the green. And Iduna held out her crimson skirt to catch the plant, and Balder threw it down, and she caught it in her lap. And since it was getting late now, they began to wander homewards.

But the gods meanwhile were none so leisurely. Rows of bearers were lined up outside Gladsheim, ready to move this movable feast. And servants were loaded with planks and benches and table-tops and trestles. And others were detailed to carry the pies and the roasts and the loaves and the flagons of mead. And others came behind them bearing braziers of fire. Meanwhile the elves had flowers in bundles, and ran about bristling with sprays and branches. And when at last everything was taken from the hall, the whole army of revellers moved over the square.

And when they came to the gate then did Hermod call, 'Heimdall, great watchman, command your servants to open the gates, that we may descend Bifrost to the lands of the dappled earth, for we are to take our banquet there, and surprise Balder in Balestrand. But do you also forsake your watch a while, Heimdall, and come down with us, and join us in our rejoicing, for long have you sat guarding our city against attack, and surely do you deserve some respite from your labours.'

And Heimdall said, 'Willingly will I command my doors to be opened. And I will also command that the bridge is shifted to the East, so that the rainbow steps may lead you to the very edge of Balestrand. And as for your final request, oh great messenger, assuredly it is a long time since I have deserted my watch, and many times have I mused on earth, for I see the beginning and the ending of all days, and when all creatures sleep there also is my watchmanship. And this being so, I will join you in your banquet.' And Heimdall turned away to climb down from the tower, and he appointed his guards to watch in his place. And he himself took the Giallar-horn on which he might blow the warning note of doom, so that if Ragnarok came, he still would be prepared.

Then did the great gates clang open on their hinges, and the guards pulled them over the metal rails, and the darkness of the archway was split down the middle. Then did Bifrost fling forth its vaulting way of colours, and the rose and fire and saffron soared on their path towards earth. And on the right were the warm hues, spangled with flecks of gold, and on the left were the cooler colours that went mingling into the sky, for the emerald and azure faded into mauve, and the left-handed purple was lost in the thin air. But then did the great bridge shudder and shift its highway, and the rainbow was given an end in the turfy meadows, and hidden among the daisies was the pot of gold.

Then did the gods begin their walk to the earth. And first of the procession went the guards bearing the tables, and they carried in pairs the great planks down, and jolted over the steps with their benches and trestles and beams. And following them came the servants carrying the feast, and they held their dishes high and took care to feel for the staircase with their feet, and the great flagons of mead were borne without splashing their golden liquid. But the elves had an easy labour, since all of them could fly, and no whit did they worry about tumbling from the rainbow, and so on the outer edge did they play at helter-skelter, and holding their garlands and branches above their heads, they sat on their bottoms and slid down the rails of the bridge. And then came the rich gods themselves, for Hermod took the leading bearing his messenger's staff, and white-haired Niord tottered in the middle, and last of the party, taking him by the arm, came the gay ladies, leading Heimdall down. And Heimdall smiled and allowed himself to be led.

But in Balestrand, meanwhile, another set of gods were hastening, for the great ship Ringhorn was pulling into the shore as the obliging breezes swept it its last mile home. And when it was moored at anchor then did the mighty Thor get ready to disembark, and he said, 'Friends, we are now reaching the end of our journey. Lo before us Balestrand, where we started out with Balder. And see, even the grand bridge, Bifrost, that glimmers with all the colours of earth. How strangely near it seems in the sunniness of this Spring day! But come then, Loki, let us get our cart off the ship, and rattle towards that bridge and so on up to Asgard!'

And so did the travellers leave the ship Ringhorn. For Ladislav jumped down, and helped Sigyn the country maid. And Thor guided down his sure-footed goats who dragged the cart clattering over the gangway to the shore. And lastly did the disgruntled Loki step glumly into the waters, and stumbling on the slimy pebbles, make his way to dry land. And he fumed that Thor had made him take Sigyn on the journey, and he looked at her evilly, as though he might stab her in the back.

Yet Balder and Iduna were still making their way out of the wood. And before they reached the glade where Sleipnir had been tethered, Balder turned to his wife and said, 'There will be little other time than this to speak a few words together. What will happen this day there is not one of us who knows. Therefore, my dear love, let us prepare to meet the worst, for in that way are we defended against the shocks and attacks of mischance. If I should not come back, but Hell should hold me for ever, then are these our bodies to be perpetually apart. Wherefore remember me, when the night is coming on, and think of the brief times we were together. And so, my Iduna, farewell, indeed farewell.'

But Iduna replied, 'If you were to be stayed in Hell, do you think that I would keep long from your side? No, you are my lord and my love and my husband, and not Hell can sever the bonds of a true match. For you have I married to follow in whatever fortune sends, and if fate should conspire to hide you under the dark mountains of death, then I will come a-searching, and not rest till we are together. In you is all my bliss, and my peace, and my homeliness, and the spirit of life itself, which cannot be resisted, will bear my little body once more into your arms. And therefore Balder, farewell, indeed farewell, for you will journey faithfully, and we shall meet again.' And then did they embrace and kiss at the edge of the wood. And so did they walk to the glade where Sleipnir was.

But when they came into the glade they saw such a sight that long did they gaze at it, unsure if it were real. For all the Aesirs were sitting ready for a feast, and the tables were before them, set with all kinds of fare, and the bushes which they had left sprouting small buds in the sun were now covered over with the thick blooms of mid-May. For the white-thorn and the black-thorn were sewn with the checkered flowers, and the crab-apple and the wild pear seemed to froth with the chalky petals. Everywhere was tumbling with luxuriance and abundance.

And Balder, when he saw this, gasped and exclaimed, 'Is this some dream or does some enchantment mock me? And yet Iduna, you surely see it too. For I fancy I see before me the whole company of gods. And those that we left but a while back at my door are here all littered like leaves over the lawn. And how also does this glade come to be sprung out in flowers? Iduna, have we been away a century, like men magicked in the mountains, who go back to their villages to find their friends all old? Yet the goddesses especially look as young as they ever did. And see where Thor stands, as astonished as we are. And look if my father is not there also! Oh truly this is the most incredible of slumbers!'

And each then looked about, gaping at the wonders. For away to the left down the meadow towards the fiord were Thor and Loki, and two other people beside. And away to the right was Odin, the gloomy god, and he gazed back at them with a look of kindliness. And the blossoms were scattered everywhere, for everything was in flower, from the cascading fruit-trees to the wriggling rows of hedges, from the pink-veined cherry to the blushing dog-rose, and the meadowsweet and cow-parsley raised their creamy heads, and the rank-smelling elder loaded the air with dizzy fumes. And long did the Aesirs gaze upon each other, while the rainbow bridge of Bifrost reared up beyond the trees.

But then at last did Odin address them and say, 'In trouble and in grief there shines still fellowship, and here are we all gathered to forget our cares a while. Wonder no longer, Thor, what we are doing here, nor, Balder, puzzle yourself how Gladsheim has shifted its ground, for I came a little earlier, and these pranksters have explained. For this is Balder's wedding-feast, not in Asgard, but on earth, to greet him and Iduna, united after long trouble. And in this fairest of groves you may all be happy a while, for the elves have brought everything to flower in the sun.'

And then did the red-bearded Thor laugh boisterously and say, 'Why, you mad Aesirs, what a homecoming is this! But let me introduce now the guests that I have brought. Wonders enough have I to tell you, as you to tell me. For this is Ladislav, a man, that was once a thrall to Thiazi, and this is Sigyn, a country maid from Telemark. But who will not be surprised when I tell you her station in life? And how fitting will this wedding-feast be, when I announce that she is Loki's wife! She found us by accident, and now has him for ever. My home I see before me, my friends are all about me: Aesirs, Balestrand, Bifrost, Asgard. But where is my wife now? Let me give her a smacking kiss!' And with these words did Thor hug her a mighty hug.

And lastly did Balder smile at them and say, 'Alas now, I repent that I must go on my journeys, for this feast looks set to be one of the best of Asgard, and from it must I fly, as soon as it is noon. Yet are you all mad lunatics, and what a hall is this! The sky is our Gladsheim, and living trees our walls. And comrades, forgive me too, for I have frustrated all your plots to have a party, and this magnificence have you mounted in my despite. Helpful is the proverb; scrap and scrape again!' And with these words did Balder laugh, and the gods cheered as he led Iduna to the table. And the lovers sat down among their friends.

And then did old Niord come forward, and he took from Thor the great hammer Miolnir, and bore it reverently to the pair. And when they were standing beneath the archway of white blooms, he placed the hammer before them, and bade them lay their hands upon it. And so did they swear to be true to each other as long as life would last. And when they had spoken these words, Niord lifted up the hammer and blessed them, and they knelt down before it, and reverently kissed. And so was the marriage of Balder and Iduna made good. The Aesirs smiled and the elves fluttered about them. And behind them near the bench was a tall-growing crab-tree. Its red and white petals were dappled with shoots of green, and these it rustled, and seemed mad with joyfulness.

And then did old Niord lift up his hands to heaven and say, 'Praise be that these roving lovers are at last united! Thanks indeed that it has been done according to custom, and Miolnir was here to sanction it. For there have been times when I thought that never would they be joined together by any honest means. For Aesirs, think, how troubled has this match been! For were we not all in despair five days ago, when we met in Gladsheim? Well, I bid you gods, at last with a clear conscience, lift up your drinking-horns and let us toast this happy pair.' And Niord held up his goblet, and the Aesirs drank to the bride.

And so did the feast begin and all was laughter and jest. And many were the comments shouted across the table, and much was Balder badgered by the quips of the feasting gods. And great was the din of talk too in that leafy glade, for everyone had a story to tell, and everyone had many questions to ask, and so did they lose themselves in the chatter of exchanged news. And the butterflies and dragonflies flitted across the table, lured by the jangling colours of the dishes of the gods.

But then did Odin arise from his place and say, 'Aesirs, it is time now for me to ask a question, for a certain prophetess this morning threw doubt in my mind over a certain thing, and this I must ask Balder, to see what his reply should be. But at the ripening of a feast is it good to hear tales, and I do not wish to throw gloom on this celebration, and so my question I have framed in the shape of a request, and that is for Balder to tell us all a story. For I would wish to know what happened in Vanaheim, when Balder went wooing for this sweet one here, Iduna. It surely will be a story that will be eagerly heard by you, and by it I may ponder what the witch meant in her prophecy. Though I hold no hope of a secret to crack our doom, yet it is well to be completely forewarned, and so be prepared for the ills that are falling upon us.' And Odin then fell silent, and the Aesirs applauded his words.

And Fricka now turned towards her husband for the first time, and frowning on him she said, 'My lord Odin, I have not spoken to you till now for reasons which are obvious. Moreover, I have been astonished at the coolness with which you come to this feast, after the things you have said about us lately. But as to your speech just now, I am prepared to compliment you upon it. It is indeed high time we heard of Balder's wooing, for it has been long kept secret, without any reason at all. And if he is going to condescend to tell us of it at last, perhaps he will also add to it an explanation of where he is going today? For all this bustle and haste is done for his sake, so that he may go on some unmentioned journey. Balder, prepare yourself then, and let us know the truth. And these questions especially answer about your time in Vanaheim: what were the apple-cores by the little black gate, what is the tree in the centre of the island, and – something I have remembered since that time – what were the scorched marks of burning in the grass?' And raising her finger at her son Fricka was silent, and they all waited for his reply.

But Balder sighed again, and at last he said, 'If Iduna will consent to tell you of our wooing, then you shall hear it, as we both shall spin the tale. And as to my journey, it is only right that I speak of it now. But this I warn you all: you will not like what you hear. There lies Sleipnir, and on him must I shortly go, and the place that I must journey to is the dark region of Hell. To Hela's realm must I fare to fetch back Iduna's golden apples, for they are the thing lost which the witch Groa bade me retrieve. And on them do the life of the Aesirs depend, for they are the apples of immortality. I see you look sombre. Indeed it is a sombre thing. But to Hell must I go this day, and nothing can prevent me. And if you now listen, I will tell you why this is so.'

But Fricka could not remain silent at what she heard, and she broke out and cried, 'Balder, what is this you tell us? You are to journey into the depths of Hell? You cannot do so much. You must not be allowed to think it. Such a journey is certain death, there is no other way. Are you to kill yourself, and we to let you before our eyes? Aesirs, I see you are with me on this. Look how they gaze aghast. Balder, you have gone madder now than ever. None of us will consent to you even beginning such a journey. I myself will plunge a dagger in my heart sooner than allow you to go forth.' And Fricka crashed her hand down on the table, and turned to Odin with an accusing look.

But Balder spoke again and said, 'Mother, contain your own rashness. If you wish to stab yourself, that is your own foolishness. But do not throw doubt on my mind, because I will take up this venture for your sake. It is a bitter thing to journey into Hell. For Hell is the region which every man dreads most. And yet I am to do it. This plant of mistletoe will give me safety. And from Hell will I fetch forth the apples that will give us hope. But now be silent, and let me tell my tale. For the golden apples are what happened in Vanaheim. And the golden apples are the key to all our woes. And the golden apples will give us life at last. So will you consent to hear why this is so? And will you consent, Iduna, to help me tell the tale?' And Balder gazed about him, quizzing the pale-faced gods.

But a while they were silent, pondering his words, but then did they nod one by one and consent, first Hermod and then Heimdall, and even Fricka last of all. And when they had agreed did Iduna nod also and blush. And so he began the tale of Iduna's wooing.

And Balder said, 'Long had I been questing in the Southern regions, and home came at the end of last summer, weary with butchery and loaded with gold. Ringhorn we left where she is moored now, and brought from her hull much treasure to brighten Bleidablik. But my heart was restless and sad after the journeys among the dwarves of Svartheim, and the riches of their cities had stirred in me strange feelings. And so did I brood upon the life I had been living, the exultant pastimes of pitching strength against strength, the fever of conquest, and the joy of overcoming. And I seemed to be rebuked by the treasures I had plundered, for they seemed to celebrate the things that I had destroyed. For here did I feed upon the glories of the dwarves, that in no way overshone them but in speed and battle. And so did I think upon the purpose of my life, and threw a cloud of doubt over all my proceeding. And yearning to glimpse again the cities that had lured me, I climbed up the mighty hill of heaven, to steal a glance from Odin's throne.

'Now Hlidskialf has the power of granting him that sits in it a vision of the whole of earth. And, father, forgive me for it, but here did I creep that day. No sooner had I sat but I saw the world before me: the frozen limits of the North, the trembling fires of Muspelsheim, the mountains of Jotunheim, the rolling steppes of the East. And I saw also below me the cities I had sacked, of Luna and Pisa, and the coast of Aquitane, Seville that gave us Arabic gold, and the damask of Valence. But as I gazed on them my heart yearned again to be questing. I envied them in defeat, for theirs was a life more delicate than ours. And I sighed again, and felt a soul-sickness, for the yearning was within me for something – I knew not what.

'Turning my eyes away then to the West, I spied the land of Vanaheim, and in its seas a certain isle. This was Apple-Isle, of which you have heard much. Now it is known to us, then it was unknown. And by the magic of the throne, I gazed down into its hills, and there did I see fair woods and apple-hung orchards, blazing among the idle waters of the sea, and the leaves were now turning as Autumn came apace.

'Among these leaves I saw an auburn-haired maiden. She strolled amidst the trees, plucking the burnished apples. A basket she carried, and placed the ripe fruit there, and as she turned I saw that her cheek was ripe with rose. In the way that she garnered there was a great stillness. Nothing seemed to take her thoughts but the orchard in the mists. And my eyes followed her, as a child would follow its mother, easy in her waywardness, free because assured. Each step she took, each reaching of her hand, increased the lulling spell she threw over my body. The sun was sinking after a day of weary toil. I felt I had lived a life there before.

'When the eyes meet the soul stands naked. Diffidence, fear, resentment, these can all be seen, though with our words we speak nothing but friendliness. What is there more holy than the surrender of a glance of love? Then we see into the soul, and give our hearts entire. Meeting, talking, loving but renews that intimacy. With that look from that maiden, she that sits at my side, all the yearning in my heart ebbed and flowed away. And from that day I began a new life.

'Yet how I began also to suffer ten times worse than before! When I stepped down from that throne I was in torment till I stepped back again. Many times I did so, skulking up to it again and again. I longed now to sweep over the miles of ocean and reach that place. Yet I dreaded the journey that would keep me so long from her sight. Then did a thousand fears sweep into me, that the maiden would never love me. She was married or betrothed. Perhaps she loved another. If she saw me might she not hate me?

The cities of Svartheim might have spoken ill of me to her. Would I not seem rough to her and crude? How could she love me, an adventurer, a plunderer of cities? How could I ever win her by weapons of sudden surprise? I repented that my whole life had not been dedicated to apples. And so I fell sighing, and a prey to restless nights, and poor Hodur, my brother, I wearied with my groans.

'Well, as you know well, and my parents especially, Lord Odin and Lady Fricka soon noticed the change in their son. But the cause of my sickness, that could they not find. Long I kept it a secret, pining within. But I talked in my sleep: this gave me away, and Hodur reported that I had been burbling of far-off maidens. And soon had I confessed the whole love-story to them. They were slightly disgruntled, but neither of them opposed to it, and when, after some time, my sickness saw no signs of abating, they summoned a servant named Skirnir, and despatched him to Vanaheim. He was to plead my case, and propose a marriage between the two races. For it was deemed a good thing that the Vanas and Aesirs should mix. But how this Skirnir fared is perhaps best left to my wife. Tell them, Iduna, how you greeted his embassy.' And Balder laughingly looked towards his bride, and she for a while blushed as scarlet as her robes.

But then Iduna sighed, and thus she began to speak, and said, 'Balder, as usual, has rushed me into things, and I am not sure how or what I should tell you. I have little skill at speaking at great feasts, and indeed until I came to Asgard had never been to one. But if I am to tell you how I greeted Skirnir, I shall seem ungrateful, unless I first go back into the story. For Balder has told you how he saw me from the air-throne in heaven, but what he has not told is how I saw him. For when he looked down at me across the thousand miles between us, I saw him also, enthroned in the golden clouds. And that vision was to shape my whole conduct.

'Aesirs, you are used to great deeds and making. You go forth into the years shaping earth as you think fit, for yours is a life of will and fierce faith, and great achievements you love to achieve, which shall be renowned down the years in song. Alas, that we in Vanaheim have no such energy. We live from day to day, doing much the same as ever, and all our delight is in little things, and we pick out our lives dependent on Mother Earth. I was happy in my orchard, tending the golden apples, and I knew that if I was threatened I would have a great defender, for in a cave in the bowels of Apple-Isle there dwelt a monstrous dragon, who would arise if my heart was troubled. And so did I neither fear or hope, but lived out my days enjoying whatever the wind blew in.

'Yet one thing must you know, for this also has a part in the story, and that is my true origin, or what of it I have been able to find out. For I am truly only half a Vana, and the other half of me is a mystery even to me. For the story goes that my father lived on my island, and by magic arts did he reach contact with hidden things, and at the summit of his life he called a great spirit: a goddess of another world, that lives not as we do. And she did he love and he lived with her on the island. Now my father was a Vana, and mortal in our way, but she, the goddess, was such that she could not ever die. And when my father grew old she conceived from him a child, and that child was myself and she bore me on Apple-Isle. But alas for mortality, my father died as soon, and never did I see him or know what he was like. And when I grew up my mother left tending me, and withdrew more and more into the realm where she lives for ever. So have I had till now a solitary life, and yet I have friends enough in the animals of Apple-Isle.

'But think, though, how I had never seen a man, and how often must I have thought what my father could have been like. And in my childish fashion, I imagined him like my mother, and just as she does I thought of him hovering in the air, growing clearer from the sunset sky, or rising from the splashing waves. For my mother can merge herself from any beautiful thing, and it is but a trick of the light and I will see her, sitting upon a bank of new flowers, or billowing like a sail over the morning sea. When I saw that handsome man in the throne on the Eastern clouds, I thought he must be my father, and I gazed at him with love.

'When Skirnir came, I did not think him as handsome, and what he proposed jarred on my feelings. I wanted no match with a far-off race, to leave my sweet Apple-Isle and my man in the clouds. And so I refused him when he wooed me on Balder's behalf. The rich things he promised me I had no desire for. The bitter things he threatened me with held no fear for me. I told him my heart was gone another way. And so he left me, and I thought no further about it.

'A little after this, one of Ran's daughters came to see me, and I told her of the embassy and the offer of marriage to one Balder. When she heard of it she agreed I was wise to refuse, for the Aesirs, she said, were all doomed soon to die. Their enemies were growing stronger, and their strength had begun to fail, and if I were to marry this Balder, one of their leaders, I would soon be swept away in the deluge which would meet them all. I thought I was very wise therefore in keeping out of their way. But I felt a little sad that I had not seen my cloud-man for so long. I am sure this is the silliest tale that anyone could tell, and I am ashamed to admit how slightingly I thought of the Aesirs. But for what happened next, I think Balder should take over again.' And Iduna hid her face in her hand.

And Balder smiled, and began his tale again, and said, 'Haphazard is this tale, but you asked for it, Aesirs. It flies from me to Iduna like a ball in a game children play. It suddenly shoots forward, then does it die away. It soars into the air, and then bumps lamely along the ground. Let me see if I can gather up the threads of what happened next. I think it would be best if I tell you merely what I did. For now has the story a little more action. For when I heard of the failure of Skirnir's mission, far from being more depressed, I was fired by his refusal. It is gratifying sometimes to meet with defeat, for it gives you the spirit to go on and accomplish. I leaped from my sickbed, moony no more. I went to Frey, the god of Alfheim. I borrowed his magic boat Skidbladnir, and floated away at once at top speed for Vanaheim. And soon did I sail merrily into the little bay at the foot of Apple-Isle. The day was warm. The sea was calm. How happy did I feel to put in at that kindly haven! At last I would meet this wondrous creature, and speak to her, face to face.

'A fine welcome I found there! When I leaped from the ship, and walked up the sandy beach to go into the island, I found my way blocked by a black little gate. I turned the handle but it was locked. I felt rather hurt that where Skirnir was let in, the prince he was pleading for was not even allowed access. But, as I say, failure inspires, and I climbed up the bars of the gate, prepared to leap over them. As I climbed up they seemed to grow higher. I thought in a few heaves I would reach the top, but after shinning up numerous feet, I found that the top of them still dangled over my head. At length I gave up, for it was obviously enchanted. I turned to the wall that ran round the island. I clambered its crags. It was just the same. With horror I staggered back onto the beach, for I realised there was no way I could get in to Iduna's orchard. I grasped the bars of the gate, and shouted into the garden. And then I waited to see if anyone would come.

'Oh then began my penance and my grief. At the boundaries of her bower, I could get no further forward. In sight and sound of her I was further away than ever. I called to her who I was, how I loved her, begged her to come to me. All my pleading vanished into the air. I knew Iduna was there, for I sometimes caught sight of her, afar off in the orchard. And after some days of grieving and starving, she began to leave me apples to eat, rolling them through the gate when I was asleep. But never once did I see her plainly. Never once did she speak to me. In one so lovely, I could not believe there was such stubbornness. I cried out at her harshness, but there was nothing I could do.

'Well, I soon grew sick of my feeble state, and determined to call my plaints no more. And since there was no way of getting on to the island, and nothing I could do, I merely sat there in silence, and waited, and waited. It was fortunate for me that I stumbled thus on the best weapon against women. Girls can brook your insults, but cannot stand your silence. And so did I linger, a hush at the gate. To make it more complete, I would lie flat on my back, as if overtaken by a sudden stroke. And so I went through the most frustrating, but restful time of my life. As I lay there through the days, gazing up at the sky, I seem to grow contented with just being there. I shall always remember that idle, happy time. And at last one day, I heard the little latch turn, and Iduna will tell you what happened.'

And Iduna looked at him reprovingly, but thus she continued: 'Yes, it is best to admit, I was caught by this clever device. It is never until we lose a thing that we realise its true worth. So was it with me, with this talker at the gate. For I had grown used to his plaints, and would listen to them eagerly. I would sit against the wall out of sight, and the tears would stream down my face, for I quite took sides with him against my cruel self. And yet for all that, I never thought I should free him. For my heart – was it not given to the handsome man in the clouds? But when he fell silent, a fear overcame me. At last I went to him in daylight. I saw his body stretched out. I unlocked the door, and went to see if he were dead. And so did I discover I had been tormenting my cloud-man.

'But oh that beast, and what a fool he made of me! He let me weep over him, and beg him to live, and all the time he was laughing at me inside. How innocent I was in those far-off days! I think I have learned a little now of the great world. At any rate I kissed him, and he opened his eyes, and smiled. And then he kissed me. He asked me to marry him. And I said yes. By leaving the island, I too would become mortal, and my marrying Balder be engulfed in the doom of the gods. But of this I kept silent, for it did not seem important. I was ready to go at once, but we stayed for a while on the island, for Balder was lazy, and wanted to dally a while.'

And Balder sighed and nodded his head, and said, 'Ay, that I admit, Aesirs. For love is a strange thing, and my time with Iduna had already softened my brain. To tell you truly, in my heart I forsook you all. I resolved to have done with warring, and take up the post of apple-man, and though I did not say it, meant to dwell on that island for ever. Indeed it was a shameful thing. And there was more shame too. For I intended to become this girl's husband, whether or not there was anyone to marry us. But there was something on that island that soon put paid to that. Harken a little further, and hear what drove us away, and then shall you also know why Iduna brought her apples.

'For as my wife has told you, there was a dragon on that isle. She put it rather delicately, but the truth of the matter is thus: that the dragon would be aroused once an islander felt lust. I do not know why these creatures have such delicate morals, but it seems this eager feeling offends a good deal of people. At any rate our life was not to be tranquil for long. Having chosen to live for ever on that isle, I turned back a little to my old ways, and Iduna did I leave now and then to tend the burgeoning apples. And I too went straying to see how the island was made. And soon I was thinking of plans of building houses, and making new cities, and founding a new race. But sooner or later my love would lead me back to seek Iduna's footsteps, and each time I re-met her she seemed even sweeter than before. Till then I had loved her purely, with none of the element of earth. But then did my kisses grow much like anyone else's, and I came to desire what we all enjoy from love. We were embraced beneath an apple-tree when we felt the tender fire, and no sooner had we felt it that the dragon was aroused.

'Forth from its cave came the lumbering monster, pouring black smoke from its scaly nostrils and mouth. Iduna shrieked with fear, and I jumped up in a panic. I had been a languishing lover for so many days that my sword and all my weapons I had left on the ship. I broke off a branch and prepared to fight the beast. I strode towards it swingeing the air like a windmill .And soon I was grappling with the demon himself. I have not fought many dragons. But the art lies in avoiding the flames. I kept nipping behind him and going for the soft part of his neck. For a long time we fought, and both were growing weary, when with a butt of his head he threw me down a bank. It was as I ran back up it that I faced a sudden light. I remember no more, for I fell down swooning. And Iduna will have to tell you the rest of the story.' And so Balder looked again towards his wife.

And then did Iduna speak the last part of her tale, and she said, 'As radiant as ever I had seen her, came then my mother to me, and such was the blazing light that made Balder swoon. And me she looked at smiling and sad, and I felt my heart ache at the perfection of her beauty. For she came in a golden light, a halo round her head, and a blue gown of softest cloth swept round her lovely form. She spoke then many a sweet thing to me, and recalled the steps which my love had taken. She told me I was to go forth into a greater world. For of my own free will I had been willing

[204]

to go to Asgard. And of our mutual lust were we now both banished the garden. She bade me to awaken Balder with a kiss, and go with him in his ship. She bade me take twelve apples from the central tree, and bear them with me to Asgard and keep them safe. She told me that with my burden I should keep the Aesirs from death. And so did she bid me farewell, and bid me be of good heart, for now was I to go forth and be a woman, and so would I need her no longer as my guide. Alas, I could not forbid the tears, which coursed down my cheeks. And what pain it was to bid my mother thus adieu! But she faded at last from the mistiness of the air, and I saw my love stretched out, and the dragon lumbering home. And so I awoke Balder again with another kiss, and I told him to make ready the ship, for we must be on our way.

'How tearful it is to say goodbye to happy days, to turn our backs upon our youth, and look away from innocence! Yet the pain is a sublime one, because it must be so, and the life we then run into has harder but deeper riches. And so have you heard, gods, how Balder came to woo me, by what strange ways I loved him, and how we were reconciled. And now, alas, I think you know also the worth of those golden apples. And I fear that all the fault is mine, that they were so lost, when I was snatched away. For I thought that I would keep their great burden to myself, and so would the gods' safety be unchallenged because unknown. Alas, I see once more, I put faith in innocence. And now am I to suffer for the wrongs of long ago.'

And when Iduna's story was finished, the gods were silent a while, but then did Fricka say, 'Why, you are a true daughter, both of your mother and me, for you do not trouble yourself with worries and doubts, but when you see a thing you do it, and no more moaning about it. I always said you were an enchantress, and I see that you partly are, but what I did not see was that it was Balder who dallied. He would still be on that isle, if it was not for the dragon's vigilance!' And Fricka ceased speaking, and glared at Balder once more.

But Balder chuckled, and smiling he said, 'Assuredly, my mother, you never miss a chance to scold. But what you have said is right, and my heart is glad: for Iduna is indeed a true-hearted wench, and she does it with quietness, and makes no deal of fuss. Well, our story is over, and you have heard what happened. Now do you know what that great tree of golden apples bore. Now do you know who ate those apples at the gate. Now do you know what dragon burnt that path. But in quest of those apples we brought must I soon go and leave you, for the sun is mounting quickly up the sky, and soon will Sol the sun-maid be reaching the zenith of noon. Therefore since we have now all eaten, let us leave these trestles and lie about the grass, and let those of us who will play games and strive in sport. For see how this place is a paradise of green.'

And the gods murmured approval, and straightway they pushed back their benches, and leaving the littered food, they took their goblets and moved away. And the elves got down and flew rejoicing in the air. And the servants went racing in the meadows, and wrestled and played with a ball. And now in the soft breezes came the petals of fruit-trees a-flying, for pink petals and white petals danced in whirlwinds along the tables, and the swallows swooped among them, skimming the rows of hedges. And so did the Aesirs lie about on the soft, warm grass, and they sipped their goblets lazily, and chewed the shoots of sedge.

But old Niord dallied a while and he said, 'My friends, before I sit down, I would have you all drink to lovers and to love. For what is more appealing than when young faces are lit with kindliness and lasses and lads laugh, and shun to be foul and quarrelling? Ah, happy times are the times of youth indeed, for then is the heart frank, and the spirit undissembling!' And old Niord lifted up his glass, and the Aesirs drank with him.

And when the gods were seated about on the grass, for a while there was silence, but for the humming of bees. And the Aesirs watched far off on a hill before the forest the servants running races over the tumbling fields, for they had mapped out a course with clothes tied upon bushes. And the sounds of their shouts went echoing in the air, filling the woods with a lazy music, and hovering over the bleak surface of the lake.

And Hermod smiled as he leaned on his elbow, and said, 'Where could you find a better feasting-hall? The Spring is out, and now we dot the grass with couples. Look, we are like those deer there, that gaze at us from the distant wood, for so do they pair off, when the beeches spread their leaves. Who is there we could wish here, who is not here now? No one, I think, unless it be Frey. For all else by good luck have come to the wedding. I think we did right, gods, to choose this day for a picnic.' And Hermod lay back, and gazed up at the sky.

And the Aesirs sat idly, musing on various thoughts. For Balder lay with his head in Iduna's lap, and she was drawing on his face with a blade of grass. And further off sat Freya twining a daisy chain. The butterflies flapped round her, lured by her yellow robes. And the sound of a cuckoo came towards them through the woods.

But then Odin began to speak, and he peered deep into his cup and he said, 'Yet life is sad, gods, life is sad. Be cheerful how we will, there is still fate to cope with. We sit here about this meadow. We drink the honeymead. Yet Balder, my son, is to journey from us into Hell. And thus it is the fate of death hangs over us all. Look, there is a cloud already on the horizon. In just such a way does our death bring us its darkness.'

And the gods gazed away to the horizon over the fiord, and there in the East they saw a streak of grey. And tethered to the bush stood Sleipnir, awaiting the journey.

But afar off then did they hear a jingling of bells, and a shepherd came past them, leading his flocks by the shore. With a hat of wide brim, and stuck over with wild flowers, did the shepherd stride along, and play a warbling pipe. And the nodding sheep with sheep-bells clattered after his step. And so did he pass on without once seeing the gods.

And Balder arose and said, 'The noon is come now, and it is time to go. And I would go quickly, the quicker to return. Farewell then, my friends. Farewell, my dearest love. Unwillingly I leave you, the farther way to fare. Nor do not follow me now, but stay feasting as you are. This memory I will bear with me, even down into the dark of Hell.' And Balder took up the mistletoe, and placed it in a cleft of the saddle, and he took the rein of Sleipnir, and began to unfasten it from the bush.

But at that point there ran into the clearing five thralls of Thor who had been sporting in the meadow. And they cried out to him that they were playing a game of throwing, and they wished to challenge him to a test with his hammer or with spears. And first Thor shook his head and denied them. But then did he think again, and have a happy idea.

And he took Balder's other hand and stopped him a while, and turning to the gods he said, 'Aesirs, we must do all we can to forestall our hero's going, for there is plenty of time to fare forth on journeys into Hell. Much of the day is before us, and we have yet to play some games. Wherefore I say, let us have a new sport, which will give us all great mirth, and has a fine part in it for Balder. For do you not know that he is invulnerable to all objects on earth? Let us have a throwing match then, for all the Aesirs, gods and goddesses alike, and for our target we will have the young Balder himself. For much fun did I have in Jotunheim with throwing things at him, and it did my heart good to see how they bounced away. For truly it is a wonderful sight, to see the fine hero stand, and all weapons but drop from his breast. All of you watch now, as I show you what I mean. And when you see what a failure I am, do you then try to better me.'

And so did Thor lead the reluctant Balder aside, and he stood him carefully in front of a hawthorn bush, and he made him put his hands down at his sides, and then did Thor walk a distance away. And Thor picked up a spear, with a sharp iron point, and as the gods watched with puzzled faces, he hurled the spear at Balder's breast. Then did all the Aesirs gasp and cry out, and some of the goddesses screamed, and some of the gods seized their weapons. But the spear when it reached Balder bounced back from his skin, and they saw Balder smile a weary smile, since he had not been harmed at all.

Then did the gods fall open-mouthed with wonder, and a grin of delight crept over their gazing faces. And Thor urged them to try the spell themselves, and they pressed forward a little to test with small knives and daggers. But soon were they merrily hurling rocks and stones at Balder, and they laughed to see the missiles bounce off and Balder sigh at enduring this silly sport. For Freya flung at him pins and brooches, and Vidar and Vali also flung their weapons. And old Niord tried it, for he was slightly drunk. And

Forseti tested it, driving forth his spear with thoughtful attention. And Ladislav fell to it, and Sigyn the country maid, and the elves too swarmed about Balder hurling everything they could find. And it grew to such a pitch that they were flinging loaves of bread at him, and the air was filled with the laughter of the crowd.

But Loki meanwhile, with the mistletoe spear in his hand, sat still at the tables, and had not gone onto the grass, for he was plunged in gloomy thoughts and was angry at Sigyn's coming, and he stared at her among the gods, lamenting his forced bondage. And Loki said to himself, 'What a pack of fools they are to be playing these stupid games! And look how that idiot Balder stands bouncing their shots from his body, for he is like an Aunt Sally at the fair, that all men fling stones at, and try to knock over. This is what he has come to: the great adventurer. And see what I have come to also: a married man stuck with a nattering country wife. Oh, I have grown weary of them all, and of myself. For years I have tried to injure them, and wasted much effort upon it, and haring about have I gone all over the world, and nothing have gained from it but trouble and strife.' But as Loki was thinking these thoughts, he felt a tug at his arm, and he saw Hodur beside him, straining his ears to hear what was happening.

And Hodur said to Loki, 'Loki, I think this is you, for it feels like you, and these are the clothes you wear. Why do you not go yourself, and throw things at Balder, since from the sounds of it they are having a merry game? And yet alas, I would so wish one day to play games. It must be so merry to leap across streams. Have you not a spear to hurl at my brother? Would it not be fun, Uncle Loki, to do that?' And Hodur turned his face again towards the sounds of glee, and he listened to try and hear what was happening at the game.

For Balder now had taken off his tunic, and he hung it over the may-bush behind him, and he allowed his bare chest to be assailed by the objects, so that they all might marvel how the skin was never broken. And Iduna went to him with a little fork from the table, and she tickled him with it, and wandered away again. And the thralls of Thor were flinging spears from a long distance, and though they were good shots, the lances fell clattering down. And then, pressed by his thralls, Thor threw his hammer, and the hammer bounced back and fell by a loaf of bread. But when the god Balder saw the hammer and the bread, then did his face darken, and he gazed at it puzzled. And afar off stood Fricka, who doubted the whole game, and that some small object would not have taken the oath.

But Loki now felt a little sorry for the blind god, and at last he stood up, and took Hodur's hand, and said, 'Come then, little blind god, and Uncle Loki will look after you. And you can have my spear, and I will guide you how to throw it. For it is no joke seeing everyone sporting, and yet sitting apart yourself, unable to join in their games. It is easy for these gods to laugh, because they have health and homes. But you and I, Hodur, are not so fortunate in our fates.' And Loki led Hodur forth, taking him by one hand, and in his other hand he held the mistletoe spear.

And when Loki came forward, the gods made a place for him. And they all fell silent, and Loki guided Hodur's hand. And he aimed the blind god's throw, and then told him to hurl it. And Hodur flung forth the mistletoe-spear, and it sped towards Balder a little unsteadily. And it missed him by an inch or two and sunk into the earth.

But Iduna felt sorry for the blind god Hodur, and she quickly picked up the spear, and guided him to Balder. But Balder saw before him a woman's hand on a spear. And he saw the bread again, with Thor's hammer lying on it. And he remembered five days ago how he had dreamed of such emblems, and Odin had told him they were the emblems of his death. And then did he notice his own tunic in the may-bush, and this was the third of the emblems of his death.

But Iduna led Hodur, and drove the spear into Balder's breast. And the spear stuck fast, and the wound poured blood. And Balder staggered, and fell upon the grass. For a long while the gods gazed at him, unsure what had happened. And the sun in the silence began to descend to earth. But then did Iduna faint, and fall to the ground.

But Fricka ran to Balder, shrieking out in anguish, and she fell on her knees at his side, and stared at the blood that seeped from the spear-point. Then did Thor rush forth, and he took Hodur by the arms and he cried at him, 'Hodur, what is this? What did you do?' But Hodur began to weep and cried, 'Uncle Thor, why do you grip me so? What is it that has happened? I do no know myself. Have I struck my brother Balder? Have I hit him with the spear?' And Hermod strode up and said then to him, 'Too well you have struck, Hodur. For Balder is wounded grievously. A spear is there stuck fast in his breast which was never bound by any oath. One ride quickly on Sleipnir's back to the thralls in the meadow, and fetch forth the healer with his herbs to tend the wound.' And Heimdall, hearing this at once rode to the fields.

But then did Thor come to Balder and kneel down beside him, and he gazed at the wound unbelievingly and said, 'How can it be so? For he was protected against all objects. It cannot be that anything should have harmed him, for was not everything bound by Fricka's oath?' And Fricka thus cried, 'Then what is this blood? Is it wine? Is it a prank? Oh you dull god, why do you have no brains?' And Thor when she said that began at once to weep, and lamenting he cried out, 'Alas, that I ever came to this feast! Alas, that this spear did not pierce me rather than Balder! For I have deserved it indeed. I began this game. Oh, how shall I bear to live, when I have done this to my friend?'

But now did Sleipnir return swiftly from the meadow, for he flew with the speed of lightning, and brought Heimdall again and the healer. And the healer was rushed forward and put down beside Balder, and at once he set out his herbs and his ointments, and fell to studying the wound in Balder's breast. For the spear was still in him, and bore down with its weight. But the healer began then to pour some ointment into the wound, and with gentle hands, he sought to sway the spear a little to one side. But Balder then cried out in a hoarse voice, 'Do not touch it. It is useless. The point has sunk deep. It will only kill me quicker if you move it at all.' And then did he groan aloud, and cough up blood.

But now did Iduna recover from her swoon, and she raved and cried wearily, 'Have I been hit? Is the cage open?' But then did she come to herself, and remember. And she looked at Balder and buried her face in her hands.

[211]

But then did Balder suddenly struggle to his feet, and bending over the spear, he ran away towards the horse Sleipnir. And he cried out as he went, 'Stay for me here, Iduna. I will fetch your golden apples.' And Hermod leapt up and seized Balder by the shoulders, and tried to restrain him from attempting to mount the horse. But Balder had gored himself with the weight of the spear, and he collapsed on the ground again, retching and coughing the blood.

And Iduna ran to him and weeping she cried, 'Oh Balder, do not move. Stay still, and ease the wound. It cannot be a bad wound, for I gave it you myself. Oh God, I am no warrior, nor Hodur, who is only a child. No man can die from such a playful blow.' But Balder sighed and replied to her then, 'Nay, my sturdy wife, but I feel this is my death-wound. The mistletoe that released you was the bringer of my death.' But as Balder tried to speak more, the blood came forth in gushes.

And so did the gods stand in anguish about them. For the healer had shaken his head, and denied that there was any hope. And all of them were numbed by the accident from thinking of any remedy. For Thor walked sadly to Balder and knelt down beside him again, and his face was stained with the big tears running down. And Fricka was distracted and paced up and down on the grass, and she rounded on Odin, who sat by merely slumped in grief. Sif sat apart, and she was white as the may-flowers. And Hodur went round the gods hoping for some comfort.

But now did Balder rage in his pain, and he fought against death, and refused to give up the ghost. And he writhed with his body and twisted this way and that as the blackness came over him and the numbness in his limbs. And to save him from goring himself more, Thor with his mighty hands broke off the shaft of the mistletoe spear. But Balder thrust Thor aside, and he stood up on his feet once more. And there was a mad look in his eye that filled all the Aesirs with fear, and none of them dared to go to him as he staggered forth on the grass.

And then did Balder gaze about him into the sky, and he seemed to see strange things, and he stared past the gods themselves. And he shouted up into the sky with a choked voice, and said, 'Ay, I have seen your emblems. Now do I see your selves. The hammer and the bush and the spear have passed before me. Now do I see the monsters that will bring our death upon all. Ay, you slobberer, you flickerer, you writher, I see you in your fylgies, shaped in the vaporous air, haunting with visions, that will soon be here indeed. Gods, to arms, to arms! The bringers of doom have come. You are surrounded. See them. Well, I can ride in their hosts!' And with a sudden rush did Balder race towards the steed Sleipnir yet again. And as the gods looked on, too horrified to move, Balder seized on the horse's reins, and put one foot in the stirrup, and began to heave himself up to climb into the saddle. But now did his heart-strings snap, and his life failed him at this task, and he slipped backwards from Sleipnir's warm sides, and reeling from the stirrup, he fell on the grass and died.

And the glade was still, and all leaves and flowers motionless, and the sun herself seemed to stop in the deep sky. For the black flies ceased buzzing about the white hemlock and they froze upon the buds, and looked through all their eyes. And the bees ceased humming among the wild-cherry blooms, and the dragonflies stood still on the lake-lapped stones. Only a lonely cuckoo flew calling his husky song as he winged along the echoing valley, his villainy being done.

But now did the true shapes of monsters show themselves, and what Balder alone had seen took form in the air. For hovering in the sky appeared strange wraiths of cloudy shapes that set forth a pageant of the terrors of the earth. For the white vapours South-ward were like Surt, the fire-demon, that wields his flaming sword in the heats of Muspelsheim. And the wispy vapours Westward were like Jormungand, the world-serpent, that showed his face towards them and his body tapering away. And last was Fenris, the wolf, that chases Sol and the sun-maid across the sky, and he slob-bered with his great jaws, and the whole sky became dotted with cumulus blobs of his spit.

And Heimdall, seeing at last the enemies of his watch, raised up the winding Giallar-horn to his mouth, prepared then to sound the long, dread note of doom. But Odin strode forward and placed his hand on the horn, and with a shake of his head he restrained

[213]

Heimdall from blowing the warning note which would summon all the allies of the Aesirs to the fight.

And then did Odin turn back to the gods and say, 'Aesirs, these phantoms are merely phantoms. Fear them not. Nor in such a way will they come at the time of Ragnarok. And so for the moment, ignore them, and instead listen to me, for I would ask you all questions to ascertain the depth of our doom. And so Fricka tell me this, for there can be no point in keeping it hid: what were the words of the oath that you took from the creatures on Balder?' And Fricka straightway answered him and said, 'That all creatures in the land, in the waters or in air, swear never to harm Balder, the god of sunlight.'

And next did Odin turn to Iduna, who stood by, and Iduna gazed before as though all life had fled from her too. And Odin asked her and said, 'And Iduna, tell me this, for you of us all would know it: what was the charm that was put on the enchanted cage, and which as Balder told us was released by the spear that killed him?' And Iduna answered the lord of the gods and said, 'That nothing could unlock the latch that was on the land, in the waters or in air.'

And then did Odin turn to them all and say, 'Fate is more cunning than ever has been man. And the best of all our planning is still the sport of fate. Twice was Balder served by the branch of mistletoe, for first it brought him joy, and now it brings us grief, and there it lies detached, untouched by mortal force. But now I have two more questions that I must put to the gods. And the first of these, Aesirs, is who brought this spear to this point? Hodur, my youngest son, that can hear my words well, how did you thus bring forth the mistletoe spear of death?' And Hodur answered him and said, 'Loki gave me it.' And then did all the Aesirs turn to gaze on Loki.

And Odin looked also, and then did he say to him, 'This final question have I to ask this Loki. And this my question is: Loki, will you weep?' But Loki remained silent, and thus did Odin say: 'Seize him then, Aesirs, and bind him in unbreakable chains. For in that he will not weep will he be confined in the darkness of Hell. There will he be locked in adamantine chains, and there will he suffer the punishments of fire. Bind him, Aesirs. Bind him, I say!

For he has long been plotting this, and has now brought my son death. And this was it he swore to do that night at the feast in Gladsheim.' And Odin pointed at Loki with the lance Gungnir, that held the runes of life, and the Aesirs seized on him, and tied him with leather straps. And when Loki was fully bound and could not move, then was Odin satisfied.

And Odin turned then, and looked back at the monsters in the sky, and thus did he call up to them and say, 'And, great monsters, let me turn to you. And yet what should be the worry, for I see you are yet but air? Fenris, you are but a ghost as yet, and Sturt, you are but made of wind. And of vapours are you also, oh writhing Jormungandr. Wherefore I say to you, offspring of Angur-boda, return to your lands, and leave these vain shows of cloud. For not until seven days have past will you have the power to do us battle. Return then, and appear to us only when you are ready to fight, for we have no wish to go tilting at phantoms of sky.' And having spoken these words, Odin turned away from the monsters, and just as he turned his back did the cloud begin to disperse, and the shapes of the three demons faded from the sky and were gone.

And then did Odin speak again to the gods and say, 'And so, Aesirs, we may attend to our other tasks. For my son is to be tended, and his body is to be burnt. And so let there be some gone into the woods, to fell down trees for the pyre of Balder's body. And let one be gone upon Sleipnir to summon from Niflheim the four ice-giants, for theirs is an ancient promise to guard my son's bier. And when have the goddesses made clean Balder's body, then let them see to these tables, and take this feast back into heaven. For soon must we all hie to Asgard once more, and fortify its battlements against the coming days. And Balder's funeral will we hold in seven days' time. Why do you dally? Be off you thralls and guards. For now is no longer a time for dalliance.' And Odin moved away then, and went towards the shore, and taking thralls with him he went down to the side of the waters, and he searched out a place for the building of Balder's pyre.

And when he was gone did old Niord say, 'Assuredly now, Aesirs, is our last hour come upon us, for terrible were those phantoms, though yet they are gone away. For Balder, he is dead, that was our hope against such things.' And Niord held up his hands, and wrung them together.

But black-browed Fricka exclaimed in grief and said, 'I curse the day that ever brought us on this path, that brought Loki to the Aesirs, that ever Iduna was seen. I curse my own womb that brought Hodur into this world, blind, unfortunate, useless, and now damned!'

But Hermod went to blind Hodur, and to Fricka he said, 'Fricka, you wrong your son, who has more affliction than any of us. In no way is the lad to blame for the throw he flung or the lance he held, for we are all instruments of the net of fate.' And Hermod clasped the blind god about his shoulders, and drew him to him.

Yet Hodur for all his misery spoke and said, 'My mother has spoken true, Hermod. This deed is surely mine. For I have cast my darkness onto my own dear brother. Alas, that I had not killed myself from despair before this day! For now will the name of Hodur be cursed by all generations, for I shall be held the murderer of my brother. You Aesirs think I am young, but I tell you in grief am I old.' And so did Hodur turn away, stumbling as he went.

But Thor had come now, bearing water in a wooden bowl, and when he came to the gods he rebuked them, saying, 'Fie, gods, why do you stare at Balder's body, when it is all so foul, and gored and bloody? Move back, so that I may bathe his wounds. For Balder was beautiful, and fairer than any god has been.'

And then did Thor grasp the head of the mistletoe-spear, and this he tugged from Balder's breast. And the blood flowed after it, for the body was still warm. And Thor's great hands were steeped in the blood. But then did he busily begin to wash the stains away. And from the god's muscled ribs, and his biceps and smooth belly, did Thor clean the blood so that Balder was once again fair. And the red-bearded Aesir laid out Balder's limbs so that he seemed at rest. But when he came to look on Balder's face, his hands fell down slackly, and grief overcame him, and suddenly did he hug Balder's body in his arms, and wept.

And thus did Thor cry: 'Oh Balder, my dear friend, why could not I have died for you? For Thor's day is done, and his greatness is long passed. Thor is slow-witted, and now is he also old. And how much fitter to live and lead were you!' And Thor clasped the body, and his shut eyes streamed forth tears.

But Iduna knelt next to him, and touching his shoulder she said, 'Great god, is it so? Will Balder come no more? For never have I looked upon death, and do not know much of it, coming from Vanaheim. And surely is it not just that Balder is swooned or asleep? For see how his face is tender, his hands are warm. Assure me then, oh strongest of gods, is Balder not merely asleep?'

And Thor looked upon her, and his tears were stopped. And he said, 'Alas, no, sweet maiden, for Balder is surely dead. And who am I to weep, when you are the deeper wronged? Oh, let there be a black cloud come cover us all in forgetfulness, for surely this day is the evillest in time, and now is all joy and hope from this place for ever fled away.'

But Iduna then fell to tending Balder's body. And she laid out his hands. And she settled the folds of his clothes, and in all ways did she see to him, as a mother does with her child. And then did she speak to him in a quiet voice, rebuking, and said, 'No one but you, Balder, could bring me such pain. For in my orchard had I been innocent and happy, and from your wooing have I had nothing but heartache and care. For love felt like agony, and pleasure brought shame. It drove me from my homeland, to live among unknown gods. I suffered imprisonment, brought to me by your comrade, among such rough ones as I had never seen. And rescued thence was I born on a violent journey, and had as brief a wedding as was ever given a maid. All this am I to thank you for, that brought me these painful ways. But alas, was this nothing to this final hour. For now have you left me, a bride of not one day, and to suffer a grief such as no one could ever have known. What then shall I say to you? With what words shall I vex your ghost? Only this, Balder: you cannot hurt me further. For that in the whole world alone am I sad.' And so did Iduna gaze at his silent face.

But now did the thralls come back from the forests, and they bore with them on runners and sledges the great logs for Balder's pyre. And when Odin saw them, he instructed them what to do, and they cleared a space on the beach, and made a platform of stones and pebbles and then did they place the long logs across it, and built up a tower to the height of a man's breast. And they laid branches and twigs to weave a bed upon the top of it, and fill the insides and the spaces with catching tinder.

But then did the Aesirs themselves bear forth Balder's body. And they made a bier of lances, threaded in and out, and placed his corpse upon it, and lifted it up by the shafts. And Thor led on the one side, and Odin on the other, and the blond hair of Balder lay between their russet and grey. And the Aesirs carried their load down to the grey-cold shingle of the shore. And upon the pyre did they set that bier, and laid upon Balder his glittering arms. The breastplate flashed forth its gold over the bleak water, and against the side of the logs did they lean his mighty shield.

And the goddesses then came down to the wintry beach, and they bore in their hands the wilting flowers of that sudden Spring: the bluebells of the woods, with blue and purple streaked, and blood-speckled cowslips, snipped from the springy meadows. These did the goddesses wind about the bier, and they threaded them in among the hard twigs and branches.

And old Niord stood with the goddesses, and thus did he say: 'How soon is the hero laid before us a pale corse! Alas, such is mortality! Such is the fate of man! For his mind can hold whole empires and his body is all too soon dust. Where is the laughter of the feast and banquet now? Where is the gay sound of the poet's harp? How hollowly they would murmur, as we stand on a desolate shore. The gulls shriek in the breezes. The hawks hang above in the clouds. The souls of long-dead sailors call us all from the wastes of the deep. Short is joy, they tell us. Long is man's deathly sleep.' And old Niord threw then the blossoms of the blackthorn, but the wind streamed them sideways away, and they littered the slabs of the strand.

But now from the Northwards there came a rumbling sound, and the ground began to shudder, as if with some mighty dread, and towering above the hills and the woods did the Aesirs then see the frost-giants approaching. For the giants were monstrous and gleamed with snow and rime. Their mighty hands were chalk white with cold. Their cascading beards billowed downwards like avalanches, and spread over their green-shadowed chests the tumbling hairiness of many blizzards. And strange was the creaking of ice from their steps.

And when Odin had seen them, he spoke to them and said, 'Welcome, oh frost-giants, that hold to your ancient treaty. For thus was it we ratified in the dark of long ago. You see here before you the body of my dear son, killed by a spear of fate, brought hither by an evil one, and there he lies for seven days till we burn him. Wherefore, oh frost-giants, do you stand at the bier's four corners, and guard him with your iciness against any decomposition or decay. And when the seven days are passed will we Aesirs come again. Upon the ship Ringhorn will we then place this pyre, and in the manner of our ancestors push the burning ship out to the West, and thus shall be his funeral rites, worthy of all the Aesirs. Take then your position, and guard my dear son well. For we will leave you and the pyre now alone, and go back to Asgard, and the hall of Valhalla, and there will we hold conference about the coming doom.' And Odin ceased speaking, and held his spear towards the pyre.

Then did the four frost-giants tramp towards the pyre. And as they moved they set up a freezing wind. And the Aesirs wrapped their cloaks about them, and stood back from the wintry blast. But the waters of the lake began to crackle into glassy strips. And frost also appeared on the flowers and branches of the bier. Each one of them was overlaid in the silvery rime, and the sparkling hoarfrost turned their blues and purples into white. And so did it also settle on Balder's blond hair, and it coated it in powdery snow, as if he had suddenly grown old. And the four giants gazed outwards, protecting the corse from all foes.

And then did Odin speak to the Aesirs and say, 'Now gods, let us go about our business, and put out of our hearts henceforth the weakening work of grieving, and the lethargy of tears. And the goddesses now, let them attend to the things of the banquet, and take back to Asgard the things that belong to Gladsheim. And gods, do you come with me this instant, and let us speedily retrace our steps to Asgard, and in the great hall of Valhalla meet and discuss our doom. For much is there to be done now that tragedy has come upon us.'

But before the Lord Odin might lead the Aesirs forth, did Iduna come to him and meekly stand in his way, and she said, 'Yet mighty Lord Odin, will you forget not the golden apples? For labour as you might, it is there that our fate lies now, and I fear the coming doom may be forestalled by them alone.'

But Odin looked grimly upon her, and thus he answered: 'Are the mighty Aesirs to take their lives from plucked apples? Woman, I scorn to hold my life at so base a cost. Nor are we to dote on such idle things, for the sake of a fairy tale that our lives come from thence. For henceforward are the gods to rely on themselves alone. If the apples remain in Hell, then neither can we nor our enemies profit, if indeed there is any profit to be gained from a bunch of sweets. Let them stay in Hell, for that is the best place for them. And now, warriors and Aesirs, let us go about our tasks.' And Odin then strode on, leaving Iduna cowed, and the Aesirs followed him, united once more behind their stern master.

But when Odin entered the gate, with the Aesirs at his heels, the lodge was swarming with men who pressed towards them anxious to hear news, for rumours were already flying about heaven and it was felt there was some catastrophe, though none as yet knew what. And these were guards from the walls, and those who move the gate, porters who keep the keys of heaven, and those with good eyes who help Heimdall in his watch. And they pressed about the lesser gods, whispering to them to tell what had happened. But Odin was aware of this, and bade them sternly keep silence, and he told them to gather all by the great square before Valhalla, where he would address them, and give them orders for this day.

And when the Aesirs went further into heaven they met the gossiping Valkyries that spoke beside their horses, and they streamed towards Odin and bade him tell them what had happened. But Odin bade them silence, and to go to the square by Valhalla, and to fetch there also the ranks of the Einheriar. And the Valkyries rode away to do their lord's bidding. But Odin swept on and came to Valhalla, and the thralls therein set it ready with torches on the walls, and under orders from Odin they erected a platform outside it, and Odin mounted the platform to wait for his forces to come.

Then did the Valkyries come with the troops of the Einheriar, and they swept onto the great plain of Idavold, and drew up in ranks before the hall. Their grey helmets gleamed, their lances were like a forest of pine. And the guards came also, and the watchmen from the walls, and all was haste as they hurried to hear the news. And some came running pulling on their leather jerkins. And the ranks were a sea of faces gazing towards Odin.

And thus did Odin speak and call out to them all: 'Warriors of the Einheriar, the chosen fallen of earth's battlefields, bravely did you die in earth's battles, and bravely have you fought in the fights of Asgard. Now does a sterner duty lie on you than you have ever known, for a fight greater than all worldly fights is to be accomplished, wherein shall clash in bitterness and death the whole of the forces of the terrors of the world! And this shall Odin tell you, warriors, this shall your leader speak: that fight shall we win, and be triumphant over all! Too long have we sat cowering, waiting for the coming of doom. Now is it near. Now does it dog our heels. Too long have we sat pondering what manner of thing might avert it. Nothing can avert it. Now is it upon us. Too long have we lain in lethargy and fear, dreading the oncoming darkness, shoring what we could against its might. But this is the way we shall face doomsday now. Ragnarok shall come, and we shall overcome it! Screw up your courage, warriors, for the fiercest of wars. Be hard. Be steel. Let each thought be the slaughter of foes. For we shall so make ourselves into granite, into iron, that the force of our legions will swarm onward against fate itself, and with the might of our utmost will shall fate itself, even fate be vanquished. Then, oh my warriors, will there dawn a better day. Then will true victory make us beneficent gods. For we shall go to earth again. There will we mix with men. Balder himself will be mediator between us, and so shall there dawn indeed a golden age. Let each man take his post and guard Asgard's walls. And do you get ready all things for the fight against our foes.' And with those words Odin paced from the platform, and suddenly was he gone into the hall of Valhalla.

And now did the troops gaze at each other eagerly, for they thought with dread and delight on the coming of the greatest of wars. And now did they murmur, and talk amongst themselves, and there was a row of voices like the sea. But their captains dispersed them, and sent them about their tasks. And the Einheriar now joined the guards along the walls. They manned all the outposts. They set up their legions, and they drew up to the walls all manner of weapons or defence. But the gods themselves went into the vaulted hall of Valhalla, and they followed Odin with a perplexed gaze. And the firelight played upon the carving of the throne, where the runes of Odin ran round the dark wood, and Odin sat there, plunged in deepest thought.

But when all the gods were assembled did Hermod address him, and say, 'My Lord Odin, well have you spoken, and the men were fired by your rule, for long it is since you harangued them and took on yourself the governing of Asgard. Yet are we much baffled by what you have told them. For no mention did you make that Balder, your son, was dead, and yet further did you speak of him as if he were still alive. My lord, what is the meaning of these words? What are we to think but that you hope to deceive the troops? For surely it will dispirit every man to hear of the death of such a god as Balder. Tell us, Lord Odin, what is behind this tale?'

And Odin looked up, and frowned upon them all, and thus did he say in a steady and sober voice: 'As many of you that have the heart for it, go now, and sleep this night well. And tell your servants to set out your travelling robes, and to get ready your horses for a long and weary journey. And do you tell them to pack you food and drink for seven days, and burnish your armour, and set all your weapons in order. And prepare you to wear them, and come so armed at the first light of dawn. And let only those of you come who are ready to risk their lives. For we are to go where no one has adventured, and to fight against creatures such as the earth has not seen. To Hell shall we ride, and the witch's own country, for Balder shall be rescued, and given to life again.' And Odin arose, and he strode immediately from the hall, and the gods gazed at each other, shaken with thrilled surprise.

But then did Thor the red-bearded address them all and say, 'Oh assuredly now this is a wondrous plan! It smacks of all daring. It fights against all powers. Is this task not better than sitting lamenting our woes? I shall be a-journeying, gods, when this tomorrow comes. I fear no devils, nor no treks throughout the dark. Why, I would tread the stars into the earth if it were for the sake of Balder, to bring him back again. Come then, let us not talk further, but go each man to his home, and let all things be made ready. For gods, now shines the spirit of the Aesirs of old!' The other gods pledged their assent and left also. And so did they stream away in the evening to their women.

But in Balestrand when the goddesses came to the tables, and looking for the last time at such flowers and such a feast, they could not find it in their hearts to clear the banquet away. For everything was as it was when they were happy. The wreaths and garlands still glowed on the pale-topped tables. The fragrant fruit and honeymead littered the grainy wood. But then at last they took to clearing away the dishes, and they gave to the servants the goblets and plates to carry. And they carried off the benches back to the bridge of Bifrost.

But when much of the feast was gone, and the people were leaving the fields, Iduna found a spray of flowers which Balder had given her at the feast. And she stooped and picked up the blue-bells and the blossom. And turning then to the shore she looked down to the gloomy pyre, and gazing upon it she could not tear herself away. For the waters were grey now, and the wind was blowing up, and all the gay colours had drained from the flowery shore. And Iduna went down to put the flowers in Balder's bosom, and she went amongst the frost-giants and gazed at her husband's corse.

But the frosts had seized him, and his hands were coated in rime. His bare breast glittered with the stars of snow, and the wound which had killed him stained the white with red. But then she took the flowers and laid them in the frosty fingers of his hand. Yet the face of Balder seemed turned into stone, and the lashes of his eyes were settled in hoarfrost. His cheek had a dusty brilliance, and his lips were sleeked with ice. And peaceful he seemed, and still as a winter's night. And the darkness grew around them, as if to take him away.

And Iduna sighed, and said in a gentle voice, 'Now, oh Balder, is the night falling upon us. Even from the sky do the deathly

[223]

frosts come down. Wherefore with these flowers must I bid you adieu. Alas, what has love brought us but pain and suffering! For the instant I saw you did my tribulation begin. They are indeed happy who never know love's ways, whose hearts are never opened, nor squander their treasures on air. For you on whom I had placed my whole joy are thus snatched from me, leaving me destitute. Ay farewell then, my love, my cruel hero. At peace beneath the rainbow you lie in winter sleep. It was in my breast I gave the greater wound.' She gazed long upon him, and then kissed his cold lips.

And Iduna left the pyre and walked towards the meadow. Then did Sigyn come to her, for the goddesses had gone to the bridge. The two girls together came to the grove of trees, and they passed through the thickets to the end of the rainbow bridge. But the colours stretched upwards now into gloomy clouds and bad weather, and the granite walls of Asgard were smoking with sentries' fires. And when Iduna gazed back at the groves of Balestrand, the curtain of the evening had been drawn across their brightness.

She sat then on the lowest step of the bridge, and as Sigyn sat beside her she spoke to her and said, 'Tell me now, Sigyn, was not this all a ghastly dream? Did I not dream of blood awhile, and death and confusion? For surely my mind now will not believe it happened. Nor can it be that I saw Balder on his bier. If I go to our room again, will he not now be there?'

But Sigyn sighed, and she would not reply. But she took Iduna's arm, and led her to rise and walk upwards on the bridge. And the two girls then began to tread the flame-hued steps, and they rose up through the dusky sky, and approached the tower of Himminbiorg. But when they were high up the spangling staircase, Iduna turned again and looked down towards the earth. And she saw now the smoky fields, and the dark hedges and trees, and she saw the blossom streaming on the wind. And by the bleak shore stood the funeral pyre, and beside it glittering arms.

And Iduna looked at it and spoke again, and said, 'Whose is this sad pyre that waits by the lonely shore? Is some great ship coming to take him for ever away? Alas, he was a great warrior. Even in the twilight I catch the glimmer of his shield. Oh, for whom is this sadness that seizes the country round? For can you not hear the wild creatures lamenting? The little foxes bay now, and the owls hoot in the wood. Surely that warrior was greatly loved on earth.' And Iduna looked down then at her breast, and she placed her hand there, as though she had lost something. Covering her face then, she walked into the gateway, and returning at last to Bleidablik she shut herself up in silence.

And now did the evening settle upon Asgard. The great halls were hushed and the walls were hid in darkness. And at the summit of the world by the ash-tree Yggdrasil, the ancient Norns wound up the last threads of fate. And they packed away their spinning wheels, and collecting their yarn together, they stood for a while gazing at the fountain, and then went away from the branching ash-tree boughs.

But as they descended came a dark-haired fylgie upwards, for this was a man's dream, and he looked like a shepherd-boy. And when he saw the goddesses thus he addressed them, and said, 'Tell me, you good ladies, which is the way to the fountain? For my master dreams of his lady-love this night, and he wishes to know if she will favour him, for a roundel has he sent her that speaks of a new love. Tell me then, I beg you, where I may drink of the truth?' And the old Norns laughed, and shook their grey heads, for this was not a fylgie such as they had ever known. And Verdandi pointed upwards, and smiled on the little dream. And the shepherd-boy went climbing up the dewy hill, and the three old crones went downwards into the murkiness of earth.

PART FOUR
Hell

ND NOW DID the day come for the Aesirs to journey towards Hell, and drear was the weather of that pitchy day. In the damp gusts were the flags streamed from the roofs, as the bugle of reveille woke the warriors from sleep. And Odin rode over the darkling fields on Sleipnir, and the streaky beams lit him as he loomed from the morning mist. And at once he led the gods forth from Himminbiorg to earth.

But Heimdall the great watchmen saw them ride through the gate, and he watched the horsemen thunder out onto the bridge, and thus did he say: 'A terrible journey you go upon, my brothers, for there is not any man who has gone to Hell's gates and returned. A sore trial of your strength is this before you, a greater test than any Aesir has known. Alas, my brothers, my heart goes with you, yet even do I fear that your mission will fail.'

But now did the great journey of the gods begin, and first they travelled through Manheim's weary ways. And they came to mossy fields which glowed with yellow light, and they rode over moors hidden in the fog, and so did they pass into the growing darkness of a forest, for pine-trees and resin-smelling firs loomed up around them. The bats were winging homewards and the crows croaked from the boughs. And they passed through twisted cliffs that overhung them with trailing moss, and the forest bedecked everything as if in a spider's web, and vast was the silence that closed round them in those woods. And so did they journey till the evening came upon them.

And Hermod rode close to Lord Odin, and spoke to him saying, 'Now are we journeying to the region of Hell, and Lord Odin, we have ridden Northwards and traversed a great forest, yet still are we fast in the clasp of Manheim. Not one of us has gone this way before, nor do we know what lands to expect, for we ride on blindly, obedient to your will. But for the sake of our doubts and fears tell us now which way do you take us, for it is best to go forward knowing the worst that will come.'

And Odin replied to him, 'Indeed I will tell you. There are two ways to Hell which from earth may be attempted. One is the way of the individual soul. There are secret places hidden about the world, whose caverns lead into the depths of Hela's realm, and to find these can only the witches and wizards help you. We go a bolder way, and this is indeed the other, for there is also a route to Hell which lies on the liberal earth. Of the nine worlds which make up the universe, one lies above and one lies below, and Asgard and Hell are those two spirit lands, opposing each other in their quest of good or ill. The other seven worlds lie all upon Midgard, the wide-ranging disc that stretches under the sky. To the far South is Muspelsheim, to the far North is Niflheim, and away to the West does Vanaheim spread its seas, and the misty islands of the creatures of happiness: for there also haunt the spirits of the earth. Yet where the lands of Midgard meet this enchanted sea, and fall into its waters with their shores of extreme heat or cold, there lies a region which hovers between all worlds, and can neither be said to be earth, heaven or Hell. We ride to such a borderland to the West of Niflheim, for there shall we find the river that leads us into Hell.' And Odin ceased speaking, and gazed forth on the way ahead.

And they left the forests and came to a land of marshes, and the evening came down over the melancholy wastes. But the Aesirs made on over the rocky causeways, and their horses' hooves threw up the mud beside the sky-reflecting floods. And the moose looked up from feeding, and reared its treelike horns, for seldom had such cavalcades of horsemen ridden through his empty realm. But now the darkness closed about them, and the yellow-streaked day waned painfully in the West.

And when they had stopped for the night and lit a scratchy fire from the green bushes and dead logs that alone could be found, they ate for a while in silence, and then did speak red-bearded Thor, and said, 'Lord Odin, now is the first of the days over from the wretched seven that we have left in freedom, and soon we must give good thought to the fight. But before that have we to ride to very Hell. Yet settle my old mind but a little, oh Aesir, for what shall we do when we come to Hell? Shall we be able to fight and fetch Balder back alive?'

And Odin considered a while, and then did he speak: 'There is a gate to Hell, set in its walls of brass. Through Hell-gate alone can men go forth and live. To this gate we shall come at the end of our long journey. Here with me in Sleipnir's saddle, just as

Balder left it, is the bough of mistletoe, which he plucked on the day of his death. By the power of that branch one of us may enter that gate, and alone he may strive for Balder's release. Yet before we resort to that, and risk one of our number, we may seek at the walls to parley or to fight. These are the actions that lie for our attempting, yet who can predict what we shall need to do?' And Odin sighed, and lay back against the saddle, and he gazed upward at the mirky sky. The night closed round about them. The weary Aesirs slept.

And the gods travelled on, when the sky was lightened with grey, and in circuiting an inlet to lie to the North and the West, they came to the seashore and rode on the gleaming sand. Quietly were the hoof-sounds deadened into the beach, and the breakers roared with a dull sound to their left. There called the sea-gulls over their heads, wailing as they flew inland to avoid the coming storm. And a few flurries of snow began to fall from the darkened air.

But as they too turned inland, Hermod rode beside Odin, and he said, 'Lord Odin, since it may be best for one of us to go into the gate of Hell alone, and to seek out Hela herself and try to bargain with her, let me be the one who should go on such a mission, for I, Hermod, am indeed the messenger of the gods. But if you grant me this, tell me then one other thing: for what have we to bargain with, that go thus empty-handed?'

And Odin looked down to the side of his horse. And he had at his side Loki, still bound by leather thongs. For Loki had not been given a horse to ride, but had been tied into a painful knot, and slung by the bonds from the saddle of Sleipnir, and so did he journey over the uncomfortable miles. And at last Odin said, 'Should such a thing come to pass, it would be good if you might go upon such a mission, for you of all the Aesirs would I trust best with that task – yea, even before myself, whose wits, I know, have grown old. Yet as for our bargaining: do you not see this prisoner? Remember well that Loki is Hela's father. Whether for love or hate she might well want him in Hell. And he do I purpose to swap for my son Balder.' And Odin looked down at the bundle which was Loki's form, and it bounced and clashed against the side of his horse. But Loki remained silent, though he could hear all.

And the gods travelled on, and the snow came down thickly, and soon were they driving through the buffets of a blizzard. The howling wind made their horses lay back their ears, for the storm came at them to tear them with white teeth. Now there teemed the frosty land of mountains, and the snow flew off the crags and drifted over the pinewoods. And so furious was the blizzard, they could scarcely see where they went. But the day wore on, and the snows grew blue, and the wastes became calm again beneath the sinking sun.

And Loki called up to Odin as the horses trudged through the snow: 'Odin, does not your heart grow fearful now? For this is a country where you have never been. Here does Niflheim spread its mists and cold. No creatures break the silence of these wastes, no eagles in its iron sky, nor no bears among its plains, and the runes of the laws of the gods in no way do obtain. But the journey that lies before you is far darker and harsher than this. Well then, do you not fear, now you have re-taken your post?' And Loki twisted about, and with a grunt he looked up at Odin's face.

But Odin looked sternly ahead of him, and grimly he replied, 'My heart is not fearful, for here has it matched its gloom. For thus does every heart go seeking for its own mirror. My heart is not fearful, Loki, though yours, I ween, should be so. For yours is this journey that goes into terror and pain. Not now are we ranging as young gods, testing the paths of an earth which is new to us both. Not now am I finding your treachery with a certain surprise. This journey have you and I been bound on long. And now am I to sweep you for ever from my sight.' And Odin called then to break their journey that day, and so did they camp among the abounding snows.

But when dawn had drawn forth the iron-grey door of the sky, the travellers made on again, and came to a mighty slope. For the snows swept upward, as if to the edge of a cliff, and beyond the edge of it might nothing clear be seen. And Odin led them forward, and they followed Sleipnir's tracks. And when they came to the edge of the cliff beside Odin they stopped in a line, and like him gazed downwards into the misty spaces. And the ground slid away even to the depths of the earth. For a river boiled before them that was black in the snows, and it roared downwards steaming in the valley, and the boulders that it crossed stood out gleaming and grey. Yet the vale had no end, but went downwards and ever downwards, and it seemed that it would not stop until it was rooted in Hell. And so far did it descend that it was veiled in mists with mystery. And a wind blew up from it that smelt of ashes and soot. And from its depths came a grinding sound, as if the earth had teeth.

And when Odin saw this river he suddenly cried out in a loud voice and lamented, saying, 'Alas, that ever I should behold this sight! For the Aesirs have I led now into the bounds of Hell! Oh Balder, my son, why did you not obey me? Why did you overrule me, and go forth on the earth? Alas, alas, that ever that day came, for as you triumphed over me, so was your life under doom. Yet I shall see you again, my dear son. Though Hell now holds you, I shall see you again. And we shall join hands in spite of death and time, and out of this our misery will all our triumphs come.' And Odin lifted up his hand and tugged from his forehead a lock of grey hair, and he cast it before him, and it flew away on the sooty winds.

And as the gods gazed at him, amazed, Odin leaned down and pulled up a leather bag from the other side of his horse, and he took forth from it pairs of linen and canvas shoes, and these he passed to be handed to each god. And Odin said then, 'Take these shoes, Aesirs, and put them upon your feet, for they are the Hell-shoes, which everyone that journeys upon this road must wear. And bind them tightly upon you, so that they might not slip off. And when you have done that, prepare for the long descent. For before you lies the brawling river of Hell, the Giurl River that flows into Hela's realm, and upon its right bank are we to make our way forward, and thus will it lead us to the very walls.' And Odin leaned downwards then, and he put on his shoes.

And when they were all so kitted, Sleipnir began the descent on the other side of the snowy cliff. And they wound their way down the face, and came to the flowing river. But whatever snows and icicles it flowed through, the river remained flowing, nor floated with any ice, and it clattered by boulders and streamed past flinty juts, and loudly did it tumble on down the endless

[233]

valley. And as they advanced the end of the valley receded, and still they could see no end but what was lost in mist.

But the stream wound downwards in a corkscrew to the right. For as they moved downwards did the turn become sharper and sharper, and the end of the stream was hidden behind the right-hand crags. And thus did they descend, winding and winding until they arrived at a place below where they had already been. And a great vault stretched over them then of black rocks, hung with icicles, and through these teeth were torn the dirty mists. And the Giurl stream hurtled downwards still into the blackening air.

Now also as they went, though there were twelve of them travelling, did they each feel that other folk went with them, for the presences accompanied them, as of great troops of people. And as the air darkened, they were aware of misty shapes that thronged the same way down by that icy path. And the gods saw then that they were ghosts going to Hell. The ghosts plodded on, of old men and women, tall heroes tramped downwards, and tottering children, weeping, all the earth's dead moved forth, with weary, desolate steps. The gods looked on amazed, and the hair stirred on their heads.

And old Niord peered at them, and thus he cried: 'See how many millions are daily journeying to death! Brief is man's existence, and soon does he tread this road. For as quickly as flowers turn up their faces to the sun, and they drink in the soft beams, and rejoice in the springtime air, but then do they wilt away and bow their petals to the ground, even so quickly, with such joy and such bowing, do the souls of men have life and then decay.'

And they trudged ever forward, the way that the ghosts were going, but the way got lighter now, for there flickered in the hazy air a brightness that came from nowhere. The passage that they travelled was filled with shimmers and glancing, and at last they saw an end to it, where the light was brightest of all. They came to a large canyon, loud with the tinkling of metal. Then did they see before them a strange wood of trees, for here was Ironwood, which surrounds the way to Hell. Nor do any trees grow there, which foist the green-ribbed leaves, but everything is iron that surges from the soil. For iron are the trunks of the trees, and iron are their boughs, and in filigrees of iron rattle the grey leaves. The gods gazed astonished at this sharp and gleaming forest, but then they followed the river again, and wound through its deep ways. And the woodpecker drilled there with a violent sound.

And when they had passed through the forest they came once more to a plain, and black was the soil through which the river flowed. Yet rearing up before them and dwarfing the wood of metal there loomed now a great cliff whose top might never be seen. Yet the roaring river surged into it, entering a cave, and there was the frothing stream lost in shadowy darkness.

Then did Odin turn to his warriors and say, 'On the other side of that vast cliff lies the underland. When we have passed through it we shall rest and take our meal, for Hell's gates will be before us, and the walls of Hell itself. Yet prepare now to pass through dangerous darkness, for the river here rushes into the Gnipa Cave, and we must travel through that cave, minding our steps by the stream, and pierce so the great barrier of denseness that encloses Hell. And now wait a while and watch, for here shall come forth a monster, such as you have never seen.'

And Odin urged Sleipnir forth to the cave-mouth, and he drew up again the bag to his side, and took forth from it a slab of cake. Now this was Hell-cake, and of a special kind, for it was drugged with a potion of potency, and if any creature should devour it, straight would the cake send them into long sleep. And with such a cake did Odin guard himself against the monster: for here was Garm, the ravening hound of Hell. Odin blew his ringing horn then, and Ironwood jangled its leaves at the note.

And at once from the cavern, splashing the river-water with its hairy paws, there ran forth the giant hound, whose head was as great and as long as a barn, and his bristling hackles stood up like daggers along his back. And bellowing from his red throat he fell barking with such a din that he made the gods reel back, appalled at the clanging thunder. But Odin flung to him the slab of Hell-cake, and devouring it in yacking bites did Garm swallow it whole. Then he grew pale-eyed, and shook his spiky head. His tail sunk downwards, and his elbows and knees gave way, and he fell in a drugged swoon, splashing into the Giurl, and there did he lie and the river flowed over his fur. And so did Odin lead the Aesirs into the cave.

Black was the tunnel now and full of dripping waters. The Aesirs dismounted their horses, and led them in by the bridles. The roaring of the river kept always on the left, and they stumbled forward, longing for the light on the other side. And when they were all most weary of the darkness, they gained the glimmering that shone from the other side. And so did they come out into the sight of Hell. And the Aesirs stood still and gazed at its ghastliness.

For the huge plain of Hell lay open before them, smoking and steaming in lazy plumes, and the air was smoggy and was stuffed. A wide-spaced city did they see, splattered out in shacks and rubbish-heaps, with stagnant pools reflecting the yellow sky, and the smoke and cinders dragged for ever over it. And the city was surrounded by a wall of stained brass, and a gate lay before them on the other side the river, and crossing over to it stretched the Giallar-bridge.

About them around the entrance of the Gnipa Cave lay half-decayed bodies set in strange forms. And the flesh on them was rank and stank, and it was haunted by flies as it slithered from the bones. And the clammy air of Hell was full of yellow fog, and a sickly jaundiced sun stained all with sulphurous light. Foul was the ripe smell that hung in that thick air, and loud was the noise of turbulence that floated to them from the city, for ringing in their ears came shrieks of lamentation, howls of despair, yells of boundless rage, and a clanging and a grating of harsh iron and of chains.

And then did red-bearded Thor cry out, 'Fie, Aesirs, what a place is this! Is this how they live under the crust of Midgard? How does it stink and how raucous are those sounds! What wretches they must be to lie in this place and let it so rot! And yet alas, for that is the city where Balder now dwells. Somewhere in those smoky walls is the one we all are seeking. Friends, we must take him hence as quick as ever we may, since for such a great hero to be lodged in such a rat-house, why, it is hardly to be borne thinking upon. Yet let us get out of this stench a while, if we are to perch and have our meal.' And Thor held his nose and rolled his eyes upward.

And so did the Aesirs retire back into the cave, for nothing but nausea could they feel outside. And Odin addressed them then, and said, 'Well, gods, ye have seen Hell. Such is your reward for such a desperate journey, and such is the reward of all, when their soul leaves earth. Is it not vile that our high hopes end in this? That when our spirit is fled, we are no more than putrefaction, rage, despair, and have for our home such a sea of illimitable baseness? Let us eat our meal, and prepare now for the worst. For this I tell you, Aesirs, and bitter it is to tell. The mistletoe is gone from the saddle of Sleipnir. When I came to the end of the tunnel and felt for it, then did I know that dark fate had snatched it away. We have only our own might and wits now to rely on. We are deserted by all but our hearts.' And the Aesirs stared with dismay upon their leader, and with small relish did they begin their meal.

But in Asgard meanwhile was all bustle and preparation, for the dwellers there were making ready against the final war. And the Einheriar went training on the field of Idavold. And about the walls also were the guards at work, fortifying the battlements and repairing any breaches in the stone. Meanwhile Heimdall kept watch on the surrounding horizons. And the Valkyries also flew out over all the earth, to collect from battles the last warriors of the slain. They returned to Asgard with the bodies slung on their saddles.

Yet when it was time for Fricka to review the troops, and to cast her eyes on the recruits of the dead, then did she refuse to come to the summons of the Einheriar. Nor might the Valkyries, whose leader she was, bring her to see to her martial duties. For Fricka shut herself away in Odin's house, and had given herself up to thoughts of despair. And Sif, that knew little of martial things, was forced to stand in for the chief goddess, and winding her mantle about her she went about and reviewed the troops, and she directed the Valkyries herself what things they were to do. And so did she tour Asgard, as armour and weapons were checked, and guards were drilled on the walls, and messengers sped between outpost and outpost.

But when she had done for that morning seeing to the troops, then did Sif think of Iduna, and she determined to go and see her.

For Iduna had not been seen by any of the goddesses for the days since the Aesirs had gone on the journey to Hell. And Sif went to Bleidablik and struck at the great oaken door. But for all the time she bided there, no answer came. And Sif turned aside and went back over the fields to her own home in Thrudvang. And as she went along all Asgard seemed gloomy, and for all the preparations there seemed to be nothing but despair. And she feared as she looked up into the iron sky above her, and the sun, though standing at noon, was obscured by thick cloud.

Yet in Hell meanwhile the sulphur sun shone down, and thickly laid everything with its sickly light. And when the Aesirs had finished their meal then did they get ready to leave, and Odin addressed them, saying, 'Now must we ride down, and cross the River Giurl, and on that Giallar-bridge must we ride steadily forward, for that is the path all creatures cross to Hell. There is a guard upon it, but she must we not dally with, and no matter what she bids us, press on to the gate. And then when we are over that river, we must go to the city to bargain.' And when they were ready they set forth again from the cave.

In a close troop they flew through the soot-dotted air, and spurned the decaying bodies that cluttered up the plain. And the hooves of their horses splashed in puddles of blood, and the steam from the river snatched at their heels. And flying all about them were the flapping leather wings of vampire bats, and they were scattered from sucking the bodies and streamed away with shrills and squeaks. And so did they reach the black arch of the Giallar-bridge. And the great arched slabs were held up by a slender hair, and on the thinnest of delicate threads dangled the vast chunks of stone.

But when the Aesirs approached the bridge, and thundering with their hooves crossed the zenith of its arch, there rushed forth from a sentry-box Modgud, the guardian, a woman of hideous looks. For she sprang from the black granite an orange skeleton, and her hair was red and stuck in tufts from her gaping skull, and there flopped by a piece of skin from her ribs two breasts with dangling nipples, and the rest of her body was a patchwork of skin and bare bone. She brandished an iron bar in one hand and in the other a tube also of iron, and she shrieked out between juddering teeth, and stood in the way of the gods to stop them.

And Modgud yelled out, 'Stay, you rumbling horsemen, and declare yourselves to me. What is your business here, and why do you ride in such a thick pack like dogs? My bridge you have set trembling as it has never shook before. Have you been eating our corpses that you are grown all so fat, that you weigh down on your horses' backs enough to break them, and set them troubling Giallar-bridge to its foundations? Do you not know that this path is forbidden the living? Turn back. Hie home. For it is but three days now and a great troop of horsemen came with a blond hero at their head, and yet for all their multitude they did not make this arch of mine shake one single tremor. But you with your fat feet rattle it all to bits.'

And Odin replied to her and said, 'We are the Aesirs, and I, Odin of Asgard, bearer of Gungnir on which is carved the runes. We are come to Hell to bargain for the release of my son, for that blond hero you saw but three days past, he is my son Balder, the god of sunlight. Let us pass then, Modgud, and we shall ride to Hell-gate, and there we shall summon your leaders to parley.'

But Modgud shrieked with laughter to hear this, and she danced round a mad dance on the Giallar-bridge, and her bones knocked each other with a dull, knobbly sound. And she cried, 'Whehee! The mighty Lord Odin has deigned to visit us! Oh bring out the best plate, maidens, and get him a dish of choice maggots. Wohoohoo, how honoured we are today! And yet how I tremble before the great one's strength! Indeed, oh mighty greybeard, you are so tough and strong, and I am but a poor bag of bones, with a few twanging sinews to give me all my strength, and I am deathly afraid that you might wish to ravish me! Do you see this bar, greybeard? This is my alarm. If I but bang this metal all the demons will swoop to the walls. Hare back, you tomboys. Go and curl your locks. For you could never make way against the hosts of Hell. Nor shall you pass Modgud. So be off from this bridge.' And the skeleton maid then shooed them away with her hand, and she grabbed the bridle of Sleipnir and startled the horse, and thus did she try to turn him back from the path.

[239]

But Odin would not be stopped, and ignoring the demon he spurred forth Sleipnir and rode over the bridge. And the other Aesirs followed him, and quietly rode on, and the skeleton maid could not prevent them. So the Aesirs approached the Hell-gate, and gazed up at its vastness. For it surged up in a mighty arc above them studded over with rusty nails, and the door had no handle on the outward side. The metal of it was sour, stained with green mould and black soot, and the mists condensed on it and ran down in droplets of blood. By the walls on either side was there slush and dirty snow, and cinders and slops and sewage lay tipped forth from the walls, and flies buzzed about it making a dreary sound.

But Modgud on the bridge had not been quietened, and when the Aesirs passed her she sped to raise the alarm. And she clanged the iron bar on the tube, and made with it a rattling noise, and she screamed out at the top of her voice that Aesirs were come to Hell. Then did the gods see the walls throng with demons, for rows of heads popped up above the battlements and laughed at the gods and gibbered at them. Some faces were red, and some were black, some sprouted horns and some had on floppy caps, and some had long fingernails that hung down over the walls. And they whistled and catcalled to see the gods outside, and for a long time was there a rowdy din.

But then Odin addressed them, and he called forth to the devils, 'Dwellers of Hell, let us into your gates, for we are the Aesirs, come to rescue my son Balder, and we would speak with your leaders and strike a bargain here. Wherefore do not sit like apes and scorn us, but open these your gates, and either let us in, or send out those who represent you to parley with us here. For a long way have we come to visit this your realm, and we do not intend to go away empty-handed.' And Odin ceased, and the Aesirs gazed up at the heads.

But the devils then began to reply in several voices, and they called down to the Aesirs and cried, 'Dwellers of Hell, let us into your gates, for we are the Aesirs, come to rescue my son Balder, and we would speak with your leaders and strike a bargain here. Wherefore do not sit like apes and scorn us, but open these your gates, and either let us in, or send you those who represent you to parley with us here. For a long way have we come to visit you in this your realm, and we do not intend to go away empty-handed.' And thus they repeated in babbling voices every word that Odin had said.

And Loki laughed out loud and shouted up to the god, 'Ha, Odin, you have your words thrown back in your face! Now have you met your match in more ways than one. For this is the trick in the game of chess to copy everything that your enemy does, and so to frustrate him and drive him into despair. Ha, these are no giants, nor no dwarves, nor no Vanas, but these now are devils that you have come against. Never will you bargain with devils, my lord god! For the substance of bargains they do not even know.' And Loki laughed on, a voice from the side of the horse.

But then did Odin cry out again and say, 'You are not children, I trust, oh devils. You have brains in your heads, and can speak on your own account. Answer me then, and learn the approval of your chiefs, for neither Hela nor her henchmen will be glad that you have spurned us. Send us an embassy at once, and grant us a parley, or we will knock these walls about your horns.' But hardly had Odin finished his speech before the devils were repeating it and jeering back at him. And they all began spitting and puking at him, and they would duck down from the walls and chew up a lump of mud, and then would they spit it forth, leaving a spray of slime. And Odin stood before them, bearing their taunts. And his face showed sombreness, for he knew not what to do. And he turned his horse and went back to the Aesirs, and they gazed at each other, unsure of themselves. And there was no sound but the sound of Loki laughing.

But then did the gates of Hell grind on their hinges, and turning back the Aesirs saw then that the mighty doors were swinging open, revealing the devils within. And forth then from the gates came a troop of dark horsemen, twelve of them, as many as were the Aesirs, and slowly they paced forward and drew up in a line before the gate. Tall were the riders, and swathed in black cloaks, and they held before them shields of a tarnished copper, and trailing on the ground they bore long and dirty lances. But though they sat upright, and seemed like warriors, yet not one of the horsemen had

[241]

a head on his body, but where the clothes ended, there was the end of the man. And they raised then their lances, ready for the charge. And then did the great gates clang shut behind them. And the Aesirs saw that they must go to battle.

Willingly then did they lay their own spears ready, and they threw back their cloaks and settled their bright helmets squarely over their heads. Then did they line up and charge at the headless horsemen. But as soon as any of the Aesirs touched their foe with spear or sword, the horsemen fell to nothing, and their clothes slipped to the ground. And instead of men, inside the cloaks were bats and cats and hounds and hedgehogs, and all manner of creature with wings to fly about on. And the little monsters and devils then swooped away in the air, and they howled at them, and shat on them, and covered the gods with muck and slime and blood. Vainly did the Aesirs seek to fight against the whirring wings, and they thrashed with their swords and lunged with their spears, but the bat-faced creatures and the long-tailed devils shrieked and flitted away, as nimble as any fly. And thus were the Aesirs mocked a second time. And the horses of the devils ran off a little way, and then did they fall dead again on the snows.

And the Aesirs retreated and drew back from the walls of Hell, and they went down to the stream to wash the filth from their clothes. There was a tall oak-tree, struck dead, with leafless limbs, that towered by the mud of the bank and stood fast by the water. Here did the Aesirs tether their sweating horses, and walking down the shore they scooped up the water with their hands. And they were all of them dismayed, and knew not what to do, and they wiped off the filth with despair in their hearts, for a kind of numbness had come into all their minds. And then did they sit and gaze across the river. And the corpses were spread before them and seemed to be mocking them, set in strange shapes of death with upraised arms and legs, and in the yellow fog did vultures hop about there, and tear up eagerly the lengths of sinew and muscle. And the bats also crowded to the water in hoards to drink.

But Odin himself went forth to another spot, and he sat away from the Aesirs further up the stream. And there did he plunge his head into his hands, and thus did he speak with himself and say, 'What a filthy place is this, and how vile are these demons! Surely, I should have realised that it would be thus in Hell. For how can you bargain with such creatures of death, and how can you hope for reason or fairness or interest or sense from devils? Oh now desert me not, my poor old tired wits! I have come through vile things in the old days with my brains. And yet in this place how easy is despair. For how will it be possible to get sense from these creatures? How can I parley with them? How can I get in there? Oh Balder, my son, my son, why did you ever fly to this wretched place, to be locked in these walls, imprisoned from us for ever, the sport of devils, the taunt of these fiends? Oh, let it not be that I am too old to rescue you, and that because of my impotence you are for ever damned. Oh, how I fear my own unworthiness, for I have led my comrades all to this putrid place! No, I must find some way. Yet my old brain cannot do it. Oh where is that will now that I drank from Od-hroerir? Oh that I might drink it here, and find my will again!' And thus did Odin agonise upon the bank, while the toiling waters of the Giurl flowed before him.

But then did Odin arise, and wrapping his blue cloak about him, he returned to the Aesirs and spoke to Hermod saying, 'Hermod, your lungs are younger than mine, and better for the blowing of this my horn. Lay it to your lips in a while, and play the horn-call which I shall whistle you, and I do not doubt that something will come from Hell. For there is a certain Dane, a Viking called Anlaf, that struck down the English once on Blackwater shore, and he, when he died his bloodless straw-death in bed, came down to Hell and was well received here. My ravens in Asgard told me Hela liked him, and for his black deeds made him chamberlain of her hall. Now the Northmen he belonged to had a certain horn-call, and since he has not for long been dead, this Anlaf will remember it if he hears it in Hell. Wherefore do you, Hermod, play it as loud as you can, and perchance Hela's chamberlain may then come to the walls. Listen then to the tune I'll whistle you.' And Odin then ceased speaking, and pursing his lips he whistled the horn-call to the harkening Hermod. And the Aesirs smiled to see their leader whistle.

Then did Hermod lift up the silver horn and blow the ringing note. And among all the roaring and buzzing and yelping of Hell did the clear, sweet note shrill out and echo from the walls. And the devils of the wall were astonished and ceased their noise. And after the Aesirs had waited in silence, and thrice had Hermod blown the horn-call, there was a stirring on the walls, and the little devils made way, and the form of Anlaf could be seen looking down. And the chamberlain in his robes stared sternly at the gods, and the gods went forward, ready for the parley.

And Anlaf spoke to the Aesirs and said, 'Why this host at the gates of Hell? Aesirs I see you are, that haunt the airy Asgard. You come here as living men and stand on the earth of death. I had been told that the Aesirs were brave warriors. When I left Midgard my folk did worship you. And now are you come here to beg me to let you in? Why else should you summon me with the sounds of my old campaigns?'

But Odin called out to him, and thus did he say: 'Across bleak wastes and down a maze of tunnels are we, Aesirs, come to speak with you. Nor do we come to beg entry or give joy, but with such an old call could we only hope to reach you, since these your troops are so ill-disciplined. Harken then to me, Anlaf, that are close to the mistress of Hell, for we have certain proposals to put to you this day, and it will be well for you to listen and hear me out. For hither are we come to rescue my son from death, Balder the beautiful, the god of earthly sunlight, and with you now will we strike a bargain for his release. What is there that you wish, which we will give you for Balder? Let me show you what trophy we can offer you in exchange. Here at my side is the arch-fiend himself, Loki, that long has lived with the lords of the Aesirs. Here we have brought him alive to the land of Hell. Who knows not that from the ogress Angur-boda Loki spawned the serpent and the wolf that rides the skies? And more did he hatch that day which, Anlaf, shall touch you near, for from the giantess's womb came forth even Hela the mistress of Hell. Would not this bundle be a prize for you to bear your mistress? A generous swap this demon will bring you, if you bring Balder now to the gate to be exchanged. Yet I see you keep your silence, and are afraid to speak.

Open your gates therefore, and let Odin come inside, for I shall put to Hela myself this bargain concerning which you are so long dumb.'

And Anlaf answered him and said, 'Are your wits crazed, old man, that you suggest such things? No one can enter Hell and come forth again, for only the dead ever travel through these doors. If you wish to cut your throat, then you may enter, but enough blood will drain from you to ensure that you stay. Away, then, with your despicable request. And as for your aim to call for Balder's release, it is all vain air, for who can escape from Hell? And as for your bargain to bring us Loki the guileful, by what strange reasoning do you think Hela would wish to see him? Tie him in tighter knots and carry him to the moon, we do not care, for who cares a damn in Hell?'

But Odin grew angry and called up to him then, 'Then bring Hela herself here, and let her tell us her will. Say that those she spoke to but last week are come now to her hall to speak with her again. Tell her we shall not leave this place until she has seen us and heard what we have to say. Tell her that if she denies to come, we shall attack your walls, and bring your realm to nothing. Tell her that if she scorns us, we will be cruel with her. Destruction shall we bring, and pain and despair. With all the might of our arms we will strike you, and we shall not cease until there is desolation.' And Odin grew furious, and he trembled as he shouted.

And Anlaf shrugged and held up his hands, and said, 'The old dog is still at his tricks, though all are grown utterly foolish. How can you bring desolation on this place? Who knows not that Hell is desolation? How can you bring pain and despair and cruelty? For Hell is pain and despair and cruelty. You cannot threaten us, for your words are but empty air. This is hell, old Aesir, this is no image of earth. On earth you say to a servant: tell your master, and he tells him. On earth you sit on a chair, and the chair lies beneath you. In Hell there is no compunction to do any of these things. For why should I bear Hela your message? Or why should these demons answer you from the walls? It does not suit them. It does not suit me. Go home, old wizard, for your days are done. Even my own folk on earth are turning from your worship. The day of the gods is done, Aesir, is done.' And Anlaf turned aside and walked down from the walls.

But when he had gone then did Odin command Hermod to mount his horse, and to ride to the gate and blow the call again. And Hermod obeyed him, and spurring his steed he stopped under the brazen archway, and putting the silver horn to his mouth sent out the note again ringing clear. And after a pause, Anlaf returned again to the wall. And Odin addressed him and said, 'Since nothing will you grant save that which appeals to you, let me offer you a bargain of another sort. For if you let my messenger Hermod come into your walls, and lead him to Hela, I will solve a riddle for you, that may intrigue you now. For I will exchange for your life-in-death, which is Hermod the live one going into Hell, a keen and hard-won bargain, which I call a death-in-life. And that shall be an amusing treaty between us. But before I grant you it, must Hermod be in the gates, and already journeying to visit Hela in her hall. What do you say then, Anlaf, will you undertake this exchange?' And Odin gazed at him with a stony face, for he could see already that Anlaf was intrigued.

Then did Anlaf at once command the gate to be opened, and he sent a demon to Hermod with a long, black scarf. And the demon bound up the messenger-god's eyes, so that he should see nothing as he journeyed through Hell. And then was Hermod led within the walls of Hell, and grating and squeaking on its hinges was the brass gate closed. And Anlaf looked forth again, and gazed at Odin.

And Anlaf said, 'It is easy for me to grant you this bargain, for it matters not much, as nothing matters in Hell. And I have granted you it, since I wish to see your trick. For Hermod is indeed now a type of life-in-death, and now will you give me on your side a death-in-life. But yet your trick must not be too tricky, for if I do not in truth see a death-in-life, then Hermod your messenger will have to stay in these walls.'

And Odin went to his bag by the horse, and he drew forth a long nail of black iron, and going to the tree, he stretched up his arms, and commanded Thor to nail him to hang from the tree. And Thor did as he was bidden, and he nailed his brother's hands together into the trunk, and Odin was left hanging upon the tree. And so did Odin endure the pains of death, for the sake of his son imprisoned in Hell.

But Loki then, who lay bound at the foot of the oak-tree, looked up at Odin's plight and jeered at him and said, 'How is it, Odin, to be cured before being skinned? For now do you look indeed like a great ham in the rafters, and at last have found your true place in the world. Truly did the witch speak, when she spoke to me, that by doing nothing would I bring the Aesirs' doom, for I but sit here and enjoy your ruin.' And Loki chuckled to himself as he squatted alone on the bank.

But the other Aesirs for very shame could not speak, nor could they bear to look at Odin in his pain. And Thor pulled up his cloak, and drew it over his head. But Odin gazed still with fierce eyes towards Hell, and beyond the walls did the vapours drag their way, and the bobbing devils' heads went to and fro about the battlements.

But in Balestrand meanwhile was the pyre of Balder guarded still by the frost-giants who stood there day and night, for the fresh suns rose over them lighting their white heads, and the nightly stars swung round them, when all the lands were still. But as the noon passed, and the sun began to sink, over the flowers and Balder's body it then came on to snow. And the little flakes fell down, and settled on the breastplates of gold, and they drifted across the grey pebbles of the beach, and they flew among the ghostly trees, and sunk on the distant summits.

Yet the golden-haired Sif, in the height of Asgard, went about the duties which had fallen upon her. And returning to her home in Thrudvang, she entered Bilskimir to take her midday meal, and the servants brought it to her, and she ate it walking about, seeing to the needs of her neglected house. But the servants led her to Hodur, who yet stayed in her home, for Hodur refused to eat since his brother's death, and willed only to die. But for all Sif's persuasion, she could not get him to eat, and she left the young god, sad in her heart for his plight. And wearily then she thought of what she must do, for now had she to go about the battlements and see to the various guard-rooms, and her spirit faltered to have to do such tasks. And when she went out of the house again, she sighed to see the day grown so drear.

For the rumour had gone about heaven that Fimbul-winter was come: the last of earthly winters before the ending of the gods. And the watchmen on the walls gazed with fear upon the sun, for Sol the sun-maid was lacking at her task, and the wolf that ever pursued her drew nearer to her fiery hems, and the shining fields of Asgard were captured by stealthy twilight. And Sif went about, trying to still the fears of the men. Yet the snow began to flurry even about Asgard walls, and the sentries brought forth braziers and sat blowing their hands by the fires, and the white smoke drifted away and over the meadows. But suddenly was there a whirring sound, and from all over Asgard the soldiers and grooms looked up. Then did they see from the hall of Gladsheim the host of elves rise up and fly away to the East. And the twilight grew deeper, as though all things were departing.

And Odin hung still upon the bitter, barren tree. Harsh were his pains that he endured for his son's sake, and fierce was the mockery of the place he saw before him. The flashing lights, the puffed smoke, the rancid smells, the bitterness, the squeaking and gibbering of thronging demons, held his mind. And the flesh swelled up about the purple wound, and the iron tore into his hands a widening gap, and from the wound the blood flowed in streams down his arms. Long did he endure the creeping minutes as they passed, while Hermod wandered forth into the unknown Hell.

But at last with a booming sound did the great brass gates grind open, and from the darkness they revealed walked forth the horse with Hermod blindfolded upon its back. And once he was free of the gate, he lifted up his hand, and took off the black scarf that bound his eyes from seeing. Then did he catch sight of Odin hanging from the tree. But Thor, as soon as he saw Hermod come forth, leapt up towards Odin to release him from the tree. And the other gods held up the body of their leader, and Thor climbed up and seized at the nail with his teeth. Pressing his hands on either side against the trunk, he pulled backwards, and his teeth shattered, but at the last heave did the black nail come away. And they laid Odin down at the foot of the tree.

But Hermod then approached and dismounted his horse, and he came before the gods and gazed upon them. For they clustered about Odin both in horror and in wonder, and they were all appalled at the fate which had brought them to these deeds. For the greatest of the Aesirs lay stricken and bowed before them, and his mighty hands were cut through and smashed and the sinew and bone gleamed white in the clots of gore, and all Odin's body trembled and shook, and his teeth chattered as though he were seized with cold. And red-bearded Thor held his head in his lap, and he too would turn aside to spit blood from his mouth. But then did old Niord come forward and see to the wounds. And he cleaned Odin's hands and poured forth a magic potion of healing into the gashes, and he bound them with cloth so that all the bleeding was stopped.

Then did Odin look up to Hermod and say, 'Do not wonder at what you see, oh messenger of the gods. Nor do not think that for your sake I have done this thing. But for my son, Balder, have I hung and suffered here, yea, and will do more, until my old frame is broken. And so let us not talk of these woes any more. Nor do not mention in Asgard how I came by these wounds. And so, oh great messenger, who of all the gods has visited Hela's realm, tell us what has chanced, tell us what has been done.'

But Hermod drew in his breath with a sigh, and thus he replied: 'A painful journey and a sour conclusion. She consented to Balder's release, but she drove a bargain. She laid on us a condition, which I doubt if we can fulfil. And thus does she play with us, giving and taking away. For Hela has set us a task, and the task is this: that we go about the whole world, and ask everything in it to weep, and if everything weeps thus for Balder's death, then we can return hither and she will give us Balder. I fear it can never be done, neither now, nor if we had time. But such was the only pledge that I could drive her to. I have failed you, gods, and my mind was not with me. Yet hear me how I journeyed to her house, and what I felt on my travel.

'When I came into her city, blindfolded, on horseback, first did it strike me what a foul place was Hell. For there all the rowdiness and turmoil of the world riots continually. Though bound at my eyes with this foul, black scarf, yet was I assaulted in my ears and my other senses by the chaos. For buffets of wind, chattering voices, sudden reeking smells and bitter tastes swirled all about me, so that I doubted if I were still on my horse. And long did this turbulence surround me, so that I could not think at all of my mission. But yet when I grew used to these frights, was I aware that I still went forward, for some unknown hand must be leading my horse, and I felt myself gradually leaving the chaos behind.

'And so did I journey then through a vast space of dreariness, and my horse's hooves seemed to clatter on some stones, and I got the feeling that I was walking on a causeway. And in the blackness of my head I began then to be afraid, for I could not tell what creature led me on, nor to what he was leading me, nor what I was passing through. And I wondered if he would not take me to an endless cliff, and there pitch me over to fall for ever into blackness.

'But I started to feel then a certain warmth on my right side, and a feeling of flickering as it touched the skin of my face. And when I turned my head that way, I could hear a bubbling and a hissing of liquids, and whenever there was a sudden puff or splurge of sound, a greater heat would flash upon my cheeks. Yet as I attended that, I felt my left side shivering, and turning then that way I did indeed feel a cold, biting blast chill my nose and mouth from that side. And then did I hear great laments and wails from the left, and these cries of woe were sharpest whenever came a grinding and creaking sound. And I tasted in the air the sleek bitterness of snow. And thus I became engrossed in the effects of the landscape about me, and it seemed only a short time before I arrived at Hela's palace. For at once was I aware of an echo thrown back from before me, and I knew then that I had reached some sort of a dwelling. I could feel myself taken into it, the horse and all, through the door, and I heard the door boom after me, and a voice told me then that I could take off my blindfold. This did I do, and gazed upon Hela's home.

'It was an old and reeky hall, this Elvidner, the house of misery. Cobwebs were strung about it, covering the stairs and the doors. The floor of it was cobbles, and strewn over with hay and dung. The demon that led me had vanished, but there appeared from a

[250]

dark corridor a slovenly servant in a blood-stained apron, and this was Idleness, her servingman. Having seen me, he sat down, and lolled on the stairs and scratched himself. I dismounted my horse and gave him the reins to look after, and since he made no stir to take them, I hooked them over his head, and so did I leave my steed, knowing that he was securely tethered to an immoveable object. And I pushed through this ante-chamber, and came to the hall, where Hela herself sat. And the vision of this did not bring me much joy.

'For Hela sat idly at a table and ate her meal. She was just as we saw her that night in Gladsheim. Her knobbly, greasy nose hung over her dish, her ragged hair stuck out all around her in a bushy fuzz, her thin lips dribbled, and one yellow tooth stuck over them, making a groove for the spit to run down, and over her wrinkled skin did the bulging warts go rioting, sprouting up their gingery hairs, and deforming the deformed shape of her one-time face. Her table was called Hunger, and her spiky knife was Greed. Her flags were strewn with bones called Anguish, and sleeping hounds lay there, titled Plague and Famine. And set over in one corner, with fleas hopping from it in flocks, lay Care, her straw bed, set on creaking wood, and the curtains about it were dusty and painted with flames. But Hela did not greet me, for she seemed in an idle mood, and she chewed her slops for a while and gazed upon me, and she picked with her long, black nails the hairy cavern of her overhanging nose.

'And Hela then did I address and say, "From furthest field, and the shining walls of Asgard, am I come hither alive to your realm, and, Hela, I come to bargain with you for Balder's life. Set aside now your waywardness, and let us speak of this sanely, for we have to offer you a good prize in exchange, nor have we come this long way to offer but idle things. Your own father, Hela, lies bound beyond Hell-gate. Him we can give you, as soon as ever you agree. And you have but to surrender us the god Balder, and Loki, the guileful, will you have in your power for ever. Now I do not need to tell you what a great prize he is, for such a father of demons is famed over all the earth. Nor do I need to remind you that he is your own sire, and from the womb of Angur-boda did he cause you

to come forth in the beginning of time. Yet think, oh mighty
Hela, how well he would grace this realm. For you and he are
like-minded, and truly bound by blood. What you enjoy he also
laughs at. What is sport for you is merriment to him. And so,
Hela, we offer him for the god of sunlight, Balder. For the Aesirs
are sad to miss their comrade of Bleidablik. Yea, and all things
on earth weep that he is gone away." Thus did I speak to her, the
ugly mistress of Hell, and as I even spoke the words, my heart
despaired within me, for my wits were cowed by the plight we had
been in.

'But the last words of my speech seemed to bring her to life,
and she looked up with a mocking look, and said, "You would wish
to swap me Loki for Balder the god of sunlight, and for me to
release the fair one to gain his ugly brother? And for the sake of
the imp who spawned me, I would drive forth Balder from death?
Do you think then it is a small thing to release a soul from death,
to make one do what none has ever done, to cross again that
barrier that once crossed cannot be broken? Why should I do such
miracles, for the sake of this grinning Loki? And yet will I do it, for
I think there is sport here. For now let me think what has happened
these last days. Did not Fricka race round the earth, and bid
everything swear an oath, and did not everything in the world swear
never to harm Balder? Yet was there one thing that wisdom had
overlooked: and the mistletoe blade killed him and sent him to me
here. And do you say now that everything weeps for Balder,
everything in the world, every single thing? Go then, and fly to
everything in the world, and if everything in the world weeps for
this Balder's death, then shall I release him, and cast him out
from Hell. I swear now by the Leipter, whose oaths can never be
broken, that if all things in Midgard weep, Balder may return. But
remember this Hermod: overlook no mistletoe." And with that
she walked from the room, and went another way, and as she
passed by the door she snorted, and her shoulders shook with an
evil laughter.

'I watched her with disgust, for thus she mocked us all, and a
tyrant that is a woman is the foulest thing on earth. And as I
passed into the passage, I suddenly heard her whistle. Down the

stairs at a gallop came then Garmlet her pet hound, and such was the vile dog she brought with her to Gladsheim. As I took my horse's reins from the neck of Idleness, I heard the witch and the dog-lover capering about in a cupboard. Her whooping laughter rang out with his fat barks, and so loud was it that the dust fell off from ledges. There appeared then the demon who had led me across Hell. His face was folded back, so that his head was mainly teeth, and two goat's horns curled round and round his bristling ears. As I mounted my fearful horse, he by his whining told me to put on again the blindfold. A weary way did I retrace to the gateway, and so at last I came back onto this shore.

'Oh Aesirs, you should have sent a better man than me, for I have got you a hard and difficult bargain, and one which I doubt we can ever truly fulfil. For Hela was mocking me, though she swore to keep the vow, and I feel she has laid on us a task that cannot be. I should have stayed. I should have argued with her. For surely the prize of Loki would have somewhat made her budge. I should have drawn my sword and sworn then to have slit her throat, or have captured Balder by force, and ridden out over the walls. Oh, gods, but a ghastly numbness overtakes me in this place. Fear and despair muffle up the mind's designs, and as in a fearful nightmare we struggle even to walk. All things on earth we must seek and get to weep. This is the only bargain I have got from the mistress of Hell.'

And red-bearded Thor then shook his head and spoke, saying, 'Hermod, you did well enough, and none of us could have done better. Reproach not yourself, that you did not bring Balder alive. Yet all this is but a spiteful plan of Hela's. And what might we otherwise expect from the hag who rules all Hell? For she knew of Fricka's hard task in bidding everything take the oath, and she knew that it is impossible to take stock of everything that exists on the earth, and thus did she lay on us this malicious task, for in thrashing ourselves to accomplish so much will we waste our strength in these last few days before doom. Ay, I see it now, for these harsh things have made me wise, and a fool I was ever to hope always for the best. For following all these prophecies have we reaped a whole harvest of pain.'

[253]

But Odin looked at him and shook his grey locks, and he laid his bandaged hand upon Thor's mighty arm, and said, 'Oh Thor, my dear brother, are you brought to say so much? And is your mighty heart hardened by the trouble of these days? Why then are we all in a poor state indeed, for the heart itself of the Aesirs has now been stricken cold. Oh my brother, how I have lacked your strength in these last few days, for if I had had your heart within me, none of this would have passed. But I lost my lasting hope when I drank of the well of Mimir. And so now have I brought us together to this place. Well then, I'll lead us forward, and from death I shall breed hope. Come then, let us to horse, and wend back our deathly travel, for we shall not shun the tasks that fate appoints. Whether we shall have success depends on Mother Earth. She at least we can have trust in, more than ever in Hell.'

And wincing he arose and stood on his feet again. And the other gods arose also, and stood up under the dead boughs of the oak-tree. And they went to their horses and untethered them from the boughs, and they led them to drink again from the boiling Giurl stream, and the horses shook their bridles and dipped in their lips to drink. And when they were mounted and stamping about in the mud, Loki alone remained, squatting on the ground.

And Odin pointed to him, and thus he said: 'Take now this Loki, two of you, and dangling him by those straps, swing him between your horses, and so cast him over the walls. For now we are to bid his like farewell, and never again will he haunt Asgard and work against us. Long has it been, Loki, the guileful, that you and I worked our separate ways, and always have you hated me and sought to bring me down. Many times has it seemed fair to me to sweep you for ever from my sight, to banish you to Hell, and have done. Yet always I stopped on the brink of your destruction. For often do we need the carper in our midst. To Hell will you be flung, where you have long been bound. And this is the punishment that waits in those walls for ye: you will be bound in chains of adamant, and set in a boiling fire, and a snake full of high venom will drip its poison into your eye. Such is the place appointed, which I have kept you from. Yet think not, Loki, that ever you might escape, for the chains that will bind you cannot be unlocked again: for nothing that exists in the land of Hell can ever unlock the lock that shall seal them. And so go to your doom, and take my curse with you.'

But then did Loki cry out from his place in the mud, and he shook with sudden fear and said, 'Nay, Odin, oh greybeard, do not do this. This you must not do, though you have brought me so far. For you must take me back and into the air again. For this place is ghastly, and appeals not to me. For surely you will do wrong if you punish me now. I tell you, Odin, I cannot be blamed for Balder's death. I will grant you I desired it. I grant you I vowed to do it. But this shall I speak to you now: I could never think how to do it. For never did he tell me how he had solved the riddle of the bird-cage. Never did I discover that the cage and he were bound by the same oath. Never did I know that the mistletoe was exempt from the vow. And thus, oh Odin, could I not have planned his death. Nay therefore, old comrade, send me not into Hell, for though I am half a demon, that place is not my home. I have lived all my life on the dappled surface of earth: about its mountains have I flown, and dwelled in its woods. Shut me not away, greybeard, from that place for ever. My curse shall be upon you if ever you do so. I swear to you, old man, my undying hate, working even in the depths of Hell, sharpened by my pains, nourished by the devils, this will you have if you thrust me into their midst. Yet pity me, leader of the Aesirs, pity me. For what should little Loki do, hemmed in those walls. Have I not cheered you, in spite of my mischief? Is it not well to have a Loki about the hall? Do not leave me here, away from the Aesirs for ever!' And Loki screwed up his face, for he winced at the fate that waited, and trying to plead with Odin did he struggle to lift up his hands, yet as he did so he tipped over upon the mud, and so was his beseeching face rolled round unto the floor.

And Odin looked with pity upon him, and sighed a while, yet shook his head and said, 'Aesirs, seize him quickly and cast him into Hell. For thus is it doomed, and thus must it be. Loki, it is impossible for you to come back to earth. For did I not bid you to weep at the death of Balder, and did you not remain dry-eyed at that hour? Thus you have made your own death sure. For how with this task can we set you again on earth, when you are the very one that would frustrate our search? Thus must it be, oh guileful one, thus must it be.'

And the Aesirs then took him, Vidar and Vali between them. And Loki did they pick up by two cords that were tied to his wrists, and dangling him betwixt their horses they rode at a gallop towards the grim-metalled walls of Hell. Thrice did they swing him back and forth, and on the third swing did they let go the strands, and thus did they fling him up into the air. Over and over tumbled the bound-up form of the fire-god, and up to the very battlements he swept, and bounced on the balustrade. Loudly did the devils shriek as they fell on his body. Horned heads and flaming-haired skulls ran along the walls to seize on the new prize, and with merry jubilation did they fling him from each to each. The fires of Hell flickered and lit their manic sports, and beside them still silent remained the watchful Anlaf. But at last did they bear the prisoner from the walls, and the shouting died away as they took Loki to his place, where the flames would lick him and the serpent's bane corrode.

And quiet was it then by the shores of the Giurl River, for the water flowed on and bore its rubbish away. And the sun of sulphur was sinking in the mists of the sky, and the lurid light faded from the streaky flanks of Hell. And Odin bowed his head and sat for a moment in silence, but then did he spur the sides of his horse, and the Aesirs followed him upwards again towards earth.

But while the Aesirs came back on the Hell-road, in Asgard did the inhabitants grow less watchful, and where once had been business and martial practice, now was there a silence, as all began to lose heart. But Sif went from her house over the fields to Bleidablik, for still had she not visited Iduna and brought her comfort. And coming again at evening to the great doors, she knocked and sent booming her summons into the hall. And at last did Sigyn come to answer, with a taper in her hand, and she opened the door to Sif the golden-haired. And Sif went in with the country maid, and spoke to her kindly, and asked of Iduna.

Whereat Sigyn replied, 'Alas, poor girl, she is too young to be a widow, and daylong does she pine for Balder. Why, I have told

.her roundly that she'll pine herself to death, and I have on many occasions forced the broth down her throat – for if she does not eat something, she'll catch some disease for sure. I have bid her be of good cheer, for her father Odin's gone to rescue Balder. But will she take notice? No, she will not. Come to her now, good lady, and do you look upon her, for if she sees you come she'll gladly change her ways no doubt.'

And Sigyn then led forth Sif into Balder's old chamber, and by the weak light of the taper she gazed into the room. But Iduna lay, still in her red wedding-dress, stretched upon the bed, and she clasped the pillow to her and buried in it her auburn hair. The flowers and garlands for the wedding-day lay withered on the walls, and a green tunic of Balder's lay twisted on the coverlet beside her. And Sif sat beside her and tried to comfort her, but Iduna would not turn nor speak to her at all. And a while did Sif weep with her, and buried her face in her hands. But nothing would Iduna speak, nor no movement even would she make, for her voice was locked within her and she could not breathe forth its power. And so did Sif leave her and went outside with Sigyn again.

But now did the trumpet from Himminbiorg clearly sound as the Aesirs returned and mounted the path to heaven. The great gate was thrown open. The horsemen clattered in. Through the echoing gateway did they pass into Asgard square. But the weary and way-spotted travellers were also astonished as they looked about, for among all the snows that muffled the walls and the fields was no wight stirring, nor any guard or watchman. The halls lay black and lonely about the whitened wastes, and the wind blew the flurries over deserted squares. And so did Odin command the messenger-god Hermod to bray forth his own bugle-call and awake the sleepy city. And Hermod lifted up the glittering silver horn and sent forth a ringing peal among the snowy streets.

But then from the halls and the walls there hurried forth watchmen and guards, and they formed up in troops at their posts. And the Einheriar came from their talk by the fires and the braziers, and they flocked into the square and set it buzzing with their voices. The Valkyries came, and the goddesses of heaven, all but Fricka that kept still to Odin's house, and Sigyn and Sif hastened over from Bleidablik, and the warrior-maidens came riding through the snow.

But Odin frowned upon them, and thus he sternly spake: 'Have ye all been asleep, and dozing by the fire? Or is it of no import that men come through your gates? Do you have to hear my horn-call before any of you will stir? Well, thus it is you guard Asgard in my absence. And where is Fricka, my wife, that should be here to lead you? For she I left with the charge to keep Asgard defended. I see too well that all of you are grown so weak and faint-hearted that much will your courage have to be sharpened to face these coming days. But now I have new missions for you to fly upon. Let messengers go at once to all the corners of earth, Valkyries on your flying steeds, now haste to our allies. Waltraute, send your sisters to Kari, the giant, and fly to Frey of the elves, and to Andvari in the caverns of the dwarves. Bid them haste here and attend to my words tomorrow. For now are each one of us to haste on a grand design. For we come back from Hell with a promise from the witch. Hela has made a bargain with the Aesirs that went to Hell that if we can get everything on earth to weep for Balder, then will he be restored to us and given to life again. Dally no longer, but take your messages straight. For the greatest quest that ever Aesirs went on is now to bring us back all the good things of old.' And Odin ceased speaking and glowered at the thronging crowds, for now there surrounded him vast numbers with flaming torches.

And Sif then rejoiced at the news, and standing by her husband's horse she seized Thor's hand. And the golden-haired goddess addressed them all and said, 'Oh well have you won, oh un-defeated Aesirs! Have you come back from Hell with an agreement with Hela? Oh happy eve, then is there hope for Asgard. For Lord Odin, we have been diligent, and we have watched by the towers and prepared. Yet these last two days has the winter come, for the pale sun has sunk low without cause, and the cold weather encased us all in ice. And greatly did we dread that this was Fimbul-winter. Yet how fine is your news now! We shall take heart again. But lonely has it been, oh gods, without your steadiness and strength to support us.'

[258]

But Odin still glowered, and thus he replied, 'And yet I cannot see why my wife should not tell me this. For, Sif, it is not your duty to see to these warlike things. But enough of this. Off then. Valkyries, be on your way. But let us gods go to Gladsheim, and there eat of a good feast. For weary are we all, dogged to the death with riding. The road has been harsh and the way has been long. Tomorrow at dawn will we meet on this spot together, and then will we hie to bid everything in Midgard weep.' And Odin set riding towards the hall of Gladsheim, and the Aesirs followed him, trudging wearily through the snow.

And so did the Valkyrie maids fly off on their separate tasks, and they went winging over the walls towards the lands of the giants, the dwarves, and the elves. But the aching Aesirs dismounted and entered the hall, and there soon were they seated about the benches that surrounded the fire. And Odin sat with a sigh in the high seat by the hearthside, and healers came to him to see to his wounded hands. And he laid them on the rune-carved arms to the throne and they salved them and drugged their pain. And soon were the warriors all feasting together, and talking of their journey in the flickering light of the torches.

And old Niord arose and lifted up his goblet, and wearily he cleared his throat and said to them all, 'Friends, let us drink to the spirit of the hearth-side, for after such wandering horrors, how sweet it is to be home! Oh black has the way been, cold and fraught with trouble, and there were times I felt that my old bones would not go so far. And desperate was Hell, most evil in its confusion, and there were times I doubted we would win anything from that pit. Seven days ago did we all feast in this hall. Then Hela came to us. Now we have been to her. Two days are left, my friends, before our foes arise. Two days before we see on the horizon the monsters of old growing strong. One day must we go questing to bid all things in Midgard weep. One day is there left then to ride down and fetch Balder from Hell. Yet the whole of earth will speak for us, and by the earth's grace shall the task be fulfilled. Oh then that will be true victory, not just for ourselves, when Balder is with us, and all things shall be well.'

[259]

The Aesirs drank to this, moved by the old man's words. The hearts of all were stirred by easy resolution. And so they fell to feasting, and thought kind thoughts again. And this was the last of all their feasts together. But when they had eaten and drunk enough, they got up from the fire and left the festive hall. Into the gloomy air they walked, and made their ways straggling across the snows. And Mani in the moon gazed down on their weary forms, for it seemed as though each one was older than last he saw them.

But Sigyn the country maid went back to Bleidablik, and she entered the hall and went into Iduna's chamber, and she sat down on the bed and thus she spoke: 'Cheer your heart now, Iduna, for I bring you great news. Did you not hear the trumpet that rang from the great black tower? The gods are all come back, even from going to Hell. And Balder is to be rescued, and brought to earth again. Well, will you not answer? Won't you rejoice at that? What better tidings could anyone ever bring you? For Hela the goddess of Hell has made a bargain with the men, and if they and Odin can get everything on earth to weep, and everything there is weeps for Balder's death, then she will set him free. Is not that wonderful?'

But Iduna then got up, and she sat on the bed, and leaning down she bound her shoes onto her feet, and then she arose and took her great cloak from its chest, and she wound it about her as if to go out in the cold. And she wound round her hair a scarf of scarlet, sewn with pink, and she muffled her neck with it and tied it into a tight knot. And then did Iduna look at Sigyn and say, 'Well then, adieu to you, and to this place, for now is my stay with the Aesirs over and done. I have lain here long enough, troubled by bitter hopes. Yet for all my praying have they not brought back Balder. And now do I know that indeed they never shall, for Hela is a cruel witch, and these things has she made to trick them. Sigyn, I thank you for tending me so well. Yet think no more of me now or for ever, for I am going on a journey into an unknown land, and this is the last you'll see of the Vana, Iduna. For I shall go to Groa, the helpful witch of the woods. Her will I speak to and tell her of my plight. One thing shall I beg her, cost me what darkness it will, that I may join Balder, wherever he may be. Tell them here in Asgard that there has Iduna gone. But as for the rest, bid them only forget it all.' And Iduna sighed, and began to stride from the room.

And Sigyn stopped her, and took her by the arm and said, 'Are you so quickly recovered, and your voice is found again? Then I shall come with you, for why should not the witch help me? I am also a woman with a husband in Hell. Tut, you are a Vana, and are used to delicate things, but Sigyn is a country wench, and has roamed the harsh world wide. It will be no trouble for me, if the witch bids me walk into Hell. So I shall indeed come with you, for two strengths are better than one, and I will be your comrade wherever you may fare.' And Sigyn pushed Iduna forth before she might answer, and the two girls left the gloomy room, and walking down the hallway came to the great oak door.

But Iduna turned back, when they had opened the door, and the bluish snows lay before them, covering their path in cold. And Iduna looked back into the hall of Bleidablik. The torches trembled gaily on the walls, nor did it seem to alter for all the joy that had left. But the cold froze her cheek and she felt the dampness of the snows in her shoes, and so she wrapped close the cloak around her, and turning to Sigyn shut the door and began the journey. Over the snowy fields of Asgard they went, and slipped from the gate of Himminbiorg by a side door. The great staircase of the rainbow, with frost-hidden colours, swept down before them to the black crags and brown woods. The far lands below them were dappled with moon-tinged snow. And the violet and the sapphire and the leafy green they descended, and brushed with their skirts the frosts that settled on the pale gold and the orange and the stain of crimsoned ice. So they entered earth again, and made for Groa's cave.

Now Groa was awake, even at this hour, and she sat in her cave by the glowing embers of a fire. Yet her cave was empty now of the leaves that kept her prophecies. She had burned them all, and the Norns had left the hill. And now Groa sat merely thinking of the past, and the events she had looked on sorted themselves into patterns in her mind, and she was filled with regret for the things she had not seen. She stared into the fire as the ashes crumbled

[261]

away. And yet out past the flames was the stillness of the woods, and the deathly snows that held them had made their silence deep. And so from such darkness came Iduna and Sigyn to consult her.

And when the two girls saw the light in the cave, they raced towards it and entered, and knelt down. And Iduna looked at the seeress, searching her face, and said, 'Indeed you are the prophetess, for so did Balder describe you. Such was the cave, and such its place in the woods. Oh then if you are Groa, let us beg you for assistance. For I am Iduna, the luckless wife of Balder, that caused him much trouble and sent him into Hell. Surely, being a seer, oh Groa, you have heard my story. And this that I bring with me is Sigyn the country maid, for she gave her love to Loki and yet now is he taken away. Oh Groa, you must have heard of the troubles the Aesirs have felt: how Balder is sent into Hell, and Loki there also imprisoned. We two are come hither to ask you what can we do, for we have no faith in the bargains which the gods have made with Hela and we are so willed to seek our husbands' freedom alone. Have pity upon us therefore, oh mighty seeress, for we have no strength, nor can muster no armies, and yet would we undertake the deathliest of tasks, so great is our yearning to see our husbands again. Is there no way we can meet them? Do you not know of any plan? Fear not to speak of terrible things, for there is no fear that can worsen the present time.' And Iduna fell silent, and gazed at Groa beseeching.

And the seeress sighed a long sigh, and thus answered: 'I am indeed Groa, and know each one of your woes. The hardships of the Aesirs have been near to me. And indeed this task of Hela's is treacherous in the extreme. I understand well what it is that brings you to me. And I would help you too, for indeed my heart pities you. But do you not know that your husbands are in Hell? That they have gone to the land of death, which can only be reached by dying? How can you determine to visit them in such a place, for are you resolved then to die for their sakes? Alas, you are faced with the commonest of man's woes: his spirit meets eternity, and yet his flesh decays. But if I should show you a way into Hell, and give you the means to go in and come out again, and if I should grant you a way to rescue your husbands, would you then undertake to do a mission for me?' And Groa looked at the two girls, as their faces grew round with surprise.

And Iduna at once answered her and said, 'Indeed we would do anything, Groa, if you could do that. To see them again would be the happiest of fates, but to see and to rescue – oh what could be more well? Should we indeed succeed where the Aesirs have failed? Might the love of weak women surpass all the hosts of Asgard? No welcomer action could there be for me, than such an act as this, that wins Balder's good will. Oh tell us speedily, Groa, what is this thing we should do?' And Iduna knelt forward, and seized on the hem of Groa's gown.

And then did Groa tell them of the adventure: 'There are two ways into Hell: by the long roads and by the short. And easy it is to slide into Hell's realm. Yet to come out again: well, that we know is hard. Take these leaves therefore, and keep them warmed in your hand, and when I tell you, be prepared to chew them both. For I shall lead you forth, and we will go into the woods, and there shall we gather a plant of mistletoe. Each of you shall have half the plant, and with it as safe-conduct may you go into Hell. Next I shall take you up the mountain to a cave, for this is one of the entrances in Midgard. There will you sit, and chew on your leaves, and when you become sleepy, get up and walk into the cave. When you feel yourself falling, think then on the one you would meet. When you open your eyes, you will see your husband before you. There you may speak with them, and tell them of your rescue. What remains then is to bring them from the darkness.

'There is a river of ice, Elivigar it is called, which tumbles its frosty flakes into a seething well. Hvergelmir is that place where it flows, a boiling cauldron, where two rivers meet. For the river of ice meets therein with Leipter the river of fire, and hence is the turbulence, when two extremes conflict. The waters of Hvergelmir feed the roots of Yggdrasil, for towering up from the ground about the well the world-ash-tree begins its long journey aloft. At the mouth of the ice-river a root falls into the soil. In the root is a knot which overhangs in a curve. Thus does it make a bower by the stream. Huge is that ash-tree, monstrous are its roots. That bower is enough to shelter you and your loves. Go therefore at Hell-dawn,

[263]

when you have found your husbands, and there join together again
the plant of mistletoe. Bearing that before you along the causeway
to your right, proceed towards Hell-gate and show your plant to
the guards. They cannot avoid then opening the gate. And so you
may leave Hell, and begin the harsh journey to earth. But this now
is your mission which you must perform for me: bring back the
golden apples, which fell from the hands of Iduna.' And Groa said
no more, but stared at Iduna hard. And then did she arise, and lead
them from the cave.

Among the moonlit fir-trees did Groa lead them forward, taking
a buried path that wound along the hillside, and as they passed the
branches the heavy snow slipped onto the ground. The woods were
held in stillness, and their trudging footsteps echoed, and they
strode through great drifts of snow, staining their skirts with
damp. They came down the valley where the oaks and birches were.
On the budding yellow shoots did the late frosts settle. They passed
beneath the gnarled boughs, the seeress gazing upward, and
touching the hoary oak, Groa showed the girls then a plant of
mistletoe, and the green waxy leaves stuck out, wearing a dense
hat of cold and heavy snow. Iduna reached out from an overhanging cliff, and scattering the snows down from its shaking
branches, she cut the plant at its roots, and cast it through the
dappled moonbeams. Groa then caught it, and slit the plant in two.
And so did they make on again, the girls each holding half the plant.

And Groa led them upward now and mounted the mountain
tracks, and soon were they travelling through rearing crags and
passes, and they left the domain of trees and came out onto barren
lands. And so did they stumble along the slippery slopes and enter
the silent land, where the snows are eternal and the quiet peaks
brood under the frosty moon. Into a valley then of brown and
jagged rocks the three women descended, hugging an icy path.
In the scoop of the vale lay a glittering glacier. Its ribbed ice
confronted them like the mountain's teeth. Moonbeams shimmered
on its slimy surface. Winding down from the heights of the sky,
it ground the boulders, and ceased at the foot of their road. They
clattered down the crags and came to its ending. Then did the
seeress lead the two girls along the glacier's base, where the dirty

[264]

ice crumbled away and left a litter of stones. Here under the glacier was a blue cave, filled with moonbeams. Here did the sibyl cease, and turn back to the girls.

And Groa spoke then, and thus she said: 'See where this glacier ends its lazy travel, and behold how it overhangs this path into the darkness. Such is the entrance into Hell. Sit in here, maidens, and chew those leaves I gave you. Hold fast each to your half of mistletoe. When you feel you are sleepy from the fumes of the chewed leaves, get up from your place and walk into that blackness. When the way down tilts so much that you start to fall, then bear in mind the man you go to seek. You will soon find them, even in the realm of Hell. But Iduna, hear you this: forget not your golden apples. Seek for them diligently, wherever they may be. And Sigyn, remember this, when you see Loki in torment: his chains cannot be undone by anything that is in Hell. The mistletoe you bear with you shall release him thus. Yet Loki is guileful, and beware his evil tricks. And Iduna keep safe your apples from his hand, for if Loki should get them, he would feed the Aesirs' foes. Go then, frail girls. Achieve this great mission. For you in your weakness have the strength to save the gods.' With these words Groa went, and the girls were alone in the valley.

Then did they diligently do all they were told, and they sat close in the cave and held their mistletoes tightly. They chewed then on the leaves, and tasted their acrid dryness. The close-packed ice above them let through the shafts of the moon. The blue light shimmered and darted about the tunnel. Hung was the cold cave with dangling icicles. Sigyn felt drowsy, and was the first to arise. She drew round her her skirts, and tiptoed into the cave. Among the freezing corridor she stumbled on the slippery ground. The tunnel grew darker, and descended in a steeper slope. The girl's feet slipped from her, and thus she began hurtling downwards. Closing her eyes did Sigyn then think of Loki, and bearing him in her mind she fell endlessly through the darkness, until about her ears there roared the fires of Hell.

Now when Sigyn opened her eyes, thus transported into the realm of Hell, she saw before her the bitterest sight, for her husband Loki was suffering his torment. Chained to a black slab of granite did he lie, with four iron chains pulling at hands and feet, and around over his body there writhed the venomous snakes. Sheeny purples and scaly copper hues did these serpents bear on their winding coils, and they bit fast on his limbs and sunk their needles in him. But above the arch-deceiver lurked the great snake of Hell, and the fire-god twisted and jerked with pain as the black oozing venom slid down from the serpent's teeth and splashed with its corroding bite into the filmy jelly of his eyeballs. Harsh were the screams that Loki there made, and yet for all his writhing could he not avoid the poison.

About him in the country round was a wide and smoking crater, for the rim of a volcano shut off the yellow sky, and the ashy slopes slid downwards to a pit of boiling lava. Violent were the molten rocks that lurched and bubbled beneath. They shot up red splodges of heat and knotted flame. They spewed up white-hot embers in showers upon Loki's breast. And again and again jumped and roared the cunning god of guile. Not one minute did he rest from the poison or the heat. And the black chains held him in an eternal torment.

And Sigyn was horrified and cried out at last, 'Loki, is this you? Is this how you are punished? Must you endure these torments, as if you were a shameful fiend?' And Loki at once turned his head to her and said, 'Get me out of these chains. Out on you, you wretch and malicious one! Will you stand there gawping at my agony? Get me out of this pain for I can endure it no longer. These chains hold me down. They can never be undone by anything that is in Hell. Fetch me, you idiot, something from earth straight. Run and fetch me a mistletoe, for that will save me alone. It is the solver of all pledges. It unravels all rules. What, will you stand there with your mouth open like a fool? If I were not on this rock I would smash ye into pieces. Set me free! Set me free! For no longer can I endure.'

And Sigyn at once ran to him, and she picked from the ashes a slab. And the slab of rock had a hollow in it like a cup. Then did she hold this under the dripping venom of the snake, and for a while she shielded Loki from the poison in his eyes. Leaning over him thus, she reached forth with the mistletoe, and one by one she touched the four chains that held him down. With the touch of the green plant they dissolved, and their adamant links were broken. Loki snatched up his hands, and pulled away his feet. Feeling himself free, he sprang away from the slate. And so with a groan did he slide into the ash, and there he lay panting, relieved from all his pain. And Sigyn went to him, and knelt at his side.

And then did Sigyn speak to him and say, 'Oh how cruel was your punishment, my husband, and how you suffered! What great chance that I came here, and was able to set you free! For I doubt if you would have been able to bear any more. The witch Groa bade me do this, for she does not think you are wicked. And she has told me how I may rescue you from Hell. For at dawn are we to meet by the mouth of the ice-river Balder and Iduna, who will have the other half of this mistletoe. And when we join it together can we all go out of Hell's gates. There now, Loki, will you not love me for this? For have I not now been a true and faithful wife? For ten years I have waited, and for many long months sought you, and here now have I rescued you from the worst pains in the world.'

But Loki drew softly away, and he slipped the mistletoe from her hand, and he placed it up on a safe place on the slope, and put both his hands slowly about Sigyn's neck. Tightly did he squeeze her then, and strangle the country girl. He grasped about her windpipe with all the fierceness his tortures brought him. Sigyn struggled against him. Faintly she tried to pull away his hands. But her breath was choked, and her blood caught in her head. Her strength weakened swiftly and her face turned black with pain. Despair did she feel then, and she died. He tumbled her corpse down the ledge of ashes. It rolled into the sea of fire, and was lapped by molten lava. In fire and steam and singeing Sigyn met her end, and Loki turned away and picked up the mistletoe, and holding it above him, he climbed out of the crater. Triumphant then did Loki stand on the rim, and the sinking sun of sulphur lit the green leaves of the plant. Then did he turn back and gaze at the smoking body.

And Loki sneered at Sigyn's corpse, and cried, 'You guileless humans, will you never learn? So do I get rid of the wife Thor thrust on me. For now am I cured of any love that held me. Henceforth I am iron-hearted, for now shall I achieve the glory

[267]

of myself and the death of all the Aesirs. For I shall scour Hell and take forth the golden apples, and the foes of the gods will I feed fat on them. Now Odin will you howl that spurned me and put me into Hell. Did I not tell you that you would reap my curse? Oh, I shall mangle and burn those soft-hearted Aesirs! I shall dig in their faces with my sharp heels. I shall have them whimper before me leading their foes. But now must I go seeking, and Balder too must I find. For his half the mistletoe must get me out of Hell.' And Loki looked out then on the smoking land. He descended the volcano and went searching the fires and mud.

But while Sigyn fell into Hell and her death, Iduna still chewed on the bitter-tasting leaves, and she did not like the taste, and could hardly stomach them. And vainly she waited for sleepiness to come. But at last she felt drugged, and she spat out the rest of the leaves, and lay back a moment against the ice-wall. But her head began to nod forward, and so she arose and went inwards. Through the shimmering tunnel she came to the darkness, and then began slipping on the steepening path. At once she found herself falling into blackness, and all the feeling drained from her outer limbs.

Then did Iduna hold fast to the thought of Balder, and she clung to him in her heart and cried, 'Oh Balder, let me but see you even in Hell. If it is only for one minute let me clasp you again in my arms. Oh let the witch be true, and let these leaves help us. For terribly I dread that some trick will come to part us.'

But now as Iduna fell, sinking slowly into Hell, there appeared to her a demon that suddenly lunged from the darkness. For a snarling dog-face she saw, with yellow fangs, and it appeared but for a second, and so took her thoughts from Balder. Then did she feel, with the flinch she made from the vision, that she twisted a little in her path, and fell from the straight descent. And before she might correct herself, she felt the ground beneath her feet. She opened her eyes to see an endless desolate plain, and grey sands were before her, blown by the gritty winds, and no person did she see there, but heard the bleak winds howl.

And Iduna felt dismayed, and instantly ran forward in fear. This way and that she searched to see Balder. But not one person could she find in that wasteland, and it seemed she was trapped in a profitless desert. But just as she trembled and was about to weep, she saw in the far distance a speck moving towards her, and at once her heart rejoiced again, and speedily she ran that way. Hasting over the sand, she saw that it was a man. Fearfully she hied on the last yards towards him, but doubtfully she saw at last the figure drawing near: for a tattered cloak he wore, and he stooped and seemed to be old. And then did she see his grey beard and know that he was not Balder. Iduna stopped in her tracks. The man did so also. Then they strode on again, despairing in different ways.

And Iduna saw then the prints of other feet, for the sand was threaded over with circling and converging footprints. And hardly had she noticed this, but she saw another speck, and hastening that way once more, she peered to see if it were her love. But a woman she saw at last, that called aloud for her son, and she hastened to Iduna, and asked her if she had seen him. Iduna shook her head, and watched her with dismay, for the woman ran on again and was lost once more in the sands. And then as she peered forth again, other figures did she see, that came thicker and thicker upon her, until soon was she lost in great milling crowds of people. For anxiously they gazed about, each searching each other's faces, and some called out for daughters, and some for husbands and fathers, and some called out for gold that they had lost, and some for homes, and some for their lords. Each figure she encountered sought endlessly and in vain. But among these whirling crowds did she never see her love, and Iduna then knelt down, and she could find no strength to go on. And the crowd strayed before her under the yellow sky.

Then did Iduna sigh and say, 'Alas, these people are all like myself, for each one of them seeks some object they loved on earth, and runs about weeping, seeking in vain. So do they show me a mirror of my soul, for such have I been all these long days. Oh shall I never find him, now I have come to Hell? Have I made this journey, still to be harshly denied? Oh thus, thus is the temper of this world: we yearn in the desert, and meet with only yearning.' And Iduna bowed her head and stared at the sands.

But then did Iduna see a man standing before her, a stranger that gazed on her with a kindly face. For the man was tall, and had on a tattered robe, and his hands were folded into the sleeves of the other arm. And he smiled at Iduna, and thus did he speak to her and say, 'Weep not, my child, for all is not lost. There is a way outward, whatever the pain may be. For do you not hold in your hand the plant of the mistletoe? And is not that plant a detachment from the world? You go seeking Balder, that came to this place not long since, and yet you see how many there are with such a longing restless in their hearts. Yet fear not, for you will find him. And I shall lead you where he is: for he too goes seeking what the realm of Hell encloses. But come now, follow me forth. Fate must be born. Hold out your hand, and take this that I give you to Balder, and then let us onward, over these barren plains.' And the stranger drew forth then his hand from his sleeve, and he held in the hand and offered her a shining, golden apple. And Iduna took it, and gazed at it with awe. For this was one of the apples which those days ago she had lost, when Thiazi abducted her from the high wall of Asgard, and this had she and Balder been seeking for so long.

But the stranger turned away before she might ask him any questions, and she saw only his long robe fluttering through the mists, and at once she hurried after, for fear of losing his guiding. Hurriedly she hastened and dogged his swift-footed steps, and the stranger led her quickly through the milling crowds of people. This way and that he tacked and steered through them, and only could she tell where she went by the direction of the waning sulphur sun. And try as she might to catch up with the stranger, always he seemed to be ahead of her, leading her on and on. And then did she see another man hastening forward, dressed in ragged clothes, with a casket under his arm. And the hastening man then passed her, and she saw that it was Balder.

With surprise and dismay, she dropped the golden apple, and it bounced upon the ground, and was kicked by flying feet. This way and that did it trickle in the crowds, and the ragged Balder seized it then and shut it in his casket, and clapped the top to with a sudden small sound. And Iduna went to him, and softly she spoke his name.

But Balder shook his head, and said, 'Leave me, you spirits. You may come in her form, and taunt me with fleeing hopes, but I shall not follow you, for you are but mist and air. I am weary now, and can haste no longer. The striving and the yearning are over now and done. For tomorrow or the next day will they come to the gate of Hell, and then must I be ready to go to hear my fate. All twelve apples that were lost are now found. If you were true Iduna, you would rejoice at that.'

And Iduna knelt down and gazed into his face, and said, 'Yet am I truly, indeed I am Iduna. Oh Balder, my love, we are surely together again. The heartache we have suffered, the pain of separation, I swear to you is banished now, and we may take our real embrace. For I am come to rescue you. See, with this mistletoe I have ventured into Hell. Tomorrow at dawn are we to go forth from the gate. For Sigyn is here also, and has gone to find Loki, and our branches of mistletoe are to be joined together, and so all four go forth, and take the road back to Midgard. For surely am I here, and we shall see earth again.'

But Balder frowned still, and his eyes roamed over her face. And he stretched forth his hand and fearfully reached to touch her. Then did he draw her young body into his arms, and long he clasped her to him, feeling at peace again. With closed eyes and salty mouths tasting of tears they kissed a long kiss. The casket of apples was pressed close between them. The mistletoe sprouted from the hand about Balder's neck. And cruel fate forgotten was in that reunion.

But Loki meanwhile, hurrying about Hell, wearied himself with vain search for the golden apples, and though he accosted many of the tribes in Hell, skirted the regions of the ice and fire, yet did he find no trace of the eternal fruit. And tiring at last of his questing, and of the bitterness of his Hell-born sufferings, he decided to forego his search, and go instead to wait at the point Sigyn had told him of: the mouth of the ice-river, where Elivigar tumbles into the cauldron. And Loki came there and found the place, and the root also he saw, arched up in an overhung bower, and feeling that this was where the lovers would come, he hid behind it and curled up ready to sleep. And so by the boiling waters of Hvergelmir, hidden behind the root of high-arching Yggdrasil, the arch-deceiver settled to await his victims.

Hither soon came Iduna, leading Balder forth, and she pointed with eagerness at the root of which Groa had spoken. The sun had sunk now, and threw their shadows far over the mud, and the ice of Elivigar shone strangely in the dusk. So did the lovers go in to wait for the dawn. They settled into the bower, and lay down on the root-hung ground. Earthy it smelt under the trunk of Yggdrasil, and cosy it was to feel each other's arms. The casket they placed between them, and the mistletoe Iduna held. And when they were lying there, they gazed into each other's eyes.

And Balder caressed her, and thus he said, 'Indeed I believe now. Iduna, you are real. For thus does it feel to hold my wife in my arms. These hands are her hands, these breasts her breasts. This face is her dear face, that I have loved so long. Why, how soon flee the terrors and loneliness of Hell! One of love's moments is enough to cure all ills. Yet alas, how I am weary, and I fear I will fall asleep. For I think I am home again, dozing by the fire. For in your arms is Bleidablik, is Apple-Isle, not Hell.'

And Iduna said, 'Sleep, my love, for now shall all be well. Not this grim place, nor that bitter day, shall we remember when we are again on earth. For new life shall have us, and fresh days begin. Did we not say so, when we last parted in the meadow? I hear the future humming, singing a song of what will be. Balder is arising, a new soul from the sun. Slumber then. I'll sing a lullaby. Into your sleep I'll creep with my song, and we shall be together in whatever land.' And Iduna hummed then one of the old songs, and Balder sighing fell asleep.

But then as she brooded, lying in his arms, Iduna heard strange murmurs and trillings in the ground. For through the roots of Yggdrasil could she catch the sap arising. Upwards they surged, the juices of earth. Under the crusty bark they soaked in the woody rings. And Nidhog could she hear also, the serpent that gnaws under the ground, and Ratatosk the chestnut squirrel, that scampers with his messages to the golden eagle, Lerad. But the humming sap teemed onward to refresh the shimmering leaves, and the sound came of nibbling from the four sky-stags: Durathor and Duneyr and Dvalin and Dain. Iduna's eyes grew heavy, and at last she fell asleep.

But now came forth the guileful one from his crouch behind the root, and he stood before the root-bower, and gazed with glee at the lovers. There did he see the half of the mistletoe plant. There did he see between them the casket that held once the apples. Stealthily he crept to the sleepers. He loosed the mistletoe from Iduna's grasp. Gently did he lift up the casket. Tiptoeing backward did he slide away from them. When he was at a distance, he opened the casket's lid. He gazed at the golden apples, and gnashed his teeth with bliss.

And looking back at the lovers did Loki sneer and say, 'Oh idiots of love, how I despise you all! For love is plain madness, and drains your life away. Born are you in strength, and grow up handsome and strong, but then are you struck like little kindly babes by the doting lust to promulgate your seed. The thought is ghastly, like a slimy taste in my mouth. Yet, you fools, you slothful weeds, you easy, slobbering, cosy cows, how shall I drive you howling from the face of earth! For the apples I have, which were to have been your strength. The apples I shall take now to all the Aesirs' foes. Jormundgandr, Fenris, Sturt, the flaming, and all: these shall I make invincible by their power and life, and Loki shall go forth to make a harsher world.' And Loki drew from his finger his ring, and he rolled it towards them and it rested by the lovers. And Loki turned away then, and crossing the river of ice, he took the long causeway that led to the gate of Hell. The mistletoe freed him. He gained the Giallar-bridge. Thus did he pass onward to spread his woe in the world.

But when dawn came to Hell, and the sickly light paled the mists, and the rising disc of brimstone showed the miseries of Hell, then Balder and Iduna awoke in their rooty bower. And when they awoke they saw casket and branch were gone, and Loki's ring beside them to show who had stolen them.

And Balder sighed and wearily he said, 'Come then, for one last duty remains. To the gate must we go to abide the Aesir's answer. And then can we rest with no more joy or pain.' And they walked beside the river, on the causeway to the gate.

But when the rosy dawn came to Asgard, and smoothed with her fingers the sloping snows, then Hugin and Munin, which were the two ravens of Odin, arose from their perch in a grey tree, and flew to the house in the groves of Glasir. For long had they been idle, not needed by their master, but now did they sense that great deeds were again to be done. And so they flew across the landscape, and landed both on the snowy window-ledge of Odin's chamber, and croaking there noisily they awoke their Lord. And Odin, when he saw them, saluted them, and threw back the pelts of bear and wolf upon his bed.

And then did the Lord of Asgard don his clothes and armour. And he fitted his chain-mail tunic over his shoulders, and took up his helmet, and set the metal wings on his head, and so did he make ready for the great adventure. Then did he pass out of his room, and the ravens watched him go, and waited for him to leave the hall. But as Odin passed by an alcove near his own, he saw lying upon a trestle-bed of straw his own wife Fricka.

So did Odin shake her shoulder, and speak to her thus: 'So you are here, my wife, and will not sleep with me now? But you lie like a slave on a dreary bed and face the wall. And is it thus you have neglected your duties while I have been away? For little has been done, so I hear, to make ready. Fricka, let me tell you, it is idle to lie and sulk, for no matter what hard things fall upon us, it is cowardly to go away, and hide from the fate that threatens. Though doom may be hastening, it is our duty to fight. For fighters are what we are, and by fighting we have achieved. And little would we have got, if we had lain in bed all day.' But Fricka replied not, and Odin so left her.

And then did he push open the door of his hall, which was clogged with snow, and go out into the white new land outside. And trudging through the ice, he made his way forward, and he whistled into the air to signal his ravens to follow. Then did Hugin and Munin fly up from their perch on the window-sill and sail across the sunny air after the new tracks of Odin. And through Glasir he went, which were groves of colourful trees. And the twigs of the trees were set like feathers with sparkling rime. Yet the sun was rising now, and chasing away the bluish shadows.

And thus did Odin arrive at the gate of Himminbiorg, and there in the square were all his troops assembled. The gods were already up, and waited in the centre. For there was Forseti, and old Niord, and Thor looked about, and on his head he sported a fur hat made by Sif. The Valkyries also clustered, and jingled the reins of their steeds. And the grey Einheriar were drawn up in their ranks, and they clinked with their chainmail as the captains strolled to and fro. But when they saw Odin did they all fall silent, and the Aesirs greeted him, and drew near to hear his orders.

But Odin called out to them, 'Greetings, comrades, and a fair morning to you. For this day begins well, when Sol rides her chariot so brightly in the sky. And well is it you are all up so early, yea, and have shamed your leader, who is the last man on parade. Yet dally a while longer, for not yet are our allies arrived. This is a tall order for Asgard alone.' And the soldiers laughed, and talked among themselves, commenting on the good spirits of gloomy Odin. And Odin greeted his brothers, and talked with the gods a while.

But then did a bugle announce an arrival at the gate, and with a creaking of hinges the door of Himminbiorg opened to the sky. Up the rainbow bridge there came then a new procession, for Valkyries hastened in with the allies that they had summoned, and so did they lead into the square the help from earth. For Kari the air-giant loomed up from Jotunheim, and Kari was huge with a drooping blond moustache, and he walked with a stout staff made of a cedar tree. And Andvari came next, the chief dwarf from Svartheim, for he is it governs the great barrows of the race, when under the ground in tumuli do they forge wondrous weapons.

And lastly came Frey, the great god of Alfheim. And Frey rode in in his blazing chariot of gold, and it was drawn by Gullinbursti, the golden-bristled boar. And Frey was a beauteous god, with a beaming face and pointed beard. And behind him about his head flocked the disparate elves of Alfheim.

And Odin then strode forward, and saluted them all and said, 'From the hearts of all the Aesirs I welcome you old friends to Asgard. For Frey, be you welcome, and Kari and Andvari, and welcome you flying elves that were our happy guests not long since. For now have I summoned you to help in one last task, to fulfil a vow of Hela's, and renew our life again. For alas, I need not remind you what sad chance brings us so together. For when Leshy and his fellows were last here was my poor son Balder alive. And surely have you all heard that he is gone now to Hell. Yet the Aesirs have made a bargain with the mistress Hela, and Hela has laid on us a task we must perform, and if we can fulfil it will she release the sun-god Balder.

'This then is the task which I wish you to help us perform: to go about earth and to ask everything to weep, and to send back your signal when all things have wept for my son. For each country must we search and each creature must we question, and all must be brought to weep and keep the oath. Wherefore the elves and the giants and the dwarves must be visited, and such are the missions I would wish you Kari, you Andvari and you Frey to perform. For each knows his country best, and best may seek its regions. If you consent to this, and will each go forth on this mission, then, oh elves, and leader Leshy, would I ask your help as messengers. For as the troops go forth to visit all lands upon earth, I would wish you to go with them, and to fly back when their task is complete. For not long have we left now to perform this difficult venture, and with all the speed we can muster would we wish it performed and reported. Such then is the mission for which I have begged you to come. Say then, oh great heroes, will you help the gods in this?'

But Frey from his chariot at once answered and said, 'We will indeed help all we can, and in the manner you have spoken of shall we be glad to do it. For the three of us met on the way to Asgard, and we have all three consented to aid you. For Asgard must be saved, that has so long endured, for long it would not be after this great fortress is fallen, that we of the elves or the dwarves or the giants suffer similar extinctions.'

And then did Odin speak again and say, 'My brothers, I thank you, for you have eased my heart, for till this day had I never truly seen that my old woes were not all my own. Come then, let us go forth, and let this be the disposition that we take. For Frey will you fly to Alfheim, and take elves on your journey to be your messengers. And Andvari will you to Svartheim and Kari to your own Jotunheim; and yet for your messengers will I not assign you elves, for do you each take one of my ravens here: Andvari have Hugin and Kari take Munin, for they are true servants and fly swifter than anything on earth, and long is it also I have left them to idle in Asgard. You hear how they croak, for they agree with me. Then my brothers and Aesirs, do you go forth in this way. For let each of you have elves to bear your messages back to me, and once have all creatures in the realm consented to weep, do you bid them fly swiftly back to me with the tidings. For I shall be seated half way on the hill to Yggdrasil, and there in that high spot will see all about the world. Then Thor, take ye Manheim, and search all its creatures well. And Forseti, go to Niflheim, bleak country, yet few creatures in it. And Niord, your own home Vanaheim visit you, and question its creatures. And Vidar and Vali go you both to the farthest lands Southward, and there search Muspelsheim, and bid all her creatures weep. Once you have all passed to the limits of each land, then you need fret no further for all else is not in Midgard. Thus the creatures of the abyss, and our own most terrible foes: they cannot be counted, though some might think they should. And so good luck go with you, whichever way you fare.

'But let these also be an aid to you in your journey: for far indeed is the whole limit of the earth, and to seek in every corner can be done by no one man. Therefore let each mission have Einheriar to aid you: for they may search all that is near to your path. And also take you with you the maiden Valkyries on their steeds, for they on their flying horses might visit the distant regions. And so will you have lieutenants to cover all types of country. Yet remember when all is done to send straight way your ravens or elves to me, for I shall have with me Hermod, that may follow the paths you take, and as soon as ever the last message is come in, then he may fly at once upon Sleipnir into Hell.

'Friends, these are hard times, and trouble plagues us round, but the sight of your hosts and the friendship of our allies gives me good hope that this time we shall win through. I rejoice that such a unity we find in our age of care. Go then, and bear our new friendship to the earth, and may she replenish it with the abundance of her tears.' And Odin held up his hand, and staring sadly before them, he bade them dismiss and the great quest to begin. And he rode away through their ranks, and took Hermod into the snows, and the two horsemen then went to climb the great hill of Asgard.

For a moment the great troops bided and looked at each other, for they hesitated as to who should be first from the gate, but then did they all surge forth from Himminbiorg, and the forces tramped to earth, and the world-task was begun. For flying in the air came the whooping Valkyries, and seething down the rainbow marched the milling armies. The sunbeams were reflected from lance, and helm, and mail, and the walking metal tossed it from each to each. The Einheriar were a border of grey iron. The elves were like speckles flowering in the midst. And jingling with their harnesses the cavalry descended the scarlet and the fiery and the gold and the lime and the turquoise and the sea-green and the sea-blue and the mauve.

But when the great army descended at last to earth, they found the land changing from its latter self. For a sound of dripping and splashing could they hear, as the sudden snows were melting under the warmth of the sun. The tinkling of icicles sounded from the wood, and the crumbling of snow-drifts beside the black-running streams. Grasses by the waterside trembled and shed their tears, and it seemed to them even that the hard rocks were weeping, for down on the gnarled crags did little rivulets run, as if the earth herself had melted in lamentation. And the armies stood still a while, overawed by the sounds, while the snow fell off the branches, and revealed the boughs that were green. And then did they make forth again with fresher hearts.

For a while did the armies walk abreast through the melting ice, but coming to a cross-roads did they divide and part, and each of the separate troops went towards their goals. Northwards did Forseti turn with his company of warriors and his cantering Valkyries. Southwards at once went Vidar and Vali, and they led their soldiers speedily down to Muspelsheim. Old Niord went seawards and coasted along the fiord, and coming to the grey breakers of the ocean, he set forth in the ship Skidbladnir, and hied to the misty islands of Vanaheim. And onward with big strides went stooping Kari, and he led his hurrying troops towards the rocky frontier of the giants' land, and Munin the raven flew after him happily, and looked down with eager eyes and beak on the slushy soil. And so one moment were the troops by the limit of Bifrost, and the next was the rainbow bridge left alone and vacant once more, and there in the tower gazed Heimdall forth, the patient witness of all that passed in the world, and he fed his eyes on the land where spring was returning.

And Thor set about Manheim, and at once questioned the creatures. For a stoat on the road he saw, and called out at once to weep. And the stoat was caught between a white coat and a brown, and eagerly he wept a little tear for Balder's death. And Thor went through Vestland, among the firs and birches, and the trees continued weeping, and the starlings in the trees. And the farmers and the huntsmen that were the friend of Thor, they wept in their long houses, as they walked about by the fire. And the Swedes of the Malar lakes wept for the riding Valkyries, and the Viking courtiers wept, as they came from Rugen and the Svold, and the eight folks of Trondelag and the skin-traders of Norland, all the tribes of Manheim wept, for the sake of their favourite Thor.

And Andvari hurrying to Svartheim, through Gotland and Zealand Southwards, sent forth his Valkyries to wide and distant lands. For they flew to Galicia and bid their stern hearts melt, and to Moorish Arzilla and Seville they raced in the air. And here did the dwarves of Svartheim duly weep, as they drew in their ships with argosies of gold. And Andvari hied through the Magyars and the Bulgars, and the rocky lands he bid weep on the path to Philippopolis. But when Southwards did he go among the industrious dwarves, to the wharves and the domes of fabled Miklagard, there did they weep indeed, and go grieving about the streets, for the deep bells boomed with a wild and solemn sadness, and in amongst their temples were the icons hung with purple. And so did the tribes of Andvari make lamentation.

And Frey pushed on to Alfheim, fluttered about by his attendant elves, for Leshy accompanied him, and saw to the combing of woods. Each toadstool did he set upon, and wring tears from each moth, and the squirrels were awoken in their bowers and bidden weep, and the lonely wolves were seized by the tail, and forced to wail and bay. And Frey followed the river, down the Dnieper and over the rapids, and he came to the Black Sea among the fierce Khazars. But also did he send his Valkyries to the Westward, and they flew to the Loire and the Garonne with budding vines, and the Nantais lamented in their high-piled fane. And Frey went through woody Weichsel, where they balance their scales at Mewe, and all things consented to weep for Balder's death.

So all day long they journeyed seeking the creatures, and all day long they met with nothing but tears. But as the declining sun began to sink in the sky, old Niord was the first captain to send word back that all was completed. For he sent forth his elves to Asgard to bear to Lord Odin happy tidings from Vanaheim: that Ran and Aegir and the daughters of the waves, that all the sea-creatures, from the huge whales to the rosy starfishes, had shed due tears for the hero Balder's death. And the elves hied in the glowing air all the way back to Asgard, and they came to Odin and told him of Vanaheim. And next to him Hermod, with Sleipnir by his side, crossed off the lands of Vanaheim, as he followed the progress with his vellum maps.

But hardly had these elves arrived, when other messages flew from the twilight air. For Hugin came winging, a dark shape from Alfheim, and he brought news from Andvari that all in that land had wept. And so did Odin hear from his faithful raven that the dwarves in caverns and on land were equally full of grief, and that due tears had come from the goats and the olives and the pebbles. And Odin smiled at Hugin, and stroked his sleek black coat, and then did he set him up to perch upon his shoulder. And he gazed forth again over the wide-spaced lands of earth, for the sunlight was rosy now, and lit them from the West, and the teeming islands seemed fair in the dusky sea.

But as Odin gazed forth, there came through the almost-melted snows the form of Fricka from the grove of Glasir, and she came to Odin and sat silent by his side, and she too looked forth over the misty world. And thus did Odin say: 'Why then, you have stirred from your bed. And here are you come to sit with your old husband once more. Why, now do you look like Fricka, the woman I married! Such dark hair had she, such a determined face. So did she scarf herself up against the dreary cold. Two messages have come so far, that Vanaheim and Svartheim weep. And Fricka, you are come. And I think you join me in hope.' And Odin turned to his wife, and smiled and touched her hand.

But Fricka looked only ahead, and thus she replied: 'No, I do not hope, for I have forsworn that drug. This task is much like a task I made. So did I busily sweep about the world, so did I call all creatures to help me. What good did that do us, but to delude us a while? And you delude yourself, Odin, to put any trust in this task. Yet in the old days we conquered by refusing defeat. And even when there is nothing to be gained, such a brave heart is it best to bear, even for its own sake, and the minutes as they fly by. And so have I come back to you. And I'll not quarrel now. For we have not long, as I think, to be together, and so let us be at peace, and cherish what we have. And is this not a fine evening that lights those distant hills?'

Then did Odin look at his wife with a frown, for he was puzzled as to whether she was scoffing at him, and he looked at her face as she gazed at the scene before her. For the hazy air was darkening now, and the snows of the far summits were steeped in drowsy light. Afar off to their left were the ranges that led to Niflheim. On the horizon of their right were the dreamy lands and inlets where the golden cities lie. And above the wealthy world did they float in eternal space. But at last did Fricka turn towards Odin with a smile. And away then in the twilight did Sleipnir shake his bridle.

But then hieing to Yggdrasil hill came the other raven, the blue-beaked Munin, and streaking across the air he flew in from Jotunheim. On Odin's knee he landed, and so communed with his master, and in the secret language of the seers he told him these tidings. For all Jotunheim had wept, and even the giants had grieved for Balder, and Kari sent to tell that his task was almost done. Yet afar off in a harsh range of mountains, Kari knew there was a prophetess that lived in a secret cave. Thurk was her name, a giant-witch. She, however, he had been unable to find, for she dwelled somewhere by the summit of Galdhopig in the plateau of Ymesfield, and yet had the Valkyries not discovered the cave. Thus there was one thing that might not yet have wept. And Odin

[281]

listened to his raven with a frown. And wearily he pondered a while, wondering what he should do.

But then did Odin arise, and he called Hermod and said, 'Hermod, do you and Fricka take up this watch. And stay for the messengers which our captains will send us. Yet do not leave for Hell until I am returned. For I am to go now on Sleipnir to visit a mountain witch. To her now shall I fly, and intend to be back before dawn, for tomorrow is the last day that we from our enemies are safe. Hugin and Munin I will take with me, and send them at once back if I am in any trouble. And so farewell. Do not ask me any further. For all speed is needed now, and I must not delay.'

And so did Odin mount Sleipnir once more. And Odin turned his steed, and whistling his ravens to follow, he spurred Sleipnir forward, and bounded into the air. And so he flew forth towards the land of Jotunheim.

But when they were there did the ravens search the snows, and they found the cave easily, for it glowed in the evening light. And croaking then both did they call down Odin to it. And so did he make his way to the cavern of the witch.

But Thurk by now was nearing the end of her days, for so gross had she grown that the cave could scarcely hold her. Her vile body filled it with roll and roll of fat, and she sat under the black roof hunched forward with her shoulders, so that her head appeared at the centre of her body. No longer could she sit up and look with ease about. And Odin flinched at what the firelight showed him.

But then did he draw in his breath and say, 'Fie, you are as foul a witch as any that I have seen. And I pity you for it, that lie such a prisoner to grossness. For how you can hardly breathe or move with all this fat! Oh surely are you visited by a foul affliction. Yet Thurk, I must address you and request you a certain thing, and urgent is this time, and I would beg swift answer. For I am Odin, the Lord of Valhalla, and Hela has granted that my son shall be freed from Hell if everything in Midgard weeps that he is dead. Already has all Jotunheim wept and fulfilled the pledge. Only you remain of all that live in this land. Then pity my sad case, unfortunate Thurk, and give me your tears now, to bring back Balder from Hell.'

[282]

But Thurk wheezed for a long time, and then she replied: 'Dry tears alone shall Thurk weep for Balder's death, for neither in life nor death did he make me glad, and so let Hela keep the prey she has. Yet are you a fool, Odin, to come so far for this. For did you not know that Thurk was the one who cannot weep? Nor might you ever get my tears to trickle down. For as long as I live now my eyes shall be dry. Loki has tested me, that came here this other day. For Loki knew a prophecy told by the wind-witch Hyndla: that the gods would be destroyed by one that cannot weep. He tried to bring my tears to test the strength of my curse. He slaughtered my own daughter. Yet still did I not weep. And thus was he satisfied that I was true. I am the tearless one, and thus I destroy the gods. And now you may leave me, Odin, and despair.'

But Odin grew enraged, and thus he replied in wrath: 'So, you connived with Loki that this last trick he should spring! Though manacled in Hell for all eternity, thus does he have his last stab at the gods. Again then has cruel fate out-tricked the might of the Aesirs. Again has some petty, noisome hitch cankered all the plans we have made against our doom. Again is Odin faced with his own grief: that the chances he foresaw have bereft him of all power. Well, I have learned something since, and thus do I deal with fate. Let all the omens gang up in hordes against me. Still do we have our desperation. Still do we have our undying will. You will weep, Thurk, or you will be gone from here. For I also can out-trick the wiles of malignant fate. Everything in Midgard must weep for Balder's death. Then everything that will not weep shall be in Midgard no longer. I give you a choice then, Thurk. Shed your tears or prepare to die. For if you weep not, I will blot you from the terms of the pledge.' And Odin drew forth then his shining sword, rune-embossed, and the blade of it flashed in the warm light of the fire.

But Thurk then sighed, and groaning did she speak then, and she shoved forth with a massive foot a stool towards Odin, and left it by the fire. And then did she draw in a wheezing breath and say, 'Sit down, old warrior, and listen to my tale a while. For you sound now as you did when you were young, and knew nothing of the wisdom of the world, but thought that if you thought a thing, then you could do it straight. Put down your sword a while, and leave threatening my life. For what I do to you is merely the way of fate, and idle is it, as you used to know, to offer any resistance to what must surely be. Come then. Be sober. And gaze into my eyes, and you will see why I mark the commencement of your doom. And you will see why I speak of the olden days. For do you not know me, oh grey-bearded man? Is there no glimmer in your old heart for me?

'Far in the darkness of the troubled past, when all was confusion and strife between minds, you, Odin, were young, and had a young man's fire. Fiercely you desired might in the battle-line, and so fierce was your will for it that you journeyed far. For the fire in the soul drives all men forward, and however far they get in the world that is the length of their fire. Yet you were not satisfied with your own strength, though great, for you wished to be a leader and found a great clan of heroes. And thus did you go seeking for superhuman strength. To Od-hroerir you came then, the great drink of will: that which would give you all the might you ever sought. And you cared not how you got it, so it was yours to drink. Do you not now remember me, deep in the dark of your mind?

'Od-hroerir was a mighty potion, made from the giant Kvasir's blood. Suttung had hold of it, a giant with the power of birds. Gunlod was his daughter, and she watched over it in a cave. Women are different from armies in the field. War you win with foul words, but love you win with fair. To Gunlod then you went, Odin, wrapped in the guise of a lover. For the sake of Od-hroerir then did you win her heart. You aroused the might of the love-god for the sake of gaining power. And when you had hold of that potion, then you could leave all your wooing, and the Gunlod you seduced you left to weep alone. Far from her cave you flew and founded Asgard, and Suttung you burnt when he pursued your steps. Yet the forces men use cannot be turned off at will. And whatever spirit you conjure for some end, that spirit must you live with, and bide its own reprisals. So after long time must you pay for unfaithfulness. For I am that Gunlod, turned to ugliness as you see.

[284]

'Ah, Odin, you have reaped much now of the evils you brewed in gaining so much power. When you drank of the well of Mimir, and gained the wisdom only granted to seers – for that in your insatiable way was the next gift you hied after – then did you suffer at once from the conflict that made with your will. For the fire in your heart that burned only for power was seen in your wisdom to be but a will-o'-the wisp. And thus did it make you impotent and drear. And I meanwhile have also suffered corruption, for all that grows older undergoes decay. Once left by my lover, I gave way to anguish. Your desertion made me into the giantess Angur-boda, and Loki then did I attract, for he was lured by the pain with which you had left me. To him I bore the monsters which are your foes. And so from them declining am I become this grossness here.

'So do you see, Odin, why it is that I am your end? From love and rage and dullness have I journeyed to this hour, and having witnessed all things am now past all moving. Thus I cannot weep, for what space is in me for tears? Thus I cause your anguish, and return your gift to you. Long are the years between our first meeting and this. Teeming has the earth become, on the brink of a new age. Now are you ending, where you once began. And such is my story, greybeard. So do I bring your doom. Put back your sword, for it is no use to kill me: I have refused to weep, and thus is the pledge broken. Nor would it now be of any use if I wept, for have you not heard the news yet? Loki is escaped from Hell. He flies to your enemies, with unweeping eyes, and he gives them the golden apples, which were to have been your strength. Finish then, Odin. Your long reign is done. Fly, fly to Asgard, and abide for Ragnarok. Great has your strength been, and not ignoble your name.' And Thurk with a sigh ceased speaking and was still.

And Odin sheathed his sword, and sat for a while on the chair by the fire. The cave was gaily flickering, but the snows were cold outside. And Odin said, 'Why then, all's done. For the dark night before us now we must prepare, and all the bright Aesirs go to their long sleep. Alas then, it is finished, the mighty feasts and walls. The grand campaigns are over, and the halls where we were glad. Why, truly have we Aesirs shaken the world, since we came from our first Asgard in the rolling Caucasus. All before our power have fallen or fled. For ours was the will, and that conquers all. Yet is that ended, and others glory now. Farewell then, Thurk. Farewell, Angur-boda. Farewell, Gunlod that loved me in old days. Though you have sealed our doom with your dispassion, yet Odin parts with you as with an old comrade. And so for all time, bide you well.'

And then did Odin leave her, and mounting his horse he flew up into the sky and led his wheeling ravens forth towards the East. Thurk did not move, but let fall the bloated eyes, for now was done the purpose of her long life. And the fire before her dwindled into embers. And now was the night air filled with flitting things, for the elves that were the messengers were hieing like Odin to Asgard, and thus did they bring their news of weeping home. For Frey had now sent word, and Forseti from Niflheim, and the elves from Vidar and Vali came back, bringing news that all Muspelsheim wept. And there remained only the messenger from Thor. But at last came Leshy with his minions, and he flew up to the messenger god, and told him his news: that all things in Manheim had wept for the dead Balder, and Thor in his journeys on earth found all men willing.

But just as they rejoiced that all had met with success, a trumpet rang from Himminbiorg signalling Odin's approach. But as Odin entered at the gate he wearily slipped from his horse. Then did Hermod and Fricka hasten down towards the square, and they came upon Odin held up by two of the guards, and when they looked upon his face, it was as though he had suddenly grown old.

But then did Odin sigh and speak at last saying, 'They tell me they are all come in, the messenger-elves from the Aesirs and our friends. The whole earth weeps then, and grieves with us for Balder. Yet alas, can all the tears in the world never wash back the dead from their graves! Hermod, mount now this good and faithful horse, and ride you at once upon that awesome journey. Seek my son Balder, and tell him if you can: that Odin has drained for him all draughts he ever drank, and yet no strength has he found to shatter death. The witch would not weep, wife, and so our son is gone. Nay more, for she told me that Loki's escaped from Hell. He would never weep for us, but has taken strength to our foes. Hie then, Hermod, unwearying god. Tomorrow shall we burn Balder on his pyre, and set him in his ship Ringhorn, and cast him outwards to sea. Haste you with our message, and meet us by the shore. For one day have we left to be together and at peace, and then must we face the menace of our doom. Go then, for in truth this is so. Nor need we have much wonder, for long has this hour been approaching.' And Odin stretched out his hand, and laid it on Hermod's shoulder. Then did Hermod turn aside and mount the sweating horse. And he drew in the reins and bounded from the gate. And Odin and Fricka went wearily to their house.

Once more on that weary journey fared the messenger-god, and he flew Northwards through the fir-woods, and along by the gleaming shore, and he crossed again over the wild and dreary snows. Down the great Hell-valley did he swoop on the hurtling horse, and rightwards into those circles which lead that river to Hell. And when he had followed the Giallar, he crossed the Giallar-bridge, and alighting on the foul soil he stood once more before Hell.

But a shuffling figure did he see approaching the gate, and something in the uncertain gait made Hermod fancy that he knew him. For the man was young, but faltered with outstretched hands. And Hermod dismounted and led Sleipnir towards him, and coming abreast of the figure he saw that it was Hodur. Then did Hermod stay him, and gaze at him with grief.

And Hermod spoke then to Hodur and said, 'Hodur, are you now here, under this sickly moon? We knew not in heaven when I left of your death. Alas now, our woes come thick, and all is drawing towards the final night. For Odin has sent me to seek Balder with ill news. But Hodur, can it be you? Of what illness did you die? For surely no violence could have despatched a blind god.'

But Hodur answered him sadly and replied, 'No illness took me, Hermod, nor no rash blade. Myself I sent hither, by my own hand. For once that I had heard that Balder could not be saved, I threw myself from the battlements of Asgard, and so did I come to this land quicker than you on your horse. Now is my dark journey almost at its end. Pity me not then, Hermod, for here shall I rest at last. Lead me, therefore, as far as to the gate. For once I have passed that point I shall have no need of eyes.'

And Hermod sighed and embraced the blind god, and said, 'Poor, blind Hodur, how unfortunate is your fate! For we that are now doomed have at least seen life's fair things. Yet have you sat darkling, banished our sports and our battles, and a corner do you sit of everything we enjoy. Yet are you too bound for this region, with no more hope than we. For those that have revelled and those that have wept come to the same dark grave and abiding. And blind are you still, even in death. For there is no progress on this side of the grave.'

But then did Hermod break from his embrace and lead Hodur by the hand towards the brazen gates, and they stood by the huge doors and banged on them to open. And a watchman looked out through a hatch in the gateway, and when he saw the dead man there he clapped the shutter to. Then was there a clanking and the great gate was unlocked, and the smoking region unfolded before them. And beneath the great archway that led to the icy rivers, with their hands interlinked, were Balder and Iduna.

And Hermod at once cried out and said, 'Hate me not, Balder, for bringing you this message, for I come with bitter news that the Aesirs have failed. For though we searched diligently, and went to each of Midgard's seven worlds, and though all creatures wept for you, all things in all lands, yet was there one that wept not, and so are you doomed to hell. And so is all the might of the Aesirs passed away.'

And Balder smiled then, and thus he replied: 'So is the pattern of the things of this world, and so does men's glory shine and spend itself. Grieve not, Hermod, for these things must be. For in striving for my life have we embroiled ourselves in trouble, and all our actions did but spring from fear of the dark. My duty is done now, and I have no further care. Not Hell I go to, but death, but only death. Therefore fret not, oh god, at what you see before you. Hell is no more but the battle of death with fear. And death has the victory, and this is but a dream. And so blessed Hermod, messenger of the gods, bear this last greeting from Balder to the Aesirs: for their concerns he thanks them, and bids them fear no more.

'Yet one thing still must I now beg you to do. For Iduna you see with me, that came to Hell for my sake, and here is now bound

[288]

by the same oath as I. Yet since the land of Hell cannot keep the
bodies of true men, the corse of Iduna does not lie in this country.
Go therefore to the land of Voss, where the Rundal runs by the
witch Groa's cave. There by the bank of a glacier will you find her
body still. Take it and place it beside mine on the pyre. And so and
for all time, Hermod, farewell. And by the mistletoe, remember me.'

And so did Balder bid his adieu. And then he stretched out his
hand towards his brother Hodur, and Hodur took it, and he led
him into Hell. Then did the great brass doorways grate again, and
sliding over the landscape they shut upon the gods. Hermod stood
before them, grieving at all that had passed, but then did he mount
again the great steed Sleipnir's back, and walking beside the river
he retraced his steps towards earth.

But when the dawn had come to the shining towers of Asgard,
and struck with her sunbeams the turrets of Himminbiorg, then
Odin arose to see to the burning of Balder, for but one day remained
of the Aesirs' safety on earth. And he summoned the forces of the
Einheriar to make ready. And he called forth the goddesses from
their halls. And they assembled in the square by Himminbiorg,
drawing together across the dewy fields. But Sif, that was astir
before any of these gods, came to them now from the columns of
Bleidablik, for she had gone once more to visit the forlorn Iduna
and yet for all her seeking she could find no sign of her. Coming
then to the Aesirs she told them of this, and the goddesses wondered
what might have become of her. But the dawn drew on, and the last
day came, and the doors of Himminbiorg were thrown open to the
East. So did the gods descend once more the rainbow, and tread the
pale grasses that clung to the cold earth.

But now from the bounds of Midgard there returned the mighty
Aesirs that had gone to bid all weep. Forseti came from Northwards, his beard set hard with ice, and Vidar and Vali, sweating still
from Southern fires. And they hurried towards the goddesses, eager
to hear news. And now came old Niord, leading his iron troops
from seaward, and they rode up from the beaches, having sailed
to the Vana's realm.

And before any of them might speak, or hear news of what had
chanced, laughing and running from Manheim came Thor with his

thralls hurrying after, and he called at once to the Aesirs, and hailed them in cheery voice: 'Hail, great gods. Now are we all back home. And I hear it by the winds that the air and the land and the seas have wept, and that everything is sorrowful for the divine Balder's death. Shall we see him again now? Is Hermod gone down to Hell? Will the young hero rise from the grave, and lead us to victory?'

But Sif, the golden-haired, shook her head and said, 'Nay, that will not be, for one thing did not weep. Gone is Balder for ever, and we shall see him no more. And now do we go to bury him in Balestrand. But Thor, have you met – since you travelled in Manheim – any sign of Iduna, for she is gone from Asgard? And alas, that we neglected her, for she has suffered most! But I see you have not, nor have any of us here, and where the Vana is vanished is once more a mystery.'

But then did Odin stride forward and say, 'Aesirs, we have suffered, and have still more to suffer, nor have we any hope of ought but pain and grief and death. Yet let not our afflictions paralyse our wills, for though the case is hopeless, there's still the here and now. Wherefore let us scorn now to worry or care. Let us not count our troubles, and start at each new woe, for though the wings of doom beat about us, are we not still Aesirs, and are we not still great? Let us therefore on this last day, be everything that our history has made us: mighty in our actions, grand in our heartedness, and since now we have to bid farewell to Balder, and tomorrow to commence the stoutest fight that has ever been, then let us remember that Asgard is strong and ready, and to spend that time truly before we mount our watch, let us make this funeral the grandest the world has ever seen. Call then down all forces of heaven, to bear my son forth and burn him on the sea, and let all Midgard resound to the Aesir's valediction. For here is our epitaph. It shall be writ with fire: our mighty fortress blazed the circling world, nor even death could veil our exultation!' And Odin stretched forth his rune-carved spear, and forth then went the Aesirs to the fiord.

With full hearts then the gods began the funeral of Balder. And now did the squadrons of the fallen march down to the bier.

And the Valkyries also drew up in their nodding troops, and the air was filled with the clatter of hooves on stone. The frost-giants drew back, withdrawing the icy air, and they strode to the headland to bide the ship's sailing to sea.

So did the Einheriar lift up the pyre, and grasping the interlaced branches they bore it out above the waters. With their leggings steeped in the fiord and their mail wave-lapped, they lifted the bier into the hull of the ship. Down like a curtain fell the white and crimson sails, greeting the pyre of Balder with a fall of glory from heaven. Then was all got ready in the ship to embark seaward. And the thronging troops set their hands to the pitchy boards to launch it.

But before the ship might sail forth and Balder be gone, there came winging from the South Hermod upon Sleipnir, for he brought with him lying across the saddle in his arms the red-robed body of Iduna. And landing before them with roaring pinions, he dismounted from the steed and brought the body in his arms and said, 'The witch Groa bids me greet ye, and here releases her charge, for in journeying in vain for the apples of our glory, Iduna gave her life, and with Balder was reunited. Thus did she leave her corse in the land of Voss. From Balder's lips I am commanded to place her with him on the pyre, for him did I speak to before the gate of Hell, where he did bid me an eternal farewell.' And Hermod bore down Iduna to the ship. Then did they place the wife beside the husband.

And Odin nodded, and sighing he addressed them: 'Come then, Aesirs, for now is all fulfilled. The maiden has shown herself as much a warrior as we. And sad but fitting it is she clasps the hero in death. But let the ship go forth, and let all our troops attend them. Let the Einheriar go to the headland, and with the giants salute his passing. Let the Valkyries escort him seaward, and bring him to the breakers of ocean. And let the ship with the sun-god be burned in the sea-mew's realm. But we, oh Aesirs, shall go to the summit of this peak, and from Langedals Brae yonder bid farewell to our departing hero. For there shall his progress to the sea be viewed at last, and we shall see the sun-god go down with the sun.'

And Odin led the Aesirs to the height. And when they were gathered on the summit of Langedal, the rune-covered Gungnir he stretched up to give the signal, and thus did the troops stir to their tasks.

For the Einheriar heaved then the great ship down into the waves. The sail shook and flurried, obedient to the winds. Then did the Valkyries launch thundering into the air. They circled and wheeled at the stern of the floating ship. In lines of glinting mail the troops marched by the sighing rushes, and reaching the cliffs, they formed in their battalions.

Then did the Aesirs see the ship gather speed with the wind, and she cut the waves keenly as she drew by the ranks of mourners. Now were the rearing valleys set ringing with wails of Valkyries, and among the woods of silver birches, and the black crags their cries echoed. From the length of the scooping channel came the billowing of mists, and the lonely head of Vangness was grieving under cloud. Out of the East then flittered, rallied by Leshy from their missions, a cloud of chattering elves, pricking the gloom with woodland colours.

But the sun grew weaker now. Its disc became tinged with blood. Hail came tumbling out of the sooty air. And now did they see Ringhorn rock to the waves of ocean, for the ship had gained the breakers, and set out on a last sea-voyage. The Valkyries turned away and streamed in the sky towards Asgard. The giants moved Northwards, trembling the ground to Niflheim. And the flocking elves rose up and whirred on their dappled wings, and they passed by the Aesirs, seeking Alfheim's teeming woods.

But the troops that steered the ship made ready to set it on fire. They bound the rudder fast, and set the mainsail before the wind. Then did they lower the skiff by the side. Busily then they piled the golden arms and treasure beside the pyre. Then with a tinderbox did they set the kindling alight, and fired the catching wood that peered through the crevices between the logs and branches. So did the matchwood crackle, and black smoke came pouring from within. Then did the men clamber down the ropes to the skiff, and untying the row-boat, they struck out through the waves to the shore.

Alone then on the boat of death did the flames creep in the branches. There was no sound now but the sea and the hissing twigs. The violets grew brown and the lilies writhed into ashes. The golden narcissus were puffed in fragrant clouds. And the flames invaded the lovers' embrace.

And now did a greenish twilight take great hold over all the land. The fiords and craggy headlands were curtained in murky air. Sol sunk backward into the jaws of the wolf. But blazing into the dusk Ringhorn tricked out its rigging in flame. Beneath the bridge of Bifrost she gleamed and stained the rainbow. The fires lit up Asgard as she brooded over her son.

And now did a streak of blue in the sky receive the rising smoke from the loving warmth of the ship, glinting in its spaces with a mother's brood of stars. The sea then teemed with the daughters of Ran, for the mermaids with their pearly scales surged from the weedy depths and peered forth with dripping tresses into the sunset air. Seeing the burning boat they thrashed their tails towards it. Laughing did they thrust it with furrow tumbling gold. To the realm of Apple-Isle they took the lovers home. The Aesirs now saw nothing but a spark upon the sea. Then did the peace of darkness hold all the mountains round.

Also published in Unicorn

THE KING OF ELFLAND'S DAUGHTER

Lord Dunsany

The King of Elfland's Daughter is the story of the men of Erl. Although mortal men, they desired a magic lord and to please them Prince Alveric armed himself with a special sword and crossed the misty frontier into Elfland, where time and the cruelties of time are unknown.

He brought back the king's daughter, Lirazel, who loved him and bore a son. But Lirazel was unable to forget Elfland and disappeared. Prince Alveric went in search of her, but the frontier of Elfland always receded before him.

Their son, Orion, grew up and hunted unicorns and just as Lirazel believed she would be content in Elfland for ever, she heard the sound of a horn . . . For the men of Erl, who had wanted magic, came the realisation that there can be too much magic in the world.

'Dunsany displayed an extraordinary imagination; he was not interested in the robots, rays and machinery that for so long filled the pages of his successors, but in the effects on his characters of some slight but vital distortion of their familiar world.'
BERNARD LEVIN

'Dunsany stands dedicated to strange and lovely worlds of fantastic beauty. To the truly imaginative he is a talisman and a key unlocking rich storehouses of dreams.'
H. P. LOVECRAFT

'Perhaps the strongest single influence in the development of fantasy fiction in the present century.'
L. SPRAGUE DE CAMP

THE LAST UNICORN

Peter Beagle

The unicorn, who possessed 'the oldest, wildest grace that horses never had', lived in a lilac wood and she lived all alone. She could never belong to anything or anyone mortal enough to want her, not even King Haggard, with his dreadful hunger for a beauty that can never escape him, and his crippling knowledge that nothing is worth loving because everything dies in his hands.

UNFINISHED TALES

J. R. R. Tolkien

Unfinished Tales of Númenor and Middle-earth is a collection of narratives ranging in time from the Elder Days of Middle-earth to the end of the War of the Ring, and comprising such various elements as Gandalf's lively account of how it was that he came to send the Dwarves to the celebrated party at Bag-End, the emergence of the sea-god Ulmo before the eyes of Tuor on the coast of Beleriand, and an exact description of the military organisation of the Riders of Rohan. The book contains the only story that survived from the long ages of Númenor before its downfall, and all that is known of such matters as the Five Wizards, the Palantíri, or the legend of Amroth.

Writing of the Appendices to *The Lord of the Rings* J. R. R. Tolkien said in 1955: 'Those who enjoy the book as a "heroic romance" only, and find "unexplained vistas" part of the literary effect, will neglect the Appendices very properly.' *Unfinished Tales* is avowedly for those who, on the contrary, have not yet sufficiently explored Middle-earth, its language, its legends, its politics, and its kings.

Christopher Tolkien has edited and introduces this collection. He has also redrawn the map for *The Lord of the Rings* to a larger scale and reproduced the only map of Númenor that J. R. R. Tolkien ever made.

'Moments of mythic grandeur.'
THE SUNDAY TIMES

'A series of essays, snatches of stories . . . another monument to the incredible imagination of Tolkien.'
THE SUNDAY TELEGRAPH